UNINTENDED CONSEQUENCES

SCOTT BURNELL

Fulton Books, Inc.
Meadville, PA

Published by Fulton Books 2021

ISBN 978-1-64952-506-2 (paperback)
ISBN 978-1-63710-117-9 (hardcover)
ISBN 978-1-64952-507-9 (digital)

Printed in the United States of America

ANDY

Andy DiPaola is an opposition researcher specializing in up-and-coming politicians at every level in government. He started the business after developing, by accident, an algorithm software to track people who are currently in politics and those who are seeking a political career. The software also collects data on activists and high-profile government officials. He has been gathering dirt information for seven years and holds leverage over numerous politicians and officials.

The software scans an individual's social media and any other online site that lists the person's name. It then searches all followers, family, or anyone associated with the person to look for incriminating information. The company then collects evidence on the incriminating information and stores it for future use. When hired by a political party or an opposition campaign, the information is updated and sold.

Andy gained notoriety as a trainman on the Arizona Pacific Railroad. He smuggled Cuban cigars through Mexico, utilizing friendships with US Border Patrol officers. He also became a union boss after a mysterious union election where the trainman who held the position for forty years died during a freak accident on the job. Andy got his start in politics when he used his newfound software to conduct information gathering on a San Bernardino County sheriff who was running for reelection. Andy hated the man and was willing to do anything to make sure he was not reelected. He compiled a list of incriminating evidence against the sheriff, then took it to his challenger. The challenger did not have much money, so Andy gave him the information with the understanding that favors were owed if he won. Andy wields power, money, and influence. He is loved and feared. He is both predator and prey.

Andy is twenty-eight years old, six feet three inches tall, and weighs 195 pounds with black hair and brown eyes. He has never been married and doesn't date often (because of his business position and because he's afraid of a setup or a #MeToo issue, which would destroy his business). He is an active outdoorsman and loves the mountains and deserts. He hates lawyers, people who abuse women and children, and corrupt cops and politicians. He freely speaks his mind and is not politically correct and despises anyone who is. He drinks craft beer and whiskey and smokes a cigar a day. He is down-to-earth and wears shorts and T-shirts when possible. He doesn't like formalities and hates pretentious and rich people who look down on everyone else.

THAT FATAL DAY

"999! Shots fired. Shots fired! Officers down! Fifth and Lincoln, two male Hispanics armed with an automatic rifle in a silver Chrysler 300 headed north on Fifth. Get EMS! I'm hit bad. My partner's been hit and is not moving!" Dep. Lavon Jones screamed into the mic.

"Sam Alpha 1. En route less than one." The radio chatter lit up with numerous units stating their positions. "Sam Alpha 1, clear this channel. Responding units, go to TAC 2," Sgt. Dan O'Rourke ordered over the radio.

Dispatch: "All responding units go to 2. Sam Alpha 1, we are receiving numerous 911 calls. The deputies need—"

Sergeant O'Rourke cut her off. "Dispatch EMS and notify LAPD and surrounding agencies and get an air unit up! Sam Alpha 1 1097."

Sergeant O'Rourke was the first unit on scene. When he arrived, he noticed one deputy sitting in the driver's seat of the unit. When O'Rourke approached the deputy, he asked, "Where are you hit?"

"Sir, I don't know. I can't feel or use my left arm or left leg," Deputy Jones responded.

"Hang in there. I have help on the way. Where is your partner?" O'Rourke asked.

"Sir, he's on the other side of the unit. Sarge, I tried getting to him, but I couldn't move," Jones said as he started crying.

"Don't worry about it, son. We're getting you help right now." When O'Rourke ran around the front of the unit to the passenger's side, that was when he went numb. "Oh god, no!" he yelled. He knew the deputy was gone. A portion of his skull was missing, and another round went straight through his nose. "Sam Alpha 1. Where is EMS? We have a mess down here!"

Dispatch: "Sam 1, EMS is staging."

"Tell them to get in here ASAP. The scene is secure." O'Rourke started barking orders to the other arriving units for them to rope off the scene, collect witnesses, and keep the media out. When EMS arrived, they had a hard time removing Sergeant O'Rourke from the deceased deputy. O'Rourke refused to give up hope that there was a chance of survival. It took several deputies to pull him off so the paramedics could work on the deputy.

"Lincoln Alpha 1. Can I get an update?"

"Sam 1. Lincoln 1, unless you're on scene, go to TAC 2 and keep this channel clear for emergency traffic!" O'Rourke demanded.

"Lincoln 1. Sam 1, advise on an update."

"Dammit, Lincoln 1. Go to TAC, and you'll get your update," O'Rourke barked.

"Ida 1, Lincoln 1, Sam 1. Go to TAC. Ida 1, Lincoln 1, are you 97?"

"Negative, sir. Still 5 out."

"10-4. Ida 1, Sam 1. Do you have the resources you need?"

"No, sir. I barely have enough for crowd and media control. The ME and homicide are en route. However, I haven't received an ETA from either."

"Ida 1, dispatch, get an ETA from the ME and homicide. Also, do we have an airship?"

Dispatch: "10-4, Ida 1, and affirmative on the airship, and FYI, the airspace has been cleared."

"What the fuck is your problem, Sergeant?" Davis yelled as he approached him.

O'Rourke was sitting on the hood of his unit with his bloodied hands holding his face. "My problem, *sir*"—and O'Rourke emphasized *sir*—"is that I have a dead deputy, another critically injured deputy, and two very dangerous suspects on the loose, and you're demanding a fucking update on an emergency channel!"

"That was to be taken as an order, Sergeant."

"I heard your order, and you could have gone to TAC like everybody fucking else!"

"I'm bringing you up on charges for this. You'll be lucky if you don't lose your fucking job."

"Fuck you!" O'Rourke replied.

Division Chief Dixon witnessed the exchange as he walked up to the scene. "Sergeant, Lieutenant, that is enough! This will not be played out on the radio or in public. There is a time and place for this, and here and now is not it."

"Yes, sir," they both replied.

"Lieutenant, I want you to take this scene over until homicide relieves you and expand this scene so we can push the media back even further. I don't want the deputy's family to see him like this."

"Yes, sir," Lieutenant Davis responded.

"What the hell is wrong with you, Dan? I have never seen you act insubordinate to a superior before. I know this is stressful, but we've been through this before."

"Chief, it's Brian," Dan said as tears filled his eyes. "It's my son lying in that street dead. How the hell am I going to tell his mother and sister?"

"Oh my god, Dan, I'm so sorry. We have to get you out of here."

"With all due respect, sir, I'm not leaving until my son's body is out of that gutter."

"Dan, you know what protocol is. The lieutenant is handling this, and homicide will be here shortly, but I need to get you out of here."

"I know, Bill, but I can't leave my son in the gutter. Can't I wait until he is removed?"

"Protocol is going to kill me on this one, but I think I can defend it. Ida 1, dispatch, what is the ETA on the ME?"

Dispatch: "Sir, I've been told the ETA is four hours out."

"10-4. This is unacceptable. Dan, let me make a call."

"Yes, sir, Sheriff," Bill said as he explained the news to Sheriff Duncan. "Sir, I would consider it a personal favor if you would authorize an airship to pick the ME up in Antelope Valley and get him here sooner. I've known that deputy since the day he was born, and I would like for him not have to lie in the gutter for four more hours. I would rather his family not have to see this on the news. It's bad enough that his father was the first unit on scene."

"Who is the deputy?" the sheriff asked.

"Brian O'Rourke," Bill responded.

"You mean Sergeant O'Rourke's son?"

"Yes, sir."

"Oh god, Bill, I'll do better than an airship! Give me a few minutes, and I'll call you back."

"Thank you, sir." Sheriff Duncan placed a call to the head ME of the county, and she agreed to respond although she doesn't do much fieldwork anymore. Duncan sent a unit to her office to pick her up. She was on scene in less than twenty-five minutes.

"Lieutenant, you shouldn't be so hard on the sergeant," Deputy Dombrowski said.

"Why not? No one has the right to be insubordinate. I know it's a stressful scene, but Sergeant O'Rourke has been around a long time and has handled this exact scene plenty of times. He knows how to handle himself."

"With all due respect, LT. He has never handled a scene like this one. That's his son lying on the ground over there."

"What the fuck! Oh shit, that's Brian?"

"Yes, sir," the deputy replied.

"Shit, he was supposed to be off today. He came in as a favor for me because I couldn't get anyone else to answer their damn phones. He worked mids last night and agreed to work the day shift for overtime," he said. "Can this shitstorm get any worse?" the lieutenant asked himself.

"Bill, I know what the procedure is, but is there any way we can transport Brian in an ambulance instead of a meat wagon? I would rather not have Mary and Heather watch him get carried out of a plain white van. I think an ambulance might help with their future mental state." As O'Rourke finished that question, Lieutenant Davis approached.

"I don't think I can pull that one off, Dan," Bill said.

"Pull what off?" Davis asked. Bill explained Dan's request. "Chief, I can make that happen. I'll call Chief Fairfield at fire precinct 42. My wife is his secretary. He will approve it."

"That would be very much appreciated, Lieutenant."

"Listen, Sergeant, I am sorry about our little blowup. I had no idea it was your son that was killed. Chief, I do not want to push an inquiry into what happened earlier. Having the facts, I don't think the sergeant's actions were inappropriate."

"Lieutenant, this can be discussed later. However, that's not your decision to make. Sergeant O'Rourke will have to answer for his actions, but he will be given due process and have a chance to explain himself. But for now, let's concentrate on getting these two mother-fuckers off the street so they can't kill any more cops or civilians."

The ME and homicide arrived within minutes of each other. Lieutenant Davis explained to Captain Silvers where the investigation was at, and the scene was officially turned over to homicide. The ME cleared Brian's body for transport, and Sergeant O'Rourke watched the body of his son loaded into the back of an ambulance. To deny the media the ability to film his emotions, a circle of LASD and LAPD officers who were on scene surrounded him.

"Marsha, what's wrong?" Mary O'Rourke asked as Marsha walked into the O'Rourkes' home. Mary was on her treadmill when Marsha called her and told her that she needed to come over and tell her something. They walked into the study, and Marsha had Mary sit on the couch. Marsha Dixon was the wife of Division Chief Dixon and had known the O'Rourkes for over thirty years.

"Mary." Marsha started crying and with broken words said, "Brian has been shot and killed."

Mary immediately broke out in tears. "Oh god, no, Marsha. Tell me no. Tell me no, Marsha."

"I'm sorry, Mary."

"Every day of my married life, I have prayed for Dan to come home safe to me. And then when Brian started working there, I did the same for him. I knew that job was dangerous, but the both of them thought it was their calling. Now look where it's gotten me. I just lost my only son. I gave birth to that boy. How in the world am I going to tell Heather? She is going to break down. She loved her big brother. How did it happen?"

"I don't know all of the details, but it was a traffic stop at about 1:30 PM. And before Brian and his partner even got all the way out of the car, the suspect open fired on them with an automatic rifle, killing Brian and critically injuring the other deputy."

"Is he in custody?"

"There were two of them, and no, they haven't found them yet."

"Who told Dan?"

"Mary, there's something else."

Mary started shaking. "Marsha, tell me Dan's okay. Did something happen to him?"

"Mary, Dan was the first unit on scene. He was the first person to see Brian that way."

Mary, still crying and now breathing heavily, stared up at the ceiling and asked God, "Why? We are a good family. We haven't done anything to anybody. Why?"

*****

"What's wrong, Mom?" Heather asked as she, Marsha, and Mary were in the vice principal's office. He had allowed them the use of it to tell Heather the news privately. She started crying knowing something wasn't right. "Mom, something's wrong. I can see it in your eyes."

"Heather, your brother was shot and killed today."

"No!" Heather screamed at the top of her lungs, a scream that could be heard halfway across campus. Heather was crying and shaking so hard they couldn't get her to calm down. All the office personnel who had already been made aware of the news broke out in tears after hearing her scream.

Stacy Hanna, Heather's best friend and teammate, heard the scream as she walked into the office's reception area. The school had asked her to bring Heather's personal items to the office. Stacy noticed that everyone in the room was crying, so she started tearing up realizing something bad happened. "Where's Heather?" she asked the secretary.

"She's in the vice principal's office" was the reply. Stacy didn't even ask permission to enter. She just opened the door and walked right in. She saw Mary and Marsha standing over Heather, who was sitting in a chair with her elbows on her knees and her hands covering her face. She was sobbing uncontrollably.

"Heather, what happened?" she asked.

Heather looked up at her. "Stacy, they shot and killed my brother. Brian is gone."

"No, oh god, no." She started shaking. She dropped everything she had in her hands and fell to her knees. She put her hands over her face and broke out in tears.

Heather got out of her chair and knelt down in front of her. They both held each other and cried for another five minutes. No one said a word.

*****

Prior to going to the hospital, Dan drove to the station, cleaned up, and changed into street clothes. When he turned the corner to the hospital, he noticed hundreds of police cruisers and motorcycles lining the street. They all had their red and blue lights flashing. He had texted Mary to let her know that he was standing by the entrance waiting on the ambulance. A few minutes later, Mary, Heather, Stacy, and Marsha walked out of the hospital and walked up to him. Mary was leaning on Marsha for support, and the two girls were holding each other. "Oh, Dan, how could this happen?" Mary asked as she gave him a hug.

"I'm sorry, Mary" was all the words he could muster because he was crying.

"Dad, did you catch the guy who did this?"

"Not yet, sweetheart."

"Dad, promise me that you will catch him and make him pay."

"We will get them."

As the ambulance started making its way up the street, a news cameraman broke the police barrier and headed toward the O'Rourkes. He wanted a shot of the grieving family as they watched Brian get pulled from the ambulance. He hadn't gotten too close to them when a deputy tackled him. LASD had orders not to allow the media anywhere near the family. They filed a complaint with the sheriff for violating their First Amendment rights but were told that they didn't have any right to be wherever they wanted if it interfered with police business.

As the ambulance made its way to the entrance, hundreds of officers were saluting it as it passed by. Most of them had tears in their eyes. "Why are all the cops saluting, Mom?"

"That is to show Brian proper respect for laying his life down in the line of duty." Every one of those cops realized that it could have been any one of them in the same position on any given day.

SAN DIMAS, THE NEXT DAY

"Joe, we have to talk," Bella said as Joe popped the top on his first beer. Joe Duncan was the sheriff of Los Angeles County. He was in his second term. He had been with the department for twenty-six years and made a lot of political friends, so five years ago, he ran against the incumbent sheriff and won. Joe was five feet ten inches tall and weighed 175 pounds. He was of Irish descent with reddish-brown hair and brown eyes. He stayed in shape but was by no means muscular. He was a handsome man with an outgoing personality that women loved. He earned a good reputation in police work while working in narcotics.

Bella was beautiful and of Mexican heritage. She was born in California when her mother crossed the border to give birth to her, so she was given US citizenship. She was only thirty years old and five feet six inches tall with black hair and brown eyes. They had been married for only six years. When Joe first decided to run for office, he was single. He liked chasing skirts, and he didn't want to be tied down. His political advisers convinced him that he needed a girl because it would make him more electable. So he found Isabella and married her basically for arm candy. He had her sign a prenuptial agreement mainly for the house and property. He had just gone through a brutal day and a half where one of his deputies was killed in the line of duty and another one critically injured in the same incident. They had arrested the suspected driver, but the alleged shooter was still on the loose.

"So what's on your mind, Bella?" he asked.

"My brother Oscar is here," she replied with a squint in her eyes. She knew Joe would not like to hear that; he hated that piece of shit.

"He had better not be, Bella. We've discussed this, and we can't afford to have him anywhere near us. He is a convicted felon, and not to mention, he is an illegal alien. What did he do this time, sold more drugs to kids, raped someone, or has he finally moved up and shot someone?" he asked.

"Joe, he was the one who shot your deputies yesterday," she said with a squint in her eyes.

"Are you fucking serious? Where is he right now?" he demanded. Joe went into the kitchen drawer and pulled out his Glock. He grabbed his cell phone and started searching for a number.

"Who are you calling?" Bella asked.

"I'm calling the San Dimas station to get some units over here to arrest his ass," he explained.

"Put the phone down, Joe," she demanded.

"I'm not going to allow that little shit to cost me my career or my political future."

"Joe, if you don't put that fucking phone down right now, I'll make damn sure both of those careers are over tonight."

Joe saw the serious look on her face, so he said, "How do you think you will do that?"

"Joe, we both know this is a sham marriage. It's a marriage based on convenience. You need me, and I need you, but if you don't let me help my brother, then I will go to the news and give them all the information on your previous secretary, who you were fucking behind my back, who you got pregnant and had to pay for her abortion, and who we had to pay off to keep her mouth shut and go away. Oh, and I'll add in that little slut Marta you've been fucking for the past six months. Rumor has it she has STDs. I guess she'll fuck anything that has money and power."

"You've been spying on me?" Joe asked angrily.

"Like I said, Joe, we need each other, and for me to have skin in the game, I need leverage. It's not personal."

"This is bullshit, Bella! Are you willing to risk your entire life and future to protect a cop killer?"

"I know this is hard for you, and it's hard for me, but he's my brother who's had a shitty life. Just let me get him to Mexico, and let him disappear for a while. I know eventually he'll have to face his consequences, but I'm just asking for a little time."

"You're not asking, Bella. You're extorting."

"So you'll help?" she asked.

"Like I have a fucking choice. Just get him the fuck out of here, and, Bella, no more of this shit. I will let my future go down if you pull any of this shit again."

"Fair enough," she replied.

"So how do you plan on getting him out of here?"

"That's the easy part," she said. "He's a Mexican citizen, so I can just drive him over the border. I have a valid visa and go see my parents all the time. The tricky part is if you put a warrant for his arrest and publicly identify him."

"How much time do you need?" Joe asked.

"Two to three days to let things cool down."

"Okay, I can withhold that information that long."

Salt on the Wound

"Sergeant O'Rourke, myself, and Chief Dixon have reviewed the facts in this case and have affirmed internal affairs' assessment of your insubordination. As you are aware, punishment for insubordination can include termination."

"Yes, sir, I am well aware of that."

"Given your cooperation and the fact that you fast-tracked this investigation by not involving legal representation that you are entitled to by law and the fact that you did not contest the outcome of the investigation, also considering the fact that Lieutenant Davis admitted some fault in not following procedure on an emergency channel, we will not be seeking termination. It is well-known that Chief Dixon here is a friend of yours, but his integrity won't be compromised, so he deferred the punishment to me.

"Sergeant, I have been in law enforcement for over forty years, and I have never been in a position where a father had to be the first person to see his own deputy son murdered in the line of duty. This is a first for me. I cannot fathom what was going through your head, and I won't pretend I can, but insubordination is insubordination. So I had to figure out a punishment that the Civilian Review Boards would buy and not try to override, so here's my offer. You will be placed on paid medical leave until such time as you and the county doctors feel you are good to go. This is not psych leave. We will classify it as extended grievance, so it will not be reflected in your personnel file. You will, however, have to see a county psych just so we can make sure that your head is straight.

"Sergeant, take the time off. Spend it with your wife and daughter and start the grieving process without having to worry about this place. On a personal note, if I may, if it weren't for the fact that this was all recorded, we wouldn't be here. Dan, you're an excellent cop, and what happened to you was unfathomable. Bill, do you have anything to add?"

"Dan, go spend time with Mary and Heather on the county dime. They need you with them right now. Do you have any questions?"

"Just one. What if the Civilian Boards doesn't like it? Will they go after more discipline?"

"Dan, let us handle that. We are willing to go to court over this, and they won't win. What judge will rule against the circumstances in this case?"

"Chief Alexander and Chief Dixon, I appreciate everything you have done for me. I seriously regret my actions towards Lieutenant Davis, and while not making an excuse, I never imagined a scenario where I would have to be faced with that. So thank you."

"Dan, take your time coming back. There is no limit," Chief Dixon explained.

"Yes, sir, and thank you."

FIVE YEARS LATER— THE OFFICE

"Andy, you have a young lady here to see you," Cindy Davis said. Cindy has worked for Andy since the beginning. She found him after her husband Mark was blackballed out of law enforcement by the corrupt San Bernardino County Sheriff's Department. On patrol one night, Mark witnessed his field training officer beating a cuffed detainee while investigating a report of domestic violence. When the internal affairs department investigated it, they attempted to force Mark into changing his original report to state that the use of force occurred prior to the handcuffs being put on the suspect and was justified by the suspect's actions. Mark refused to change his original report and was terminated. Cindy and Mark had three small children at the time. Mark had a hard time finding law enforcement work, so Cindy had to find a job.

"Cindy, I don't have any appointments this afternoon. I am heading to Arrowhead to go fishing." Lake Arrowhead was a picturesque resort paradise set on a deep high mountain lake in the San Bernardino Mountains. It was commonly referred to as the Alps of Southern California. The lake and surrounding properties were private. Andy owned a small cabin in the woods.

Cindy knew he wasn't going fishing. He was going to Arrowhead to take out the love of his life, Jenny. Andy spent a lot of time with her. On Thursday afternoons, to avoid the weekenders, he would take her cruising on the lake while enjoying a Padron 7000 Maduro cigar and Four Roses single barrel bourbon. Jenny was a perfect fit for Andy. She was beautiful and elegant. Jenny, of course, was his seventeen-foot 1955 Chris Craft Runabout that he had restored. Andy enjoyed the Americana that went with the boat and the history of Lake Arrowhead.

Cindy tried explaining to the attractive young woman that she would not be able to see Andy. The woman insisted and stated that she drove all the way out from UCLA and missed her literature class just to meet with him and that a mutual friend suggested she do so.

Cindy explained the circumstances, and Andy allowed the meeting. Always fearful of being alone in a room with a woman, Andy requested that one of his investigators be present. As the young woman entered his office followed by his investigator, Andy could not help but notice that this was a very attractive girl. She stood five feet eleven inches tall. She had long light brown hair with beautiful light blue eyes. She was wearing a white floral print summer dress with thin straps and low pump shoes. She had a beautiful tan.

Andy introduced himself and his investigator to her. She identified herself as Heather. Andy offered her a seat and asked her what he could do for her.

Heather began. "I was sent here by a mutual friend who suggested that I speak with you about a problem that I am having."

"Who is this mutual friend?" Andy asked.

"I'm not at liberty to say. I gave my word that I would not say anything," she said.

Andy had an idea who sent her. However, he just wanted to test her loyalty and her ability to keep a secret.

"Mr. DiPaola," Heather said after looking at the investigator, "I was hoping we can speak in private. What I have to ask you is a very private, sensitive matter."

"First of all, Heather, I prefer to be called Andy. And secondly, Ben is in here for my protection," he explained. "Unfortunately, in this day and age, being alone with a woman, especially a very attractive woman such as yourself, can put a man and his career in jeopardy if even the slightest accusation of something inappropriate is said. You have to understand my position. I can assure you anything you say in this room will always stay in this room."

"Mr. DiPaola—I'm sorry—Andy, I know you don't know me, but I am not a bad person. What I have to talk to you about is very personal, and I was hoping I could do it in private. I am not here to hurt you, and I certainly am not going to make up any accusations. You have to believe me."

Andy looked at Ben for a sign of whether he should trust this girl or if she was some kind of a setup. Political operatives would love nothing more than to capitalize on a false sexual harassment accusation against him, but Ben just shrugged his shoulders as if to say, "I don't know."

Andy looked into Heather's eyes, and something told him she could be trusted, so he asked Ben to leave the room. But prior to Ben leaving, Andy had him take Heather's purse and scan her for any type of electronic signal.

Andy tried to explain to Heather the reasons for this, and she stopped him midsentence and said, "Andy, I completely understand. You need to trust me."

"So now that you have my full attention, what can I do for you?" he asked.

"About five years ago, my brother was murdered in Los Angeles. He was a sheriff's deputy in a two-man car, and they conducted a traffic stop. During the stop, a gunman opened fire on both deputies with an AK-47, killing my brother and critically wounding the other deputy."

"I am well aware of that case, but how do I fit in with it?" he asked.

"The suspect, Oscar Garcia-Hernandez, fled to Mexico where he has been 'hiding'"—she used finger quotes—"in the open for five years. We constantly contact LASD's homicide department for answers and have been brushed off."

"And what do you need me for?"

"I am under the impression you might have connections in Mexico so we can grab Garcia-Hernandez and bring him back here to face justice."

Andy became a little annoyed, which wasn't easy. While it wasn't a secret to everybody that he used to smuggle in Cuban cigars through Mexico, it was only known to a handful of people who were very loyal. How she knew of this information concerned him. One of his close friends opened his mouth by telling someone outside the group about his connections, especially a young girl. "Heather, there is nothing I can do for you. If the investigation points to this Hernandez guy, then the US Marshals will pick him up, especially if he's not in hiding. It seems to me that there is some sort of holdup in the case where no arrest warrant has been issued."

"A warrant has been issued for his arrest, but no one will follow up on it, and no one knows why. There is rumor in the agency that LASD is purposely stalling the case," she replied. "They have already prosecuted the accomplice, so I don't understand why they won't go to Mexico and get this guy. Our family friend is pretty influential, and he can't understand it either." Just then, Andy confirmed what he already knew who their mutual friend was.

"Then you need to let it play out. Besides, connection or no in Mexico, there is nothing I can do for you."

Heather's face dropped, and small tears started to fill her eyes. "Andy, I am begging you. I was told that if anyone could help us, it would be you. We have no one else to turn to. We are desperate. If there is anything you can do to help, we would appreciate it. I just want justice and for my family to be able to go back to being somewhat normal considering the circumstances."

Andy stood up and said, "Heather, I am a political researcher who finds dirt on people in an attempt to keep corrupt officials from holding public office. I cannot help you. I'm sorry." Andy turned his back to her to mull a small angle he might be able to help her with. Also, he didn't want to see her tears. Andy didn't like it when girls cried.

He was mulling options when Heather pleaded. "Andy, please, I am begging you. I don't have much money, but I'll do anything, anything for your help."

After hearing that, Andy turned around to see that Heather had stood up, dropped her dress, and was standing partly naked in front of him. She had a slender, toned, and tanned body. Her breasts were firm, and she was not wearing a bra. She was wearing white panties.

Andy originally thought to call Ben back in but decided against it. He felt that this young lady was acting out of desperation and not for political reasons or a setup.

Andy walked around his desk toward her and said, "So you are willing to do anything?"

Without looking at him and while staring straight ahead, Heather replied, "Anything."

Andy walked behind her while she remained looking straight forward. He placed his right hand on her right shoulder and felt her tense up. Andy could smell the fear on her. He felt tiny droplets of sweat forming on her body. He bent down and grabbed the dress straps and pulled her dress back up. He slipped the front over her breasts and had her put the straps back on, and he zipped up the back.

Andy had her sit back down, and he returned to his chair. "Do you always offer your body to get things you want?" he asked.

Heather, unable to look Andy on the face, looked down at the floor, started shaking her head, and replied, "No, I have never even had sex before."

"Why not?" Andy asked.

"I just haven't found the right guy."

"So you drove all the way out here to see a man you had never met and determined that I was this right guy?"

"I don't know why I just did that. I am so embarrassed."

Embarrassed and afraid, tears started to stream down her face, and her body started to shake uncontrollably. She tried to speak, but the words were broken up. She felt numb.

Andy offered her a bottle of water and tried to calm her down. He touched her shoulder and asked her to calm down. Always a smart-ass, Andy stated, "I normally get that reaction from women after I have sex with them but never before." Andy had always found that humor was the best in tense situations, and he usually used himself as the punch line.

Heather looked up at him, and a slight smile came across her face, then a giggle. She looked him in the eyes and felt safe. She felt very comfortable and started to calm down.

Andy sat back in his chair and let her speak. As Heather started to speak, tears started to fill her eyes. She explained to Andy the toll that her brother's death had taken on her family. She expressed anger toward LASD for not pursuing the case more aggressively. She hated the fact that Garcia-Hernandez was partying in public in Mexico and that the authorities knew where he is, but they were not getting him.

Then the conversation turned to her father and the hell he went through that fateful afternoon and the hell that LASD was still putting him through. "My dad is a patrol sergeant as he was the day my brother was murdered. After that incident, they placed him on paid psych leave and left him there for six months. He was finally cleared for full duty and went back to patrol.

"Every day on his off time, he would go to homicide and ask for update statuses on the case. And for about a year, they talked to him about it. Then suddenly, they refused to give him any answers. And now that it has been five years, it seems that they have dropped pursuing Garcia-Hernandez. In my free time from school, I would go by homicide and inquire. They were always polite to me but would never tell me anything.

"Recently, my dad was told by the homicide captain to lay off and let them handle it. They warned him that if he continued, then they would discipline him for obstruction. He recently went to the union and explained everything, and they told him that they were going to file a vote of no confidence against the captain and to not to worry about his job. They did warn him that he was probably being watched, so if he screws something up, the department would go after him.

"Andy, I don't know if you know this, but my father"—and as she continued, the tears started again but this time heavily—"was on patrol that day when the call came out as 'Shots fired, officer down.' My dad was less than a mile from the scene. He was the first unit to arrive.

"Garcia-Hernandez had already left. As my dad ran to the two officers, the one bleeding in the driver's side front seat was still breathing. On the passenger side of the car, lying in the gutter was his…son." Heather started shaking, and at this point, Andy felt tears starting to well up in his eyes. "My dad said he knew he was gone, but he tried CPR anyway. People have told me that when the paramedics arrived, it took four officers to pull my dad away from my brother so the medics could try to help him."

Andy got up and looked for tissues only to learn that he didn't have any. He reached into his go bag and pulled out a clean T-shirt. He walked around his desk, sat in the chair next to Heather, and handed her the shirt. Her makeup, what little she used, was running. The front of her chest and her dress were soaked with tears. Andy turned to her, grabbed both of her shoulders, pulled her to him, and gave her a comforting hug. He didn't know what else to do. He didn't like to see her cry, but deep down, he was trying to grasp the enormous pain that her family had endured. He also didn't want her to see him cry.

"So apparently, it wasn't any better the second time!" Heather smirked.

Before she left the office, Andy asked her if she brought any makeup. "I can't let you leave this office looking like that. Anyone out there who knows me will think we did have sex."

"Remember I was the willing one," she replied.

"You're quick," he said. With a hug and a smile, she left with instructions to never tell anyone of this meeting and to not contact him anymore.

One-Year Anniversary Four Years Earlier

Standing at the podium for the press conference of the one-year anniversary of the killing of Dep. Brian O'Rourke was Sheriff Joe Duncan, DVC William Dixon, and Sgt. Dan O'Rourke. Dan's wife, Mary, and their fifteen-year-old daughter, Heather, were sitting in the front row. The sheriff spoke. "As you are all aware, one year ago today, DS Brian O'Rourke was killed in the line of duty during a routine traffic stop. Dep. Lavon Jones was critically injured in that shooting and, unfortunately, because of the nature of his wounds will not be returning to work. We have identified the suspects, and one of them, Anthony Fernando Sierra, is currently in custody and is awaiting trial for those crimes.

"The second suspect, who we believe to be the shooter, has been identified as Oscar Garcia-Hernandez. Our intelligence has determined his whereabouts in Mexico, and my office is currently working with the Mexican government to have him extradited back to the United States to face prosecution. There are no further suspects being sought. Unfortunately, we have yet to recover the weapon that was used in the shooting, and that portion of the investigation remains open. Other than the apprehension of Garcia-Hernandez and the recovery of the weapon, we consider this case closed. I will entertain a few questions. Yes, go ahead, Ron."

"Sir, Ron Hart, Fox News LA. Sheriff, can you explain the holdup with the extradition? It seems it should be fairly simple."

"Sure, Ron. I am looking for an extradition agreement where the death penalty is not taken off of the table, and so far, the Mexican government refuses to extradite with those conditions."

"But, sir," Ron continued, "the Mexican government never extradites one of their citizens if there is a possibility of the death penalty."

"I understand that, Ron, but there are two ways to handle that. One, we can negotiate it and explain that Mexican citizen or not, no one should be able to gun down an officer here, in Mexico, or anywhere without having to face the ultimate punishment. And secondly, if negotiations fail, then we will wait until he crosses back into the United States. He has many connections in the LA area, and it won't be long before he gets rambunctious and returns. And when he does, we will be waiting for him, and we will scoop him up. Go ahead, Alice."

"Sir, Alice Holden-Fritz, ABC LA. Wouldn't it be wise to cut a deal with the Mexican government, offer them life without the possibility of parole, and get this guy in custody? Because let's be frank, Sheriff, even if he were to receive the death penalty, the likelihood of it being carried out here in California is practically nil."

"Alice, I understand your point, but not at this time. What would my deputies, my department, and the citizens of Los Angeles County, whom I serve, think of me if I allow a cop killer the freedom to live just because he ran to Mexico? Not on my watch. Go ahead, Jerry."

"Jerry Jansen, *LA Times*. Sheriff, rumor has it that there was a shake-up in command staff in the homicide Division. Is that true?"

"There was no shake-up. I rotate my command staff from time to time to get them to experience all aspects of the LASD. Capt. Jose Garcia was brought over to homicide from the criminal courts division, and Capt. Jeremey Silvers was transferred from the homicide division to the criminal courts division. They are both excellent captains. No, there is no shake-up. People, can we keep the questions to the Garcia-Hernandez investigation? Any of these other questions can go through my press liaison office. We don't need to waste the O'Rourke family's time with these nonrelevant questions. Yes, Melanie."

"Melanie Ferguson, NBC LA. Sheriff, has there been a warrant issued for Garcia-Hernandez? Because I cannot seem to locate one in any court system or through any of my police contacts." There was a hum in the room. The other reporters were whispering to one another, and the consensus was that no one thought to check that out. Everybody just assumed there was one. NBC apparently was on top of it.

"Melanie, I am under the impression that there is an outstanding warrant for his arrest, but I have not personally seen it. I will research it and get back to you."

"But, Sheriff, how can you be talking to the Mexican government as you claim when there isn't even a warrant issued for his arrest?"

"Again, Melanie, I will look into that ASAP. I am quite confident there has been one issued. There will be no further questions at this time."

"Sheriff!" Melanie blurted out. "Can you have one of your people check while we wait? It shouldn't take but a few minutes of your time." Sheriff Duncan ignored the question.

Ron Hart asked a question, yelling over all the commotion. "Sheriff, how can you close this investigation when, A, the suspect is still outstanding and, B, when you don't even know how he got to Mexico or if he had assistance?" Ron turned to Mrs. O'Rourke. "Ma'am, my apologies to your family. I know it is a rough thing that you are going through, but the sheriff's answers simply don't add up."

The sheriff turned to Ron and with a somewhat disgusted voice said, "Ron, we have one suspect in custody and the other one identified. There are no further outstanding suspects. There is no reason to spend any more taxpayer's monies chasing ghosts. The last thing a sheriff wants is an unsolved homicide case, especially involving one of his deputies as the victim. The case is closed pending the arrest of Garcia-Hernandez."

The sheriff turned toward Dan O'Rourke, shook his hand, and said, "Dan, we will get him if it's the last thing I do."

"Thank you, sir," Dan replied. Sheriff Duncan walked over to Mary and shook her hand and reiterated the same sentiments. When he reached to shake Heather's hand, she grabbed onto her mother's arm and refused. The sheriff, stunned, said "That's okay" and walked off.

*****

As the O'Rourkes were driving home, Dan looked in his rear-view mirror at Heather in the back seat and said, "That was pretty rude what you did to the sheriff, Heather. Why did you do that?"

"Dad, you have always told me not to trust anyone if my gut felt something was wrong."

"Yes, honey, but I meant that for strangers and when you are alone and feel uncomfortable, not for my boss."

"Dad, I don't like him, and I don't trust him. I can't tell you why, but I just don't." She looked into her dad's eyes in the rearview mirror deadpan and said, "If I had my pepper spray, I would have sprayed him in the face and called 911 like you taught me."

Dan looked at her in the eyes and could tell she wasn't kidding. He thought, *Am I missing something? My daughter senses danger just like I taught her, but I don't.* "It's okay, Heather. Never second-guess your gut feeling," he said.

THE FUNERAL

The funeral mass was held at St. Peter's Italian Catholic Church in Los Angeles. Dan and Mary had been going to it together their entire married life, and Mary had been going to the church since she was born. The church was only able to handle 230 people, so seating was set up by invitation only. Family and close friends were given priority, then the remaining seats were given to politicians and upper-brass law enforcement. Outside the church, several televisions were set up on the church grounds. All in all, approximately 1,200 people showed up for the services with most of them being law enforcement officers dressed in class As.

Every state and major law enforcement agency were represented. Ironically, no one from San Francisco or Oakland was present. To accommodate the number of police cruisers present, N Broadway Street from Bishops Road to Cottage Home Street were shut down. The parking area for Cathedral High School was also utilized. The media was pissed because they were confined to areas outside the road closures. The past two days prior to the funeral, a wake was held in which only family and invited close friends were allowed. Due to the nature of Brian's injuries, the wake was closed casket. The mass was a standard Catholic funeral mass. First, there was a greeting by the priest followed by a procession of the priest, coffin, then congregation. Holy water was sprinkled during the procession. Next were opening songs and prayers followed by readings from the Bible. Holy Communion was offered followed by more prayers. After the prayers were finished, the coffin was taken back down the aisle and out of the church. The pallbearers consisted of the LASD honor guard. They were very skilled and professional. Unfortunately, this wasn't the first officer funeral that they served in, and it wouldn't be their last.

The hearse turned left out of the church parking lot toward I-5 south followed by two limousines carrying the O'Rourkes, Stacy, Chief Dixon, Judge Fallon, and Heather's grandparents. LAPD, LASD, and the California Highway Patrol coordinated for the road closures from the church to the cemetery in Covina Hills about twenty-five miles east. Although it was Saturday, that was a remarkable feat. Leading the procession was twenty-one motorcycles from all three agencies. Following the funeral party was the rest of friends and relatives followed by approximately one thousand police cruisers. They merged onto I-5 south for approximately one and a half miles before merging onto I-10 east toward San Bernardino. As the lead motorcycle entered the San Bernardino Freeway, the last units were barely leaving the church.

The drive on I-10 was approximately twenty-two miles and traveled through the cities of Monterey Park, Rosemead, El Monte, and West Covina. Each of those agencies were tasked with blocking off all entrances to the I-10, and they did an excellent job. For the entire trip, they only encountered a half dozen cars on the freeway that somehow managed to get on. Fire department units were utilized at the clover leaf of I-10 and I-635, the San Gabriel Freeway. At every overpass, there were hundreds of people waving American flags and holding homemade signs. "We love you, Brian," "RIP, Brian," and "Thank you for your service" were just some of the many different ones. The procession took the Via Verde exit in Covina, and conveniently, the cemetery was right off the end of the exit ramp. It only took one and a half hours from the time the funeral procession left the church until the priest started the Rite of Committal.

"Mom, Dad, can I have a private moment alone with Brian please?" Heather asked as they were walking away from the gravesite.

"Is everything okay, honey?" Dan asked.

"I'm fine, Dad. I just wanted to say a few words to my brother without anyone else around."

"Okay, sweetheart. We will be right over there if you need us." Heather turned around and walked back to the gravesite.

She stood there with the California sun glistening off her hair and addressed her brother. "Well, big bro, you know I've always considered you and Dad to be my supermen, and although the both of you explained that something like this could happen, I never believed that it actually would. I know you don't want me to feel sorry for you, but you are still my hero. And I will never forget you, nor will I allow anyone else to do so either. I will not allow you to be just another statistic. You have my word on that. I don't quite know how I will accomplish that just yet, but I promise you that it will be done. Don't worry about Mom and Dad either. I'll take care of them."

She stood there for half an hour by herself talking to her brother. They couldn't hear what she was saying, but her body language spoke volumes. Initially, she just stood there and acted like she was having a normal conversation, even laughing at some point. Then they saw her with her hand on her left hip and her finger pointing at him as if she was scolding him for something, then back to both of her hands on her hip. At one point, she stood there with both of her arms across her chest as if she was being defiant. Judge Fallon walked up to Dan and Mary and asked, "Do you want me to go talk to her?"

"No, Tim," Dan responded. "I think she needs this. I don't see her breaking down. I just think she wants to get some things off her chest. You go ahead of us, Tim. We will meet up with you at your house when's she's finished."

About five minutes after Fallon left, Heather got down on her knees to pray. Stacy, realizing that her personal conversation with her brother was over, walked up and knelt next to her best friend. Heather turned, and they both hugged each other, then turned back to the coffin and prayed together. When the prayer was through, they both stood. Stacy put her arm around Heather's shoulders, and they walked back to Dan and Mary.

"Everything okay, honey?" Mary asked.

"Everything's fine, Mom. I just had to talk to Brian about some stuff, and I didn't want it to be on the six o'clock news."

"Sorry to have to tell you this, sweetheart, but it probably will be on the news," Dan said as he pointed to the remaining news vans with telescopic cameras.

"Why can't these people just leave us alone?" Heather asked. "I don't know what sane person can just prey on people's misery and suffering and make money from it. You'd have to be mentally deranged to be in the media."

SAN DIEGO

Rosa's Taco Shop was a small family-owned mom-and-pop shop that had been passed down for three generations. Only family members worked there, and they had never expanded, even with the popularity of it, nor did they plan on doing so. At lunchtime and on the weekends, people could wait up to one hour to get served. The California burrito was Andy's favorite. It came with carne asada, french fries, guacamole, pico de gallo, and sour cream. Apparently, it was created in San Diego by surfers in the early seventies to get protein and carbs while surfing. Most of the time, Andy would never consider putting that much crap in his body, but Rosa's was not to be missed. It was ten thirty when Andy walked in and saw his old friend Rick already munching on a burrito.

"What the hell, man?" Andy asked.

"I couldn't wait for your late ass any longer," Rick replied.

"We were to meet between ten thirty and eleven."

"Yeah, and it's ten thirty-two now, so you are late!"

Andy had met Rick when Andy was a conductor for the Arizona Pacific Railroad and Rick was a border patrolman just south of Yuma, Arizona, working the San Luis point of entry inspection station. They met in a bar when Andy got off a train one night, and they hit it off. They developed a close relationship and eventually started smuggling Cuban cigars in through Mexico. After Andy's dad was killed, Andy left the railroad and perfected his software and quit the cigar-running operation, but Rick still did it, and Andy would still hook him up with a list of clienteles. Rick was now the station chief at the Calexico point of entry in Calexico, California, just across the border from Mexicali where Garcia-Hernandez was living. Rick was a big man—

six feet four inches and 225 pounds—and still worked out. However, his love for Mexican food and beer kept a belly on him.

Andy walked up and ordered his burrito. He sat down across from Rick, and the two started talking generalities. "So how's the wife and kids?" Andy asked.

"The wife is still a nag, and the kids are doing great," Rick said.

"Isn't your oldest one a senior this year?" Andy asked.

"Samantha, yes, and as a matter of fact, she was just accepted into Stanford."

"Stanford! Jeez, Rick, that cigar racket you have going must be doing better than I thought. Isn't Stanford like $85,000 per year?"

"Not that well, Andy. If it weren't for her academic scholarships, she definitely wouldn't be going to Stanford, I can assure you that. Andy, I was going to ask a favor of you this summer, but I might as well do it now."

"Anything you need, Rick. You know that."

"When Sam takes off to college, she's going to be close to your neck of the woods, and I was wondering if you could be there for her if she needs something."

"Rick, that goes without saying. Give her my number, and if she ever needs anything, I'm one phone call away."

"Thanks, Andy. I appreciate it. It's going to be hard on me when she leaves. I'm just worried for her because, as you know, she is a very quiet and shy girl, and Palo Alto is going to be a huge culture shock for her."

"We will get her through it," Andy replied.

"Now listen, Andy. I know you don't like talking on phones, but I also know you didn't drag my ass all the way over here from Calexico to ask about my life. What can I do for you?"

Andy explained what he was looking for. After a brief description, he asked, "Is that something that can be accomplished?"

"Of course it can, but I have a few questions. What is your interest in this?"

"A mutual friend of ours sent the deceased deputy's younger sister to me asking for help, and he told her that I had connections in Mexico."

"And you agreed to this? Does this girl know you are here?"

"Of course not. I told her I would see what I could do for her and told her that she can never come to my office or have any contact with me."

"And you trust her?"

"I do," Andy replied. "I conducted some research, and she checked out."

"I don't know why you even agreed to that," Rick said. "This makes it pretty sticky for me knowing someone other than you might know what is going on, and you have a great life going for you. If you get caught up in this, it will be ruined. Are you sure you want to go through with it?"

"Yes," he replied as they worked out the details. As they were winding down, Andy handed Rick a cell phone with one number programmed into it. He told him to use it to contact him if necessary and when it was over to destroy the phone.

"I know how a throwaway phone works, Andy." When Rick stood up, he said, "She sure must have been a great piece of ass to convince you into doing this." Andy looked at him and just laughed. "You didn't, did you?" Rick barked.

"Of course not," Andy replied. Both men shook hands and went their separate ways.

The Party— Mexicali

Mexicali, like a lot of American towns, had its good side and its bad. In its early history, the city was an agricultural hub for Northern Mexico. It was now a building boom for assembly plants for parts from the United States that were built there, then the finished product was returned to the United States for sale. Garcia-Hernandez had been living in the El Cóndor section of the city west of Calle Novena in the eastern part of the city. The area was known for high crime and gang activity.

On that warm night, Garcia-Hernandez was hanging out with a guy he had just met two weeks earlier, and they hit it off right away. They were in the backyard of an abandoned house. Garcia-Hernandez was currently living in the house. He bounced from house to house and stayed with friends when he could. Isabella told her brother when she dropped him off to not go near their parents and put them in the middle of it. Oscar promised her that he wouldn't, and up to this point, he had not.

They were drinking Bud Light and smoking weed. As the night wore on, Garcia-Hernandez was getting shit-faced. His friend started asking him questions about the LA shooting. "Hey, Oscar, tell me about how you killed that cop in LA."

"Shit, man, that was nothing," Oscar responded. "Those motherfuckers are always jacking with us, so I finally had had enough. When me and my homey Anthony got pulled over, I told him, 'Fuck it, I ain't taking this shit no more.' I had two warrants for my arrest, and I wasn't going back to jail. I had just picked up an AK from a friend, and I told Anthony I was going to level those pigs. He told me to stay calm, but when the two cops got out of their car, I got out of the passenger's side and started spraying. I knew I hit them both. The black one tried to fire back, but he couldn't raise his arms, and the white boy was gone."

"Cool, man," said the friend. "Everyone around here thinks you are a hero. How'd you get away?"

"We took off and hit the hood. Anthony dropped me off at my homey's house, and he took off. They got him about two hours later. I got a ride from my homey to my sister's place in San Dimas. She took me in for five days, then she drove me here."

"Aren't you afraid of being arrested and brought back to LA to be prosecuted?"

"No way, man. My sister has a lot of juice, and she won't let them come for me." When Oscar walked away to urinate on the side of the house, his friend picked up his beer and poured a few grains of a powdery substance in it.

SHUT UP

Joe Duncan walked into his kitchen when he arrived home for the day to find his wife cooking dinner. "Bella, you have got to get ahold of your shithead brother, and tell him to lay off social media and go find a place to disappear."

"Why, are they getting ready to arrest him?" she asked. Bella made Joe promise her that if or when they were going to arrest Oscar, he would tell her so she can tell him to go into hiding.

"We should be, but no. I held a press conference this morning on an update with the case, and I was hammered with questions of why we haven't arrested him yet and that it shouldn't be difficult because he is partying in the open and bragging about it on social media. I should have never agreed to this. I should have arrested him the moment you told me he ran here to hide."

"Joe, calm down. It'll be all right. I know it sucks, but he is my brother, and I don't want to see him locked up for the rest of his life."

"Bella, he murdered a deputy, one of my deputies. So you think we are just going to let him go free?"

"No, Joe, I know his time will be up, but I'm just not ready for it to be now."

"Tell him to get the fuck off of social media and hide. Better yet, tell him to go to Cuba where we don't have any extradition."

"I'll talk to him," she replied.

THE CROSSING

About two minutes after Garcia-Hernandez passed out, an unmarked Crown Victoria pulled up in front of the house. Four men got out of it, picked his limp body up, and threw him into the trunk. They climbed back in and sped off. The informant looked around to see if anyone saw it and determined that no one did. He waited three minutes and walked two blocks, got into his car, and drove off.

The Crown Victoria drove fifteen miles east to an unsecured area on the border. It had barbed wire, but it was mangled and stretched to the point that anyone could cross. The area did have cameras and trip sensors. They were given instructions to not go within two hundred feet of the fence until exactly 0120 hours and that they had exactly fifteen minutes to get Garcia-Hernandez through the fence to a waiting truck. The border patrol's IT department was doing a security software upgrade, and the cameras and trip sensors would be disabled for fifteen minutes.

Two men pulled up in a black Ford F-150 on the American side. As they got out of the truck, the four Mexicans opened their trunk, pulled Garcia-Hernandez out, and dragged him to the fence. The four of them picked him up and literally threw him through the barbed wire, not giving a damn if he got caught in it or not. In Spanish, one of them told the two Americans, "Here you go. You can have this piece of shit. We don't want him back. Thank you." The four climbed into the Crown Vic and sped away toward Mexicali. The two men dressed in black picked him up and threw him into the bed of the truck. The F-150 headed west to the rail yard approximately ten miles north of the point of entry in Calexico. They pulled up alongside an intermodal train and threw him into the well area.

They zip-tied each of his wrists to the handles of the door of the container, pinned a note on his chest, and drove off.

"AP2310 border patrol."

"AP2310, go ahead."

"Sir, can I get a 5 mph roll by?"

"AP2310, 5 mph roll by here we go."

This was the radio exchange between the conductor of the Arizona Pacific train and border patrol agents on the ground. The intermodal train was leaving the Calexico rail yard en route to Yuma, Arizona. The train had already cleared customs at the Calexico point of entry earlier. However, it had been parked for ten hours waiting on a new crew. The agents were standing on lifted platforms on both sides of the train. When the train was about two-thirds past the agents, they spotted a rider in an intermodal well.

"Border patrol, AP 2310. Bring her to a stop."

"AP2310 stopping." The agent radioed the container location to the agents on the ground. They immediately swarmed the railcar to make sure the rider didn't jump and run away. Two agents were immediately on the railcar when the train came to a stop.

"AP dispatch, AP2310."

"AP2310, go ahead."

"What is the holdup? I need that train rolling."

"We are stopped for border patrol activity."

"AP dispatch, US Border Patrol Calexico."

"Border patrol Calexico, go."

"How much longer will this train be stopped? I have a very tight window to get it to the main line."

"Sir, we have a unique circumstance here. I am waiting on supervisor permission to proceed. I will do everything in my power to get you going as fast as I can."

"Thank you. AP dispatch out."

"West sector 8, Sam 3."

"Sam 3, go ahead."

"Sam 3, can you call me on my cell?"

"10-4. Stand by."

Sgt. Alicia Reyes was sitting at her desk when she called. "What's up, Danny?" she asked.

"Sarge, I have a rider in an intermodal well who is zip-tied to the container, and he has a note pinned to his shirt."

"What does the note say, Danny?"

"Ma'am, it says, 'Wanted for the murder of Los Angeles deputy sheriff Brian O'Rourke.'"

"Are you fucking serious?" she asked.

"Yes, ma'am."

"Okay, Danny, stand by."

She quickly punched the deputy's name into the system and was shocked to see what it said. "Danny, does he have any ID, or did he tell you his name?"

"No ID, ma'am, and he appears to be under the influence of something, so I cannot understand a word he is saying."

"It's quite possible you have Oscar Garcia-Hernandez. He has a murder warrant out of LA for the deputy's death. He also has a felony warrant out of Bell Gardens for possession for sales of a controlled substance and another felony warrant out of East LA for sexual assault of a minor."

"What are your orders? Do we leave him here and get investigators to secure the railcar?"

"No, Danny. I am getting my ass handed to me by Arizona Pacific and my captain. We have to get that train rolling."

"I understand, Sergeant, but under this suspicious circumstance of obviously someone tying him down, don't we want to further investigate?"

"No, Danny. My orders are to get that train rolling. Cut him loose, and bring him to the station. I'll have a nurse waiting for him when he gets here."

"Yes, ma'am," he replied. The agents cut him loose, lifted him off the train handcuffed, and placed him in the back of a unit.

"AP2310 border patrol."

"AP2310, go ahead."

"Sir, agents are clear from your train. You may proceed."

"Yes, sir. Confirming still a 5 mph roll by."

"Negative highball."

"AP2310 clear of Calexico Border Patrol highball. Thank you."

"AP dispatch, AP 2310."

"AP2310, go ahead."

"You have a thirty-minute window on a twenty-five-minute run. You are green-lighted to the main line. You will be placed in a siding in Glamis for a small wait for a west-bound hotshot, then you will be green-lighted to Yuma."

"AP2310, copy."

"AP dispatch, US Border Patrol."

"Border patrol, go ahead."

"Thanks for your assistance."

"AP dispatch, thanks for your patience."

When the agents arrived at the Calexico Border Patrol Station, several other officers drove up. Word had already leaked that they might have captured a cop killer. There were twelve officers waiting for the unit to stop so they could pull Garcia-Hernandez out themselves. It took an order from Sergeant Reyes to control their emotions. Agt. Hector Ortiz, a former army ranger who stood six feet six inches and weighed 260 pounds, was the one to open the door. He reached in and grabbed Garcia-Hernandez by the back of the neck and jerked him out of the car. He practically held him up with one hand while a second agent put his arm under the suspect's handcuffed arm, placed his right hand on Garcia-Hernandez's left shoulder, and pulled up. Ortiz did the same thing on his right side. They lifted him off the ground and headed to the station door.

The nurse was standing there with a wheelchair and requested that they place him in it. Ortiz walked by her and said, "Fuck that! He didn't need a wheelchair when he killed that deputy, did he?"

"Ortiz, calm down," Sergeant Reyes ordered. "We don't even know if it's him."

"Yes, ma'am, but I'll bet my next paycheck that it is," he replied. They brought him into the nurse's treatment area for an evaluation. She drew blood and gave an overall assessment.

"From the looks of it, he seems to be under the influence of fentanyl and definitely alcohol, probably more, but I won't know further until the blood test comes back," the nurse told the sergeant.

"Is he bookable?" the sergeant asked.

"Under heavy watch. I'll be here until 0600, and then day shift relief will be here with more resources."

"Thanks, Maria. Okay, Danny, Hector, he's all yours, and, Hector, I expect you to uphold the honor and integrity of the border patrol."

"Yes, ma'am," he replied.

Danny and Hector grabbed his arms and basically dragged him to the booking area. They immediately fingerprinted him. Less than five seconds went by when they confirmed his identity. They in fact had arrested Oscar Garcia-Hernandez with three felony warrants out of Los Angeles, including for the murder of DS Brian O'Rourke.

"Nice pinch, Danny. Beers are on me," Hector said as he slapped him on his back. "I can't wait to call my cousin about this."

"That's right. I forgot she's an LA deputy, isn't she?" Danny asked.

"Not only that, she went through the academy with O'Rourke. She was still working the jails when he was gunned down, but after they graduated the academy, she said she tried on numerous occasions to get him interested in her, but he would never ask. She told me that they would always be around the same people, so one day, she tried to strike up a conversation to find out more about him. All he would tell her was that he had a younger sister who was heavily into volleyball and that she was very good at it, so he didn't want to miss any of her matches. My cousin was happy that he opened up about his personal life, so she figured that the next time they were together, she would inquire more about him. I think she really liked him, but then two days before they were supposed to meet up again, this shithead killed him." As he said that, he smacked Garcia-Hernandez in the back of the head, knocking him to the floor.

"I'm sorry to hear that, Hector, but easy on our detainee."

"You're right. Sorry about that. It was just a reflection."

"Captain Reyes here. Sorry to bother you again tonight, but I think you would like to hear this."

"That's okay, Alicia. What do you have?"

"Sir, we just picked up and confirmed Oscar Garcia-Hernandez, who is wanted for the murder of an LA sheriff's deputy five years ago."

"Are you serious? Great job, Sergeant!"

"Thank you, sir," she replied. "Captain, all of the booking process has been done. Do you or the chief want to call LASD and advise them?"

"No, Sergeant, you do it. This is due to the hard work that you and your guys do while the chief and I are in bed. I'm coming in, but go ahead and notify LASD Homicide and have them get their guys en route."

"Will do, Captain," she said.

"Alicia, great job."

"Thank you, sir."

"Becky, you up?" Hector asked when she answered the phone. Becky was in bed in her apartment in Covina. She was a Los Angeles County sheriff's deputy and worked the midday shift in Region 3.

"Hector, is that you? What time is it?" she asked.

"Three AM," he replied.

"Are you okay? Did something happen?"

"Everything's fine, but I have some info that I thought you would like to hear."

"At three AM? This better be good. I've only been in bed for an hour and a half," she said.

"Oh, it's good. Are you sitting up? We just picked up Garcia-Hernandez," he said confidently.

"Who?" she asked.

"You know. Garcia-Hernandez, the guy that killed Brian O'Rourke." Dead silence. "Bec, are you there?"

"I'm here, Hector. I'm just trying to determine if I should scream or cry. How?" she asked.

"Well, it wasn't me. Danny was the first one to get him. But I did get to be the one to drag his ass out of the unit and book him. Our sergeant is on the line with LASD Homicide right now to arrange transportation."

"Hector, you are the best. Well, I know the O'Rourke family will be very happy come morning. It's been a long wait."

"Aren't you happy, cuz?" he asked.

"Oh, I'm happy. I'm happy for the O'Rourkes, and I'm happy that that asshole has to face justice. But I'm a little sad in thinking that I don't know if me and Brian would or would not have hit it off, and I'll never know. Don't worry about it, Hector. It's a girl thing. Tell Danny and the rest of the guys thank you, and when you come into town this weekend, beers are on me."

THE SCOOP

At 3:20 AM, Andy was asleep in his Rancho house when a phone rang. He didn't immediately recognize the ring, which meant only one thing: it was the throwaway phone and Rick. Andy answered with a "Yep."

"Rosa's at noon. Go dark."

"Okay." Nothing else was said. Andy was supposed to be in Boise, Idaho, today at 2:00 PM for a business meeting with an incumbent congressman who was facing a serious primary challenger. Andy had the goods on the challenger that would knock him out of the race, and this afternoon would be an easy $45,000 plus expenses. He would have Cindy call the congressman first thing to apologize and reschedule the meeting for tomorrow. He picked up the phone and left a message for Cindy and explained that he would be unavailable and uncontactable until later tonight. Cindy never questioned him. Andy lay back down and tried to get a few more hours of sleep.

Going dark meant that Andy would need to leave all his cell phones and electronic devices at home and get a car that was not registered to him for the trip to San Diego. At 5:00 AM, he got up, worked out, ate breakfast, and showered. He then removed the SIM card from the throwaway phone and destroyed it. He went into the garage and took a hammer to the phone and smashed it into hundreds of pieces. At nine thirty, he had an Uber pick him up and drive him to the closest car rental place. He rented a nondescript silver Hyundai Elantra. By ten, he was on the road to San Diego. To avoid Los Angeles traffic, he took the I-15 south instead of the I-5. As he was driving and listening to the radio, he wondered how many Americans could just give up their smartphones and drive two hours in peace. He guessed he was probably the only one.

Andy arrived twenty minutes early, so he went inside for a beer while he waited. Rick arrived at exactly 12:00 PM. "You're late," Andy said.

"Fuck you," Rick responded. "You were late the last time we talked, so I'm just getting even." Rick ordered a burrito and a beer.

"What, you're not eating, Andy?"

"No. I had a big breakfast. I'm not hungry." Andy was hungry, but he wasn't going to fill up on fattening foods. The beer was bad enough. They bullshitted until Rick's food arrived, and then Rick changed the subject.

"Well, you will be happy to know that LASD is currently at my station picking your boy up."

"You got him. Thanks, Rick."

"You're welcome. However, we didn't have to do much. It was a piece of cake. That guy is a real piece of shit, and besides, Mexico was happy to rid themselves of him. For someone wanted for murder, he was living a happy and outgoing life. Andy, this hasn't hit the news yet, but when it does, it's going to blow up."

"Any fallback for us?" Andy asked.

"Not really fallback per se." Rick smiled.

"What did you do, Rick?"

"We just had a little fun with him because he killed a cop, so it's going to make the media go nuts. Andy, this girl you are doing this for, how is she going to react when she finds out?"

"Rick, I don't know exactly. However, my gut feeling is, she won't say a word to anyone."

"I've got to take you at your word for that, Andy, but that is not the reason I dragged your ass all the way down here."

"There is more? I was happy with what you just told me."

"Shit, I could have said that in one sentence on the phone. Andy, this Garcia-Hernandez fellow might have some sort of political connections with LASD."

"Why do you say that?"

"Without getting into too much information to protect you, prior to snatching him up, he was getting drunk at a party with one of our informants. So the informant brought up the shooting and told Garcia-Hernandez that it was cool that he shot a cop and got away with it. Well, the dipshit started bragging about some stuff. He told the informant that after the shooting, he ran to his sister's house in San Dimas and hid out for five days. He then said that after the five days, she helped him cross the border and drove him to Mexicali. He made mention that she was protecting him from prosecution. Unfortunately, we had a strict timeline to get him over the border, so he was juiced up, and we didn't get any more out of him. I don't know if it means anything or not, Andy, but I thought it was worth your time to tell you, but it couldn't be done over the phone."

"Rick, I am going to follow up on this. I think you are on to something with that info. The girl that came to see me said that rumor around LASD was that someone high up was stonewalling the investigation, and now it seems that this little shithead might be confirming it."

"Andy, this is something you have to do on your own. I don't know how you are able to get the dirt that you do, but this sounds like it's right up your alley. You know this information can never get out as far as where you heard it."

"Rick, I am offended that you felt you even had to tell me that."

"Oh, grow up, snowflake!" They both laughed. "You know, you should have been a cop, Andy."

"No way. It doesn't pay very well."

"You're right about that."

"What do I owe you, Rick?"

"Owe me? Are you serious? I thought we were friends. We do stuff for each other all the time."

"I understand that, but I asked you to do something for me on behalf of someone else, so there was added risk."

"Andy, unknown girl or not, this was a noble thing we did. And if somehow we were to get caught, it was well worth it. Hell, we have taken bigger chances than this for less reasons."

"Thank you, Rick." The two men shook hands and headed their separate ways.

He Did It!

"Ah! Oh, thank God!" Heather yelled.

"What is it, Heather?" Stacy asked. Stacy Hanna was a six-feet-two-inch tall, pretty, blond-haired girl with deep blue eyes. She was of Swedish descent. She had a slender body and long legs. "Hold on a second, Mom," Heather put her hand over her cell phone and explained to Stacy that the border patrol picked up Garcia-Hernandez.

"What a relief," Stacy stated as she and Heather hugged.

"So what are you two girls doing tomorrow? I want to put together a little celebration."

"We didn't really have anything planned. We will be there. What time?"

"How about one o'clock?"

"Great, Mom. We will see you then." After she hung the phone up, Heather sat on her bed and broke out in tears.

"What's wrong, Heather?" Stacy asked. "This is a good thing, isn't it?"

"These are tears of joy," Heather explained. "I just can't believe he did it," she stated out loud.

"Who did what?" Stacy asked.

Realizing she said that out loud, Heather replied, "Oh, nothing. Come on, let's get some lunch."

*****

"Ma'am, is it possible that I might speak to Division Chief Dixon?" Dep. Rebecca Ortiz asked after identifying herself. She was not on duty and was in street clothes. The secretary had been around a long time and knew proper protocol.

"Have you spoken with your captain and received permission to go up the chain of command?"

"No, ma'am. This is not LASD related. It is a personal matter reference the O'Rourke family." She asked Becky to sit while she talked to the chief. A minute later, the secretary came out of the office followed by Dixon. He walked up to her and offered his hand.

"Deputy Ortiz, Bill Dixon. Come on in." They walked into the office. He offered her a chair, and they both sat down. "What can I do for you, Deputy?" She explained her connection to Brian and the fact that her cousin who was involved in the arrest will be in town.

"Sir, it is no secret that you are very close to the O'Rourkes, and I am under the impression that they are holding a celebration tomorrow to celebrate the arrest of Garcia-Hernandez. I was wondering if somehow my cousin and I could get an invitation to that celebration. I know it's silly, but I would just like to meet the family who could have possibly been my family, and I definitely want to meet the little sister that Brian was so attached to."

"You know, Rebecca, Brian talked to me several times about you, but he didn't think you were interested. And if he talked to me about you, then I can assure you he talked to his sister about you as well. It seems like a case of shy versus shy. I'll tell you what, are you off tomorrow?"

"Yes, sir. I took vacation time this weekend to spend time with my cousin."

"Okay. Give me your number." When she did, he called her phone. "There, now you have my number. I will text you the O'Rourkes' address. It starts around 1:00 PM, but I want you to be there around two. If you run into any trouble, text or call me. Sound good?" They both stood up and shook hands.

"Thank you, Chief. I don't think you know what this means to me."

"Oh, I have a feeling I do. I will see you tomorrow."

The Celebration

When the girls turned the corner to Heather's house, they saw the street packed with cars and the news media. West Covina PD had six units keeping the house secured and keeping the public and the media away. The girls had to park over on the next block. When they walked up to the front yard, they were stopped by an officer who explained to them that only invited guests were allowed in. When Heather explained who she was and showed him her driver's license, the officer allowed them past. The news media overheard her explanation and immediately started shouting questions at her. Hearing the commotion, Chief Dixon came out of the house, put his arms around the two girls, and pulled them inside, ignoring the media.

The place was packed—Judge Fallon, Division Chief Dixon and his wife, Marsha, Heather's four uncles and aunts, cousins, Stacy's parents, grandparents' uncles, aunts and cousins, Father Cleveland from church, Dan's close cop buddies, and Mary's church friends. All in all, there were approximately 120 people present. When Dan saw Heather in the foyer, he bulldogged his way through the crowd and gave her a big hug.

"Congratulations, Dad. Maybe things can start getting back to normal," Heather said as both of their eyes filled with tears. No sooner did Dan let go of Heather when her mom practically knocked her over with a hug. Then Dan and Mary turned their attention to Stacy. "Mom, I thought you said 'a little celebration'?"

"Well, honey, it started that way, then when the word got out, it kept growing." Heather looked into the kitchen, and there was catered Italian she figured enough to feed two hundred people. There were coolers of beer, soda, iced teas, and water. The counter had Jack Daniels and red wine, a staple in the O'Rourke house.

"Mom, we have to feed the cops outside. Can I make them a plate and bring it to them?"

Stacy's uncle Jay overheard the conversation and interrupted. "Heather, I don't think that would be very wise. If you or any member of your family go out there, the media will chew you up. I'll tell you what. Why don't I go out there and bring the supervisor in here, and you make the suggestion to feed them, and let him determine how to do it."

"Okay, Jay, thanks."

Jay walked out the front door and found the corporal in charge. He whispered that his presence was requested inside by the family. CPL Dave Finch followed Jay into the house. The media noticed it and became restless, believing something important was about to happen. When Jay brought the corporal into the foyer, someone yelled, "Oh shit, the cops are here!" The entire place burst into laughter, including the corporal. Dan, Mary, and Heather met him as Jay introduced everyone.

"First of all, Mr. and Mrs. and Miss O'Rourke, I would like to express my condolences and my appreciation of Brian's sacrifice."

"Thank you, Corporal," Dan said.

"Well, what can I do for you folks? You name it."

Heather jumped in and said, "Corporal, you are already doing plenty for us. I asked you in here to offer food and drinks for your officers."

"That's very generous, ma'am, but with all of the news cameras out there, it would put us in a bad light."

"Well, they have to eat," Heather replied. "Is it possible that you can just let one in here at a time, let them eat, and then send the next one in?"

"Are you sure? I don't want to interrupt your celebration."

"Interrupt, hell," Dan said. "The six of you are what we are celebrating."

"I will go talk to my officers and start sending them in. Thank you again."

"Corporal," Heather said, "they don't need to knock. Just tell them to come right in. The kitchen is to the left, and there is a bathroom the first door on the left down the hall behind me. Tell them to help themselves."

Heather walked into the kitchen, poured a glass of wine, and set out to look for one person in particular. She finally found him in the backyard sitting on a bench next to the pool underneath a large avocado tree, sipping on a Jack and Coke. "Well, there you are," she said. "Are you trying to avoid me?"

"Heather, get over here, and give your uncle Tim a hug." Chief Judge Tim Fallon was not her real uncle. He had been a family friend since before Heather was born, so she always called him Uncle. Fallon and Heather's father had known each other from when Fallon was a prosecutor and Dan was a new deputy. He got off the bench and gave her a big bear hug. They both sat down next to each other, and after looking to see if anyone was listening in, he said, "Well, you did it honey. How does it feel?"

"Uncle Tim, when my mom called me and told me the news, I couldn't get my emotions under control. I went from bouncy happy to crying, back to happy and then thinking that this road isn't over yet. We still have a trial to go through, but at least the process can now get started. Then as I was lying in bed last night going over everything in my head, I felt selfish."

"Selfish?" Tim asked, confused. "How in the world can you correlate selfish with what you did?"

"Uncle Tim, when I started this, I never in a million years thought of the unintended consequences of my actions."

"What are you talking about, Heather? It was set up so you would be protected."

"That's the selfish part. I mean, what does he get out of it? I go to a man and ask for help. He does exactly what I asked him to do, but he gets nothing. He doesn't even get to be here with us celebrating his accomplishment." She started tearing up. "Uncle Tim, that man provided us with a miracle. My family now has a chance at justice, and I finally get to see smiles on my mom and dad's faces again, but what does he get out of it? He gets no money, no recognition, nothing. Why would he even help to start with? He takes all of the risk with no chance of some sort of reward. I was so selfish just thinking about my family when I went to him. I never thought once about him and the position I put him in. I feel terrible. I wish I could just hug him right now and tell him how thankful I am for what he did, but I'm never going to see him again, am I?" she asked.

"Unfortunately, honey, that's how this stuff works," he explained. "I don't know what you did or said to him in your meeting three weeks ago, but you triggered something in that man's head to agree to help you, but that decision came with conditions, conditions that you accepted. But, Heather, think for a moment. You got exactly what you wanted, and he will be fine, trust me. I've known him a long time, and he knew what he was getting into when he agreed to help. Don't worry about him not getting anything out of it either. He certainly doesn't need the money, and you would have insulted him if you offered any. He just likes to do nice things for people."

"Well, can I at least go see him one last time? Please?" she asked.

"Heather, you know the answer to that question."

"Uncle Tim, I like him!" she blurted out. "I've thought about him every day since I left his office."

"Are you telling me you have feelings for him?" Heather put her head down and looked at the ground, shaking her head in the affirmative. "How? You just met him once."

"It's all your fault, Uncle Tim," she answered back.

"My fault?" he asked, surprised. "How can you blame me for that?"

"Because you never told me how cute he is and how much of a gentleman he is," she replied.

"I get it, and now you feel really strongly about him for accomplishing what you asked him to, right?" he asked.

"Yes," she said.

"Heather, not to change the subject, but why don't you try to go on a date with a guy from school? Maybe it'll take this pressure off of your shoulders because you know it can never work out between you two. I just don't see any path forward without jeopardizing his freedom, and I know you don't want that to happen. Do you?"

"No way, never! If I have to do without him, fine. I would never hurt him. But I don't want to do without him, and I am not going to go on any dates just to forget him either. Uncle Tim, can you talk to him for me?"

"Heather, I'm just as much off-limits to him as you are. We cannot be seen together or have any contact for protection purposes. You know that."

"I know, I know," she said. "Uncle Tim, all you have to do is tell me that he is a bad guy, and I'll leave it alone, although I would still like to one day thank him in person. But I trust you, and if you tell me he's bad for me, then I will drop my feelings for him."

When Tim didn't answer, she asked, "He's a good guy, isn't he?"

"Heather, you are putting me in a very difficult position right now. I can't answer your question without lying to you or getting your hopes up because I don't want to do either of them. So, Heather, are you going to let it go? You know you have to."

"Uncle Tim, you can take me at my word that I will never jeopardize what we did, but you can't ask me not to say an extra prayer every night," she said with a smile.

"Fair enough because for you to get what you're asking for would take some very powerful prayers or more like a direct intervention from God himself. Come on. Let's join the others."

BECKY AND HECTOR

As they were walking to the back door, Bill approached them. "Heather, there are a couple of people here who would like to talk to you and your parents."

"Is it the media?" she asked.

"I thought you said that you loved me," Bill said in a fake hurtful tone.

"Of course I do. Why do you ask that?"

"Do you think that I would ever let the media into your home?"

Heather laughed. "Sorry, Bill. I didn't think that one through. Who are they?"

"I'm going to let them explain it, and I'm warning you, it might get a little emotional but in a good way."

"Okay, Bill. You know I trust you. Where are they at?"

"In the study. I've cleared everyone out."

"Okay, but if it might get emotional, I'm bringing Stacy."

"That goes without saying," he replied. All three laughed. They walked in to find everybody already sitting and just chatting. Heather and Bill walked in and sat on each side of Stacy.

"What's going on, Bill?" Dan asked.

"Dan, this is Rebecca Ortiz. She is an LASD deputy. Not in your region. She works in Region 3. And this is her cousin Hector Ortiz, border patrol out of Calexico. The two of them have a connection with Brian, so Rebecca came to me yesterday and asked if I could arrange for her and her cousin to meet you folks. I felt that all of you need to hear each other out. Rebecca, if you will."

"Thank you, Chief. Sergeant and Mrs. O'Rourke, I appreciate you seeing me, and quite frankly, it's probably pretty selfish of me to even be here. Sir, I have to warn you, it's a girly thing, and I'm going to get emotional."

"Rebecca, if you told this story to Bill and he thought it was a good idea for us to meet with you, then it's probably not selfish."

She continued. "I went through the academy with Brian, and we worked in the jails together. He got out one year earlier to work the streets than I did. We worked together a lot and would meet up with other people to hang out. I liked Brian a lot, but I could never get him to ask me out. Sure, we met up with the same group of friends but never one-on-one. I thought he liked me, but I couldn't tell for sure, so I told myself that I was going to work on him until he asked me out."

"Why didn't you just ask him out?" Stacy asked.

"Because Brian didn't seem like the type of guy that would let a girl ask him. He seemed too old-fashioned for that, so I didn't want to ruin any chance with him. So every time we got together, I would ask questions about his family. He seemed to be very family-oriented, so I figured that was going to be a way into his heart. I hit the nail on the head because when he was talking family, I could tell he would loosen up. He loved his sister and her friend Stacy. All he talked about was the two of them and volleyball. We started getting really close, and I thought I might finally have a chance with him, then two days before just the two of us were to meet up for a beer, he was killed." She broke out in tears. The whole room was in tears.

Mary stood up and said, "Come here, sweetheart." Rebecca stood, and Mary gave her a mama bear hug.

"I am so sorry for coming here. I just wanted to meet the family that maybe would have...could have...should have...I don't know. I know it's silly, but I guess I just wanted to put that chapter of my life to bed."

"Why didn't you come to us sooner so you didn't have to put yourself through all that misery for so long?" Mary asked.

"Because the suspect was still on the loose, and that would have been very selfish of me to close a chapter in my life when yours was still open."

Heather stood up and gave her a big hug. "I'm sorry you had to go through that. I know Brian wanted to ask you out several times, and it was getting frustrating for me to hear him talk about you but being too much of a chicken to ask you out. He was afraid of you turning him down."

"Thank you for that. Sir, is Heather here? And if so, may I meet her? I won't bring any of this up to her so I won't upset her, but I just want to meet the little sister he was so fond of."

"You just did. She's standing right in front of you," Dan replied.

"You're Heather?" she asked, surprised.

"Guilty," Heather replied.

"I didn't expect you to be so young."

"We were ten years apart."

"Now I get it. You weren't just his little sister in the sense that all brothers say it. You literally were his little sister. So that means you must be Stacy."

"Guilty. But how did you know that?"

"Brian told me that you two were very close and that if Heather was somewhere, then you would either be close by or stuck to her hip. He said it worked both ways with you two." Everyone laughed.

"Well, you know, Rebecca, there is someone else here in this room that had a crush on Brian," Mary said.

"Mrs. O'Rourke!" Stacy blurted out, red-faced.

"So you had a crush on him as well?" Rebecca asked. "Well, I would have lost that fight," she continued.

"Why do you say that?" Stacy asked.

"Because look how pretty you are. Actually, Brian told me that the both of you were pretty, but he failed to explain that you two are gorgeous." Stacy and Heather blushed.

"You wouldn't have had anything to worry about. I was eleven years old when I had a crush on him." Everyone laughed.

"Thank you, folks, for letting me get that off of my chest, but on a lighter note, my cousin Hector was one of the agents who arrested Garcia-Hernandez."

"Really?" Dan said. "Well, thank you for that." Mary and Stacy had their eyes wide open and their hands over their mouths. Bill just sat there because he had already heard the story.

Heather sat there emotionless and, when they were done talking, asked, "How did you find him?"

"It was kind of easy. We were inspecting a northbound train when he was spotted in the well area of an intermodal railcar. We had the train stop, and actually, it was my partner, Danny, who was the first to him. He was under the influence of some sort of drug. The medical staff thinks it was fentanyl, but the strange thing was that his wrists were zip-tied to the container doors, and he had a note pinned on his shirt."

"What did it say?" Dan asked.

"Sir, it said, 'Wanted for the murder of Los Angeles deputy sheriff Brian O'Rourke,'" Hector replied.

"So that probably means he was put there and did not show up on his own," Dan said.

"That's what we figured, sir."

"Are they investigating that?" Heather asked.

"Of course they are, sweetheart," Dan replied.

"Well, actually, sir, we aren't. Danny and I wanted investigators to respond to the scene, but we were overruled and ordered to cut him loose and bring him to the station."

"Did they tell you why?" Dan asked.

"We were told that the train had to move," Hector replied.

"Well, good," Heather stated. "Did you guys beat him up?" she asked.

"Heather!" Mary barked. "What's gotten into you?"

"Mom, I hope they kicked the crap out of him and that he ended up in the hospital with broken bones and stitches," she replied very stoned-faced. Bill, Dan, Rebecca, and Hector just laughed.

"Young lady, that is not how professional law enforcement acts."

"Well, they should," she replied.

"Heather, you will be happy to know that I was the one who assisted him off the train, got him out of the back seat at the station, and assisted in booking him," Hector said as he winked at Dan. Dan just gave him a nod.

"I saw that, Dad. What was that?" she asked.

"We will talk about it later, sweetheart."

"Well, Mr. and Mrs. O'Rourke, I appreciate you taking the time to listen to my silly thoughts. Chief, thank you for setting this up, and Heather and Stacy, it was very nice to meet you," Rebecca said. "We will let you get back to your celebration and guests." She stood up and said, "Come on, Hector. Let's leave these folks alone."

"Where do you think you're going, young lady?" Mary barked. "No one comes into an Italian home during a celebration and leaves without eating and drinking. It's rude. You're not going anywhere. So what do you like to drink—beer, wine, or whiskey?"

"I'm not a big beer person, but when I went out with the guys, Brian got me hooked on Sierra Nevada Pale Ale. I don't suppose you have any of that."

"Of course we do. It was his favorite beer. Heather, Stacy, come on. Let's get these two fed properly."

"You girls go. I need a minute with Hector," Dan said.

Heather whispered into Stacy's ear, "Go with my mom and Rebecca. I'm going to stay here for a minute."

"Sure, Heather," she replied. When Heather didn't leave the room, Dan knew why she was staying, so he wasn't even going to try to make her leave.

When Stacy shut the door, Heather said, "Okay, Hector. What did you do to him?"

"Heather, your mom was right when she said our hands are tied when being rough with prisoners, but…" He smiled. "There are things that can be technically wrong but don't appear to be done with malice. For instance, after we cut the zip ties off of him, I placed him in handcuffs. Danny and two other agents waited on the ground for me to lift him over the train for them to catch him. Well, let's just say that my aim was off, and I missed all three agents." Heather smirked. "Then when we got to the station, I reached into the back seat and grabbed him by the back of his neck and carried him that way into the station. Then in booking, as I was explaining to Danny my cousin's connection to Brian and when I mentioned that they were supposed to meet up two days later, then I said until this shithead killed him, as I said that, I smacked him on the back of his head so hard that he actually fell out of the chair and onto the floor."

"Well, good. Thank you for that," Heather said.

"Guys, listen. I know today was weird, but I appreciate you listening to my cousin. No one knows if Brian and her would have ever been together, but I think she was sold on how family orientated he was. You see, she came from a verbally and physically abusive family. My uncle and aunt were very abusive parents, so she had no real sense of family until my dad took her in when she was a sophomore in high school. So that's why today was important for her, although I did warn her that doing what she did today might make it worse, you guys being a good family and all."

"Thank you, Hector, and thanks for picking up that shithead. Now let's go celebrate," Dan said.

*****

"So do you two still play volleyball?" Becky asked. She asked Heather and Stacy if they would call her Becky because she hated the name Rebecca. It always reminded her of when she was getting a beating.

"Oh yeah. We both play for UCLA," Stacy replied.

"Really?" she asked, shocked. "Brian told me that you two were good, but that's better than good," she said. As Stacy and Becky were talking, Heather noticed that Becky kept looking at Corporal Finch, who was standing by the kitchen table eating spaghetti.

"What are you looking at, Becky?" Heather asked.

"Oh, nothing, why?" she replied.

"I see you looking at that corporal," Heather said.

"Well, he is kinda cute."

"Are you interested?" Heather asked.

"Oh no, Heather. I haven't dated since before the academy."

"You mean to tell me that you haven't dated because of Brian?" Heather asked.

Becky's eyes filled with tears, and she said, "I really liked your brother."

"Becky, that's not healthy. Go talk to that corporal."

"I don't know anything about him. What if he's married or in a relationship, or worse yet, what if he turns me down?"

And that was the final straw, Stacy thought, and she saw it in Heather's eyes. "Becky, I had to go through this with Brian over you for a long time, and I could have gained a big sister a long time ago but didn't because you and Brian were too shy. Now I'm not blaming you. I'm blaming my brother for being so chicken, but you're being chicken now. Excuse me. I need to talk to someone." Stacy and Becky watched Heather walk up to the corporal.

"What is she doing?" Becky asked.

"She's getting you a date," Stacy replied.

"I'm so embarrassed right now. I don't know what to do."

"Becky, Heather was right. It's not healthy for you to not date. I understand the Brian thing, but you got it off of your chest today, and at bare minimum, you've gained a new friend."

"We don't know if he'll say yes," Becky stated.

"I wasn't talking about him. I'm talking about Heather."

*****

"Corporal, do you have a minute?"

"Of course I do, but please call me Dave."

"Dave, there is someone in this house that has an interest in you, but she is too chicken to come talk to you, so can I ask you some personal questions?"

"Let me guess. The cute brunette in the living room?"

"Yes, how did you know?"

"Because I've been watching her, and her eyes kept wandering over here."

"So are you married?"

"No."

"Have you ever been married?"

"No."

"Are you currently dating or in a relationship?"

"No."

"Do you have any children?"

"No."

"Do you come from a close family?"

"Yes. I have a very close and loving family."

"Would you like to take my big sister out to get to know her?"

"I don't know, Heather. A little over a year ago, I ended a four-year relationship with a girl that I was going to ask to marry me. I caught her cheating on me with her boss from work, so it's pretty hard overcoming something like that."

"I'm so sorry to hear that," she said. "Well, you don't have to get into a relationship. Just have a girl that you can hang out with and see where it goes from there."

"Well, in that case, I have some questions to ask of the middleman."

"Go ahead." She giggled.

"Is or has she been married?"

"No."

"Is she currently dating or in a relationship?"

"No."

"Does she have any kids?"

"No."

"Who is that big monster that brought her here?"

"Her cousin."

"Does she come from a good family?"

"Yes and no. Her parents are poster people for the worst parents of the decade, but her uncle, her cousin's dad, took her in when she was in high school."

"What does she do for a living?"

"She's an LA County sheriff's deputy."

"Really?"

"Yep, right up your alley."

"Heather, cops are notorious for cheating on their spouses." Heather then told him about Becky's connection with Brian. "You mean to tell me that she hasn't been on a date in, what, nine years?"

"No, she hasn't. She really wanted my brother, but when that was taken from her, she wasn't interested. So I don't think I'd worry about her cheating on you."

"Well, she is cute, and it wouldn't hurt to have a girl in my life, so sure, I'll take her out and see how it goes."

Heather started to walk back to Becky and Stacy when she noticed that Dave wasn't following her. She went back to him and asked, "Well, are you coming or not?"

"Right now?" he asked.

"Yes, right now. You'll never know if you will lose her if you don't seize the moment."

They walked over to Stacy and Becky. Becky's face was beet red. Dave offered her his hand and said, "Becky, my name is Dave."

"Nice to meet you, Dave."

"I don't want to beat around the bush, and I believe you already know why I'm here, but listen, would you like to go out for a beer or a coffee sometime? I'm under the impression that you are someone I should get to know."

Becky, now even more embarrassed, replied, "I would be interested in that, yes." Hector walked up and heard everything and couldn't believe it. He'd been trying to get her to go on a date for five years, but she had always refused.

"Well, because of my new promotion, I get the crappy days off. I'm off Tuesday through Thursday," he said.

"Mine aren't much better. I'm off Wednesday through Friday. Where do you live?" she asked.

"Right next door in Covina," he replied.

"So do I," she said.

"Okay, then how about we meet up for a beer at BJ's off of Barranca Avenue, say, 1500 hours on Wednesday?"

"Sounds good to me," Becky replied.

"Well, it's not good for me," Heather blurted out. "Dave, do you have a minute?"

She pulled him aside and whispered something in his ear. After a few minutes, he walked back up to Becky and stated, "Apparently, that is not the proper way to treat Heather's big sister. So if we can exchange numbers and if you'll give me your address, I will be picking you up at 1445 hours on Wednesday." Stacy stood there with her hand over her mouth, giggling. "If you ladies will excuse me, I have to get back outside. I don't want my guys thinking that I took more time than they did for lunch. Heather, thank you for this, and thank your parents for lunch. And, Becky, I will see you on Wednesday."

When he walked away, Heather excused herself to talk with Bill. "Well, I lied to you, Becky," Stacy said as Heather walked off.

"How's that?" she asked.

"I thought that you gained a new friend in Heather, but you actually gained a little sister."

"Really?" Becky asked.

"Yes, and I don't want to upset you, but what you sensed in Brian's referenced family values, you were exactly right. This family is very close, and the good thing about it is, if they like you, then you could be a part of them as well, and it looks like Heather likes you."

"I didn't come from a good family," Becky admitted. "But I was lucky enough to have been taken in by Hector's parents when I was fifteen, so that helped."

"I was lucky enough to have a good family," Stacy replied.

"Are your parents like the O'Rourkes?" she asked.

Without answering her directly, she replied, "I was talking about the O'Rourkes. Come on, big sis, let's get you another beer."

"Big sis?" she asked, confused.

"Do you think that it only applies to Heather? We are a package deal. Haven't you figured that out yet?" They both laughed.

Boise, Idaho

Andy drove back to Rancho, returned the rental car, and went home to pack for his flight to Boise. Cindy had postponed the meeting until tomorrow at 11:30 AM. Andy had to be on a flight out of Ontario International Airport at 6:40 PM. He had an hour layover in Salt Lake City, then onto Boise, arriving at 11:42 PM local time. He was to meet US congressman James Armstrong.

Congressman Armstrong was a ten-term congressman and well-respected in Idaho. However, he was facing a serious Republican primary challenger who recently moved to Boise from Fresno, California. Jake Reed was twenty-six, handsome, and well-liked in the Mormon community. Andy was contacted by Armstrong less than three months ago, and it didn't take long for him to uncover the truth about Reed. Andy called the congressman three weeks earlier and told him that he had significant dirt on Reed that would not only cost him the primary but also quite possible a relocation back to California.

The congressman was told that Andy's fee would be $45,000 plus expenses. Andy had standard expenses that he charged every client—two first-class tickets, transportation, his choice of hotel for a minimum of three days and two nights, and all food and beverages, no questions asked. One additional demand that he insisted on was that he would talk to the client alone and in person. He would not talk to aides, staff, family, or anyone else, and those people were not to be present during the meeting. The congressman agreed to those terms without hesitation because he had heard of Andy's reputation in the business, and Andy had proven to be very reliable and well worth the money.

Andy arrived on time and walked straight to his rental car. He programed the GPS to the inn at 500 Capitol to get a few hours of sleep. He woke at 5:00 AM and went to the hotel gym to work out. Afterward, he went for a morning run around the state capital and down around Boise State University. He loved the city of Boise, and he loved the Boise State Broncos. He liked the way that they beat up larger schools.

Andy showered and ate breakfast at the hotel restaurant. At nine thirty, he drove downtown and parked across the street from the 10 Barrel Brewing Company on the corner of W Bannock and N Ninth Street. Andy had been there before and loved the place. He walked around downtown and took the sights in. At eleven fifteen, he walked into the restaurant. The congressman surprisingly was already waiting for him. Andy immediately recognized him from pictures that he researched.

"Congressman Armstrong, Andy DiPaola," he said as he extended his hand. The congressman was in slacks and a polo shirt. Andy as usual was in shorts and a shirt.

"Good to finally meet you, Andy. If you don't mind, I reserved us a table in the back corner so we can talk."

"That's fine with me. Who did you bring with you, sir?" Andy asked.

"No one as per our agreement," replied the congressman.

"Good. Let's talk, Congressman."

"Please call me Jim."

"Jim, about the only thing I can find truthful about Reed is that he is Mormon and that he is twenty-six years old. Everything else including his name is a fraud."

The congressman's eyes lit up. "Really? What do you have?"

Andy spent the next hour detailing Jake Reed's life, specifically the past six years. Reed was born Jake Reed Daniels; he changed his name five years ago and dropped the Daniels. That was done in attempt to cover his past and current activities. Reed was a far-left Liberal-Progressive disguising himself as a Conservative Republican. He was recruited by the Democratic Congressional Campaign Committee and Liberal-leaning people inside the Mormon church in Fresno in an attempt to infiltrate the Republican Party and to take out the incumbent Republican congressman. They picked Boise because of the heavy Mormon presence. Reed changed his party affiliation five years ago from the Socialist Party of California to Republican, and he was an active member of the Fresno County Antifa group.

"Of course he tried to scrub all of his social media accounts under the name Daniels and attempted to build a fake life under Reed. Unfortunately for him, I was able to track all of it. Jim," Andy said, "everything is in this dossier for you." Andy handed the congressman a packet that was three inches thick.

"Andy, you have a very good reputation in this business, and now I see why. I would have paid you triple for this information."

"I could have charged you triple, Jim, but, A, I don't do it for the money alone. I do it specifically to keep people like Reed out of public office. And B, if I started charging too much, people might be hesitant to utilize my services." As an added bonus, Andy had Jim open the envelope and take out the first picture. "There he is just last week at an Antifa meeting in Fresno."

The congressman couldn't believe his eyes and asked, "You have pictures?"

"Several," Andy said. "It's all in there."

"I don't know why my people couldn't even find out any of this."

"That's why you pay me," Andy replied.

"Well, Andy, any suggestions on how to handle this? I would like your opinion."

"Sir, I generally don't give campaign advice. However, since this might be the start of a new trend, my advice would be to first take the information to the local Mormon bishop and show him what you have. I've done some research on him, and I think you will get what you need. If Reed goes afoul of the church, which once they see the proof, he will, then he is done. Secondly, I would take the information and photos and pay for ads on television and social media and do it soon. Thirdly, I would contact the National Republican Congressional Committee and tell them to be on the lookout for copycats, and use the leverage, Jim, to have them pay for your ads. That information is gold."

"Good idea, Andy, but don't you want to solicit them so you can make money?"

"Sir, you paid me what I asked for. The information is yours to be used however you choose. This might even boost your name recognition on a national level if you play it right."

"So, Andy," Jim asked, "are you going to take your wife and spend some time in our little town?"

"I am. I love this place. But no wife. Just me."

"Out of curiosity, why did you ask for two plane tickets?" Jim asked.

"Well, I normally give one away. For instance, on the flight from Ontario to Salt Lake City, a young mother with a small infant was having a hard time managing everything, so I gave the seat to her. And from Salt Lake to here, I gave it to a soldier who was in uniform. Just a little giveback, at your expense, of course." They both laughed.

THE CALVARY

"Catch anything yet, Bill?" Andy asked as he walked onto his dock carrying a couple of beers.

"I've only been here five minutes. Give it time."

Bill Dixon was the division chief in charge of Field Operations for Region 1 at LASD. He had been a cop for almost thirty-eight years. Andy had met him when he was ten years old. His dad, Jack, and Bill would fish together all the time. Bill met Andy's dad at the Lake Arrowhead Marina. He was fishing from the shore. He and his wife, Marsha, owned a weekend cabin in Running Springs, so since Lake Arrowhead was a private lake, he wasn't allowed to fish on the lake, so Andy's dad invited him onto his boat. They were friends ever since. It was in Bill's division where Brian O'Rourke was killed.

"I appreciate the invite, Andy."

"Come on, Bill. You know you never need an invite here. You can come and go anytime you want."

"I know, but I was just trying to be polite."

Andy had a few friends that he trusted, and they had total access to his cabin and boats whenever they wanted. Bill was one of those friends. After Heather came to his office, Andy initially thought about going to Bill and inquire why Garcia-Hernandez wasn't in custody. But he quickly decided not to because no matter what the reason was, the fact remained that Garcia-Hernandez would need to be on American soil.

"So, Bill, have you considered running for sheriff yet? You know, I know somebody that can be very beneficial to your campaign."

"I know you would be, Andy, and I appreciate that, but you know I cannot afford you." They both laughed. Andy had offered his services for free. "I don't know. I would like to. I know I can run that agency a hell of a lot better than the moron we have now, but he would be hard to beat. He has a lot of political friends with money."

"How long do you think those friends would stay connected to him if he were to go to jail?"

"What are you talking about, Andy?"

"Bill, I have uncovered some very disturbing information that is serious shit. Do you remember the Brian O'Rourke murder?" Andy asked.

"Remember it? Hell, I relive it every day of my life. Not only did it happen on my watch. I personally have known the O'Rourkes for over thirty-five years. I am glad that the bastard is finally going to face justice for it. Why do you ask?"

"Do you know why the case was stonewalled for over five years?" Andy asked.

"I don't know if I would say stonewalled, but the sheriff refused to cut a deal with the Mexican government to take the death penalty off the table. He wanted to let criminals know that if they kill a cop, then they would get the death penalty. But then the shithead reentered the United States and took that issue away."

"What if I told you that was all bullshit? No offense to you, Bill."

"Okay, Andy. You have to tell me where you are coming from because I know you, and you don't fuck around when it comes to this stuff. You must have something good."

"Bill, after O'Rourke was killed, Garcia-Hernandez ran to his sister's house in San Dimas for five days. She then drove him over the border into Mexicali. The sister was born in the United States to a Mexican mother who illegally crossed the border specifically to get birthright citizenship for her. The mother did the same with her older son, but her youngest son, Garcia-Hernandez, was born in Mexico. The sister is well-connected and holds a lot of sway in your agency."

"LASD?" Bill asked confused.

"Yes, sir. And when I tell you the name, you're going to be pissed because your agency has been protecting the suspect the entire time."

"You're killing me, Andy. Who is the sister?"

"Isabella Duncan," Andy replied.

"Why does that name sound familiar?" Bill asked.

"Well, it should. It is your sheriff's wife."

"Are you fucking serious?"

"Yes, I am, and that's not all. Guess who your captain in charge of the homicide division is?"

"Who?"

"Her brother."

"I know this is a dumb question, Andy, but do you have proof of this?"

"Of course I do, and I also have a list of investigative angles you can do to cross-check it."

"Well, what do we do with this?" Bill asked.

"My thoughts are, I give you the package of what I have, you verify everything so you won't have to reveal my name, and hopefully, you have a trustworthy friend in either the DA's office or the FBI that can investigate it. I have a feeling that the sheriff himself knew what was going on, and he was protecting Garcia-Hernandez from prosecution by using the bullshit excuse of the death penalty issue. I'll bet if you ask your friends the O'Rourkes if the sheriff or anyone else asked them if they would accept a life in prison sentence instead of the death penalty, they would say no. Bill, do you remember how the sheriff reacted when Garcia-Hernandez was arrested?"

"Now that you mention it, he publicly acted happy. But in staff meetings, he seemed annoyed about how the shithead was found."

"Did he go to the FBI for an investigation into how Garcia-Hernandez was arrested?" Andy asked.

"He tried to," Bill said, "but the FBI had no interest in it."

"Did anyone ever ask themselves why he would want that investigated? Let me ask you another question, Bill. Was there some sort of command change in homicide after the O'Rourke shooting?"

Bill thought about it for a moment. "I remember a huge shake-up where the sheriff reassigned the homicide captain to criminal courts and brought the criminal courts captain and placed him in homicide, but I don't remember when and why."

"Think for a moment, Bill."

Then the lights went on. "The sheriff placed his brother-in-law in homicide to protect the suspect."

"There you go," Andy said.

"Andy, this really is some serious shit."

"I think that if you go after that captain, he would be the weak link," Andy said.

"Andy, what is your interest in this? What made you get involved?"

"I would rather not tell you right now, but it is safe to say that I was intrigued by the news media accounts of how he was found in Calexico and then how long it took for him to face justice. You know me. I do things for weird reasons. Out of boredom, I guess." Andy didn't want to lie to him, but he didn't want to tell him the truth either, so he chose a middle ground.

"Well, you wouldn't be so bored if you found a girlfriend." Bill was always trying to get Andy a date. "When was the last time you went on a date, Andy?"

"It's been a long while."

"Andy, you are a good guy and have a lot going for you. Why do you have such a hard time with women?" Bill asked.

"I don't have a hard time with women. Maybe I'm just looking for Ms. Perfect, and maybe she just doesn't exist." In the back of his mind, Andy said to himself, *Yes, she does*, and he knew exactly where to find her.

"Andy, I know you don't like to talk about it, but maybe you have a hang-up with what your mom did to your dad, and you're afraid that all women do that."

"Maybe, I guess," Andy replied.

"Well, I'm here to tell you not all women are like that. I've been married for thirty-eight years. I have an idea," Bill said. "Dan O'Rourke has a daughter named Heather, and she is smart and gorgeous. She plays volleyball at UCLA, and Dan says she doesn't really date. I'll ask Heather if I can introduce you to each other. She is a little younger than you, but she is a good girl."

Andy laughed and said, "Bill, I appreciate it, but I don't need people setting me up on blind dates. Thanks anyways." Andy thought, *What a small world.*

Breaking the Rules

Andy arrived at the Pauley Pavilion located in the heart of the UCLA campus to watch one of Heather's matches at 6:00 PM. This was the third time he had watched her play. The pavilion could hold 13,800 spectators, but tonight's match with Oregon State, he estimated the crowd size at around 3,500. He knew he wasn't supposed to be anywhere near Heather, but it had been eight months since she came to his office, and he just had to see her. He sat with the Oregon State fans, so hopefully, Heather wouldn't be able to see him. If she knew he was there, she probably would be very upset. He had told her the day she was in his office that they could never have any contact or be seen together.

Andy had never been into volleyball. In fact, this would only be the third time he had ever even watched a match. The first game, he spent most of it looking at Heather and how good she looked in spandex shorts. He really didn't pay attention to her play. But the second match, he started getting into the game and learning the rules. He was actually impressed with the sport. He started watching matches at home on his computer so he could understand rotations and the rest of the rules. To this day, he still hadn't seen a double touch, yet the refs called it often.

Heather started each set as an outside hitter, then rotated to the right side, then to the service line. She stayed on the court the entire match. Stacy played middle blocker and rotated out. She was also a starter, so when Heather was at left outside, Stacy was next to her in the middle. Stacy was an excellent blocker in her own right, but when she and Heather teamed up, they were a force. Offensively, Stacy worked the slide better than anyone in the nation.

THE EMBRACE

The John Wooden Center was a multifunctional recreation center located atop Parking Structure 4 on Westwood Plaza. The women's volleyball team usually conducted their practices in that building. During a spring practice session, Andy walked into the arena and sat down behind the twenty or so people watching the practice. Heather had just finished a serve in which there was a short volley, after which the coach ended practice. Andy watched Heather grab her gear and head into the locker room. He approached a girl who was picking up volleyballs and asked her to relay a message to Heather. He asked her to let Heather know a guy named Andy was waiting for her when she finished. The girl walked into the locker room to relay the message.

Less than twenty seconds later, Andy heard Heather yell, "Andy is here?" A few seconds later, she came out of the locker room at a fast pace and saw him. She was wearing a sports bra and some sort of small sports panties both in UCLA colors complete with logos. She ran toward him, jumped into his arms, wrapping her legs around his waist, and gave him a long hug. Andy returned the gesture, but she wouldn't let go. Still holding on to him, she leaned back, looked into his eyes with tears in her eyes, and whispered, "Thank you."

This was the first time that they had seen or talked to each other since she left Andy's office and since Garcia-Hernandez had been arrested. "You're welcome," he said. Several other ballplayers, after hearing the initial scream, followed Heather out of the locker room and witnessed the embrace. Half of them were wearing the same apparel. One girl had only a towel wrapped around her. "Why is it every time I see you, you are half naked with tears in your eyes and sweating?" he asked.

"Why is it every time I see you, I get half naked, throw myself at you, and get rejected?" she replied.

The watching ballplayers giggled at the exchange, and Andy blushed. He hadn't realized how close everyone was to them. "Okay, okay, you win," he said.

"I had every intention of doing so," she replied.

"Heather, do you have a minute? I need to ask you a question," he said as he set her down.

"Of course I do." She walked to the players' chairs and sat down.

"Aren't you going to put clothes on first?" he asked.

"With or without clothes on around you never seems to improve my chances anyways, so why waste the time?" she replied. Again, the girls giggled, and Andy blushed.

Andy changed the subject. "Heather, I hate to reiterate this, but this conversation has to be forgotten about the minute I leave here. Do you understand?"

"Andy, I haven't seen or heard from you for almost a year and a half, and I gave you my word of no contact, so you can trust me, although I can't say how hard it was for me not to drive out to see you several times, especially after Garcia-Hernandez was arrested."

"I'm going to ask you to use your dad to give me a name inside the LASD that can be trustworthy and loyal. I just need a name. I can take care of the rest."

"Why? Garcia-Hernandez is in custody and goes to trial this month," she replied. "Why do you need LASD anymore?"

"Heather, you have proven to be very trustworthy and loyal, and I appreciate that, but I don't need to get you involved in this," he replied. "This is heavy political shit—I'm sorry—stuff." Andy does not like to use foul language around women, feminism be damned. "Round two is going to rock LASD, and I don't want your family being another target."

"Is it going to affect my family again?" she asked.

"Only in a good way," Andy replied. Andy gave her specific instructions on where to write the name of the official and where to leave the information. He reiterated to her that she was not to have any further contact with him until further notice. Heather reluctantly agreed and told him that seeing him today would make not seeing him even harder. Deep down, Andy felt the same way, but politics had a way of ruining someone's life, and he didn't want to see harm come to her.

With another hug and as they went their separate ways, Heather asked, "Andy, how did you know to find me here?"

Andy turned around, smiled at her, and said, "I get paid to know everything." To prove his point, Andy waved and said, "Hi, Stacy. It was good to see you."

"Who was that?"; "Is that your boyfriend?"; "He's cute. How do you know him?" were some of the many questions that Heather faced while walking back toward the locker room. She just told them that Andy was a good family friend that she hadn't seen in a long time, which was why she was so excited to see him. "Heather, if that is just a family friend and you don't want him, can I get his number?" Stacy asked.

Heather looked at Stacy with sad eyes and said, "I don't even have his number, and I don't know when or if I'll ever see him again." Stacy walked back into the locker room.

Coach Brown overheard the conversation with Stacy and walked up to Heather. She put her arm around her and said, "You will definitely be seeing him again." Heather asked how she knew that, and the coach replied, "When you two were hugging and then when you both looked into each other's eyes, I saw a spark—not really a spark, I saw a flame. And besides, with an embrace like that, he probably had a hard time walking over to the bench with you. He is not ever going to forget that."

Heather looked at her shyly and stated, "I know. I felt it."

"Whether you sensed it or not, it was very romantic. So if you don't want him, can I have him?"

"Coach Brown, you are married," Heather stated.

"Heather, hit the showers, and may I suggest you take a cold one," Brown suggested.

"Why?" she asked.

"Because the physical and emotional effects of an embrace like that are not exclusive to men," she explained.

Heather felt embarrassed and said, "Yes, ma'am." She thought about what the coach had just told her, and she felt a warmth in her heart.

Garcia-Hernandez's Fate

The Los Angeles County Clara Shortridge Foltz Criminal Justice Center was located at 210 West Temple Street in Downtown Los Angeles. It was the central hub of the criminal justice system for LA County. About 240 protesters were gathered in front of the building protesting the conviction of Garcia-Hernandez. They were waving Mexican flags and burning American flags. The jury foreman notified the court that the jury had reached a verdict. Tim Fallon presided over the sentencing phase. Under normal circumstances, this should have been slam dunk with little fanfare. However, this case was especially difficult not only for the fact that the murdered deputy was one of his best friends' son, who was also a sheriff's deputy, but also for the circumstance surrounding the capture of the suspect and that he might have had a hand in it.

Prior to the reading of the sentence, Judge Fallon told the packed courthouse that he would not tolerate any outburst for or against the sentence. Anyone who violated his order would immediately be remanded into custody for contempt. The jury foreman handed Judge Fallon the verdict. The judge read the sentence. "We the jury impose the death penalty"—there was a low hum throughout the courtroom. The judge paused for a moment and continued—"for Oscar Garcia-Hernandez for the crime of murder with special circumstances of a) a felon in possession of a weapon, b) murder of a public servant, c)interstate flight to avoid prosecution." Judge Fallon asked Garcia-Hernandez if he understood the sentence.

He turned to the audience and looked at a dark-haired woman sitting behind him, turned back to the judge, and laughed. In Spanish, he told the judge that he didn't care what he said, that the Mexican government will get him released. The judge immediately ordered him out of the courtroom.

Andy knew who the woman was, and within a few days, Oscar-Hernandez's entitled mentality and hopes of reprieve from the Mexican government would be short-lived, and that woman with the man in uniform sitting next to her would be in custody. As the crowd started leaving the courtroom, a familiar face started walking to the back of the room. Heather was with her father and mother. She saw Andy and didn't know if she was allowed to talk to him, so she did not look at him and continued walking toward the door. When she got within five feet of him, he said, "Heather, may I have a minute of your time?"

Heather looked to her dad for permission. "Heather, do you know this guy?" he asked.

"Yes, Dad. I'll see you in the hall." She walked up to Andy with a smile on her face. It was more like a grin because she didn't know who might be watching. They shook hands, and Andy whispered something in her ear. She looked up at him and said, "Are you serious?"

"Yes," Andy replied.

"How do I get ahold of you?" she asked. Andy whispered something else in her ear, and she smiled. After a short conversation, they shook hands again, and she left the courtroom.

Andy waited a couple of minutes so Heather could catch up to her parents because they were being escorted out the back of the courthouse due to the protests in the street. A deputy sheriff came up to Andy and said his presence was required in the judge's chambers.

"Why am I not surprised to see you in my court?" Judge Fallon asked. I wonder what influence you had over the mysterious way Garcia-Hernandez arrived back into the United States. Did you have anything to do with his smuggling back here?"

Instead of answering the question, Andy asked, "How is it that a young lady shows up at my office asking for assistance sent by a mutual friend that told her I had some sort of connections in Mexico that could help her out?"

Fallon looked into Andy's eyes and saw that this was going to be a tit for tat and that no one was going to be the winner, so he stated, "Fair enough. You understand, Andy, that there are a lot of people wanting answers on this. The Mexican Consulate sat through the entire trial and sentencing to make sure he wasn't given the death sentence. In the trial, I had to listen to hours of accusations from the defense that he was kidnapped by the LASD or someone working for them and brought back to the states so he couldn't avoid the death penalty. I know the Mexican government and the sheriff have talked to the FBI about a criminal inquiry about this issue. We have protesters marching in the streets, which will probably turn into a riot now that he has been sentenced to death. I saw you talking to a woman. By the way, what was that conversation about?"

"First of all, Tim, you give me way too much credit. I'm not the Mafia or a gang leader that has mysterious people lurking in the dark to do evil for me, and why would the sheriff ask for a criminal inquiry? Doesn't that seem strange to you? I just said hi to someone."

"That seemed like a long hi between the two of you," Fallon said.

"Listen, Tim, we have bigger issues than people being upset that a piece of shit mysteriously reentered the United States when he had a warrant for his arrest for the murder of a sheriff's deputy who was given a fair trial or the fact that I said hi to someone in your courtroom."

"What issues?" Tim asked.

"We need to talk, but not here. The Tap Room tomorrow at 1700."

"Why must we always go there?" the judge asked.

"Because you live right down the street, and I have other business there this weekend I need to tend to."

"What type of business?" he asked.

Andy stood up and stated, "Election season is coming up, and I believe you're up for reelection." With that, Andy turned around to walk out of the chambers.

As he went through the door, he heard Tim yell, "You wouldn't dare!" Andy had a grin on his face, but he never turned around.

WEST COVINA

Andy pulled his four-door Toyota Tundra in front of Heather's house where he parked. Although he knew her parents weren't home, he was still nervous. He was just about to ring the doorbell when the door opened with Heather standing there with a large suitcase and a duffel bag. She dropped the bag on the floor and rushed to give him a big hug. She was wearing white shorts and a light yellow tank top and sporting a perfect tan. She had asked Andy what to wear at the courthouse the day earlier, and he told her to pack casual with maybe a swimsuit and perhaps that white summer dress she wore the first time he met her in to wear for dinner. He explained to her that she could wear whatever she wanted for the short drive because she would have plenty of time to change for dinner. From the looks of it, she packed plenty of clothes. Andy himself was in a pair of shorts with an untucked shirt and boat shoes.

He grabbed her bags and loaded them into the back seat. He opened the door for her and closed it when she sat down. The short twenty-mile drive to Pasadena took fifty minutes. This was what happened when you lived in Southern California. For most of the drive, they talked about the case and the verdict. She thanked Andy numerous times for the arrest of Garcia Hernandez, although Andy would never admit he had a hand in it. She told him how her mom and dad were relieved that Garcia-Hernandez got the death penalty, although they readily admitted that by the time the state of California executed him, they wouldn't be around to see it. She explained to Andy that since the arrest, however, the department had been after her dad for some reason. He had gotten written up all the time, and the department went to the public after his calls for service to solicit complaints. Andy told her to keep faith and that it would end real soon. She looked at him and asked, "How do you know?"

"Please just trust me," he responded. Heather said to herself that this man provided her family with a miracle, so she would take him at his word. She was just happy to be sitting in a car with him and being able to spend the weekend with him. She definitely had no reason to doubt him. She smiled to herself thinking maybe he would take her up on the offer she made the first day they met. She was willing.

Andy pulled into 1401 S Oak Knoll Avenue into the Langham Huntington, Pasadena hotel. The historic hotel was built in 1914. Andy didn't like valet parking, but he knew the people there well enough that he didn't have to worry. He pulled up to the veranda, got out of the truck, and was greeted by the valet. "Welcome back, Andy," the valet said.

"George, it's always great to see you." Andy handed George the keys. The busboy came over and opened the back door to retrieve the bags. Andy held Heather's door open and offered her a hand out of the truck. He tipped both the busboy and George. They both thanked him. As they walked through the front doors, they were greeted in the middle of the lobby by Amy, the hotel manager.

"Andy, so great to see you," she said as she gave him a hug. Amy then turned to Heather and said, "You must be Ms. O'Rourke. I've heard a lot about you, including how pretty you are. It's a pleasure to finally meet you," she said as she gave Heather a hug. Amy handed them keys to their rooms and told Andy that she would go talk to Paul.

"Andy, is there anyone you don't know?" Heather asked.

"You," he replied.

"I don't think I quite believe that," she replied.

"Why would you say something like that?" Andy asked.

"I don't know. You just seem to always be one step ahead of things. I can't put my finger on it, but when you showed up to volleyball practice last month, I never told you I played volleyball or where I went to school."

"The volleyball part is true. However, that day in my office, you told Cindy that you drove all the way out there from UCLA, so that was easy. The rest was simple enough, although I noticed that you do not use social media much."

"Only for volleyball team stuff," she replied. "I hate social media." After having said that, Heather realized what just happened. As they walked to the elevators, she looked at him with a disappointed look and asked, "Two rooms?" Andy smiled but didn't answer. Their rooms were adjacent to each other. He told her that he had a short meeting to attend to while she was getting ready and asked her to meet him in the Tap Room at 1745 hours. She agreed, and they went their separate ways. Andy went to his room and put on a pair of Tommy Bahama shorts with a matching shirt. He replaced his boat shoes with another pair. He left the room and went down to meet Judge Fallon.

Judge Fallon couldn't believe what Andy was telling him, specifically how in the world he was left in the dark about it. Fallon assured him that he would watch the state cases and impose harsher bail amounts if necessary. He had no control over the federal case. They were finished with their conversation and were just enjoying a beer when Heather walked in and saw the two men together. The look between her and the judge was exactly what Andy hoped for. Heather was beautiful. She was wearing the same dress as the first day they met, her hair was perfect, and her tan made the dress stand out. She hesitantly walked up to Andy while trying not to make eye contact with the judge.

"Judge, I believe you know Heather, and, Heather, I believe you know Judge Fallon, or should I say Uncle Tim?" Andy asked. Fallon stood there and didn't say a word, for he knew what Andy was up to, and to fight him would be a lost cause.

Heather started to speak, "I am not—"

At that point, Fallon cut her off and said, "Heather, he knows."

"Uncle Tim, I didn't say anything, I promise," she said.

"I know you didn't, honey. Andy has his ways of finding information and putting two and two together, then apparently, he set up this little encounter to prove his point."

"But how?" she asked.

"Yesterday in my chambers, Andy said he needed to talk to me, so well against my wishes, we set the meeting here at five o'clock. I protested the location because we always come here. Andy told me that we needed to meet here because he also had business to conduct. I'm assuming you are the business he was referring to. What time were you asked to meet Andy?" Fallon asked.

She replied, "At five forty-five."

"And where did he ask you to meet him?"

"Right here in the Tap Room." Heather put two and two together and turned to Andy and said, "How long have you known?"

"Since the first day I met you."

"Why didn't you say something?" she asked.

"Because it was throughout this whole ordeal that I knew I could trust you."

Fallon changed the subject because he didn't want any more said on the subject, especially in public. "So are you two here on some sort of date, or was this just to get me and Heather in the same room for your twisted amusement?" Fallon asked.

"Both," Andy responded. "Heather agreed to allow me the honor of taking her out to dinner and spend some time with her, and I wanted to let you two know that you weren't that clever." At that point, Andy turned to Heather and handed her a long jewelry box.

"What is this?" she asked.

"Open it," he said.

When she opened the box, there was a stunning diamond necklace and matching earrings. Just by looking at it, Judge Fallon valued the set at approximately $35,000. Heather nervously said, "They are beautiful, but I don't understand."

Andy explained. "You have been very trustworthy this entire time, and I know how hard things have been on you for the past six and a half years. At nineteen years old, you unselfishly sought out help from a stranger and was willing to do anything"—he emphasized *anything* to get a snicker from her—"to help your family." The sly worked as Heather turned red and giggled. "You took control of a bad situation and made it right, all the while going to school full time in addition to being a student athlete, so I felt you deserved something nice."

With her eyes filling with tears, she said, "Thank you, but I cannot accept these. They look very expensive." She looked to Uncle Tim for advice.

"Heather, I've known Andy a long time, and you can take him at his word. He genuinely feels you deserve something good in your life. It's okay, honey."

Heather would always get embarrassed around money. She took out student loans for college to pay for what her scholarships didn't cover because she didn't want her parents paying for it. Unbeknownst to her, her dad and mom just paid it off every semester. She put the earrings in and asked Andy for help with the necklace. When she turned around and lifted her hair, Andy noticed her beautiful neckline. *God,* he thought, *this girl is a thing of pure beauty.*

"So let me get this straight. You are not on a date, and you two barely know each other, and she gets expensive jewelry. Just out of curiosity, what would have she gotten on a real first date?" Fallon asked. Andy didn't reply but just stood there admiring Heather. Fallon saw that he was in the way, so he stated that he needed to go. He shook Andy's hand and assured him that he would keep a close eye on the cases. He turned to Heather and gave her a hug and a kiss on her cheek and asked, "How were you able to make this happen?"

"Power prayers, Uncle Tim," she said with a smile.

He whispered into her ear, "And you were worried that he wouldn't get anything out of helping you."

"What's that supposed to mean?" she asked.

He just smiled and told her, "Watch out for this one."

"I don't think you would have sent me to him or would leave me here with him if he was so bad," she replied. Fallon just raised his hands in the air as he walked away as if to say, "I give up."

"Andy, your table is ready," Paul said. Andy introduced Paul to Heather. "Nice to meet you," he said. Paul was a great waiter, and Andy requested him every time he went to the Terrace. Paul was polite and attentive but not too attentive as to give you space but at the same time enjoy great service. They walked to the Terrace's outdoor patio. It was alfresco dining, and it overlooked the picturesque bridge and pool. Andy picked the patio to absorb the beautiful June weather, and knowing that Heather would wear that dress and the addition of the jewelry made it a perfect setting.

"Heather, what would you like to drink?" Andy asked.

"Just water please," she replied.

"I know you drink red wine. Would you like a glass?" he asked.

Heather motioned for Andy to come closer, and she whispered to him, "I'm not twenty-one yet."

Andy just smiled, then said, "I know exactly how old you are. Would you like a glass of wine?"

"I don't want to embarrass you if they card me."

Andy just realized two things about her. One, she said she didn't want to embarrass him, so she was more concerned about his reputation. And second, she had not been around this type of atmosphere where money talked and everything else was noise. She was raised well. Paul came by with water glasses and asked for their drink order. Andy took the liberty and said, "Heather would like the Crest, a Napa Valley cabernet sauvignon, and I would like the Stone IPA. Thank you." Paul walked off to retrieve the drinks.

"Do I look that old?" she asked.

"Not at all," he replied.

"Then how come he didn't ask me for my ID?"

Andy explained that she was there with him and that no one was going to card her because of it. "Besides," he told her, "a girl with the class that you portray should never get carded." Heather blushed.

After their drinks arrived, Andy started the questions. "So, Heather, tell me a little about yourself."

She had just taken a sip of her wine. She pulled the glass down and giggled. "Really, Andy? Wouldn't this go much easier if you just ask me questions in which somehow you don't already know the answers to?" she asked. "If that is possible."

"What is that supposed to mean?" he asked, although he knew she was right. "I thought this weekend we were supposed to get to know each other and to celebrate our accomplishment."

Heather looked at him straight in the eyes and said, "You seem to know everything about me. You found me on the volleyball court, you know what type of wine I drink, you knew about Uncle Tim, and you even said goodbye to Stacy."

Andy looked at her as she was talking, and under his breath, he said, "God, you are beautiful."

She tilted her head to the side and asked, "What did you say?"

"I didn't say anything," Andy replied.

"Yes, you did. You said that I was beautiful."

"I said that out loud?" he asked.

"Yes, you did." Heather was blushing.

"Changing the subject. Okay, I have two questions that I don't know the answers to. First, have you found the right guy yet?" He was referring to the conversation he had had with her in his office. "And second, is the ring on your wedding finger from that right guy?" She told him that she thought she had found the right guy, but the relationship was fairly new and complicated, so she had to give the guy time. As for the ring, her mother bought it for her to wear to keep the sharks at bay. "So this guy," he asked, "how long have you been seeing him and how is it complicated?"

"That's numbers three and four. You asked for only two, which were asked and answered," she replied. "My turn," she said. "How in the world do you know who Stacy is?"

"I have a confession to make," Andy quickly blurted out.

"What?" she asked. "Did you sleep with her?"

"No, no. Why would you think I slept with Stacy?"

"Because when you showed up at practice last month and we talked and then when you left, all the girls started asking questions about you. Stacy told me that if I wasn't interested in you, could she have your number. I told her that I didn't even have your number and that I didn't know if I'd ever see you again. My coach assured me that I would, and she was right. Then when I just brought up her name, you claimed to have a confession to make. So what is this confession?" she asked.

He debated on whether he should tell her but felt he was in competition mode with another guy. "I had been missing you and needed to see you, so last fall, I showed up to some of your volleyball matches and watched you play. I always sat in the opposing team's seats so you couldn't see me."

"What?" Heather asked in disbelief. "You explained the rules of our association in that we couldn't be seen together and that we should have no contact. You broke the rules, Andy, your rules, I might add. After you left practice last month, I cried for a week straight thinking I would never see you again. I couldn't concentrate on my schoolwork or volleyball and to find out you were cheating the whole time."

"Are you mad at me?" he asked.

"Mad?" she asked. "No, not mad. I am a little hurt, though. How would you have reacted if I were missing you—which I was, but I held true to my word—and drove to San Bernardino to see you?"

"Point taken," he said.

"You are an interesting guy, so now it's my turn to get to know you, and at least it feels good to know you were hurting as much as I was," she said. "Are you through with questions for me now?"

"No, but I have a feeling I'm not going to be allowed to ask any more," he said.

"Not for now," she explained.

They ordered dinner and two more drinks. Heather ordered the baby arugula kale salad with grilled salmon. Andy ordered market lettuce and seared scallops.

As they were eating, Heather asked, "So what are your hobbies, likes, and dislikes?" Normal questions.

"Well," Andy replied, "I'm an outdoor enthusiast. I enjoy kayaking, paddleboarding, boating, fly-fishing, rafting, skiing, sandrailing. I mean, you name it, I enjoy it. I like classic cars." Heather was thinking to herself that she enjoyed all those but really hadn't had the time or opportunity to do them lately.

"And your family, your parents, and siblings?" Andy lost his usual cheerful self, and Heather picked up on the sudden mood change. "I'm sorry if I went out of bounds," she stated.

"No, no, you didn't. I don't suppose we can bring this up at another time, maybe on a future date or something?"

"Sure, Andy. I'm sorry."

"There is nothing to be sorry for, Heather. It was just a low point in my life, and I wanted this weekend to be cheerful."

"Did you say future date?" she asked. "I thought this was just dinner."

"Well, I figured tonight would be dinner, tomorrow would be kind of a first date if you liked dinner, and see where it goes from there, but I messed up by not realizing there was another guy in the mix."

"Wait a minute. Is that the reason you were willing to take heat over breaking the rules?" she asked.

"How do you mean?" Andy asked.

"You don't seem like the type of guy who would volunteer information and take a risk at upsetting me if you didn't feel you needed the competitive advantage. So you told me about going to my matches to show me that you have always cared for me in hopes of a fighting chance against the other guy. Well," she continued, "I think I owe it to him to give him a chance since you left me hanging for almost a year and a half."

"Fair enough," he said, dejected.

"Do you want the jewelry back?" she added.

"No! That is for you and has nothing to do with this weekend."

Heather picked up on the mood change and laughed. She picked up her wineglass and, right before she took a sip, said, "I think I found a kink in your armor, Andy."

"How is that?" he asked.

"You are that right guy, silly. This is fairly new," she said as she pointed between her and him. "And it's complicated because of what we went through. Ha! So I am that clever. Uncle Tim must have been the weak link." Andy nodded. They both laughed together and toasted each other. *Was she right? Can I be broken, or can my thought processes be compromised by a relationship, or was this girl that special?* Andy thought.

"So I am beautiful, huh?" Heather asked while she was biting her lower lip in a sexy and playful way. She couldn't believe she actually brought it up. *Must be the two glasses of wine talking,* she thought. But no one aside from her dad and Becky had ever called her beautiful.

"You honestly don't see it, do you?" Andy replied.

"See what?" she asked. "That I see myself as beautiful?"

"Exactly," he said.

"I don't consider myself beautiful. I mean, I try to take care of myself. Are you saying that I'm stuck-up?"

"God, no," Andy replied. "Complete opposite. Now that I don't have to give away anymore secrets to fend off this new guy"—they both laughed—"can I give you an honest observation?"

"Sure," she said.

"Heather, you are the most attractive woman I have ever seen. You are fit, your skin, hair, nails are always perfect, you dress and act classy, but aside from the exterior beauty you possess, your interior beauty is unmatched."

Heather started blushing and said, "Gee, with all that supposedly going for me, I still constantly get rejected by you! Two rooms? Really."

Andy finished. "You care for your family and the people around you, and you are unselfish and gracious. Aside from all of that, you know what makes you perfect?"

"What is that?" she asked, now feeling embarrassed.

"The fact that you don't even see it." Heather was blushing red now. She didn't know if it was the two glasses of wine or not.

CAPT. JOSE GARCIA

Captain Garcia's personal phone rang, and he immediately recognized the number. His personal attorney, Jeff Baker, was on the line, and Jose figured it couldn't be good news. Jose had been cooperating with the DA's office and the FBI for over a year now against his sister and the sheriff. But for his attorney to call at 8:00 PM couldn't be good.

"What's up, Jeff?"

"Jose, the DA has issued an arrest warrant for you. Because of your cooperation, they are giving you twenty-four hours to turn yourself in, or they will come get you."

"Fuck, Jeff, what are my options?"

"You don't have any options at this point, but as your attorney, I recommend that you have no contact with anyone, especially your sister or the sheriff. My guess is, they are using this warrant to get you to contact them. You are probably being wiretapped and followed."

"Shit, fuck! Okay, Jeff, let's do this. Can we set up a bail bondsman and have him ready to go so I won't have to stay in custody very long? How much is the bail?" Jeff told him that it was six hundred thousand dollars cash-only bail. "What the fuck!" replied Jose. 'For a chickenshit obstruction case?"

"Jose, they charged you with felony obstruction, and they added conspiracy under color of authority and a public corruption charge."

"Shit, I can't get that kind of money."

"Jose, I think something else is at play here. I was told that this warrant was originally issued yesterday with a $250,000 bail amount, then the chief judge got ahold of it and reissued it tonight with the $600,000 bail on it. That's generally unheard of, especially late on a Friday night."

"Who is the judge?" Jose asked.

"Judge Fallon," Jeff said.

"Fuck that prick. He should have never been involved in this case in the first place because of his personal relationship with fucking O'Rourke."

"Well, you know the appeals court heard the arguments and ruled he could hear the case, and as far as O'Rourke goes, his son was murdered, and he hasn't done anything to you."

"You're right. I'm just pissed off right now."

"Well, your anger should be at your sister and your brother-in-law," Jeff said.

"Okay, Jeff, what do you recommend?"

"Jose, I would like for you to turn yourself in ASAP. I'll get an emergency hearing to try to get the bail reduced, but you might be in there for a couple of days."

"Can we do this without the media?" Jose asked.

"The DA assured me that there will be no media leaks, and Judge Fallon did seal the indictment and arrest warrant, so it's not for public view as of now."

"What if Fallon tells O'Rourke and he goes public?"

"Jose, I have known and worked with Fallon for over seventeen years, and although I think his bail increase might be excessive, his integrity should not be questioned. He has always been very hard on criminal cases involving police officers. He isn't going to say anything to anyone. Keep in mind, Jose, the bail amount might be justified. I haven't seen the warrant or indictment yet."

SAN DIMAS

Sheriff Joe was sitting in the family room of his house watching television. The room was ample, just like the entire house. The home and property had been in the family for five generations. The house was built in the forties but had been remodeled numerous times, the most recent being two years ago. The guesthouse was built in the eighties. Originally, the property consisted of 140 acres of prime horse property but was down to 15. When Joe's father passed away, he made a promise to him that he would keep the family property intact. Joe's dad hadn't been dead for three months when Joe started selling it off. He liked the money more than the property. It was 11:00 PM when his cell phone rang. Joe always carried two phones, one for work and the other for his girlfriends. It was work. "Frank, what's up?"

Frank was the undersheriff handpicked by Joe after he had won his first election. Frank was very loyal. "Joe, I just received a call from county jail, and they said that one of our captains just turned himself in."

"What's the charge, and who is it?"

"Sir, it's Capt. Jose Garcia, and the charge has been sealed."

"Sealed my ass. Call them back and demand an answer. How much is the bail?"

"Sir, I did call them back and ordered an answer, and they claim that they have no idea. They told me that it was an outstanding warrant from the DA and that the bail was set at six hundred thousand dollars cash-only."

"Who was the judge that issued the warrant?"

"I don't know the original judge, but I spoke with his listed attorney just now, and he told me that he was not at liberty to discuss the charges because of a gag order. But he did tell me that the original warrant was issued for $250,000.00 bail but was increased tonight by Chief Judge Fallon. Joe, the lawyer also hinted that there might be some fed action related to this, but when I pressed, he clammed up."

"This doesn't sound good," Joe replied. "Okay, Frank, thanks for the info."

After Joe hung up, he walked to his bar and poured what was to be many shots of Jack Daniels tonight. His mind was racing, and the only thing he could come up with was Garcia-Hernandez, then he put two and two together. There was no way in hell that the DA would let his brother-in-law turn himself in on a six hundred thousand dollars cash-only bail. They would have kicked his door in. That could mean only one thing: He cooperated.

The more the sheriff drank, the bigger the conspiracy became in his head. As he was sitting there drinking, he started reflecting on the past and tried to figure out how he screwed up. Then it hit him. He should have never married Bella. He figured he could have won the election without her. And marriage, what was supposed to be his biggest benefit had ended up becoming his biggest liability.

He asked himself, "How can you be in a fairly young marriage and your wife won't even have sex with you?" *Well,* he thought, *if I'm going to jail, I'm going to get a piece of ass first.* Joe was a sexual deviant. He sat and thought about which one of his girlfriends he would call when it hit him. There was no way he could leave his house. If they were after him, then they would surely pull him over and pick him up as he was probably being watched. Joe then realized that he needed to make sure his security systems and cameras were active. He clicked on a monitor on the wall and verified that all were working properly. As he stared intently at the monitor, he kept imagining seeing someone walking around his property, and the more whiskey he drank, the more people he saw. In reality, there was no one there.

His anxiety built up to the point of him actually thinking that they were coming for him at any moment. At 4:00 AM, he kicked the door in to Bella's bedroom. The pair slept in separate rooms, and Bella always locked her door at night. He was wearing boxers only and had a belt in his right hand.

A startled Bella yelled, "What the fuck, Joe! Get out of here!" Ignoring her, he walked to the side of the bed and grabbed her by her hair. "What are you doing? Let me go!" she yelled.

"Bella, your brother is in custody, and they are coming for us."

"What are you talking about? And let go of me."

He explained everything to her but refused to let her go. "So if I have to go to jail this morning, I'm going to get laid tonight."

"Go fuck one of your whores. Your diseased ass is not touching me."

He started to pull her down, but she fought back. She began scratching at his arm and punched him on his chest. Joe forced her face down on the bed and took the belt and began hitting her buttocks and back with it. She quit fighting. He ripped off her panties and forced himself on her. Bella lay there motionless and let him continue. Joe then tried to force himself anally on her, and she began to fight back. Joe took the belt and began the beatings all over again. When there was no fight left in her, he penetrated her anally. The brutal assault lasted until five forty in the morning. Joe grabbed her by the hair and dragged her into the kitchen. "Make me some fucking coffee," he demanded. After the coffee was made, he told her to sit at the table with him. In fear for her life, she did.

"What's going to happen now, Joe?" she asked.

"Well, right around six o' clock, they will kick our front door in and take us to jail." As he said that, he saw the HRT speeding up his driveway. "Well, they are here now," he said as he pointed to the monitor.

"Joe, please let me run to my room and get dressed. I don't want to get arrested naked."

The HRT was about to breach the front door. "Bella, you're not going to jail. You're going to the fucking morgue," he said as he pointed his Glock at her. She screamed, and Joe fired two shots into her head. "You stupid bitch!" he yelled.

Hearing the screams, the HRT breached the door and entered the foyer when the shots rang out. "Shots fried!" the team lead spoke into his mike. "Move, move!" Before they could enter the kitchen, one more shot rang out. Sheriff Joe had put the Glock two inches away from his temple and pulled the trigger.

Pasadena, the Date

Andy and Heather spent the rest of the evening strolling the grounds of the hotel, talking. After a nightcap in the Tap Room, they went to their separate rooms. Heather threw herself on her bed and thought, *Wow, is this really happening?* She had been thinking about Andy since the first time they met and nonstop since he showed up at ball practice a month ago. She could sense that there was something special about this guy.

The next morning, she walked into the hotel gym at five ten to find Andy working out. He was wearing gym shorts but no shirt. She always thought of Andy as fit but didn't realize the shape he was in. He was muscular with almost no body fat, and he was tan. His abs were impressive. Surprised to see her there, he reached for his shirt, a little embarrassed. "Don't put that on, on my account," she said. "You saw mine, so it's only fair that I get to see yours."

"I didn't expect to see you here," he said.

"Well, if it wasn't me, who were you expecting since you were half naked and sweating?"

Andy laughed and said, "No one." He explained to her that he normally liked to get his workouts in daily between 5:00 AM and 6:00 AM before he ate. Heather agreed and explained that she worked out only six days a week and enjoyed her cheat day. Andy told her that he couldn't afford any cheat days because he drank too much beer. They finished working out together and then went back to their rooms to prepare for the day. They agreed to meet in the lobby at 8:00 AM.

When Heather walked out of the elevator, she saw Andy talking with Amy. As she approached the couple, Amy looked at her and noticed that even though she was wearing a pair of nondescript shorts and a tank top, she looked stunning. "So I take it last night went okay because I see you two are headed for a second date."

"Last night was great," she replied.

"Where are you taking this pretty little thing, Andy?"

"I don't know," he replied. "I haven't thought about it."

"Oh, BS," Amy replied as she gave both of them a hug and walked away.

"She really has your number, Andy," Heather stated.

"Yes, she does. Yes, she does," he replied.

They walked out the front doors, and Andy had already had his truck pulled up out front. He opened the passenger door and helped Heather climb up. They drove to Colorado Boulevard in Old Pasadena and parked. Andy really didn't have a plan. He just wanted to spend the day with her and then weather the political storm that was brewing. They ate breakfast at an outdoor venue and spent the rest of the morning walking through shops, grabbing a drink, and talking. For lunch, Andy asked her if they could eat at a local pizza joint that he frequented. He could tell by her figure that she didn't eat pizza too often if at all. "I will eat anywhere you want to as long as you let me pay for it this time," she replied.

"That will never happen," he said.

"Why not?" she asked. "You've paid for everything so far."

"Heather, I was raised a lot different than the boys you are used to. When a man asks a lady out, the man will always pay. There are no exceptions to that rule."

"That's exactly what my dad says," she said. They found a table and ordered pizza. She told him a story about a date she had with a guy and Stacy and her date where they went to the movies, and not only did she have to pay for herself but also she had to pay for the boy because he didn't have any money. When she told her dad that story, he went on a rant about little boys and how the past couple of generations' parenting styles had neutered men. By the time the pizza came, they were in the middle of discussing Heather's next year at UCLA when her phone rang. She ignored it.

"Aren't you going to answer that?"

"Whoever it is, they can wait," she said.

"I'm pretty sure it's your dad, so you might want to answer it," he said.

She looked at him with a questioning look on her face, then looked at the caller ID, and sure enough, it was her dad. So she answered the phone. It was around 1:40 PM. "Hey, Dad, what's up?"

"Where are you at?"

"I'm in Pasadena with a friend."

"Have you seen the news?"

"No, I haven't. Why?"

"Apparently, the FBI attempted to serve arrest warrants on Sheriff Duncan and his wife at their home in San Dimas. The news didn't say for what, but according to them, before they could be apprehended, the sheriff pulled out a gun and shot his wife, then turned the gun on himself, and both of them are dead."

"Really."

"Yes, but that is not all. Apparently, yesterday, LASD arrested the wife's brother for obstruction of justice and conspiracy. Guess who he is?"

"I don't know," she answered.

"Capt. Jose Garcia, Oscar Garcia-Hernandez's brother!"

"Is this all related to Brian's case?" she asked.

"I don't know, but I'll bet it is. Who are you with?"

"I'm with Andy."

"Who is Andy?" he asked.

"The guy you saw in the courthouse."

Dan started thinking, *First, the courthouse meeting. Now the two are together when all of this goes down.* "Are you okay?"

"Of course I am. I'll see you tomorrow, Dad." Andy had just taken a drink of his beer when she hung the phone up. "What do you know about that?" she asked.

Andy played stupid and said, "About what?"

"You knew this was going to happen, didn't you? Because you told me to pick up the phone, and somehow, you knew what the news was going to be, and you knew my dad would call me." Thinking for a second, she added, "Does this have anything to do with what you told me a month ago at practice that LASD would be rocked?"

Andy looked at her in the eyes. "Yes, it does."

"Well, are you going to tell me about it?"

"Let's eat this pizza and go for a walk. Here is not the place."
Heather agreed.

SMALL WORLD

After they finished eating, they went for a walk. Heather told him what her dad had said about the sheriff and his wife. "Well, I certainly didn't know that was going to happen," Andy said.

"How much do you know, Andy?" she asked.

"Pretty much all of it," he replied. "Heather, I normally wouldn't tell you or anyone else what I'm about to tell you, but you have proven to be very trustworthy, and I have a gut feeling that you are a very special girl."

Heather blushed and said, "I am just curious how everything fits together since you mentioned it to me when you showed up to practice, and you told me that it involved my family. Then yesterday during the drive over here, you told me that the harassment that my dad was enduring would stop, but I understand if there are things that you cannot tell me. I just don't want my family to be hurt anymore."

"Heather, not once did you just mention that you were curious because you might have had a hand in it or just for curiosity's sake. All you want to know is if your family is going to be okay. What an unselfish girl. And yes, your family will be safe, and your dad's career should start getting back to normal. Heather, before Garcia-Hernandez was brought over the border, he made comments that his sister hid him in her guesthouse for five days before she drove him to Mexico. He also made comments that his sister was protecting him from prosecution, so when you told me that the rumor at LASD was that someone was stalling the investigation, you were right. So I took all that information, worked with my software, and found out who it was."

Heather jumped in. "The sister was the sheriff's wife, and the brother is the homicide captain that was going after my dad."

"Exactly," Andy said. "Remember when you came to my office—"

She interrupted him. "Remember it? I'll never forget it."

"Remember you told me that the homicide division was initially talking to your dad about the case, then about one year into it, they refused?"

"I remember that," she said.

"Well, I was told that the sheriff placed Jose Garcia in charge about one year after the shooting to stall the investigation and protect Garcia-Hernandez."

"So that's why they quit talking to us."

"Yep," Andy replied.

"So how were they able to stall the investigation so long?"

"Well, the sheriff decided to play politics. Everybody knows that Mexico will not extradite one of their citizens if they face the death penalty, and the sheriff knew that. Publicly, he demanded the death penalty to show his deputies he had their backs and that if you kill a cop, you will be put to death. But privately, he knew Garcia-Hernandez would never be extradited under those conditions."

"So that's why he was partying out in the open. He wasn't afraid of being picked up," she said.

"Yep, the sheriff was protecting him."

"So we had to wait five years for justice because of crooked cops."

"I'm sorry, Heather, but yes, you did."

"So how did the investigations start?" she asked.

"Apparently, we have two mutual friends and never knew it. I took all the research and evidence that I compiled and called up a family friend at LASD, Division Chief Dixon."

"Bill?" Heather asked. "Bill is a friend of your family too?"

"Yes, he has been for almost twenty years."

"Boy, first, Judge Tim, now Bill. It's a small world," Heather said.

"You want to hear something even more ironic than that?" Andy asked.

"Sure," she replied.

"When I invited Bill to my cabin to tell him about what I found and to give him my evidence, he told me about his connection to your family, and he even wanted to introduce you to me."

"Really? That's funny. How'd that get brought up?" she asked.

"Bill is always trying to set me up with girls, and he asked me how come I always have a hard time finding girls. I told him that I was waiting for Ms. Perfect and that maybe she just wasn't out there. Then he brought you up. I told him I wasn't interested in being set up with you."

Heather curled her bottom lip and then said, "That sucks, Andy. Why wouldn't you want me after all that nice stuff you said about me last night?"

"Because in my mind, I had already found my perfect girl, you, but time had to pass before I could act on it."

"Nice save, mister." She laughed. "Where is your cabin?"

"I have a small place up in Lake Arrowhead."

"So," Andy continued, "Bill took the ball and got the investigations rolling. He knew the head DA, and he trusted her, and then they set up a meeting with the feds. They agreed to go after the sheriff and his wife on fed and state charges and the captain on state charges. Bill then backed out and only acted as an adviser because he could have gotten in trouble for not telling his chain of command. They worked the cases, and just a couple of days ago, I was informed that they would be in custody by today. Obviously, I didn't know the sheriff would kill his wife and then kill himself."

"What's going to happen to that captain?" she asked.

"I don't know for sure, but I was told he cooperated the whole time with the investigators, so my guess is, he will be fired, possibly lose his pension, and maybe get a couple of years in prison on a plea deal. He is currently in custody on a high bail, and LASD has placed him on administrative leave pending an internal affairs investigation. One thing I know for sure is that he will never be a cop again."

"Good," she said. "Wow, Andy, you did all of this for my family. I am so grateful. I don't know how to begin to repay you. I already tried giving you something special to me, and you turned it down."

"Heather, you don't owe me anything, and don't give me too much credit either, and don't be so humble. You're the one that started this, so it was you who got justice for your family. I just did the right thing."

"Now who's being the humble one?" she said.

"By the way, tell your dad to go see Bill about those low-level write-ups. I've been assured that if there is no merit to them, then they will be removed from his personnel file."

"Thank you, Andy, for everything you have done."

"So what does my perfect girl want to do?" he asked.

"Oh, so I'm automatically yours all of a sudden?" she said, smiling.

"I didn't mean it like that, I meant—"

Heather cut him off. "Well, the way I see it, if I'm not yours, then how can the new guy have a chance?"

"You're a funny girl. I think I might have my hands full."

They spent the rest of the afternoon and evening just strolling downtown and talking. After dinner, they both changed and met at the hot tub. Andy had the waitress bring a bottle of cab for the both of them. They soaked in the hot tub and played around in the pool for hours. At ten o'clock, they went for another nightcap in the Tap Room. Andy turned toward Heather and asked, "So what are your plans for this summer?"

"Well," she replied, "I wanted to get a job to earn some spending money, but my mom wants me to relax and prepare for the upcoming school year, and my dad wants me to work on my serve. According to him, my serves pretty much suck, although I consistently have the most aces on our team."

"So why does he think you suck? I mean, I watched you play, and you seem good to me."

She squinted her eyes at that comment. "Because my serves are only average for the Pac-12, and he wants me to finish my career above average."

"I see," Andy said. "So are those the only plans you have?"

"Yeah, that and hanging out with Stacy and going to the beach and stuff. Why?"

"I don't want to sound forward, but is there any room in there for maybe some dates with me?"

"Oh, I don't know, Andy. Let me check my schedule." She lifted up a fake planner and flipped through imaginary pages and said, "I think I can pencil you in a couple of times." They both laughed.

"Heather, I don't want to push you, but I'm not the type of guy to beat around the bush. I would like to see you more often than that. I feel like I've known you a long time, and I don't want to waste any more of it."

"That's not fair because you cheated on me, and I wasn't allowed to come see you," she replied. After she said that, all ears within hearing distance looked their way and gave Andy a disgusted look. Heather noticed it and assured them it wasn't what they thought and that it was an inside joke.

"Heather, at least I cheated on you with you while I was waiting for you while you were going out with other boys," he said in a light-hearted "Gotcha" tone.

"Andy, that wasn't a real date. Stacy set it up, and we just went to the movies as a foursome," she explained.

"Heather, I was just joking. I just had to defend myself against your cheating comment."

"All right, mister, we might as well get this out in the open now because you know in the future it'll come up anyways, and I'm curious. How many girls have you dated, and how many have you slept with since you met me?" she asked.

"So since like yesterday?" he asked.

"No, since the day I showed up in your office. It wouldn't be fair for me to ask about anything further in the past unless of course you want to tell me."

Andy looked at her straight in the eyes and replied, "The answer to both of those questions is none."

"Really, you haven't even went on one date?"

"Not a single one."

"And before you met me?" she asked.

"Nice try, Heather." Andy laughed. "Okay, missy, how many have you been on?"

"Well, if you're counting the movie night as one, then three."

"So tell me about the other two."

"Well, the first one was great, and the second one is shaping up to be even better," she said.

"Are you talking about last night and today?" he asked.

"I am," she said.

"So when Bill told me you really didn't date, he wasn't kidding. Okay, and the answer to the second part of that question is?" he asked.

"Andy, you know the answer to that question," she said.

"You made me answer it," he replied.

"Okay, you want an answer," she said. "Well, there was this one guy who I tried to have sex with, but he embarrassed and humiliated me by turning me down, then that very same guy has taken me out two days in a row but booked separate rooms, so I have the feeling it isn't going to happen now either! Does that answer your question?" she asked with a satisfied smile.

"Now I'm sorry I asked it," he said.

"Andy, as you know, I was in high school when my brother was murdered. My family was an emotional mess for years, so I stayed close to my mom and dad and my volleyball family. I wasn't interested in boys until I found you. I have had more dates in the past two days than I did in all of high school and college."

"Boy, I would think that a pretty girl like you would have boys all over you."

"There were always boys coming around, but all they wanted to do was hook up, and I wasn't going to do that. None of them were interested in even a single date, just sex. So that's when my mom bought me the shark ring so I could tell all of them I was taken."

"Okay, so are we through with the boyfriend/girlfriend questions?" he asked.

"Yes," she said. "That was uneventful."

"For you maybe. I'm still reeling from your answer a few moments ago," Andy said. Heather gave him a "You asked for it" smile. "So back to my question on being able to see you more this summer."

"What do you have in mind, Andy?" she asked.

"Well, I have a lot of out-of-town business appointments this summer, most of which are in very nice places. I would love it if you would accompany me on some of those. I would only need a couple of hours to conduct my business, and then you and I can spend time together. For example, the week after the Fourth of July, I have to be in Sedona, Arizona. I figured after my meeting we could walk the beautiful trails, explore the red rocks, and take a jeep ride, anything you want. We would spend three days and two nights. I think you would love it. What do you say?"

Heather picked up her imaginary calendar, looked through it, and said, "Heck yeah, I'll go!" When they finished their drinks, Andy walked her to her room and said good night. Heather again lay on her bed holding the red rose Andy gave her yesterday, just dreaming of the day when these two can be together forever. Her mind was already made up.

SUMMER FUN

They checked out of the hotel Sunday morning, and Andy drove her home. When they got into the truck, he asked, "Where is the rose I bought for you?"

Heather's face immediately turned red. "I sort of played with it. Why?" she asked.

"I don't know. I just thought girls liked that kind of thing, and I figured you would at least take the first rose I ever gave you home with you, that's all."

Still embarrassed, she replied, "I'm sorry, Andy. I played a popular girls' game with it last night."

"What game is that?" he asked.

"I'm so embarrassed right now. Okay, last night after the Tap Room, I lay in my bed just thinking about the great weekend I just had, so I had a silly thought and played He Loves Me, He Loves Me Not." Heather put her hands over her face in embarrassment.

"I see," Andy replied. "And the result was?"

She looked at him and said, "That's something only you can answer."

They both laughed. "So are your parents home?" he asked.

"They should be, why?"

"The right thing to do is to introduce myself to them, don't you think? Especially since your dad knows you were with me this weekend."

"Or"—Heather replied, drawing out *or*—"you can just drop me off at the curb because if not, we are going to have a lot of questions to answer."

"I know, but that wouldn't be right, and I don't feel comfortable doing that."

"Okay, then what are we going to tell them?" she asked.

"Before we get into that," Andy said, "when am I going to be able to see you again? I don't want to have to wait until the second week of July."

"Andy, I am an unemployed, very available girl. You name it, and I'll be there." As they pulled up to the house, Heather noticed that her dad's truck was gone. "Looks like we are in luck. My parents must have stayed longer at church this morning." Andy stopped his truck, came around to the passenger's door, opened it, and helped Heather out. He grabbed her bags and walked her to the door. "I had a great time, Andy," she said.

"Heather, I have been anticipating this weekend for a long time. You are an exceptional girl. I thoroughly enjoyed the time we spent together. I'll call you this week, and we will set something up. Is that okay?" They gave each other a hug.

As Andy was walking to his truck, she yelled, "Don't make me wait too long like you did the last time, or I might have to find another new guy!" Andy laughed. He drove off, heading to his home in Rancho Cucamonga. He was about fifteen minutes into his drive when she called. He turned on his hands-free phone. "Heather, is everything okay?" he asked.

"My parents came home less than five minutes after you left and asked about you," she explained.

"I'm sorry I left you to answer by yourself. Do you want me to turn around and handle it?"

"No, it's okay. I'm still daddy's little girl. All he wanted to know was if I was okay and if you treated me like a lady and if I thought that you were a good guy. He never asked how we met."

"How did you answer those questions?"

"I told him that you were very much a gentleman, that you were a great guy, and that I was going to see you again soon. He was good with that. Then I had to tell my mom what we did this weekend, and she thought it was a nice date."

"I was thinking, Heather, how about we hit the beach on Thursday so we can avoid the crowds? And if you're up for it, how about a two-day drive up PCH? We'll probably stay somewhere near Big Sur and come home sometime Sunday."

"You know, Andy, I have never been on that drive, and it sounds great."

"Okay. I'll pick you up around 10:00 AM Thursday."

"See you then," Heather replied.

Heather's mom walked in her room during the last half of the conversation. When Heather hung up, she asked, "What drive haven't you been on?"

"The PCH, Mom. Andy is picking me up Thursday morning, and we are going to spend the day at the beach, then we are spending two days driving up the PCH."

"Jeez," Mary said, "I have never been up the PCH. This guy must really like you. So I will get to meet him Thursday, but your father will be at work."

MEETING MOM

Andy drove up in front of the house with his bright red 1964 1/2 Mustang convertible. His dad had it restored and had been his favorite. It wasn't all original because it was a basket case when his dad bought it. Instead of the original six-cylinder, his dad had replaced it with a modern 5.0 v8, an automatic transmission instead of the three-speed on the column, and he added air-conditioning, four-wheel disc brakes, and custom paint. Everything else was left original. He knocked on the front door. He was wearing Tommy Bahama shorts and shirt and boat shoes. Heather answered the door and asked him to come in. Mary walked into the foyer, and Heather said, "Mom, this is Andy, and, Andy, this is my mom, Mary."

Andy noticed that Mary was a very attractive woman. She was about five feet nine inches tall with a very slender figure. She had black hair with light green eyes and beautiful skin. *This is where Heather definitely got her looks from,* he thought. He stuck his hand out and said, "Andy DiPaola. Nice to meet you, ma'am."

She shook his hand and said, "So I hear you are taking my daughter up the PCH for a couple of days."

"Well, I'd like to change that if it's okay with you, Heather."

"What do you have in mind?" she asked.

"I couldn't get the hotel rooms in Santa Monica for just one night, so I had to book them for two. So can we stay at the beach for tonight and tomorrow night, then drive to Big Sur on Saturday and spend just one night there and come home on Sunday?"

"Sounds great to me," she said.

"Then," Andy added as he turned back to Mrs. O'Rourke, "that is where we will be."

"Heather tells me that you treated her like a lady last weekend and that you were honorable."

"Ma'am, I have nothing but the best intentions with your daughter, and I can assure you that I will take proper care of her. If you would like, I can give you all of my personal information, and you can have your husband run me."

Mary laughed a little at how willing he was for her to have him checked out. "That won't be necessary. I have always trusted my daughter, and when she tells me she is in good hands and for me not to worry, then I believe her. Where are you staying in Santa Monica, if you don't mind me asking?"

"I booked at the Hotel Casa del Mar."

"Nice place," she said. Santa Monica State Beach and the pier were Mary's favorite places in all of California. She had spent most of her childhood and young adult life there. She and Dan had their first date on the pier. "Andy, if you don't mind, may I have a moment with Heather?"

"Of course," he replied. "I'll just load up her luggage, and I will be outside whenever you are ready, and, Heather, we are in no hurry. It was very nice to meet you, ma'am."

Andy picked up her suitcase and duffle bag and carried them to the car. When he walked out of the house, Mary turned to her and asked, "Where in the world did you find him? He is handsome, polite, and obviously cares for you. I see the way he looks at you."

"I know, Mom. I told you he was great."

"Is he rich?" Mary asked.

"Mom! I don't know, and why does that matter?"

"Oh, it doesn't, honey. I was just asking because the Hotel Casa del Mar is very high rent." They both walked outside and saw the car. "That's your car, Andy?" Mary asked.

"Yes, ma'am. I brought it because I thought it was a perfect fit for a beach/PCH cruise."

"You know, I have never even been on that drive. I'm going to have to get my husband to take me."

"Well, I don't know what the future holds, Mrs. O'Rourke, but maybe one day we can all go."

Mary whispered into Heather's ear, "I want one."

"I hope you're talking about the car, Mom!"

Dan Finds Out

Bill explained the investigation to the sheriff. "That son of a bitch! You mean to tell me all his condolences at the funeral, the court-house, and him using me as a prop during press conferences were all bullshit? He was working against me to protect a cop killer?"

"I'm sorry, Dan, but yes."

"I'm glad he's dead because if I had found out about this earlier, I would have killed him myself."

"Well, Dan, it's over. Hopefully, Brian can rest in peace. And hopefully, the three of you can move on with your lives," Bill explained.

"Thank you, Bill," Mary said.

"Speaking of three, where is Heather?" he asked.

"She is on a date," Mary said.

"Oh, good, she finally decided to date. Who's the lucky guy?"

"I met him Thursday. His name is Andy, and he seems really nice," Mary explained. "The two have spent two long weekends together now."

"Andy who?" Bill asked, thinking it couldn't be who he thought it was.

"An Italian boy. DiPaola, I think," Mary said.

"DiPaola with a white Toyota truck?" Bill asked.

"No, he picked her up in an old red Mustang convertible."

"Really? Andy DiPaola, I'll be damned, and he broke out the Mustang."

"You know him?" Dan asked.

"Know him?" Bill replied. "I've known that kid since he was ten years old! Hell, months back, I tried setting him up with Heather because I thought the two would be perfect for each other, but he turned me down."

"What do you think of him, Dan?" Bill asked.

"Couldn't tell you. I've never met the kid."

"What?" Bill asked, confused.

"After their first long weekend together, Mary met him, but I have yet to," Dan explained.

"That doesn't sound like the Andy I know. He definitely knows better than that. I can't vouch for him on that, but I can vouch for him as a man."

"Tell us a little about him," Mary said.

"Mary, Heather has a good man with her right now. He will treat her with the utmost respect. You don't have to worry about her being with him. The kid has his shit together. He has a very successful business, a power player in the political world, yet he hates politicians, so he doesn't associate with them outside of business. And while I do not know the exact amount of money he has, it is substantial, but you would never know it by the way he acts. But aside from that, he is handsome, humble, very respectful, except with the recent thing you just told me. Let me put it this way. If my two daughters were available, I would want them with him."

"Really," Dan said.

"Yes, and I'm not exaggerating one bit," Bill said.

"Well, they will be here shortly if you want to say hi," Mary said.

"We would love to, Mary, but I have to get Marsha home because I have to meet with a county supervisor."

"Oh, really, Bill?" Dan asked. "For what?"

"He wouldn't say over the phone, but I'll let you know if it's anything worthwhile."

"Okay, thanks, Bill, and thank you for the information on the sheriff. May he not rest in peace."

"Dan," Mary barked.

"I know, I know. I'm just a little pissed about it right now."

As they walked onto the front porch, Heather and Andy pulled up. "Is that the Andy you know, Bill?" Dan asked.

"The one and only," Bill replied.

"Nice car," Dan said.

"It is, but I'm surprised he drove it because it's very sentimental to him. He must really like Heather," Bill replied. Dan looked at Bill and said to himself, "You got that from a car?"

Meet the Dad

On their drive back from Big Sur, Mary called Heather and asked them if they could be back in town at a reasonable hour because she was making Sunday gravy and invited them for dinner to meet her father. Sunday gravy was common in Italian households. It was basically homemade pasta sauce made from a recipe that had been handed down through generations. Mary's sauce was from her great-grandmother. Heather asked if five thirty to six would be okay, and Mary said it was perfect.

"So what are we going to tell my parents about how we met?" Heather asked.

"I don't know, Heather. I don't want to lie to them, but I don't want to tell them the truth either. I have an idea," he said. "If it comes up, I will tell them I saw you at volleyball practice a little over a month ago, and we kind of hit it off."

"That will work only if they don't dig any further," she said.

"Well, we're just going to have to play it as it goes. I'm pretty good under pressure."

"Oh, really, Mr. I-Have-a-Confession-to-Make," she said, remembering what he said during their first date. "Maybe you should leave it to the clever one." They both laughed. Andy pulled up in front of the house and saw that Mr. O'Rourke, Mary, Division Chief Dixon, and his wife, Marsha, were standing on the porch. Andy thought, *Something's up.* Heather noticed it too and said, "Look, Bill and Marsha are here."

When they stopped, she was excited to see them, so she reached to open her door. "Heather, please don't open that door. Let me." She saw the concerned look in his face, so she waited. Andy opened Heather's door for her and retrieved her bags from the back seat, which didn't go unnoticed by O'Rourke. Dan O'Rourke stood at six feet three inches tall and 215 pounds with a mixture of black, grey, and a hint of red in his hair. His father was Irish, and his mother Italian. Andy placed Heather's bags on the porch and extended his hand and said, "Sir, Andy DiPaola."

Dan returned the gesture and said, "Dan O'Rourke."

Andy turned to Marsha and gave her a hug and shook Bill's hand. Heather gave them both a hug. "Well, this is exciting," Bill said. "I've heard you two have been dating. That's good news. Sorry we can't stay to hear some details, but we will catch up later. Andy, walk us to our car, will you?" Bill asked.

"Yes, sir," Andy replied. Mary had already said her goodbyes and was in the kitchen checking on the gravy. "Heather, Mr. O'Rourke, will you excuse me for a moment?" Andy asked.

"Of course," Dan said.

When they got to the car, Bill turned to Andy and said, "You know, Dan and Mary are pretty old-fashioned people. I'm not here to beat on you, Andy. God knows it's not my place. But I just spent the better part of twenty minutes explaining what a great kid you are only to be told that you took Heather out on two long weekends without announcing your intentions to Dan."

Marsha jumped in. "I know you know better, Andy. What were you thinking?"

"I think it's great you two are together," Bill said, "but you can't start a relationship pissing the parents off. You know that."

"Are the O'Rourkes pissed at me?" Andy asked.

"Nice try, Andy. You know I can't tell you that," Bill said.

"Guys, I'm sorry. I knew better, but things just spun out of control fast. I'll talk to the O'Rourkes and make it right."

"We know you will, Andy. On a second note, I need to talk to you on a professional matter," Bill stated.

"Tell me when and where, and I'll be there," Andy replied.

"Okay, thanks, Andy. I'll call you. Now go get Heather, and don't let her get away. She's a good girl."

"Yes, sir."

Andy walked back to the porch, and Dan said, "Come on in."

Andy grabbed the bags and walked through the front door. "Where would you like these, Heather?" he asked.

"Just put them by the door. I'll put them away later, thanks. I'm going to get Mom."

Dan invited Andy into the study and offered him a beer and a seat. He took both. As Dan went for the beer, Mary and Heather came into the study. Andy stood and said, "Mrs. O'Rourke, good to see you again." Dan watched the chivalry and liked it. He handed Andy the beer, and they all sat.

After about twenty minutes of conversation about the PCH and Big Sur, Dan asked, "Andy, you have taken my daughter out how many times now?"

Oh boy, he thought, *Dan doesn't waste any time.* "Twice, sir."

"And both of them were long weekends."

"Yes, sir."

"Then why is it that this is the first time that I'm meeting you?"

"Dad!" Heather blurted out.

Mary knew exactly what her husband was up to and said, "Heather, let the men talk."

"Sir, I have no excuse. I knew better, and all I can do at this point is apologize."

"Apologize for what?" Heather asked.

"Heather, there are certain rules a man must abide by when dating someone's daughter, and the number one rule is, introduce yourself to her parents before taking their daughter out, especially on overnighters. These rules are not to be broken, and I broke them," he explained.

"Dad, he tried to last Sunday. I told him to just drop me off at the curb, but he wouldn't. But when we got here, you guys weren't home, and, Mom, you met him on Thursday."

"Heather, please don't. You are only going to make this worse for me."

"Did Bill and Marsha just give you the heads-up?" Dan asked.

"Sir, I wouldn't characterize it as a heads-up but more like a kick in the butt and a smack on the back of the head. Mr. and Mrs.

O'Rourke, I have no excuse, and I will accept any consequences you deem fit."

"There will be no consequences, Mom and Dad!" Heather demanded. "Who makes these rules anyways?" she asked.

"Men do," Dan replied. "That's what separates us from the boys to maintain a morally healthy society."

"Is this like what you told me in Pasadena, Andy?"

"What did he tell you?" Mary asked.

"Andy had asked me if we could eat lunch at a pizza joint that he likes, and I said yes as long as he let me pay. Andy refused and told me that if a man asks a lady for a date, then the man shall pay, no exceptions."

"That's exactly right," Mary replied.

"What do you think, Mary?" Dan asked.

"After listening to Heather's story and the fact that he knows what's expected of him, I think he has learned his lesson, and I'm good with that. Would you like another beer, Andy?"

"Yes, please."

"Well, I'm not good with that. There has to be some accountability," Dan said.

"Heather, will you come with me to grab a beer?" Mary asked.

While they were in the kitchen, Heather asked, "What was that all about, Mom? You've probably embarrassed him, and I wouldn't be surprised if he never asks me out again."

"Heather, you've got yourself a real man out there, and he is not going to stop dating you. He would sit through a thousand of those beatings to be with you. You have to understand it's an alpha male thing. Andy knew what was expected of him, which proves he was raised right, and your dad was just testing him. Andy passed the test. Let me put it this way, honey. Think about the last two weekends you spent with him. If I had to guess, he held open every door for you, he held your chair out for you, and got up when you needed to. I imagine he walked on the traffic side of parking lots and sidewalks, and even though I have only met him briefly twice, I would be willing to bet that he didn't try or even say anything sexual to you. Am I close?"

Heather was running the two weekends through her mind and answered, "Everything you just said is true."

"That is what the man rules are about. Andy is definitely someone worth having."

"That's not what they teach in college," Heather replied.

"I know they don't, and that is why you don't want to date kids that are being taught like that. Heather, if a man doesn't treat a girl right when they first meet, do you really think it will get better as the relationship goes on?"

"No, I don't think so," she answered. "Mom, I don't understand these man rules, but I really like Andy, so please promise me he's not going to leave me because of this."

"Heather, trust your mother. He isn't going anywhere."

When they returned to the study, Dan and Andy were talking about Andy's Mustang. "I have a classic convertible also," Dan said to Andy.

"Really? What is it?" Andy asked.

"A 1969 Camaro," he replied, "but she is in need of a complete restoration."

"Something that's probably never going to happen," Mary stated.

"I'll get to it, Mary," Dan answered. Dan spent five minutes discussing the Camaro.

"So did you two work out your issues?" Mary asked.

"I figured it out. For violating the most basic of rules, I punish you by demanding you eat my salad tonight. I hate salad with my pasta, yet Mary always serves it to me," Dan replied.

"Really, Dad? This is stupid," Heather said.

"Heather, please don't try to defend me. It could have been worse. Yes, sir, I accept."

During dinner, only basic questions were asked. "Where do you live, Andy?" Mary asked.

"I have a place in Rancho Cucamonga and then a cabin in Lake Arrowhead."

"Do your parents live close by?" Dan asked.

"Dad!" Heather said, and when he looked at her, she just shook her head no.

"It's okay, Heather. Sir, I don't have any parents," Andy explained.

"I'm sorry, Andy. I had no idea," Dan replied.

"Don't worry about it, Mr. O'Rourke. There was no way for you to know." Heather now understood why Andy didn't want to talk about it.

"The dinner was excellent, Mrs. O'Rourke, thank you."

"You're welcome. Why don't you and Dan go into the study while Heather and I clean up?"

"Ma'am, I'll get the dishes," Andy said.

Mary laughed and asked, "Why would you do dishes?"

"Well, the way I see it, if someone does all the hard work by preparing the meal, then the other half should have to clean it up. It's a two-way street," he explained.

"I like what I'm hearing," Mary said while looking at Dan.

"Is that in your little rule book?" Heather asked sarcastically.

"No! It is not," Dan blurted out.

"Well, I think it should be," Mary said.

"Andy, I accept your offer, and I know someone that would be more than happy to help."

"Okay, Mom, I'm on it." Heather jumped up, just happy to be next to Andy.

"Not you, honey. I think your dad should help."

"Really, Mary?" Dan said as he gave Andy a sideway look.

"Yes. Heather and I will sit right here and enjoy some wine and watch you two. This ought to be fun."

"I was going to forgive you for breaking the rules, but now that I'm stuck with dishes, I'm not," Dan said to Andy.

Heather took a sip of wine. "Needing forgiveness for breaking rules. I wonder where I have heard that before," she said out loud as she looked at Andy with raised eyebrows.

"Dan, I believe the way the rules work is that if a man has paid his debt, then it is to be forgotten. Andy ate your salad, and now it's over," Mary said.

At 9:00 PM, Andy thanked the O'Rourkes for dinner, shook their hands, and walked out to his Mustang to go home. Heather went with him. They talked for thirty minutes. "Andy, I'm sorry about what Bill and Marsha and my parents did to you earlier."

"Heather, there is nothing to be sorry for. I was wrong, and they called me on it. Trust me, it could have been worse. Your parents could have asked me not to see you anymore or at least for a while."

"Are you serious?" she asked.

"Yes, I am, but it didn't come down to that, so I'm thankful."

"You are going to see me again, aren't you, Andy?" she asked.

"Of course I am. Why would you think differently?"

"I told my mom when we went to get that beer that I thought they embarrassed you enough that you wouldn't want to date me anymore."

"Heather, I have waited a long time for you, and every minute of time I spend with you proves that my wait was worth it. There is no way in this world that I'm going to give you up that easy."

"Andy, you have said a lot of wonderful things to me these past two weeks, but that has to be the sweetest thing you've said." She smiled and gave him a hug.

"Heather, tell me about your dad's Camaro."

"What do you want to know?" she asked.

"When your dad was telling me about it, I could tell something was missing in the story."

"You're pretty observant, Andy. My dad and my brother went in halves and bought the car. Their plan was to restore it as a father-son project. The only thing that Brian loved more than being a cop was working on cars. They had this crazy dream of driving a bigwig or a celebrity or even a supermodel in the Rose Parade."

"First of all, that's not a crazy dream. And secondly, let me guess. After Brian was killed, your dad abandoned the project."

"Yes, he did, and he never talks about it. I'm surprised he brought it up tonight. Why do you ask?"

"I like old cars, and it was just interesting to me, that's all."

Andy walked her back to the door. "You don't have to walk me to the house," she said.

"Yes, I do," Andy explained.

"Let me guess. It's another one of those rules."

"Yes, it is, Heather, and get used to it if you're going to spend any more time with me." Andy gave her a hug and told her he would call her during the week.

When she walked back into the house, her dad asked, "Did he walk you back to the door?"

"Yes, he did, Dad. Well, what do you guys think?" she asked.

"Heather, why didn't you warn us about his parents?" Dan asked.

"Dad, I didn't know. I asked him about his family on our first date, but he asked me if we could not talk about it. He said it was a low point in his life, and he hasn't brought it up since. Now I know why."

"Well, I like him," Mary said. "He is well-mannered, handsome, and he treats you great."

"Dad, what about you?"

"Well, I thought I was going to like him until he pulled that dishes stunt."

"Really, Dan, don't be such a baby," Mary said. "I thought it was nice, and I get the feeling it wasn't a stunt. I think he was raised that way. He doesn't seem to be trying to impress anyone. He seems genuine."

"Dad." Heather started to tear up. "Andy told me that you guys could have asked him not to see me anymore. Please tell me you wouldn't do that to me."

"Come here, honey." Dan gave her a big bear hug. "I guess technically we could have, but that thought never crossed my mind. That's some real old-school man rules. Somebody taught that kid well. Heather, after his comment about Bill and Marsha beating on him, I wasn't going to do anything to him. I figured he had enough, but I just used the salad thing because I really didn't want to eat my salad. It had nothing to do with Andy. I talked with your mother Thursday night, and she told me about him, and Bill had nothing but high praise for him. So I was comfortable with that. Heather, I think you've got a good guy there, sweetheart. I mean he didn't even give me an opportunity to screw with him. He immediately accepted responsibility and didn't even try to make any excuses like kids nowadays do. Heck, he wouldn't even let you try to defend him. If I had to guess, he would have introduced himself when he saw us at the courthouse, but I'll bet he didn't because he thought it would have been inappropriate because of Brian, but I will be watching him."

"I'll take that, Dad, thanks."

Mary asked Heather if they could talk about their date, so the both of them went into Heather's room. Heather told her about the great time they had at the beach and the things they did on Santa Monica Pier. "Mom, the Casa del Mar is a beautiful hotel and, you were right, very expensive. Then we stayed at a hotel in Big Sur that overlooked the ocean, and the drive was beautiful. You have to get Dad to take you on that trip." She told her how Andy was a gentleman the whole time and treated her like a princess.

"Wow, sounds like he's really into you, Heather."

"I think he is, Mom."

"Well, honey, don't go too fast. I can see and tell by your actions that you are already falling head over heels in love with him. I just don't want you to get hurt."

"Mom, I know that I haven't dated, and you think this is some kind of schoolgirl infatuation, but it's not. I could go on a hundred dates with a hundred different boys, and all of them combined would not equal one date with Andy. I don't know how to explain it."

"I do, Heather. It's called being in love," Mary said.

Heather smiled and said, "I hope so."

For the next two weeks, Andy picked Heather up a couple nights during the week for dinner dates. On the weekends, they would spend the days together but no major trips.

"What do you have going for the Fourth?" he asked.

"I talked to my parents about that, and since it's on a Wednesday this year and my dad has to work, we aren't going to do anything."

"Well, if you would like, the Arrowhead Lake Association puts on a great fireworks display every year. So if you're interested, you can come to my cabin for a couple of days, and we can watch the show, and I can show you around Arrowhead."

"I would love that, Andy."

"I'll pick you up on Tuesday. I don't know exactly what time because I have some appointments that I have to attend to, so it might be later in the afternoon."

"Well, just give me a call with an approximate time to expect you, and I will be ready," she said.

FOURTH OF JULY, LAKE ARROWHEAD

When Andy pulled into the driveway of the cabin, Heather noticed that his cabin was no small place in the woods. It sat on one and one-fourth acre of prime Lake Arrowhead real estate with 175 feet of lake frontage. The front of the home had a grand entry complete with two separate front doors and an open sitting room with a baby grand piano and fireplace. Two rocking chairs sat outside the smaller of the entry doors. To the right was a formal dining room. To the left of the sitting room through a small hallway was a laundry room on one side and a half bath on the other. A small hallway led to the four-car garage.

There was a curved staircase leading up to the loft and three bedrooms each with their own bathroom. The loft overlooked the great room with a floor-to-ceiling river rock fireplace and an open-air chef's kitchen with a center island, which seated six. There was a butler's pantry between the kitchen and formal dining room. In the kitchen was a smaller dining table and a French door that opened to a covered patio complete with an outdoor kitchen. The back of the cabin had tall all-glass A-frame windows overlooking the grounds and lake. The master bedroom was large with a fireplace and a separate stone walk-in shower with no doors.

French doors also opened to the back patio and grounds. The entire outside was manicured and landscaped like in a picture book. There was a hot tub and fireplace on the patio. The double boat dock had covered slips, and there was another hot tub built into a rock formation at the lake's edge. There was a four-car attached garage and a four-car detached garage. The house and grounds were immaculate. They had arrived later than Andy wanted to, but he had two late appointments that he needed to attend to. He then had to drive to Rancho for some items, then to West Covina to pick Heather up. Traffic was terrible. They arrived at 7:00 PM, so Andy changed plans and cooked for Heather instead of taking her out. They talked until 10:00 PM when they both said good night to each other.

*****

"You still miss him a lot, don't you?" Heather asked. Andy was in the detached garage, wiping down his 1964 one-half convertible Mustang that his dad had left him. He had a cloth in one hand and a cup of coffee in the other. That surprised Heather because Andy had told her that he hated coffee. Andy had told Heather about the garage yesterday when he gave her a tour of his cabin and grounds, but they never went into it. He said that he built it to store his dad's stuff and other items in it.

He saw her looking at the coffee cup, and he stated, "Yeah, I don't like the stuff, but my dad would always get up in the morning, grab a clean cloth, and with one hand polish the car and drink a cup of coffee with the other."

Andy had never told her about his dad. It was brought up a couple of times, but it always seemed like he didn't want to talk about it. She had called Uncle Tim, who explained to her that Andy's father and stepmom had died in a car crash on the mountain. He told her that a drunk San Bernardino County sheriff's deputy in an unmarked unit had rear-ended them and sent their vehicle through a guardrail and down a two-hundred-feet embankment, killing them both.

"I'm sorry, Andy," she said. "I should have never come in here. I was looking out the front sitting window and saw you come in here, so I thought I would join you. I know what happened to your dad, and this must be a very special place for you. It certainly wasn't my place to violate your space. I had no ill intentions. I'm so, so sorry."

Andy walked over to her and grabbed her by her elbow and said, "Let's finish that tour from yesterday." He walked her around the garage and showed her the 1949 Chevrolet pickup, a chromed-out Harley-Davidson Breakout, and other mementos of his father. She had already driven in the Mustang. There was another car under a car cover, and Heather asked what it was. Andy told her that he only took that one out when he needed the big guns, but he didn't show her. She assumed it was a sensitive matter, so she didn't push it.

After the garage tour, the two went for a jog around the neighborhood. The sun was up and was starting to bake the pine needles, which put off a very pleasant aroma. Andy had always enjoyed it. When they got back to the cabin, they went for a swim in the lake. Heather initially thought the water was too cold, so she was going to opt out.

"Is the water too cold, or do you not feel that you're athletic enough to keep up with a man?" Andy asked her as a challenge.

Not one for having her athleticism challenged, she replied, "Really? Wait here, and let me get changed. I'll be right back." When she returned to the dock, Andy was just lying on a lounger, soaking up some sun. "Are you ready?" she asked.

"I'm ready. So what are the rules?"

"Well, I'm not familiar with the lake, so you point out which way to go, how far out, and which way to return."

"Since it's a busy holiday, we should stay in the bay here. We will swim to the end and turn around. Should be about twenty minutes each way. You should stay at least twenty-five yards offshore. We will pace together, then when we get about fifty yards away from my dock, we will race back, and no impeding the progress of the other swimmer."

"Okay, fair enough for me. But I'm warning you, Andy, I swim like a girl, so you better be able to keep up." She laughed. They both dove in and headed to the end of the bay. Swimming was a little difficult because boats were starting to leave their docks into the open water, so they had to navigate around all of them. It took about thirty minutes to reach the end. They turned around and headed back toward Andy's dock. When they were about twenty-five yards out, they kicked it into high gear. Within ten yards of the dock, Heather pulled slightly ahead of him; and when she was within a few feet of the dock, Andy grabbed her ankle and pulled her back, allowing him to touch the dock first. He climbed out of the water, and when he reached for her hand to assist her, she refused and climbed out on her own.

"What was that?" she asked.

"What was what? I touched the dock first," he replied.

"You cheated and broke the rules. Come to think of it, you seem to have a pattern of breaking rules," she said as she had both of her hands on her hips.

"Oh, come on, Heather. It was just in fun. You beat me fair and square."

"Ha! I told you to keep up. You got beat by a girl," she teased.

Andy noticed that she had goose bumps on her skin. "Do you need a towel?"

"I'll be okay once the sun dries me."

"I have some right here," he said as he opened a cabinet door built into the rock formation of the lakeside spa. He handed her one.

"Thanks, Andy. Boy, this towel is very warm."

"I keep them at around seventy-five degrees," he replied.

"You have heated towels?" she asked, surprised.

"Of course. They really come in handy after soaking in the spa in the snow."

"That sounds delightful," she stated. They both walked to the cabin and showered separately. Andy had her stay in the master bedroom, and he stayed in one of the upstairs bedrooms. When they were both dressed and ready for the day, she asked, "So what are the plans for the day?"

"I had to change plans. Bill just called and said he needs to talk to me and that it was important. I told him that I was up here with you, and he asked if they could come up for the afternoon, so I invited them for an afternoon grill. Is that okay with you?"

"That's fine with me. I love Marsha and Bill, although I'm still a little upset with them over what they did to you a couple of weeks ago."

"Heather, you have to let that go. Everything worked out fine," he replied.

"I know, and it's not like me to hold onto something this long. But I waited a long time for a chance with you, and I honestly thought that night you would leave me, and I didn't want it to end so soon."

Andy walked up to her and gave her a big hug and said, "When you agreed to go to dinner with me that first night, I told myself right then and there that I wasn't giving you up. There's nothing Bill or Marsha could have said to me to change my mind, unless of course they told me that you made out with that boy at the movies." Andy laughed.

Heather pushed herself away from him and said, "You never asked me if I made out with him. You only asked if I slept with him," she said as a "Right back at you."

"So you did make out with him. I thought you told me you didn't even consider it a date," he said.

"Andy, be serious. Stacy invited me to a movie with a couple of guys she knew. I had to pay for one of their tickets, and we didn't even sit next to each other. I sat next to Stacy. So the answer is, no, I did not make out with him."

"Okay, that went in a different direction than anticipated," he stated. "Well, then," Andy continued, "after Marsha and Bill leave, we will jump in the boat for an evening lake cruise, and then we will watch the fireworks show. Then after that, if you want, we can sit in the spa and enjoy the mountain air."

"Sounds great to me," she replied.

Every year, the Arrowhead Lake Association had a fireworks display in the middle of the lake. Visitors from all over Southern California came to the mountains to watch it. That was why it was best seen in a boat because only property owners were allowed on the lake.

"But for now, let's get the boat and go get some breakfast so I can introduce you to Jenny." Heather dreaded this. He had told her that she needed to meet Jenny, his love, on their drive up the mountain yesterday. She asked herself, "What if Andy had to choose between me and Jenny, or what if he is just using me to make Jenny jealous?" She quickly discarded the latter thought because, although they have only been dating for a month, Andy did not seem to be the type of guy who would take advantage of women. He certainly had an opportunity with her and turned it down. Andy maneuvered the boat up to the docks and tethered it just below the Waffle Works. The restaurant was small, but it offered lakeside outdoor seating and very good food. Andy helped Heather out of the boat. They walked up the dock and a small set of cement stairs and walked into the restaurant.

They were greeted by Amber, who was the owner's daughter. "Hello, Andy," she said as she walked up to him and gave him a hug, a hug Heather thought was a little too long. She wondered if she was Jenny. She thought that there were a lot of pretty girls working there, but unfortunately, none was wearing a name tag. Amber brought them to Andy's favorite table outside on the patio.

Heather couldn't get comfortable. Andy noticed it and thought maybe the air was a little too cold for her. "Is it too cold? You want to eat inside?" he asked.

"No, it's great weather," she replied, so Andy dropped it.

They ordered their meal and started to eat. He noticed something strange about her behavior. She was constantly looking around, specifically at the waitresses. This was not her usual self, and she wasn't eating much. "Are you okay?" he asked.

"Yes, why?" she replied.

"You just seem uncomfortable. You're looking around everywhere, and you haven't eaten much food. Is something on your mind?"

"Yes," she said. "Who is she?"

"Who is who?" Andy asked.

"Jenny," she said. "You said you were going to take me to breakfast to introduce me to your *love*"—she emphasized *love*—"and I cannot figure out which one she is. Andy, tell me, please. It's killing me."

Andy started to laugh but didn't push it because he could tell she was really hurting. "Look down at the dock. She is right there," he said.

Heather, in clouded confusion, saw a woman in a yellow bikini getting into a boat. She looked a little older, but she couldn't really tell. "That's her?" she asked.

"Yes, Heather."

"And you like her?"

"Very much so."

"Have you slept with her?"

"Yes, we have slept together."

Heather's face turned red. "You told me you haven't slept with anyone since you met me. You lied to me, Andy?" she asked in a hurt tone. She stood up and told him she was going for a walk.

He stood up and walked around the small round iron table and grabbed both of her hands. He looked into her eyes, which had a very disappointed and hurt look in them, and said, "Jenny is my boat."

She looked at him, confused, and said, "Your boat."

"Yes, my boat," he replied.

"But what about that woman down there?" she asked.

"Purely coincidental," he said. At that point, Andy got a firmer grip on her hands just in case she was going to use them to beat the shit out of him. She had spent most of her life punching balls around, and he wasn't going to take any chances.

"Why would you do that to me?"

With a small laugh, he said, "I don't know, Heather. Maybe I was giving Mr. Right Guy a chance."

She remembered her playing him when they went on their first dinner date. "Okay, you got me," she said.

"I had every intention of doing so," he replied. He cautiously released her hands. They finished their breakfast and walked around the village shops. While they were walking, Andy reached for her hand, and she gave it to him. This was the first time they had held hands in a romantic way. Heather smiled and rested her cheek on his shoulder. Andy released her hand and put his arm around her waist and pulled her closer to him. As they were walking past the Rocky Mountain Chocolate Factory store, he stopped, turned Heather toward him, and stated, "I am sorry about what happened back there. When I hatched this scheme, I was just going to tell you at breakfast, but I didn't figure out that it was upsetting you."

"Well, you were just getting me back," she replied.

"I don't want to get you back for anything. I saw the disappointed and hurt look in your eyes, and that killed me. It killed me the very first time we met when I told you that I couldn't help you. I don't ever want to hurt you, and that little schoolboy stunt I pulled back there was over the line. Did you really think I would bring you up here to spend a couple of days together and introduce you to a girlfriend, especially after I told you that I haven't been on a single date since I met you?"

"I didn't think so," she said, "but you played it up pretty good."

"I'm good at that," he said. "I have a knack for using words and letting people use their imaginations to figure out what I meant."

"Andy, don't worry about it. I forgot it the moment you held my hand." As they continued walking, she asked sarcastically, "Who sleeps with a boat anyway?"

As they were walking around the village enjoying the beautiful weather, Heather asked, "Is there a shop that sells swimwear? I only brought one suit, so I'd like to pick up another one."

"Several of these shops do. What are you looking for in particular?" he asked.

"Just a standard two-piece like what I was wearing this morning."

"I know just the place, but I have to warn you that the owner is very outspoken and can sometimes be rude, but deep down, she is sweet."

"Well, we don't have to go there. We can go to another shop," she explained.

"Yeah, but this will be the place that has good quality stuff. Don't worry about it. I will try to control her." He laughed. They walked to the lower lakeside shopping area and walked into Joanne's at LA. The *LA* really stood for Lake Arrowhead, but Joanne wanted a Los Angeles chic feel to it.

"Andy DiPaola, where the hell have you been?" Joanne yelled from across the shop as he and Heather walked in. "Young man, I haven't seen you in months!"

"I've been a little busy, Joanne," he replied.

"I can see that. Who is this?" she asked.

"Joanne, this is Heather. Heather, this is Joanne. She owns this place and the restaurant we ate at earlier."

"Nice to meet you, Joanne," she said.

"You don't look familiar. Where are you from?" she asked.

"I'm from West Covina," she replied.

Joanne looked at Andy. "West Covina? Really, Andy, a flat-lander?" she said with a scorned attitude. "What's wrong with a mountain girl, not good enough for you? Does Amy know about this?"

Heather started to feel uncomfortable. "Andy, I don't need another suit. I can just use the one I have. I didn't mean to cause any trouble."

"Joanne, you're being very rude," Andy stated.

Realizing the way she came across, Joanne said, "I'm sorry, Heather. I meant no ill towards you. It was directed at Andy. I don't know if you know this, but Andy is the most sought-after bachelor on this mountain, and a lot of girls would give anything to be in your shoes right now, including my Amber," she explained as she hit Andy on the shoulder. "There's going to be about eighteen to twenty girls very upset with you, Andy."

Needing to change the subject, Andy said, "To answer your question, yes, Amy is well aware of Heather and has met her already."

"Well, I will be calling her tonight to talk about this," Joanne responded. "So are you two boyfriend and girlfriend right now?"

Andy looked at Heather, who in turn looked at him, because they had never talked about it. "We have been spending a lot of time together," he replied.

"Well, I do have to admit you are a very attractive girl," Joanne told Heather. "Sorry about my little blowup. Let's get you suited up." Heather spent only twenty minutes finding a suit. The problem was that she couldn't make up her mind between four of them. She liked the yellow one, but it was the most expensive at $400, and the black one was only $150. Always mindful of money, she chose the black one. When she walked up to the register and took out her credit card to pay, Joanne responded, "Your money is no good here."

"Why not?"

"Well, I can tell you haven't known Andy that long, and good, by the way. Maybe Amber still has a chance. Andy would never allow a girl to pay for anything so long as she is with him." As she said that, she rang up all four suits and placed them in a bag. She handed Andy his card back and told them to enjoy the holiday.

They walked out of the shop hand in hand. When they were far enough away from the entrance, Heather stopped and said, "What was that all about? It was kind of embarrassing for me."

"Which part?" Andy asked, confused.

"The entire part from the bachelor statements to Amber and twenty other girls to you paying for everything. Is Amber that girl that gave you a long hug at the restaurant?"

"Yes, she's Joanne's daughter. Let's get the paying thing out of the way. When you said you needed a suit, I brought you to a shop to get you one. I don't understand the confusion."

"Andy, you buy me everything! I appreciate it, but I feel weird because I don't want you to think that I expect it. And besides, you bought all four, not just one. That's a lot of money."

"The way I see it is, now you have extras, so maybe I can convince you into staying another night or so."

Heather's heart melted. "Andy, I'll stay as long as you will have me. That is, so long as you don't invite Amber over." They laughed.

The rest of the morning was spent walking around the village and pushing Heather on a lakeside swing. Heather really enjoyed the swing and the views it had. When they finished, they took Jenny to the other side of the village and parked by the resort. They walked to the grocery store for food to grill. Andy picked up some steaks, lobster, scallops, fruit for a salad, and some fresh vegetables. He carried the groceries in one hand while holding Heather with the other one. They loaded the boat and drove to the cabin. "Well, that's a first for me," Heather said.

"What's that?" he replied.

"I have never drove in a boat to go grocery shopping before."

"Believe it or not, it is a lot faster than getting into my car and driving around the lake to the village."

"I like it. The weather, the views, and the smell of pine trees are breathtaking."

HELP

Marsha and Bill arrived at about 12:20 PM. All four of them exchanged greetings. They sat in the great room. Andy brought the girls a glass of wine and a beer for Bill and himself.

"So how's the dating between you two going?" Marsha asked.

"It's great. Andy is wonderful," Heather replied. Heather briefly explained Pasadena, Santa Monica, Big Sur, and the great time she was currently having.

"Andy," Bill turned to address him, "I'm sorry for having to barge in on your time with Heather, but there are some things I need to ask you that simply cannot wait."

"Fine. We can go on the patio if that's okay."

"Sure," he said.

"Bill, would you mind if I speak with Heather privately for just one minute?"

"Of course not."

"Heather, you have a minute?" he grabbed her hand and walked into the master bedroom.

"Are we going to do it now?" she asked.

"No." Andy said. "But listen, Marsha is a terrible cook. And when Bill and I go out back, she is going to want to prep the food. Please do everything in your power to not let her touch the food."

"I know she can't cook, but how can I stop her?"

"I don't know. Maybe have her cut fruit for the fruit salad and wash and cut vegetables. Just stall her as long as you can, please."

"No problem, Andy, but while we are in here…"

"Bill's waiting, funny girl." Heather curled her bottom lip and walked out of the room.

The boys went out back and sat on the patio. "First things first, Andy. How in the world did you and Heather meet?"

"Bill, I'm going to tell you something that very few people know or will ever know, but I know I can trust you. Heather came to me a while back and asked for help with Garcia-Hernandez, so I... helped," Andy said with a big grin.

"So you two are the ones responsible for him being arrested on American soil?"

"In a nutshell, yes," Andy said.

Bill broke out in laughter. "That is classic Andy. So that is how you had that inside information about what the little shit said in Mexico that you gave me."

"Yes, it is," he replied. Bill was one of the few who knew about Andy's past smuggling operations. Jack, Andy's father, and Bill were always smoking Cubans while fishing. "So," Andy continued, "when you asked to set me and Heather up, I had already met her and wanted to, but I had to wait for time to pass to make sure she would be protected if something went astray. Then I showed up at the sentencing hearing to see what the shithead got. I had every intention of asking Heather out that day, and I also intended to talk to her parents. But after the hearing ended and when I saw them walking up the aisle, I asked myself if I was being selfish. They had just gone through another emotional hearing, and their son finally got justice, so I felt it was inappropriate of me to interfere with that. Of course my dumb ass didn't abandon asking Heather out."

"Did you tell the O'Rourkes that?"

"No way. I told them that I knew better and offered no excuses."

"What did Dan do to you?"

"He made me eat his dinner salad."

"What?" Bill asked. "That must have meant he liked you."

"Bill, Dan, and Mary don't know about how Heather and I met."

"Are you telling me Heather asked for your help by herself?"

"Yes, she did."

"I told you, Andy, you two are meant for each other. She's a good girl. She's smart and very attractive. She gets her looks from her mother. Andy, there is something else she gets from her mom."

"What's that?" he asked.

"She can be very witty and very feisty."

"Tell me about it. Our first weekend together, I had asked her a personal question, which I already knew the answer to, and she knew I knew, but I forced her to answer it anyways. Well, let's just say the answer she gave me made me regret asking it." They both laughed.

"Don't worry, Andy. I won't say anything to anyone."

"So what's on your mind, Bill?"

"Tomorrow, I will be voted in as acting sheriff by the county board of supervisors," Bill said.

Andy reached his hand out and said, "Congratulations. You are the best man for the job."

"Thank you. The position is temporary, and I have been told that I will receive three of the five votes. They will vote again in a month to fill the seat until the next election in three years."

"What do you need from me?" Andy asked.

"I am being told that they chose me because they didn't want the undersheriff because he was handpicked by the sheriff and that I had the most experience and had the cleanest record. But three of the five are on the fence for the permanent position because they think they should hold a special election instead of an appointment."

"I see," Andy said. "So you are looking for one vote?"

"I'm looking for three votes but will settle for two."

"Why so many?" Andy asked.

"I'm looking to the future, Andy. If I can get voted to fill the vacancy and bypass a special election, then the more supervisors I get to vote for me now will lock their hands come election time."

"Okay, got it. So you are telling me I have less than one month?"

"Sorry, Andy. I just confirmed everything late last night. I just thought of something. Andy, there is no way in hell Supervisor Harris will vote for me. She is the biggest public racist I've ever known, and because I'm not black, I will never receive her vote, so I guess we cannot waste any time on her."

"Yeah, I don't know how she keeps getting reelected. I have been waiting for someone to challenge her so I can sell the information that I have been sitting on."

"You have dirt on her?" Bill asked.

"Bill, I have more than dirt. What I have is enough to put her behind bars."

"Really? Why are you sitting on it?"

"I was waiting on a challenger, but no one wants to step up."

"Am I allowed to hear what you have?"

"Bill, you know I trust you, but it would be better to keep you in the dark on this one till I make my move, you being the sheriff and all." They both laughed.

"So how are you going to deal with the information I obtain?" Andy asked.

"I don't know, Andy. I am not schooled in politics, so I was hoping for advice," Bill said.

"Do you have any support behind you?" Andy asked.

"I have all of the various sheriff associations and DA associations yes," he replied.

"Do you have any bulldogs in that group?"

"I don't understand, Andy."

"Bill, when I get dirt on these guys, we need a delivery system, someone who can go to them and explain that it would be in their best interest to vote the right way."

"I see, and it'll have to be done in a way it won't be viewed as extortion."

"Exactly," Andy said.

"And that's assuming you can find something," Bill stated.

Andy broke out in laughter. "Really, Bill, they are politicians. They will have dirt. The only question is how dirty it is. Here's what we'll do. You find a messenger to handle the fence riders, and let me handle Mad Max."

"Thanks, Andy, I really appreciate this."

"Bill, you're the best man for that job. If I thought you were a dirty politician, I wouldn't be helping. Now let's go get Marsha away from our food."

"No shit," Bill replied.

*****

"Heather, did you know that I tried setting you two up, but Andy turned me down?" Bill asked as they were eating.

"Yes, Andy told me that, and he also told me that you are always trying to set him up with girls."

"I try, but he never takes me up on it."

"Well, Bill, you know I love you, but that practice is going to have to stop."

Although Heather was serious, everyone else laughed. Bill picked up on the seriousness of it and said, "Of course, Heather. I would never do that now that you two are together. I always have your best interest at heart."

"Thanks, Bill," Heather said.

After the late lunch, Bill and Marsha said their goodbyes and left.

First Kiss

When the sun started going down, they headed back onto the lake. They circled the barge a couple of times and found a perfect spot. Ironically, it was only twenty yards off Andy's own dock. For one, it had one of the best views on the whole lake for the fireworks show; and secondly, it made it easier to navigate home after the show. Andy poured Heather a glass of wine and poured himself some Four Roses. They sat next to each other in the front seat with Andy placing his arm around her shoulders.

When the first firework lit off, Heather jumped. The echo and the noise off the water and surrounding mountains made for an extra-large boom. Heather finally got used to it. They sat there holding each other and watching the excellent display when Andy took her glass from her and set his and hers down on the floorboard. He turned sideways toward her, stared at her in her eyes, and brushed the back of his right hand softly across her left cheek.

"Are you okay, Andy?" she asked.

"I'm perfect, and so is this night, and so are you." And without another word spoken, they locked lips in a deep, passionate kiss, all the while the sounds and sights of the fireworks show going off around them. About halfway through the show, Andy fired up Jenny and pulled into his dock. "If we hurry, we can change and get into the spa to finish the show," he explained.

"I'll be ready in less than three minutes," she said.

"Would you like a glass of wine?"

"Yes, please," she replied.

Andy put his trunks on and grabbed a bottle of cabernet, a bottle of Four Roses, a cigar, and glasses and headed to the patio spa. They sat there enjoying each other's company until the show ended.

"Andy, can I ask a favor of you? I know you have done a lot for me, and I'm in no position to expect a favor, but I need to get this off my chest."

"Anything you need, Heather," he said.

"Andy, you have already proven to me that you are a great guy. Actually, I figured that out the first day I met you by the way you treated me. And I'm not naive. I realize that other girls like Amber and apparently twenty others would be foolish not to have an interest in you, but, Andy, I'm a good girl, and I wish that you will just give me the opportunity to prove it to you. If I can't show you that I'm someone that you would be interested in, then by all means look elsewhere, but please just give me a chance."

"Heather, Amber has had a crush on me since she was twelve years old, and I think it has more to do with Joanne than her. My dad helped them both out when she went through her divorce, so I believe Joanne feels she owes me something. Besides, I've known Amber since she was born, so it would be kinda weird. Anyways, I'm not looking for anyone else. I know that you are a good girl, and my sole concentration right now is focused on you and you alone."

"Thanks, Andy. Oh, and by the way, I figured out what Joanne meant by flatlander."

"You didn't know that term?" he asked.

"I've never heard that before, so when she said it and was being mean, I thought she was making fun of my breasts."

Andy laughed. "What's wrong with your breasts?"

"Well, I'm a little self-conscious of them. I think that they are a little small."

"Heather, your breasts are perfect proportion for your body type," he explained.

"Really? Thanks, Andy."

"Okay, my turn to ask a favor."

"Sure, Andy, anything."

"Can we consider ourselves boyfriend and girlfriend?"

"Only if you're willing. I've always been willing." She laughed.

"Settled. I can now consider you my girlfriend, which means no more hard times about me spending money on you. Deal?"

"I'll honestly try, Andy, but it's going to be hard. That's something I'm not used to and wasn't raised that way, but I promise that I'll try hard."

"Fair enough," he replied.

"So are you going to tell Amber, or am I?" she asked.

Andy laughed. "No need, Heather. When Joanne calls Amy tonight, Amy will set her straight."

"Who's Amy?"

"The lady you met at the Langham in Pasadena."

"That Amy. I like her. She seems nice."

"She is, so I don't know what Joanne thinks she is going to gain by talking to her, but oh well."

"So tell me about Joanne and Amber," she asked.

"Joanne and her now ex-husband, Chris, were personal friends of my dad. Chris was the local banker, and he and Joanne bought out the Waffle Works when the owners wanted to retire. Well, Joanne caught Chris having a threesome in their hot tub with two of his coworkers from the bank. Joanne was supposed to be down the hill that weekend to spend time with Amy but came home early because she wasn't feeling well. Joanne kicked him out and filed for a divorce. She got the restaurant, the cabin, and her car and child support.

"The mountain was torn between loyalties. Everyone liked the restaurant, but they also relied on Chris at the bank for loans and such. Well, Chris decided to be stupid and let it be known that any local who patronizes the restaurant would no longer be able to rely on him for banking support. Joanne's business started to suffer. You see, all these shops up here can do good business from the weekenders, tourists, and summer activities, but the restaurants rely on locals during the off-season and weekdays to stay in business.

"My dad didn't want to see Joanne go out of business because not only was her food good but she was now a single parent with a daughter to raise. So my dad started holding all of his meetings with his clients at the restaurant, and when the locals found out that my dad was eating there every day, more and more showed up. He volunteered his off time to the restaurant—going over inventory and making suggestions on employees. He even convinced Joanne to have Amber work there on the weekends to save money on employee expenses. Joanne's business was making a profit again. When Chris found out about it, he became enraged."

"Why would he be mad? Sounds like your dad was just being nice."

"He was, but Chris felt my dad was being disloyal to him, so he threatened him with cutting off future loans to his clients. My dad had a lot of money in that bank. That threat proved to be Chris's downfall. My dad was a very nice guy. Everybody liked him. He was referred to as a gentle giant, but if you cross him and more importantly hurt his clients, my dad was ruthless. He pulled all of his business out of the bank and made new relationships with three smaller banks on the mountain. He could have gotten any bank he wanted down the hill, but he was very loyal to the mountain and wanted mountain money to stay here.

"So after my dad's death, I moved back to the mountain and helped out in the restaurant, taking over where my father left off. Then as Amber got older, she started taking more and more control of it. Joanne never liked food service and had always been into fashion, so she came to me, and I helped her open her own shop. When Amber graduates high school, she is going to take total control of the restaurant. She actually has some brilliant ideas to expand her customer reach. She's pretty smart."

"Sounds like it, but she's still in high school?" Heather asked, confused.

"Yes, she graduates this year."

"So what happened to Chris?"

"When his bank called my dad to find out why he pulled his money, my dad told them the truth. They conducted an investigation and demoted Chris and transferred him to Riverside."

"Sounds like he deserved it."

After the hot tub, they both showered separately and said their good nights.

The next morning, they both got up and went for a jog; and after that, Heather challenged Andy to another swim race. "I let you win yesterday, so don't expect the same treatment today." He laughed.

"Andy, I want a do-over because I will not be satisfied with a win by default."

"Okay, but I'm warning you, I'm going to turn on the afterburners today."

"I'm not worried about that," she replied. "I saw how you swim, and I think I can take you." They both changed and met at the dock. "Same route and rules as yesterday, mister, and please try hard not to break them this time," she said with a smile. They dove in and swam down the bay. They were neck and neck on their way back. Andy noticed that Heather swam like a dolphin. Her strokes were smooth.

At about forty yards out, he hit it hard, but he couldn't pull away from her. At about twenty yards out, she pulled away and hit the dock a whole six feet in front of him. She climbed out of the water and offered Andy her hand. He took it, but instead of climbing out of the water, he pulled her back in. "You're a brat, Andy," she said as she splashed water in his face.

"Come here," he demanded, and when she did, he hugged her and planted a big kiss on her lips. She returned the gesture. They climbed out of the lake, and Andy retrieved some warm towels. "Heather, where did you learn to swim like that? I mean, I watched you, and you are very skilled."

"Well, thank you for noticing, Andy. Swimming is my number one workout routine. It keeps my core and just about every muscle group worked out."

"So by just swimming every day you became that skilled?" he asked, confused.

"Not exactly. I've been working out with both the men's and women's swim team at college for the past three years."

"What?" Andy asked in disbelief. "You cheated?"

"Absolutely not," she replied. "Don't be upset with me because you got beat by a girl twice." She laughed. "What's on the agenda for today, Andy?" she asked.

"Well, I don't know how to ask you this, but Joanne called late last night and asked if we can eat breakfast with her and Amber."

"Sure, I'll do anything you want to," she replied.

"Really?" he asked, surprised. "I figured with what happened yesterday that you wouldn't want anything to do with them."

"Andy, although yesterday was a little weird with Joanne and even more upsetting with that stunt you pulled on me at breakfast, I had a wonderful day. I got to beat you in a swim race, one that you challenged me to by the way, then you held my hand for the first time, then we had our first kiss underneath fireworks in a classic wooden boat on a mountain lake. And when you told me last night that you would give me a chance with you and you made me your girlfriend, that's all I needed. I'm not worried about Amber or any other girl, and although Joanne can come across pretty rough, deep down I think she was just looking after her daughter's best interest."

"Thanks, Heather. You made this easy on me. I thought I would have to tell them no." They both showered and changed for the day. They took Jenny to the Waffle Works and went inside.

"There you two are!" Joanne yelled from the kitchen door.

Amber walked up to them and introduced herself to Heather. "Heather, I'm sorry about my behavior yesterday. I should have known my manners and introduced myself to you, but I want you to know, when I hugged Andy, it had nothing to do with getting at you. I always hug him like that, but when my mom called Amy, she explained to me how it probably came across, and I'm sorry."

"So where is my hug?" Andy interrupted.

"You are dating Heather now, so out of respect for her, there will be no more hugs," she replied.

"Amber, I appreciate that, but you can hug Andy anytime you want."

"Seriously, you won't get mad?"

"Not one bit," she replied.

When Amber turned to give him a hug, he refused. "I don't want one now." He pouted.

"Andy, you're such a brat," Amber said. "Let's eat. Andy, we can't sit at your usual table because it's too small, so we will use the bigger one next to it."

"Sure, why not. First, you take away my hugs, and now my table." They all laughed.

As they were waiting for their food, Amber started to speak. "Heather, the reason we invited you here was first to apologize, and second, I would like to ask a favor of you."

"No need to apologize for anything," Heather said. "I will admit, yesterday was a little awkward for me. But last night, Andy explained your families' history, so it made sense. So what favor can I do for you?"

"Heather, I realized yesterday you were put in an awful spot, especially after I heard about what my mom did to you." She looked at Joanne with a scorned look. "But I am asking you to please not take Andy from us. We need him."

"I don't understand. What do you mean by take him from you?"

"Heather, I know you know about my interest in Andy. Apparently, my mom beat it into you several times yesterday." And again, she gave her mother a stern look. "And you have every right to tell Andy not to be around me anymore, but I am asking you to please don't do that. I can promise you that I will never get in between the two of you, but I really need him not only personally as a friend but the restaurant needs him also."

"Amber, there's nothing for you to worry about. I would never dictate to Andy who he can or cannot see, male or female. It's not my place. I know about the history you two families have, and it would be rude and selfish for me to do something like that. I realize Andy had a life before me and people he's attached to and apparently twenty other girls up here who are also interested in him, but I can't change that, nor would I ever try. I'm not the jealous type. I learned the hard way that life is way too short and precious to waste time trying to change things that are out of my control."

"What twenty other girls, Andy?" Amber asked.

"I'm not the one who said it," he replied.

"Well, then who did?" she asked. And before anyone could answer, Amber turned toward Joanne. "Mom!" she blurted out. "Thank you for this. Heather, I truly didn't expect this outcome, but Amy convinced me into trying. She said that you were a sweetheart, and as always, she was right."

"I'll take that Andy hug if you don't mind," Heather stated.

Amber got up and hugged her. "Thank you for this," she said.

"I have a question," Heather said as they both sat down. "What is Amy's connection in all of this?"

"You don't know who Amy is?" Joanne asked.

"I have met her a few times, and she seems like a very nice lady, and she really keeps Andy in line. But that's all I know."

"Well, the whole story you'll have to get from Andy. It's not my place. But I can tell you that in my lifetime, there has been only two people who are so loved and respected on this mountain that when they speak, you listen. Amy is one of those two."

"I see," she responded. "So who is the other one?"

Before Joanne answered, Amber blurted out "Mom" while shaking her head no.

Joanne looked at Andy, and he nodded. "The second one, my dear, was Andy's father."

Heather grabbed Andy's hand. "I'm so sorry, Andy. I didn't mean to pry."

"It's okay, Heather. Don't worry about it."

SEDONA

"I have never sat in first-class seats before," Heather said to Andy as they sat down for the short flight from Ontario to Phoenix. Andy was meeting with the current governor of the state to give him details on his November general election challenger. Gov. Bruce Davis was well-liked in the state and was seeking his fourth term as governor. At the beginning of the year, he held a comfortable 14 percent lead in the polls. However, with the election less than four months away, the polls showed him with a slight 3 percent lead well within the margin of error, so he contacted Andy.

After landing at the Phoenix International Airport, Andy and Heather drove the two hours to the L'Auberge de Sedona spa resort in Sedona. "Is this where we are staying?" she asked.

"Yes, it is."

"Let me guess. Separate rooms," she replied with her bottom lip curled in disappointment.

Andy just chuckled but didn't answer. "Heather, while I'm in my meeting, why don't you get a facial and a massage?" he asked.

"That would be relaxing, but no thanks."

Andy knew she was concerned about money, so he said, "Heather, we've talked about this. You have to stop worrying about money. Remember, when a man—"

"I know, I know. Asks a lady for a date, the man will always pay, no exceptions," she finished the sentence.

"Andy, you are always spending a lot of money on me, and I get embarrassed."

"Heather, I do it because I like to. You're my girlfriend now, so of course I'm going to do nice things for you. Plus, you promised me that you would try."

"Well, I wasn't your girlfriend when you bought me expensive jewelry on our first dinner date," she tried reasoning.

"In my mind, yes, you were."

"You're so sweet."

"Settled. A facial and a massage."

"Andy, I don't want to sound ungrateful, but can you make sure I get a woman masseuse? I'm real private with my body when it comes to men, and I don't want one massaging me."

Andy laughed. "This coming from a girl who practically got naked in front of a stranger and offered her virginity."

"That's right, and although that stranger not only decided I wasn't good enough for him, he then further humiliated me by putting my clothes back on for me, but for now, he is still the only man allowed to touch me. For now," she emphasized.

Andy, feeling stung again, said, "Bill was sure right. You are very feisty!"

Heather blushed and bit her bottom lip in a sexy, shy way. "Andy, I take my body and innocence very serious, so when you make jokes about it, I have no choice but to defend my honor. Besides, with a boyfriend like you, I'm not worried about losing it anytime soon!"

"All right, all right, you win. A woman it is. Jeez." He kissed her, and they walked into the resort.

*****

"Governor Davis, good to see you again." Andy had worked with him on the last election cycle to fend off a primary challenger. Although the challenger stood no chance at upsetting him, Bruce wanted to send a message to future challengers not to take the risk.

"Andy, you look like you never age. Must be living the good life." After Andy was cleared by the governor's security detail, the two men went into an office. "Okay, Andy, what have you got? When I hired you, I just needed you to get enough dirt to keep me ahead in the polls, and I agreed to the $30,000. But when you called me back and said you could destroy him but it would cost me $70,000,

I became curious. I agreed to it because you have a very good reputation, and of course, you helped me out last time."

Andy ran down all the chickenshit, little things—selling cocaine in college for money and a bar complaint on taking a client's award monies and spending it all. "Stuff you probably already knew about," he said.

"Actually, Andy, I didn't know any of that stuff."

"Governor, the bar complaint is public record."

"Apparently, I need a better research staff."

"But," Andy said, "here is the kicker. When he was in his last year of law school, his younger sister came to visit him. He got drunk and raped her."

"Oh god," Bruce replied. "Andy, can you prove that?"

"Bruce, I don't charge seventy thousand dollars for speculation, but this gets worse. He raped her for a week straight while she stayed with him. She couldn't tell anyone. She was embarrassed, and she didn't want to ruin his chances at the law firm that wanted to recruit him. So she stayed quiet. He then got her a job at that firm as a secretary. The two started a secret love affair for five years."

"Andy, this keeps getting better and better," Bruce said.

"I'm not done," he replied. "She ended up pregnant." Bruce couldn't believe what he was hearing. "She decided she didn't want the emotional baggage that comes with an abortion, so she kept it."

"You mean to tell me he fathered a child with his own sister, and the kid is alive?"

"Yes, sir."

"This is going to crush him. Wait a minute. If I go public with this, it will ruin his sister. I don't know if I want to go that low."

"You have her blessing, sir," Andy replied.

"You talked to her?"

"Of course. I had to verify my findings. Bruce, she is scorned. During the pregnancy, he took care of her and put her in a nice home in Tempe. But when he decided to run for public office, he felt that she would be a liability, so he abandoned her. She ended up in a women's shelter when the baby came. They eventually helped her get into low-income housing. Bruce, she is currently on welfare and food stamps, but you know what the ironic thing about this is?"

"What's that?"

"She's a very intelligent girl who wanted to follow in her brother's footsteps and become a lawyer, and he destroyed that dream. So she agreed for me to go public with this information. She feels she can avoid a lot of humiliation by claiming rape and Stockholm syndrome in this era of #MeToo. She figures that may be her way out of her shitty life, or she figures she can stay in the shadows the rest of her life. She wants her brother to pay. The baby has been put up for adoption in an undisclosed state so he can have a future. Everything you need is in this file, including a taped consent and interview."

"Andy, that extra forty thousand dollars was well worth it. Thank you."

"Well, Bruce, that extra money isn't for me. When I found out about her, I raised your bill because I'm giving that money to her."

"You're very generous with my money, Andy." They both laughed. "Well, would you like some lunch?"

"Sure, but I have someone with me, though."

"Well, I hope so with those two first-class seats you made me buy. Besides, I think you can afford it."

"What? We had an agreement that all expenses will be paid for."

"Andy, it was a joke. Lunch is on me."

When they walked to the restaurant area, they noticed Heather sitting at a patio table next to the creek, sipping on a glass of water. As the men approached her, she noticed several of them coming toward her and felt a little nervous. Heather stood up when Andy got close. "Heather, this is Gov. Bruce Davis, and, Governor, this is my girlfriend, Heather O'Rourke."

"It's a pleasure to meet you, Heather."

"It's an honor to meet you, sir."

"You can call me Bruce. Did you enjoy your facial and massage?"

"I did, yes. They were both excellent," she replied.

"Well, Andy, we have a table set up inside for lunch. Are you ready?"

"Of course. Heather, we will be having lunch with the governor and his staff. Is that okay?"

"Sure. I've never had lunch with such an important man before, but do you want me to change? I feel a little underdressed."

"Heather, you look stunning the way you are. And besides, don't consider me too important. Andy here is much more important than me. Trust me." As they were eating, Bruce asked, "Andy, you didn't tell me you are engaged."

"We're not, sir. Why do you say that?"

"I see that ring on Heather's wedding finger."

"Oh no, Bruce. My mom bought it to keep the sharks at bay so I could concentrate on my schoolwork and volleyball."

"Well, tell your mother that it didn't work," Bruce said.

"Why do you say that, sir?"

"Because you landed the biggest shark with the biggest bite there is," he said as he was pointing toward Andy. Everyone laughed, even Heather, but she didn't quite understand the joke.

"That's where I know you from," Tom, one of Bruce's staff members, said. He leaned over and whispered into the governor's ear.

"Really, number 4, that Heather O'Rourke?" Heather's face turned red. "Heather, you have to do me a personal favor."

"Yes, sir."

"You have to keep our lunch here a secret. You cannot tell anyone in this state that I had lunch with you."

"Why not?" Andy asked, a little concerned.

"Because your girlfriend here came to my great state twice last year and literally kicked the crap out of the girls from both our big universities. If the citizens of this state found out I had lunch with her, I wouldn't have to worry about you coming after me. They would throw me out of office on their own." Everyone laughed. "You are, what, five feet ten inches, eleven inches? How do you jump so high?"

"My dad said that I was born with springs as toes," she replied.

"And that powerful spike you have," Bruce continued. "Andy, I wouldn't want to be in your shoes if you somehow make this girl mad at you."

"Tell me about it. I have already had that thought once before."

"When did you think I was going to hit you, Andy?" she asked.

"At breakfast on the Fourth of July," he said.

Heather turned red and said, "Well, you would have deserved it, but I would never hit you. Governor, I won't say a word to anyone, I promise."

"Heather, I am just joking. But in all seriousness, what would it take for you to transfer to either the University of Arizona or Arizona State? Both of them could use a player like you."

"That's very flattering, sir, but I can't leave my UCLA family."

"Well, you can't blame a governor for trying."

After lunch, Heather and Andy went to their rooms and changed into swimsuits. They went to the poolside to swim and catch some rays. "Andy, do you mind?" Heather asked as she handed him a bottle of suntan lotion. She rolled over onto her stomach. As he applied the lotion on her back, she asked, "Can you undo the bikini strap? I don't want a tan line." He undid the strap and finished with the lotion. When he went to stand up, she asked, "What about my legs? I don't want to burn."

"Where do you want me to put it on?" he asked.

"Anywhere you see skin," she replied.

"With the suit that you are wearing, that's pretty much all I see." He laughed. He rubbed it on the back and outside of her legs.

"Andy, you're doing a terrible job," Heather barked.

"What? I think I got it everywhere," he said.

"Well, you missed my inner thighs and the sides of my butt," she said. Andy was already hard, but if he continued, it would start throbbing. "Please," she begged, "I can't because if I get up, people will see my boobs." Andy gave in and started rubbing lotion on the parts. When he was finished, she asked, "That wasn't too bad, was it? Thank you."

"You're welcome."

When he didn't immediately get up, she asked, "Are you just going to sit there and block the sun?"

"Give me a minute, please. I sort of have an issue." She started giggling. "You did this on purpose, didn't you, Heather?" he asked.

"Did what?" she replied shyly.

"Um, hmm," he said. Heather thought that if they have to sleep in separate rooms, she was going to make him wish that they weren't. "So you can't get up right now?" Andy asked.

"Not unless you put my top back on. Why?"

"Just asking," he replied. He placed his hand on the back of her leg and started rubbing it like he was smoothing out the lotion. He thought that her body was very firm and very sexy. She lay there with a smile on her face, just happy that he was touching her when he did it.

"Stop!" Heather yelled as she was laughing. Andy had grabbed her inner thigh and started tickling it. She couldn't get up, but she kept wiggling and kicking her legs to get him to stop. When he finally stopped, she said, "You're a brat."

"A brat, huh?" he started tickling her sides.

"Andy, this isn't fair," she complained.

"Neither is seducing me with tanning lotion," he replied.

"Okay, okay, you win."

Andy stopped and laughed. "Heather, don't you ever worry about guys staring at you?"

"I used to, but not anymore. Why?"

"Well, look around. I can count twelve guys that were hoping that you did lift up while I was tickling you."

She just laughed. "Andy, they can look all they want, but they can't touch. During my freshman year, Stacy showed me a website that gave me the title as the hottest college volleyball player in America. I was curious, so I looked at the site, but all the pictures were of my butt or of me bending over or a close-up of my private parts or going up for a swing and looking up my shirt at my bra. Initially, I was a little freaked out about it, but then I figured, boys will be boys. I'm not naive, so I figured if that's what it takes to get more people interested in watching volleyball, then fine with me. That's also the reason I shied away from dating and boys in general, because all they wanted to do was have sex with me so they can claim they slept with the hottest volleyball girl."

"Actually, Heather, you have held that title for three years in a row," Andy told her.

"You watch that type of stuff, Andy?" she asked.

"Heather, type your name in any web search bar and see what comes up. You'll find UCLA stuff, but they aren't even listed in the top ten. It's websites of hot volleyball players."

"Really? Oh well. What can a girl do?"

MAD MAX

Maxine Harris was the most publicly outspoken, unapologetic racist that Andy had ever dealt with. She would not vote for anything unless it helped the black community more than any other race. She was chronically being censored at board meetings. When Andy walked into her office, he told himself that he knew he couldn't win her vote, but he wasn't taking any of her shit either. Dwayne Brown, her chief of staff, introduced Andy to Supervisor Harris.

"Supervisor, this is Andy DiPaola. Andy, this is Supervisor Harris."

"Nice to meet you, ma'am," Andy said.

Maxine just ignored him and sat down. "Dwayne tells me that you are a very serious man and that I need to respect you because you can make or break careers. Is that true? I mean, you can't be that powerful because I have never heard of you."

"Ma'am, I am here on behalf of a very good friend of mine. Sheriff Dixon has been friends with my family for over twenty years."

"So what does that have to do with me?" she asked.

"Tomorrow night, the board of supervisors will hold a vote to either allow the sheriff to fill the term until the next election cycle or hold a special election."

"Yes, and?"

"What I'm looking for is your vote to let Bill hold that position for the remaining term."

Maxine let out a loud laugh. "Are you kidding me? I was asked to see you because you were an important man, but you come in here and ask me for a vote for a friend of yours. I'll tell you what, Andy. You find me a black deputy to vote for, and I'll give him that vote, but I will never vote for Sheriff Dixon."

"Ma'am, Bill is a great cop with an impeccable career, and he has the full support of the black deputy's association."

"What's in it for me?" she asked.

"Supervisor, it would save the county taxpayers a lot of money if you don't spend it on a special election."

"I don't care about that. What's in it for me?"

"Ma'am, if you are suggesting I pay you or do some sort of favor in exchange for your vote, then I have wasted my time coming in here. I will not break the law for a vote, and any suggestion otherwise, quite frankly, is insulting."

"Get out of my office. Dwayne, show him his way out!"

Andy stood up and said, "Thank you for your time, Supervisor." Maxine just waved him off. As Andy was walking out the door, he turned back to her and said, "Oh, by the way, say hello to your brother Leroy for me please." He kept walking. Dwayne's face hit the floor. He warned Maxine not to fuck with him, but she did it anyway, and Andy just dropped a bomb on her. Dwayne walked back into Maxine's office and slammed the door.

"Boy, don't you be slammin' my door."

"Aunt Max, I warned you not to mess with that man. I have a feeling you just lost your career, me my job, and worse yet, my dad his business."

"Dwayne, I'm a county supervisor, and that mild-mannered teddy bear that you are so afraid of can't do shit to me."

"Auntie, that teddy bear has taken out US senators, US congressmen, governors, sheriffs, chiefs of police, plus countless others. He is not worried about your career. My dad is going to be pissed."

THE VOTE

Dwayne Brown saw Andy walk into the supervisor's chambers about twenty minutes before the meeting was to start. The place was relatively empty considering the important vote that was about to happen. He walked up to Andy and offered him his hand. Andy shook his hand, and Dwayne said, "Andy, I apologize for the way you were treated by the supervisor yesterday. Whether she agreed with you or not, no one should be treated that way."

"Dwayne, don't worry about it. If you think that was the first politician to treat me like shit, you would be mistaken. Listen, Dwayne, I know about your political aspirations of running political campaigns, and so far, what I have on you is very minimal, so may I make a suggestion?"

Dwayne looked him in the eye and knew he was serious. "Sure," he replied.

"Do yourself a favor and take the rest of the week off effective immediately. Take your wife and kids out of town."

"Why?" he asked.

"Dwayne, you know who I am, right?"

"Yes, sir, and I tried explaining that to the supervisor."

"You mean your aunt?"

Dwayne wasn't going to try to lie. "Yes, my aunt. Just so you know, Andy, after you left the office yesterday, I blew up at her, and then I tendered my two-week resignation."

"Has that been made public yet?" Andy asked.

"No, I was going to wait until my last day. Why?"

"Dwayne, I would suggest you do it immediately. Use your media connections and get that out there fast. It could very well minimize damage to your reputation."

"She's going down, isn't she?" he asked.

"I'm not at liberty to answer that, but if she does, do you really want to be on that ship?" Andy asked.

"No, I don't. Thanks, Andy."

The chairman of the board just heard public comments reference the issue of the sheriff appointment or a special election. Most of the comments leaned to not spending the money on a special election. Then there were the usual nutjobs who demanded the abolishment of the agency. She was just about to close the public comment period when Andy addressed her. "Chairwoman Klein, I am not a resident of LA County. However, may I address the board on a personal level?"

Before Klein could speak, Supervisor Harris blurted out, "Do not let that man speak. He is personal friends of the sheriff, and he came to my office yesterday and tried to bribe me into voting for him."

"Mrs. Harris, you do not get to determine who speaks in my hearings. I alone have that authority, and I would appreciate it if you keep decorum with no further outbursts." Turning back to Andy, she said, "Sir, is that true?"

"Ma'am," Andy replied, "the only thing true in her comment was that I was in fact in her office yesterday, and I am a personal friend of the sheriff. Nothing else is true."

Supervisor Kathy McSally requested permission to speak. "Granted," Klein said.

"Madam Chairwoman, I personally know of Mr. DiPaola's professionalism, and he does not conduct business in the way Supervisor Harris has stated. Although he is to be feared in the political world, his mannerisms should not be questioned. But don't get me wrong. Don't take his handsome looks and his exceedingly behaved manners as a sign of weakness, because if you do, well, let's just say you will lose."

After that comment was made, Dwayne looked at his aunt and gave her an "I told you so" stare. For the first time in her political life, Maxine Harris started to feel nervous.

"Heather, what does Andy do for a living? Why is everyone afraid of him?" Mary asked.

Heather was sitting in between her mother and father in the third row behind Bill. Andy suggested that he sat elsewhere for political reasons. "I don't know, Mom. We have never talked about it. I know last week when we had lunch with the governor in Arizona—"

"You ate lunch with the governor of Arizona?" Dan asked, shocked.

"Yes, Dad. Andy had a meeting with him at a beautiful spa resort in Sedona, and when the meeting was over, we all ate lunch together. Bruce is real funny."

"Who's Bruce?" Mary asked.

"The governor, Mom," she replied.

"You call him by his first name?" Mary asked.

"He demanded that I do. So when I found out I was having lunch with the governor of Arizona, I got excited and told him that I'd never eaten with an important man before. He assured me that Andy was way more important than he was, and he kept making comments about how afraid of Andy he was. Then he asked us if we were engaged because he saw the shark ring, so after I told him the story behind the ring, he told me to tell you that it didn't work because he said that Andy was the biggest shark with the biggest bite. I still don't get that one, but all of his staff laughed."

Dan sat there thinking how Bill had told them Andy was a power player. The governor of Arizona was afraid of him, and now this supervisor was saying that everyone in politics should fear him. *What the hell does he do?*

"Mr. DiPaola, you have the standard three minutes."

Andy briefly talked about Bill's career and what the agency meant to him. He then spoke of tragedies that he went through and how Bill and Marsha were always there for him. His final words were the saving of the money on a special election. "Supervisors, by the time you hold a special election and a new staff gets put in place, then it will be time for another election. Sheriff Dixon has completed all of that, and I believe it would be foolish to go through that process again. Thank you for your time and the opportunity to speak.

I do realize that you didn't have to allow me the time, and I really appreciate it."

"Now I know what my colleague means by using your handsome looks and great mannerisms. You're welcome, sir," Klein replied.

"Mom, those two ladies better stop calling him handsome. He's mine, not theirs."

"Heather, calm down. They are just being polite. What's gotten into you? You are not the jealous type," Mary said.

"I'm sorry, Mom. I don't know what's wrong with me."

"Any other public comments to be heard?"

"Yes, ma'am." Dwayne Brown stood and requested time.

"Mr. Brown, you have three minutes, sir."

"Thank you, ma'am. I'm here to set the record straight. Mr. DiPaola did in fact come to our office yesterday asking for Supervisor Harris's vote for Sheriff Dixon. He explained everything yesterday to us just like he did here tonight with the exception of his personal tragedies. It was Supervisor Harris who demanded a bribe, and"—there was a long gasp in the room—"and when Mr. DiPaola refused and told her that he was insulted by any such criminal request, she threw him out of her office. For that reason, after he left the office, I tendered my two-week resignation. Now having witnessed what I heard here tonight, I can no longer be associated with Supervisor Harris, and I am making my resignation effective immediately. Thank you for your time."

"Thank you, Mr. Brown."

"There may be some hope for this kid after all," Andy said to himself.

"I am going to call for a brief fifteen-minute recess so I can talk to the county attorney's office on a procedure issue," Klein said.

During the recess, Mary turned to Heather. "Tell me about the Sedona trip you went on." Heather told her everything—the massage and facial, the lunch with the governor, the jeep trail ride, and the stargazing on the red rocks.

"What happened in the meeting with the governor?" Dan asked.

"That I don't know, Dad. I wasn't present," she replied. She then told them the story about the governor's comments on her volleyball play.

"He actually watched you play?" Mary asked.

"Yes. He said he goes all over the state to watch different sports. He said everyone's normally only interested in college football and then basketball and baseball if the school is doing good. He said he enjoys watching all the other sports as well, and he even said that he doesn't think that women's college sports get enough attention, so he makes it a point to go to them to bring attention to the girls. He then tried to recruit me, but I turned him down."

"That's funny, Heather," Mary said.

"Well, I have his personal phone number if I change my mind." Heather laughed.

"You have the personal phone number to the governor of Arizona?" Dan asked.

"Yes, right here," she said as she showed her parents her phone.

"Why would he give you that?" Dan asked.

"He told me that so long as I was Andy's girlfriend and whenever I'm in Arizona, if I ever needed anything, to let him know. I told you, Dad. He is afraid of Andy."

While Heather was talking to her parents, Andy and Bill talked in private. "Thanks for the speech, Andy, but you didn't need to do that for me."

"First of all, Bill, yes, I did. You vouched for me with the O'Rourkes, so I was returning the gesture. And secondly, I wanted to let the two fence riders understand that I was in your corner. A scare tactic, if you will."

"Boy, Andy, this political shit is nuts."

Andy laughed. "Tonight was child's play. It gets way worse than this."

"So after hearing what happened in Mad Max's office, I take it she won't be voting for me?" Bill asked.

"She was never going to vote for you in the first place. I just went to her office to drop a bomb, if you will," he said.

"What was the bomb?" Bill asked.

"Let's just say come tomorrow afternoon, Mad Max will have her life turned upside down. And shortly thereafter, your county won't have to deal with her anymore."

"I don't want to know." Bill laughed.

After all the supervisors took their seats, the meeting continued. "Supervisor Harris," Klein started, "in light of the accusations leveled against you this evening, will you be abstaining from this vote?" The county attorney advised her to do so until an investigation was conducted.

"Chairwoman, I will not abstain," Harris responded.

"Very well," she replied. "I am calling for a vote. The vote will be to allow Sheriff Dixon to fill the vacant seat for the remainder of the term. If that vote fails, a follow-up vote will be to authorize a special election in accordance with county election rules. As relating to the first vote, all in favor, four ayes. Any opposed?"

"No," Mad Max said.

"The vote passes 4–1. Congratulations, Sheriff. I know you will make this county proud."

"Thank you, ma'am, and thank you, Supervisors."

NOT AGAIN

Andy had just finished an eleven o'clock meeting with the mayor of Arcadia when his personal phone rang. It was Stacy. "Stacy, is everything okay?" Andy asked.

"Andy, I'm sorry to bother you. Heather asked me not to, but she's pretty upset."

"What happened?" Andy asked.

"Her parents called her and told her that the guy that shot her brother was going to get some sort of new trial, and Heather's afraid of her parents having to relive it all over again," Stacy told him.

"Oh, jeez, where is she now?" Andy asked.

"She's in her room crying," she said.

"All right. I know just how to cheer her up. What are you guys doing this afternoon?"

"We didn't have anything planned other than catching some rays."

"Okay. Do you feel like going out to a late lunch?" Andy asked.

"Sure, I'll go," Stacy told him.

"I'm in Arcadia, so depending on traffic, it shouldn't take me too long to get there. Don't tell Heather. Let's surprise her."

"Okay, Andy, thanks, and I'm sorry to have called you," Stacy said.

"I'm glad you did," he replied. "I'll see you in a bit."

The distance to UCLA was only about thirty-five miles, and during rush hour, it would take close to two hours to get there. But at this time of day, Andy figured more like a little over one hour. He had to make one stop and one phone call. Andy arrived less than an hour later, parked his truck, and walked to their dorm. As he walked past the front desk toward the elevators, he was stopped by a dorm monitor.

"May I help you?" a kid named Justin asked.

"No thanks. I'm good," Andy replied.

"May I see your student ID?"

Andy replied, "I'm not a student here. I'm just here to pick up my girlfriend for lunch."

"Well, sir, you can't go in there unescorted," Justin demanded.

"I've been here several times picking her up, and no one has ever said anything to me before," Andy explained.

"Who is your girlfriend?" Justin asked.

"Heather O'Rourke. May I continue, or is there a form I need to fill out or something?"

"If you step one foot towards that elevator, I'll call the police," Justin said.

Frustrated, Andy pulled out his phone and called Stacy. Stacy was in Heather's room when the phone rang, and when she saw that it was Andy, she excused herself and went to her room to answer it.

"Hey, Andy what's up?" she asked.

"Stacy, I'm down in the lobby, and the front door guy is telling me that I can't come up there unescorted."

"Let me guess," she said. "A little pip-squeak with a funky haircut named Justin."

"That's the guy."

"I'll be right down." When Stacy walked off the elevator, she said, "Sorry, Andy. Justin here picks and chooses which rules he wants to follow. Did you tell him who you were here to see?" she asked.

"I told him I was here to see Heather."

"That's the problem. Justin thinks Heather is his girlfriend," Stacy explained.

Andy turned to Justin and extended his hand. "I'm sorry, Justin. I didn't know you and Heather were an item." Justin shook Andy's hand, at which point Andy returned a manshake.

"Ow, that hurt," Justin said as he pulled back his hand.

Stacy grabbed Andy's hand and led him to the elevator and told Justin to grow up. On the way to the room, Stacy explained that Justin went around telling everyone who would listen that Heather was his girlfriend and that they were going to get married right after he graduated. "We all just laugh at him."

"That's funny," Andy said.

"Heather, I have something that'll cheer you up," Stacy said as she walked into her room.

"I'll be fine, Stacy. I just can't believe we might have to go through this all over again. I'm beginning to think this is never going to end." As she said that, Andy walked into her room carrying a small bag. "Andy!" Heather jumped off her bed and into his arms.

"Stacy called me and said you needed some cheering up, so since I had nothing better to do, I stopped by," he said.

"Thank you, Stacy," Heather told her.

"You're welcome, Heather. That's what best friends are for. I'll leave you two alone."

Andy whispered into Stacy's ear, "We'll leave in about thirty minutes if that's okay."

"I'll be ready," she replied as Andy shut the door.

"Well, missy, I brought you some things." He reached into the bag and pulled out a box of tissues and handed it to her. Heather held up a tissue as if to say she already had one. "Yeah, but you don't know the significance of these. Remember the last time we had to deal with this situation? I didn't have any tissues, so this time, I came prepared. I call it my Heather's Emergency Kit." Heather quickly realized he was talking about the first time they met, and she giggled. "Or," he said as he reached back into the bag and pulled out a T-shirt, "we can keep it original." Next, he pulled out a bib. "This is to keep the tears off of your clothes, but it looks like I'm a little late for that, and these…" He pulled out a set of plastic handcuffs and asked her to put her hands out in front.

"What are you doing?" she asked.

"Just let me see your hands." She put her two hands in front of her, and he put the cuffs on.

"These are so we can make sure you keep your clothes on this time." Heather went from giggles to a straight-out laugh.

"Thank you, Andy," she said as she gave him a kiss.

"Listen, Heather. I talked to Tim, and he said that there will be a hearing on whether or not Garcia-Hernandez will be allowed a second sentencing hearing. Apparently, the Mexican Consulate in

LA filed for the appeal based on his attorneys not bringing in enough witnesses to show what a crappy childhood he had, so maybe they can get sympathy from a jury and get the death sentence reduced to life in prison. He is still convicted of the crime and will not see the light of day."

"So will my parents and I have to retestify?"

"No, not at this next hearing, but if a new sentencing hearing is ordered, then possibly but just victim impact statements."

"Those are the worst, Andy," she said.

"I know, sweetheart, but let's cross that bridge when we get to it, if we get to it, okay?"

She gave him a kiss. "Thanks, Andy. I can always count on you," she replied while holding his hands.

"What about your other boyfriend? Why can't you count on him?" Andy asked.

"What other boyfriend?"

Andy didn't answer. "Let's get you cleaned up. I'm taking you and Stacy out to a late lunch/early dinner."

"That sounds wonderful. It'll get me away from these four walls."

"Chop, chop. The bus leaves in twenty minutes," he told her. Heather bounced out of bed, grabbed some clothes, and headed to the bathroom.

"I heard her laughing," Stacy said to Andy as they were in the living room waiting for Heather. "How do you always manage to cheer her up and so quickly?"

"I don't know. I guess when you know someone so well and have figured them out, you can use that information and turn it into jokes. Laughter really is the best."

When Heather got out of the bathroom, Stacy asked, "Did Andy tell you about Justin?"

"No, what did that little jerk do?" she asked. "Wait a minute, Andy, was that the boyfriend you just asked about?"

"How many more are there?" he asked.

"Be serious," she replied.

"Boy, Heather, I thought you said I was handsome, but after looking at your other boyfriend, you have terrible taste in men!" The three of them laughed. As they were headed down in the elevator, Andy asked, "I know this sounds weird, but can the three of us walk out arm in arm to screw with Justin?"

"That's not weird," Heather said. "I think it will be fun."

As the door opened, both girls had their arms wrapped around Andy's. When they walked past Justin, Andy said, "They are both mine, so stay away."

"You hurt me!" Justin yelled back.

"You hit him?" Heather asked, concerned.

"No, I just shook his hand," Andy responded.

"That guy creeps me out," Heather said. "He's a borderline stalker."

"Are you afraid of him?" Andy asked.

"Not if all I have to do is shake his hand," she replied. They all laughed. As they walked out of the building, they ran into their teammate Jasmine.

"Jazz!" Heather and Stacy blurted out at the same time. Jasmine Dubois was a six-feet-four-inch tall, slender Cajun girl from Baton Rouge. Her mother was black, and her father white. She had long black hair and beautiful skin. "Jazz, I want you to meet my boy-friend, Andy," Heather said.

"Nice to meet you, Jasmine," Andy said as he offered his hand.

She offered her hand and said, "Nice to meet you, Andy. I have heard a lot about you, and I mean that literally. Heather goes on non-stop." Heather blushed. "Where are you guys headed on a threesome date?"

"What does that mean?" Stacy asked.

"Well, I see Andy here likes pretty girls. He has two of them hanging on him."

Stacy realized that she was still attached to Andy and let go and said, "No, we just did that to screw with Justin."

"What did that little shit do this time?"

"He wouldn't let Andy see Heather and threatened the cops on him," Stacy replied.

"There's something wrong with that kid," Jazz said.

"I apologize, ladies, I forgot my manners. Jasmine, we are headed out to a late lunch. Would you like to join us?" Andy asked.

"For real?"

"Of course, if you have the time. We will be gone awhile," Andy replied.

"I would love to. Can you give me a few minutes? I have to go upstairs for my wallet."

"You won't need it unless you just want to bring it. Lunch is my treat," Andy said.

Jasmine looked at him and thought, *This guy doesn't even know me, and he's offering to pay for lunch.* "Let's go, then," she said. As they were walking to Andy's truck, Jasmine said, "Heather, your boyfriend might need a third arm." They all laughed.

On the drive there, Andy had to endure the three of them talking nonstop volleyball. He couldn't get there fast enough. They pulled up to valet, and George came to greet them. He opened Heather and Jasmine's doors for them, and Andy opened Stacy's. "How are you, George?" Andy asked.

"I'm great," he replied.

Andy and the three girls walked into the lobby of the Langham. "Andy!" Amy yelled from behind the counter. "Wait for me, will you?" When she finished talking to a customer, she walked over to Andy and gave him a hug. She turned to Heather and gave her one also. "Andy, what's going on here? Are you not satisfied with one pretty girl? Now you have to have three?"

Andy turned red. "Amy, this is Stacy, Heather's best friend and teammate, and this is Jasmine, Heather's friend and teammate. And, ladies, this is Amy. She runs this place." Amy shook their hands. "We are here for lunch and to give these girls a break from school," Andy explained.

"Well, Paul is off today, but Marissa is here. I'll talk to her and have her seat you," Amy explained.

"Thanks, Amy," Andy replied.

"Have fun, ladies. And, Andy, one at a time please," Amy said with a scorned look.

"That woman keeps you in line, Andy," Heather said.

"Yes, she does," he replied. Andy ordered two bottles of wine and some appetizers for the girls. He turned to Heather. "Will you ladies excuse me for about twenty minutes? I have a quick meeting, and I will return."

"You're leaving?" Heather asked, shocked.

"Just to the Tap Room, sweetie, for a meeting, and I will be back before you even finish your appetizers."

"Okay, Andy. I'm sure we can find something to talk about." Heather laughed.

Andy excused himself and walked into the Tap Room where Judge Fallon was already drinking a beer. "Thanks, Tim, for meeting me, and thanks for not giving me a hard time over the location."

"Hell, Andy, I've given up trying. You have some sort of special connection to this place, so I'm done fighting."

"Thanks, Tim," Andy replied.

"Andy, I thought about our conversation reference plan B. Are you sure you want to go through with it?"

"No hesitation," Andy replied. "Tim, the O'Rourkes have gone through a lot, and I will not allow them to go through any more. People shouldn't have to be constantly victimized because of lawyers and loopholes. That piece of shit was given a fair trial, received a fair sentence, and all the Mexican government wants to do is remove the death penalty. What difference does it make? California is never going to execute him anyways. He'll die in prison. But a good family will have to relive that fateful day all over and relive the six years of pure hell that they went through for what? No way."

"I'm on your side, Andy. I don't want to see the O'Rourkes go through that again either. But you are taking a big risk."

"Tim, if you handle your end and I handle mine, then the risk is very minimal if really any at all."

"I agree," Tim responded. "But, Andy, only if plan B is needed," Tim warned.

"Of course. If the O'Rourkes are left alone, then there will be no need," Andy replied.

"I know Dan and Mary may never know what you have done for them, Andy, but on their behalf, thank you," Tim said.

"The O'Rourkes have a great friend in you Tim," Andy replied. "I'm grabbing some lunch. Would you like to come join me?"

"We're right here, Andy. Just order something," he said.

"No, in the Terrace. I have a surprise for you."

"Okay, but you're buying. Your place, your money," Tim said.

*****

"Heather, I don't want to be rude, and please tell me if I am, but is your boyfriend rich?" Jasmine asked.

Stacy was nodding when Heather replied. "I don't know, Jazz. We don't talk about his finances. Why?"

"Because when he asked me to join you guys for lunch, I thought fast food or maybe pizza or something, but not a place like this. This place is expensive. I mean, he doesn't even know me," Jazz replied. "Where did you find this guy?" Stacy looked at Heather because she had asked her that same question several times and felt she never got the whole story.

"Ironically, Jazz, right here. And knowing Andy, that is why he brought us here today to cheer me up."

"Really," she replied.

"Yes, Andy's a very thoughtful guy, and knowing that we are all friends and teammates and the fact that we had our first date here, he probably—" Heather never finished her thought because she saw Andy walk back into the patio with Uncle Tim. Heather got excited. "Uncle Tim!" she said out loud as she left her chair to give him a hug.

Next, Tim walked to the table and gave Stacy a hug. "It's good to see you, dear. How's your parents?"

"They are good, Mr. Fallon."

"Stacy, I've known you since you were a baby. You can call me Tim."

"Uncle Tim, this is—"

"I know exactly who you are, young lady," he said as he looked at Jasmine. "You're the Jazz. It's a pleasure to meet you in person,

Jasmine." Tim loved women's college volleyball and went to as many UCLA games as he could.

"Sir, the pleasure is mine," she replied.

"It looks like I made it back before you gals finished appetizers. Have you ordered yet?" Andy asked.

"Not yet, Andy. We were too busy talking," Heather replied.

"Well, does everyone know what they want?" Andy asked. They all nodded. "And you, Tim?" Andy asked.

"Really, Andy, you make me come here so often I can recite the menu to you," he answered. They all laughed.

They finished their meals and wine and said their goodbyes to the judge. As Andy was waiting for his truck from valet, he had a terrible thought. He thought, *I've got to drive three girls back, each with a couple of glasses of wine in them, and listen to volleyball. Great.* When they got back to campus and as they walked into the dorm building, Andy noticed two officers talking to Justin, and paramedics were looking at his right arm. "That's him, Officer!" Justin yelled out as he pointed at Andy.

The first officer turned and saw Andy. "I'll be damned. Andy DiPaola," he said.

"Brett Grissom, how are you?" Andy asked as they shook hands.

"I've been great, but it appears that you are doing a hell of a lot better. I took this job for the pretty girls, but it looks like you are gobbling them all up just like old times."

"Really?" Heather asked as she raised her eyebrows to Andy.

"Heather, Jasmine, Stacy, this is Brett. We played football together in high school."

"I know each of these ladies. Well, not personally. I police all of their home games."

"What's going on here, Brett?" Andy asked.

"This kid claims that you assaulted him and that he has major injuries," Brett said.

Stacy got worked up and started to speak, but Andy calmed her down. Andy relayed the story step-by-step and word for word to Brett, and Stacy confirmed what she witnessed. "That explains why he won't tell us how you assaulted him. He just told us you hurt his arm," Brett told them. "This is not the first time he's pulled this stuff. This is the third dorm job we've had to deal with him already this year, and the story always seems to be about the same. So which one of you is his imaginary girlfriend?" Brett asked.

"Guilty," Heather responded as she raised her hand.

As the paramedics were finishing up with Justin, Brett relayed the story to his partner, Bob. Bob didn't look surprised. He pulled out his phone and made a call. Brett asked the paramedics for a status, and one replied, "I can't find anything wrong with his arm."

"What about his hand?"

"Nothing," the medic replied.

After Bob finished his phone call, he walked up to Justin and asked point-blank, "Did Mr. DiPaola just shake your hand?"

Justin looked up and said, "Yes, but very hard."

Bob released the paramedics and apologized for wasting their time. Bob looked at Justin and said, "Justin, this is the third time we've been through this with you this year, so here's what's going to happen. You will be issued two citations, one for misuse of 911, and the second is for filing a false police report. They are both misdemeanors, so you will have to show up in court, or a warrant will be issued for your arrest. Do you understand?"

"I don't have to talk to you. I know my rights," he replied.

"That's fine. Secondly, I just got off the phone with student services. You are hereby banned from this dorm as well as the other two. If you return, you will be arrested for trespassing. Do you understand?"

"Still not talking," Justin replied.

"And thirdly, I need all of your card swipes. Student services have just placed you in suspension pending an investigation and a copy of my report."

Justin grabbed ahold of them hanging from his neck and wouldn't release them. "You need a warrant to take these," he yelled.

"Justin," Bob said, "either you hand them to me right now, or I will place you in handcuffs and take you to the station." Justin thought about it and handed them over.

As the officers escorted Justin out of the building, he turned to Andy and said, "You're an asshole. You'll be hearing from my dad!"

After a few minutes, Brett came back inside and apologized to Andy. "Don't worry about it, Brett. I don't know how you guys do what you do."

"It's interesting to say the least," Brett replied. "Ladies, it was a pleasure to meet you personally. Let's get together one day for a beer, Andy," Brett stated.

"Call my office and set it up," Andy replied.

"That was interesting," Stacy said.

"Yeah, it was," both Jasmine and Heather replied at the same time. Jasmine thanked Andy for the lunch and said it was good to finally meet him.

Stacy, Heather, and Andy went back to their rooms. "I'll leave you two alone. Thank you, Andy, for lunch and for cheering up my friend," she said.

"You're welcome, and thanks for letting me know."

LOVE YOU

Heather and Andy went into Heather's room. "So, Andy, I guess Thanksgiving is your favorite holiday," she stated.

"Why do you say that?" he asked.

"Because apparently, you have a history of gobbling up pretty girls!"

Andy chuckled. "So how is my perfect girl feeling now?" he asked as he brushed the back of his hand across her cheek.

"She feels likes she needs to hear the gobble-gobble stories," she replied.

"Heather—" Andy started.

She cut him off. "I'm just joking, Andy, but it definitely wasn't something I thought I'd hear today, that's for sure." She thought for a moment and decided to take a gamble even if she got shot down. To her, it was worth the risk. "Andy, I'm sorry about my behavior just now and for the way I treated Bill at your cabin on the Fourth when we talked about other girls and you and for my comments at the board of supervisors meeting."

"What comments did you make at the meeting?"

"I got mad at those two ladies who called you handsome," she answered. Andy laughed. "For a couple of months, I have been trying to figure out why I was like that because it is not in my personality to be that way, then today when your cop friend made the gobble comment, I figured out what my issue is."

"What is that?" he asked.

"Andy, I love you. I fell in love with you a long time ago. I know this seems too soon, but I can't change the way I feel about you. So I just figured out that I was getting jealous every time another girl is mentioned, whether she was real or perceived, and I don't want to be like that. I'm not asking you to feel the same way, but I just wanted you to know why I was acting like a little girl, and you won't see me act like that anymore."

"Well, Heather, you don't know what a relief it is to hear that. I have been wanting to tell you how much I love you for a long time, but I didn't know when it was or when it wasn't appropriate. Contrary to what people like Brett or even what you may believe, I am not experienced in dating, and I don't know what I'm doing. That's why I screwed up by not talking to your parents first and by bumbling in Pasadena when I asked to see you more. I have never been in a real relationship before, and I certainly have never been in love before.

"Heather, I have wanted to tell you that I love you several times. I could have said it in Pasadena at any time during our first weekend together, in Santa Monica, or Big Sur, on the Fourth, in Sedona. Heck, I wanted to tell you that when I saw you at practice when you had your legs wrapped around my waist. It almost came out when I was staring into your eyes. I have loved you since day one, so to make sure I do this right, Heather, I love you." They both embraced and kissed for a long time.

"Boy, Andy, out of all the romantic things you've done for me, I have to admit, saying it during our embrace at practice would have topped them all."

"Yeah, but would you have reciprocated?" he asked.

"Without hesitation," she replied. "Now back to the answer to your earlier question, your girl is feeling a whole lot better thanks to a very caring and loving boyfriend. It could not have been any better, and with the exit of that little jerk in my life, it was a stress-relieving afternoon."

THE CAR CONSPIRACY

"Oh, by the way, did you talk to your mom for me?" Andy asked before he left her dorm.

"I did, and she wanted for me to tell you that your offer is very sweet and generous, but she said she cannot accept it."

Andy had asked Heather if he could have her dad's Camaro restored for him, and then Heather and Mary could surprise him with it for Christmas. Then with any luck, they could get it placed in the Rose Parade. Actually, the parade was the easy part with his political connections, but the hard part was, they were running out of time. Andy felt it would be a nice gesture because he knew the attachment he had with his dad through his Mustang, and he felt that Dan could have the same attachment with Brian. "Well, tell her that I won't take no for an answer."

"Seriously, Andy, you want me to talk to my mom like that?" she asked.

"I didn't mean it like that. I just feel that it would do your dad some good and maybe let him move on from the nightmare he's been living and remember the good things about Brian, that's all."

"That's very nice, Andy, but my mom is old-school and Italian, so it's pretty hard to change her mind once she's made a decision."

"Well, I'm going to work on her Friday night at dinner if that's okay with you."

"It's fine with me, Andy. But I'm warning you, my mom is tough, and she won't be afraid to tell you you're wrong."

"I'll take my chances. Besides, I'll have you on my side, won't I?"

"Andy, I love you, and what you are trying to do is very sweet. Of course I'll help you try to convince her, but promise me that if she is firm in her denial that you will back off."

"Yes, of course. I don't want to upset her. I'm trying to do a nice thing. What time does your dad get home from work on Friday?" he asked.

"He pulls up normally around six."

"Okay. I'll pick you up at three, and then we will have time to talk to your mom before he gets home."

*****

Andy and Heather pulled up at the O'Rourkes' house at 4:30 PM. Traffic out of Westwood was terrible. They walked in the front door and noticed several red rose arrangements everywhere. They walked into the kitchen and found Mary. Heather gave her mom a hug, and Andy told her it was good to see her again. "What happened, Mom? Did dad cheat on you or something?"

"No. Why would you say something like that?" she asked.

"What are all these roses for?" she asked. "It looks like Valentine's Day threw up in here. I just figured he must have done something really bad to buy all of these."

"Those aren't for me, sweetheart. Those are for you."

"Me?" she asked, surprised. Heather had never received roses from anyone before, nor had she ever even received a Valentine's flower, except from her dad.

"Yes, dear. At least, that's what the card reads," Mary said as she handed it to Heather.

She opened the card, and all there was inside was a note that said, "The challenge is for you to figure out the meaning behind the roses. I love you Heather. Andy."

"I love you, Andy," she said as she wrapped her arms around his neck and gave him a kiss.

"Love?" Mary asked. "That's the first time that I've heard either one of you say that. So does that mean your relationship is moving forward?"

"I hope so, Mom," she replied. "Andy, these are beautiful, but why so many?"

"That's the challenge, Heather. There is a meaning behind them, and I want to see if you can figure it out. I'll give you a hint. There are seventeen arrangements, each with a dozen roses, then there is one arrangement with just six roses in it."

"Andy, I have no idea what that means. Tell me please."

"You can't give up that easy. You're a smart girl. Think about it."

Changing the subject, Heather asked, "What's for dinner, Mom?"

"Well, with you two health nuts, I decided to try wild salmon-stuffed portabella mushrooms with grilled veggies and a salad."

"That sounds great," Andy replied.

"I think so too, but Dan is going to kill me because I told him he could grill steak, and he hates mushrooms. Andy, have you broken any man rules lately?" Mary asked.

"I don't think so, ma'am, why?"

"Because then I can tell Dan, and he can make you eat his salad again, so he won't be so ticked at me."

"I would prefer not to have to get beat on again, but if it'll help, I'll take one for the team." They all laughed.

"Andy, would you like a beer?" Mary asked.

"Yes, ma'am, thanks."

They all sat at the kitchen table. "So Heather tells me that you are here to try to change my mind on the Camaro restoration. Listen, Andy, your offer is very kind and very generous, and I appreciate it. But you just spent a lot of money on a new car for Heather, and I couldn't ask you to spend more for this family, so again, it is something that I just cannot accept."

Heather needed a car because her 2009 VW Bug would break down at least once a month, and finally, it could not pass the stringent state of California emissions testing. So by law, the car could not be on the road. You know, for environmental reasons. Ironically, these cars end up being sold in Mexico. Andy always wondered why California officials allowed that. A good southern wind would drive the pollutants right back into California.

Andy insisted he buy her one for her birthday, and she thought she would get a cheaper, used car. Heather had always been a little uncomfortable about the amount of money Andy spent on her. She didn't want him to think that she was with him because of money. She had relayed her concerns to him, but he insisted he never thought of her that way.

He told her absent the jewelry he gave her on their first date that everything else was responsible spending. Andy even tried to justify the jewelry by telling her that it was payback for making her wait a year and a half. Andy really bought the jewelry because he wanted her to wear it with that white summer dress and her gorgeous tan. It was as simple as that. The jewelry didn't make Heather beautiful. Heather made the jewelry look beautiful. The brand-new all-wheel drive Subaru Outback was reasonable, Andy explained, because he felt more comfortable with her in it on the mountain roads when she came to see him.

"Mrs. O'Rourke, will you at least let me try to explain myself?" he asked. "If you still say no, then I will respect that and drop the subject. I am not trying to offend you."

"Mom, Andy has good intentions. Can he at least tell you about them?" Heather asked.

"Go ahead, Andy. The least I can do is hear you out," Mary said.

Andy started. "Ma'am, your family has been through hell for almost seven years, and Heather told me the story of why that car was bought and for what purpose. Now that Garcia-Hernandez is locked up, wouldn't it be a great idea if Mr. O'Rourke were to stop living the nightmare and start celebrating Brian's life? I think restoring that Camaro would be a great start." Andy noticed that Mary had begun building up tears. "Mrs. O'Rourke, I'm not trying to upset you or bring up old wounds. I'm just trying to do the right thing. My thoughts are, we get the Camaro restored, you two give it to him as a surprise Christmas present, I will be able to get it entered to be used in the Rose Parade, and then Mr. O'Rourke can start living again."

"Andy, that's very sweet, but how much will something like that cost?"

"I've spoken to the same company that restored my Mustang, and to go all out, the least it would be is about $23,000, and the most about $35,000. It could be considerably less depending on the current condition of the car."

"Andy, there is no way I can allow you to spend that kind of money on that," Mary said.

"Let me make you a deal that might make you feel more comfortable. What if I were to increase my fees to my clients by 10 percent to cover the costs?"

"So you want to raise your prices just to pay for a car for us? That could ruin your business."

"No way, ma'am. My clients aren't using their own money. They use rich people's monies in the form of campaign contributions for their campaign expenses. They need me way more than I need them, trust me. The rich get the tax break, and the candidate doesn't personally spend a dime. Consider it this way. We will be putting their money to use for a greater purpose than electing politicians.

Mary laughed. "You have a way of selling ideas, Andy."

"So is that a yes, Mom?" Heather asked, confused.

"Yes, if Andy makes me a promise that the monies will come from where he just said that they will and not out of his personal bank account."

"Ma'am, you have my word, but just to be honest, I will have to lay out up-front money so we can get this started fast to make sure it will be done in time, but it will be paid back to me way before the restoration is done."

"Andy, it's none of my business, but you can make that kind of money that fast?" Mary asked.

"Mrs. O'Rourke, I can make ten times that amount even faster if I wanted to. There are always new politicians and causes just waiting to spend money. It really is dirty business, so don't feel bad about taking their money. I never do."

"I just thought of something," Heather said. "How are we going to get the car out of the garage and make it disappear for three months without dad knowing?"

"Good question," Andy said.

"You two let me handle that. As a nagging Italian wife, that'll be easier than you think." They all laughed.

"Mrs. O'Rourke, do you have any idea of how they wanted to restore it? I mean, like color, that sort of stuff."

"Andy, in the glove box of the Camaro is a notebook with everything you need to know. Dan and Brian spent a whole year drinking beer in the garage staring at that car and agreeing on its restoration. It used to drive me nuts. Two grown men staring at a pile of junk and making future plans and talking about her as if she was a person. It was all crazy talk to me."

"I don't think that's crazy," Andy replied.

Heather and Mary laughed at how serious Andy was. "Wow, Mom. I don't think I have ever seen you change your mind before. I told Andy that he wouldn't be able to get you to."

"Heather, be nice to your mother. Andy sold me a convincing story, and quite frankly, I think it will really help your dad. He seems to have given up on life since Brian's death, and I believe this will boost his morale, and maybe I will get that PCH drive we have talked about."

Dan pulled up the driveway and walked in the house. Heather gave him a hug, and Andy stood and shook his hand and said, "Nice to see you again, Mr. O'Rourke."

"You too, Andy. Is the grill going? I'm starving. I didn't get my code today because of a long accident investigation." Code 7 was lunch.

"I changed my mind, Dan. We are having wild salmon and stuffed portabellas."

"Why, what happened to steak?" he asked, confused.

"I changed it after Andy and Heather agreed to come to dinner the other day. You know they watch what they eat."

"You know what, Mary? That sounds good. A steak would be too heavy, and go ahead and leave the mushroom with mine. I'll try it." Heather asked herself, "What the heck is going on around here? My mom caved in to Andy, and my dad's eating mushroom." As the four of them were eating, Dan asked, "How's business, Andy?"

"Sir, in my line of work, business is always great. There is a never-ending line of idiots who want to be the next political superstar, and their competition pays me to crush their dreams."

Mary spoke up. "Dan, I need to get your Camaro out of the garage so I can have more room. I talked to my brother, and he said the offer to put it in his storage building still stands."

"I've been thinking about that car, Mary. Why don't we just sell it?" he asked.

"Dan, you had plans for that car. Why would you sell it?"

"I would like to restore it, but I don't know when I'll get to it or if I ever will get to it."

"Well," Mary said, "let's move it to my brother's, and you can decide whenever you want. Storage is free, and it's not hurting anything."

"Okay, fine, Mary. It would be nice to be able to move around in that garage."

"I'll have my brother pick it up sometime this week."

YES AGAIN

Andy had just dropped Heather off at her dorm and was headed to Rancho when his phone rang. "Tim, what's up?"

"Andy, you are not going to be happy. We need to talk."

"Name it," Andy replied.

"Oh, so I finally get to pick somewhere," Judge Fallon said in a sarcastic tone.

"I'm just leaving Westwood, so tell me where."

"Fine, you win. The Tap Room in two hours."

"I knew you liked that place, Tim. You just like to give me a hard time. Oh, and by the way, Tim, you picked, you pay. I'll see you there," Andy said with a laugh. Traffic was moderate, so Andy made it in an hour and a half. After dropping his truck off at valet, he went in to say hi to Amy. When he walked through the front doors, Amy was standing there to greet him. "How do you always know when I'm here?" he asked.

"I always have my eye on you, young man, you know that," she replied. She gave him a hug, and they spoke for a few minutes. Andy caught her up on his and Heather's relationship, his business, and the restoration project. "You know, Andy, that's a very nice thing you are doing for the O'Rourkes' Camaro, and I know why you are doing it. You're so sweet," she reached up and gave him a kiss on the cheek. When they were through talking, Amy said, "Behave out there, Andy." She told him this as she walked away.

"I don't have a choice, do I, Amy?" he yelled back.

Without turning around, she responded, "No, you don't!"

Andy walked to the Tap Room and ordered a beer. Fallon was about fifteen minutes late. He walked in and immediately started complaining about traffic. He ordered a beer, and they talked. "Andy,

I got a call from a colleague that sits on the district court of appeals, and they are granting Garcia-Hernandez another sentencing hearing. It hasn't been made public yet."

"Why, what was their reasoning?"

"They said that his defense team was inept in regard to his childhood, and they want a jury to hear about it."

"When will this happen, Tim?" Andy asked.

"After the appeals court makes their ruling final and notifies all parties, I will hold an informal hearing and set a date. I'm looking at some time next March." Andy just looked at Fallon in the eyes, waiting for him to talk. Tim knew what Andy was looking for, so he said, "The answer is yes to your question." Nothing else was said. Plan B will move forward.

"So how are you going to tell the O'Rourkes?" Andy asked.

"I don't know, Andy. It's only a week away from Thanksgiving. Do I wait until afterwards? But then it will be Christmas season. Are you going to tell Heather, or am I?" Tim asked.

"I'll tell her," Andy said. "I kind of have her prepped already, so I think I can break the news with minimal emotion. She has a volleyball match tomorrow, so I will wait until Friday afternoon when I pick her up for the weekend."

"Okay, then. I will invite myself to dinner with Dan and Mary and tell them Friday night also. Where are you guys going this weekend?" Tim asked.

"That's going to depend on Heather and how she takes the news. Thanks, Tim, for the info." They finished their beer and went their separate ways.

Heather's last class on Friday ended at 11:50 AM. Andy was waiting for her outside her dorm building when she showed up. She saw him sitting on a bench, so she ran up to him and gave him a hug and a kiss. "I thought you were picking me up at one."

"I was, but traffic, for some reason, was flying this morning. Are you packed?" he asked.

"Not yet, but it'll only take a few minutes. Come on up." She grabbed him by the hand and went inside.

As she was packing, Andy was talking to Stacy in the living room. Stacy was telling him about the amazing game she had last night and how it was the best she had been this season. Andy wanted to tell her that he knew because he watched the whole thing, but since she was so excited, he just listened. Heather came out of her room with the same suitcase and duffel bag that she always used. Andy stood up and gave Stacy a hug and told her to have a great weekend. "I'll see you on Thanksgiving." Andy was invited by the O'Rourkes for Thanksgiving this year, and oddly, he accepted. Stacy and her parents were also invited. Since his father's death, Andy really didn't celebrate the holidays. Jack, Bill, and Amy always invited him, but he always turned them down. His father loved the holidays, so Andy was always reminded of him when the season came around. But now with the addition of Heather into his life, he was slowly changing.

"So what are the plans for the weekend, Andy?" Heather asked.

"Well, you name it. Rancho or Arrowhead?"

"Arrowhead of course," she replied. "Crisp fall mountain air, a burning fireplace, a hot tub, and you. What more can a girl ask for?"

"I want one," Stacy replied.

"You'll get one, Stacy. Just be patient," Andy assured her.

Andy started driving toward the Langham. He reached over and grabbed Heather's left hand and kissed the back of it. He figured he would take her there because she was always happy when she was there. "Heather," he started, "I have some news that you are not going to like."

"I think I know what you are going to tell me," she replied.

"How do you know?" She reached down and grabbed the Heather's Emergency Kit off the floorboard and held it up. "Yeah, I brought it along, but I figured it probably could only work once."

"It's okay, Andy. When this was brought up a couple of months ago, I told myself that it was probably going to happen anyways, so I prepped myself for it. I'll get through it because I know I have you by my side." She squeezed his hand. "Do my parents know yet?" she asked.

"No. Tim is going over there tonight to break the news."

"My poor parents. It seems like they have to keep losing their son over and over again. The three of us have talked about this day, so I know they are expecting it. We will get through it together as a family."

"The three of you are a very close family. You'll be fine," Andy told her.

"Andy, I was including you in that as well." She continued, "Listen, Andy, I don't know what the future holds for the two of us, but whether or not we remain a couple, you will always be a part of my life and my family." She reached over and kissed his cheek.

"That was very sweet, Heather, but do you have thoughts of dumping me?"

"No way. I didn't mean it that way."

"I know you didn't. I know what you meant. Well, I was going to take you to lunch at the Langham to cheer you up, but now that you made that easy on me, you get to pick where to go."

"Why don't we skip lunch, if that's okay with you, and grab an early dinner in the village. This way, we can avoid all the traffic heading east."

"Great idea," Andy replied.

*****

"Well, we were expecting this," Dan told Tim after he explained everything to them.

"I guess I'll call Heather and let her know," Mary added.

"That is being handled already, Mary," Tim replied.

"Are you going to tell her?" she asked.

"No, I had Andy do it."

"Andy?" Mary asked in disbelief. "Why would you bother that boy with this mess?"

"Andy doesn't live under a rock, guys. He probably knows more about this case than the three of us combined. Besides, he is the only one who could calm Heather down fast if she gets upset. Dan, Mary, whether you see it or not, Andy is connected to your family already, and he is definitely someone you want on your team. I know it's only been, what, five or so months since they started dating, but those two are connected at the hip, and Andy's very loyal once he attaches himself to someone or something." Mary thought that now she understood his insistence on the Camaro restoration.

"I'm going to predict for you right now that you will have a son-in-law, and it will be Andy. I can't tell you when. Only Andy knows that. But it could be tomorrow. It could be two years from now because Andy plans everything out, but it will happen, unless, of course, when the time comes, Heather turns him down."

"That's not going to happen," Mary said. "She's been in love with that boy for a long time."

"Well, the two of you might want to start preparing for a wedding."

CHRISTMAS

Heather and Andy pulled up to her parent's house around 8:00 AM. They had asked Mary if she could take Dan out on the back patio for coffee so he couldn't hear them pull up. At first, Dan complained because it was a cool morning, but Mary had her ways of getting him to do what she wanted. Andy had rented a car hauler trailer to pull the Camaro on. They walked into the house and to the back patio to get Dan. "Merry Christmas, Mom and Dad," Heather said.

"Merry Christmas to the two of you," Mary responded.

"Are you ready, Mom?" Heather asked.

"Ready for what?" Dan asked.

"Your Christmas present, Dad," Heather explained. They walked into the house and up to the front door. Before they opened it, Heather said, "Okay, Dad, you have to close your eyes, and don't open them until we say so. Mom and I will walk you outside, and, Dad, no peeking."

"Heather, I'm not six years old. I won't open them until you say so," he replied.

They opened the front door and led him onto the porch. "Okay, Dan, open your eyes," Mary said.

Dan's eyes opened wide. "Is that what I think it is?" There sat his convertible 1969 Camaro painted in Corvette yellow with dual black racing strips down the middle of it.

"It sure is, Dad," Heather replied.

"It is beautiful," Dan said as a small tear ran down his face.

"Let's check it out," Andy said. "Dan, your checklist didn't address a couple of items, so I took the liberty to make the changes. I hope you don't mind."

"What did we forget?" Dan asked.

"Well, in your notes, you mentioned installing air-conditioning, but there was a question mark next to it, so I made the decision to have it installed. Then you never addressed rims, so I put the original RallySport wheels on it. Was that okay?"

"We couldn't make our minds up on the AC because of the additional cost that it would have taken, and that's the same reason we didn't address wheels. We wanted the rally sports, but they are hard to find and very expensive," Dan explained.

They walked around the car and opened the hood to look at the engine, and Dan sat in it. He turned the key, and the engine came to life. It purred like a kitten. He turned it off and did another walk around. He had a smile on his face the whole time. When he walked to the back of the car, that was when he saw it. "Where did you get that number?" he asked Andy as tears started running down his face.

"What number, Dad?" Heather asked.

"The license plate number, sweetheart," Dan replied. "How did you get that?" he asked again.

"What's wrong with it?" Mary asked.

"Mary, do you know what that number is?" he asked as tears were still running down his face.

"No, I don't, Dan," she replied.

As Dan started choking up, he said, "That's Brian's badge number." Andy had custom plates put on it.

Mary put both of her hands over her mouth and started crying. Heather had tears running down her face.

"Are you upset with me, Mr. O'Rourke?" Andy asked.

"Andy, you just lifted a five-hundred-pound gorilla off of my back that I have been carrying around since Brian's death. I never thought that it would ever go away. I will always have a connection with my son through this car. I can't thank you enough," Dan explained. He walked over and shook Andy's hand.

Mary walked over to him and gave him a hug, "Thank you for this, Andy. This was more than just a car restoration to you. Now I see why you did it."

"You're welcome, Mrs. O'Rourke," he replied.

"Well, you guys get to just hug him. I get to kiss him," Heather said as she walked up to him and gave him a hug and kiss.

"Mary, why don't you grab a couple of jackets, and let's take her for a spin," Dan stated.

After the drive, Dan couldn't wait to get the car into the garage and wipe her down. The four of them were sitting in the study when Stacy and her parents arrived. Andy walked over to the Christmas tree and removed two wrapped presents. He handed the first one to Stacy. "What is this?" she asked.

"It looks like a Christmas gift to me," Andy replied.

"I didn't know we were doing a gift exchange."

"We aren't," Andy explained. "I just wanted to do something for you, that's all. Open it."

Stacy opened the box and saw three thick envelopes. She opened the first one and saw that it was a two-night stay for two in San Diego to swim with the dolphins. "I don't understand," Stacy said.

"Just open the next one," Andy replied. It was a two-night stay at a dude ranch in Colorado for two people. Heather figured out what Andy was up to, and she started tearing up. Stacy opened the third one, and it was a weekend in Mammoth Lakes to go snow skiing. Each package had all hotel accommodations, airfare paid for, all meals, and even spending money for both Stacy and Heather.

"Andy, this is great, and thank you, but I still don't understand."

At this point, Heather had tears running down her face. "What's wrong, Heather?" Mary asked. Everyone turned and saw the tears.

"I know exactly what this is, Andy," she said. "I thought we agreed no outlandish gifts, and we already had our gift exchange at the cabin."

"These are for Stacy, so I kept my word."

"If that's the case, then why do all the tickets also have my name on them?"

"Loopholes," he replied.

"I still don't know what's going on," Stacy blurted out.

"Stacy," Heather started as more tears started down her face. Stacy, seeing that her friend was crying, also started crying.

"What is going on with you two?" Mary asked. "How can three trips make you cry?"

"Mom, these aren't just three trips. Andy somehow figured out the three trips that Stacy and I didn't go on in high school, so he is sending us on them now."

"What three trips?" Mary asked.

"Mom, Dad, during our junior and senior years, the volleyball team did some fundraisers and set up three trips. One was to swim with the dolphins, one was a ski trip to Mammoth Lakes, and the other was a weekend cattle round up. I didn't go or even tell you about them because of what you were going through with Brian. I needed to be here for you, and Stacy didn't want to leave me behind, so she stayed with me and gave up her chance at going." Stacy's mom, Kathy, and Mary both teared up. Heather walked over to Andy and gave him a hug and a kiss. "Thank you, Andy, but how did you know?"

"You know I can't tell you that. You already made me give up a secret during our first date. I'm not going to do that again." Heather giggled.

Stacy stood up and gave Andy a hug and a kiss on the cheek. "Thanks, Andy. I had forgotten all about those trips."

"There's more." Andy handed a small wrapped box to Stacy as she sat back down.

"Andy, that's enough. I can't accept any more."

"You want to turn Santa down on Christmas day?" he asked.

"You might as well open it, Stacy. He won't take no for an answer," Heather told her.

She opened the box and saw a set of car keys. "What is this?" she asked as she pulled them out of the box. Andy reached for her hand, and when she gave it to him, he pulled her up off the couch and led her to the front door. He opened the door, and there sat a brand-new white Toyota Corolla Sport with a big red ribbon on the hood. "Are you serious?" she asked.

"I overheard your dad telling the O'Rourkes at Thanksgiving that your car broke beyond repair, so with permission from your parents, I offered to buy you one."

"Andy, I don't know how to ever thank you enough."

"Stacy, you're welcome, and the look on your face is thanks enough for me. Listen, you have been the greatest best friend to Heather that anyone could hope for, so if Heather is happy, that makes me happy. In my world, loyalty deserves to be recognized, that's all."

"Heather, do you mind if I take your boyfriend for a spin around the block?" Stacy asked.

"Of course not," Heather replied.

While they were gone, the rest were sitting in the study when Dan spoke. "Heather, Andy has spent a lot of money on all of us, and while I appreciate it, I can't figure out why he's doing it."

"Dad, I know, and I get embarrassed every time he does something like this, so that's why I thought we had an agreement together. But he somehow figured a way around it."

Stacy's dad, Steve, said, "He did the same thing to us. When he asked permission to buy Stacy a car, we agreed because he sold us the story on how loyal she is to you, Heather, and how that makes him happy. But we told him something cheap, like a Corolla or something. Apparently, he loopholed us also because we didn't specify used cheap."

"Well, I'm going to call the judge because I don't want Andy going broke thinking he has to buy expensive things for us, and the judge is the only person that I know who can talk to him," Dan said.

He picked up the phone and called Tim. When Tim answered, Dan put him on speakerphone and told him who was all present. After the holiday greetings, Dan relayed the story about what just happened.

"So what?" Tim replied. "Dan, do you remember what I told you last month about him and loyalty? Well, you guys have front row seats to Andy's show. He is very loyal when he gets attached, so enjoy it. There is no ulterior motive to his actions. When he explains why he did what he did, and I'm quite confident he has told you his reasoning, then don't second-guess him. He means exactly what he says. Andy knows Heather went through a rough time in high school, and Stacy stood by her side the whole time, so if I had to guess, Andy is just trying to make the girls feel better about losing some of their childhood. And as far as the car goes, it's just a car to Andy. Stacy needed one, and making Stacy and, in turn, Heather happy was his only goal. Steve and Kathy, I don't want to sound rude, but Stacy is twenty years old. Andy doesn't need your permission to buy her anything. I imagine he sought your permission out of respect."

"That's true," Steve replied.

"Uncle Tim, then why would he agree with me about not buying expensive gifts, then turn around and do it anyways?" Heather asked.

"Andy plans everything far in advance, and he makes sure everything goes according to those plans. I'm confident that he had those trips planned and purchased way before you asked him not to, so when you put restrictions on him, you left him no choice but to agree with you. If he didn't agree with you, then he probably felt that he would have put you in a position of having to buy him something expensive, and Andy would never do that, so he agreed knowing he had a way out and just gave them to Stacy instead. The end result was the same in his mind. Dan, as far as him going broke"—Tim paused and laughed—"well, let's just say that's never going to happen. Guys, and specifically you, Heather, don't give him a hard time over it because you will embarrass him and make him feel bad about it. He isn't trying to win you over with money. He just likes doing nice things for people he cares about."

"Thanks, Uncle Tim, and I promise I won't."

"I know, Heather. You always keep your promises." Heather blushed.

"How do we get him to at least slow down?" Dan asked.

"Well, the way I see it, you only have two choices: The first one is, Heather can break up with him, and the rest of you can kick him out of your lives."

Heather blurted out, "That's not ever going to happen. I told him that no matter what happens between him and I that he would always be a part of my life and my family."

"You told him that, Heather?" Tim asked.

"Yes, I did, and I meant it. Andy could dump me today, and I will always consider him family."

"What's the second choice?" Dan asked.

"You guys can learn to accept it. Dan, take me off speakerphone and go into another room please," Tim said. Dan took the phone into the kitchen. "Listen, Dan, remember what I told you and Mary about having a son-in-law? Well, I didn't tell you everything because it's not my place, and you can never tell anyone I told you this, but when Andy marries Heather, you guys will be the only family he has."

"Please tell me you're kidding," Dan said.

"I'm not. He has friend families like me and Bill but no relative family."

"What the hell happened to him?" Dan asked.

"Dan, it's not my place to say. That's for Heather and you guys to get out of him. But when the time's right, he will tell you."

"Thanks, Tim, but now I feel like a complete ass for having brought this up, but at least I have a better understanding of why he is doing it." After Tim hung up, Dan walked back into the study.

Mary asked, "If that's the case, what was the connection to the PCH vacation for? I understand your gift, Dan, because he knows the story behind the Camaro, but there's no story behind mine."

Heather thought about it for a minute and said, "Yes, there is, Mom. Do you remember the first time you met him?"

"Of course I do."

"Well, you told him that you have never been on a PCH cruise and that you would have to get Dad to take you. Andy replied maybe one day we will all have a chance to go."

Mary thought about it and asked, "Do you mean to tell me something triggered in his mind that very day that he was going to do something like this for me?"

"I'd be willing to bet, Mom, and with Dad's car being restored, Andy just needed an excuse, and he used Christmas."

Dan addressed everyone. "Guys, let's just drop this and be appreciative of what Andy's done for us. After all, it is Christmas, and since when do we question someone's giving? And, Heather, no giving him a hard time about money, okay?"

"Sure, Dad. It's just that I get embarrassed. I don't want him to think that I'm with him because of his money."

Mary jumped in. "Heather, Andy is with you because of you. I don't believe money plays any factor in your relationship. That boy loves you, and I am confident that he doesn't believe you are with him because of money. If I had to guess, if he thought that way about you, he wouldn't be with you."

"I never thought of it that way, Mom, thanks."

Embarrassed

After dinner was completed and the girls were in the kitchen cleaning up, Dan, Steve, and Andy were in the garage admiring the Camaro when Dan excused himself to use the restroom. "Andy, I just want to apologize to you for what happened earlier," Steve said.

"What happened earlier?" Andy asked.

"Well, when you gave that car to my daughter and I saw that it was brand-new, I didn't appreciate the fact that you spent so much money on her. But then after we spoke with Judge Fallon about it, I realized that I might have overreacted."

"When did you speak to the judge?" Andy asked.

"When you and Stacy went for that drive," he replied.

"Why did you call the judge?"

"We all did. We just wanted to see if he could talk to you about not having to spend so much money on everybody," Steve said.

"Was Heather there?"

"We all were on speakerphone with him."

"Steve, do me a favor and tell the O'Rourkes and your family to have a merry Christmas." Andy turned around, walked out of the garage, jumped in his truck, and drove away.

Dan came out just in time to see Andy driving away. "Where is he going?" Dan asked.

"I don't know. He just told me to tell our families to have a merry Christmas and turned around and walked out."

"What the hell happened?" Dan asked.

Steve told Dan the story of how he tried apologizing to Andy. Dan yelled at him. "Why the fuck would you do something like that?

Was it not made perfectly clear that we were to drop this and not embarrass him?"

"Why are you yelling at me?"

"Fuck, Steve, I don't know what is going on in Andy's head right now, but I guarantee you just caused a whole lot of hell for us and particularly for Heather."

After hearing the commotion, the girls came out to find out what was going on.

"Why is there so much yelling and cursing?" Mary asked.

"Where's Andy?" Heather asked.

Dan explained to them what happened, and Heather immediately started crying. She ran out of the garage to see for herself that Andy had left. She ran into her room to get her phone and keys because she was going after him, and that was when she saw the text.

"I still don't understand what's going on," Stacy said. Dan explained to her what happened while Andy and she were on a drive earlier. "Let me get this straight, Dad. Andy buys me a car out of the kindness of his heart because you refused to, and you tell him it wasn't appreciated? Great." Stacy started to cry. "Andy's probably thinking that I don't appreciate it either. If you would just treat me like a daughter for once in your life, then none of this would have ever happened." As she started walking off, she said, "Dad, you don't know how pissed I am at you right now. I'm going with Heather."

"Now what do we do?" Mary asked.

"I don't know, Mary," Dan said. "I'm not quite sure if there's anything we can do."

"Well, we can call Tim again. He knows Andy better than anyone that I know of," she said.

"Do you think that is wise?" Dan asked. "We already called him for advice earlier, then we turned around and ignored his advice, which put us in the position we are in right now."

"Mary, do you mind finishing up the dishes? I'm taking Steve home before he causes any more trouble," Kathy said.

"That's probably a good idea, Kathy. I don't think either one of the girls are happy with him right now."

"Heather, I'm so sorry for what my dad did," Stacy said. "Come on, I'll go with you, and we will find him together." Heather, still unable to talk, showed Stacy the text.

> Heather, I love you, but please don't come look for me because you will not find me. Please tell everyone that I am sorry. I didn't mean to offend anyone. I just wanted to do nice things for you guys, that's all. You are the best thing in my life, and I certainly wasn't trying to upset you. I love you.

Heather responded.

> Andy, I am so, so sorry for what I did. This is all my fault. I should have never made an issue over those three trips, then none of this would have ever happened. You are the best thing that has ever happened to me in my life, and I screwed it up. I just want to let you know that I love you, and I meant what I said about you always being a part of my life and my family even if we aren't together anymore. I just hope one day you can find it in your heart to forgive me. I love you, Andy.

Mary and Dan walked into Heather's room. "Aren't the two of you going to look for Andy?"

Stacy showed them the two texts. "Oh, dear God," Mary said as she started to cry.

"What have we done?" Dan asked.

"Heather, maybe he just needs to cool off. He will be back," Mary said.

Heather, still crying and shaking, said with broken words, "He told me not to look for him because I wouldn't find him. That doesn't sound like he's coming back to me."

"Have you tried calling him?" Mary asked.

"Several times. No answer. That text is the only thing we got from him," Stacy said.

"I'm calling Tim. He has to know what to do. The only problem is, I'm in for a royal ass-chewing, but I deserve it," Dan said.

"What the fuck, Dan!" Tim yelled after Dan relayed the story. "How the fuck did you let that get out of control?"

"I thought I had it handled, but apparently, Steve didn't want to let it go."

"That guy is fucking brain dead. For being a college-educated CPA, he sure is stupid."

"What can we do?" Dan asked.

"Oh, so now you're asking me for more advice when you didn't fucking listen to the first advice I gave you?"

"Tim, I know, and I'm sorry. You have every right to be pissed at me, but I need to straighten this out for Heather's sake. My little girl is crushed."

Dan read both texts to Tim as he put him on speakerphone. "Guys, this isn't good." Heather started shaking harder. "I've been through this with him before, years back. After Andy's dad was killed—"

Dan interrupted. "His father was killed?"

"Yes, Dad," Heather said through sniffles. "Him and Andy's stepmom were rear-ended by a drunk San Bernardino County sheriff's deputy on the mountain and forced down a two hundred feet cliff, killing them both."

"Oh god, can this get any worse?" Dan replied.

"So Andy's dad's best friend and his wife helped Andy get through the hard times, so Andy wanted to reward them for their loyalty and pay for the new cabin they had just built. When they refused, Andy did it anyway. He wouldn't take no for an answer. They gave him such a hard time over it that he became embarrassed and disappeared. We couldn't find him for five months until one day, he just showed up and apologized to the couple for offending them. To this day, we still have no idea where he went, and he's not going to tell us either. The good news in that story is that they remain great friends to this day. You know, guys, that ever since Andy's dad was killed, Andy hasn't celebrated the holidays. He has refused every invitation that he received. This is the first time he has accepted a holiday invitation."

"Uncle Tim, I am sorry for messing this whole thing up. I had a great guy, and I lost him. Do you think he will ever forgive me?"

"Heather, I think you are misunderstanding what is happening here. Andy is not mad at you or anyone else. He is embarrassed and now has to find a way to be able to show his face around you guys again. Last time, it took five months."

"I know I'm being selfish, but do you think there's a chance that I won't lose him?"

"Heather, you are not going to lose him over this. I guarantee because of his feelings for you, he is fast-tracking a way to get back to you as we speak. If I had to guess, the rest of you might not see him for a while."

"Judge Fallon, in my defense, I was with Andy when all this happened. He certainly can buy whatever he wants for me," Stacy said. Everyone let out a small laugh.

"Well, we certainly should be the ones who are embarrassed. I know I am," Dan said. "Is there anything we can do or say to him?"

"Not really. The only saving grace is Heather."

"Uncle Tim, he won't speak to me or even return texts."

"He will, sweetheart. Just give him time."

"Thanks, Uncle Tim. I feel a little better. I just wish I could hold him right now and tell him how sorry I am."

"Stacy, take me off speakerphone and talk to me."

"Yes, sir," she replied.

Stacy walked into the hall, and Tim said, "Maybe you should tell Andy what you just told me."

"What, that he could buy me whatever he wanted to?"

"Yes, tell him that."

"Tim, I was just joking. I would never tell Andy something like that."

"If you text him that, I have a feeling you will get him to laugh and calm down."

"Really? But what if it backfires?" she asked.

"It won't, trust me, dear."

"Okay, sir, I'll do it."

"Just to set the record straight, you can buy me whatever you want to," Stacy texted Andy.

"That's funny." Andy immediately texted back. Stacy couldn't believe she actually got a response from him. *Now what?* she thought. *Do I say something else or let it go?* Before she could respond, he texted again: "How's Heather? Is she mad at me?"

"Heather is very upset, but why would she be mad at you?"

"Because I offended her and her entire family."

"Andy, do you mind if I call you?"

"Please do," he replied.

She walked out the front door and called him. "Andy, thanks for taking my call."

"Well, I figured you were the only one I didn't upset today."

"Andy, you didn't upset anyone."

"Yes, I did. Do you realize that when we went for that drive, they called Judge Fallon and discussed the gifts? And then your dad made it clear that he didn't appreciate the car until after they had spoken with the judge. So I know he's offended."

"Yes, they told me the story after we found out that you left. Andy, listen, my dad's an idiot. None of this would have happened if he didn't go around telling everybody that my car was shot and that I wouldn't get another one until I got out of college and got a job to pay for it myself to teach me a lesson about life. Do you know how embarrassing it was for me for a month to have to rely on Heather for a ride? I'm twenty years old, and my dad has money. He just won't spend it on me. This is obviously a tricky subject with you, but can I just be honest?" she asked.

"I would prefer that," Andy replied.

"Andy, you obviously have a great deal of money, which is none of my business, but you have to understand that people like us don't have that kind of money, so they feel a little embarrassed when they receive expensive gifts. They appreciate them, but they just feel that they could never get you something as nice back. It's human nature for them to think that way. It's like if I were to buy Heather something for her birthday and then take her out. Well, when my birthday comes around, she will feel obligated to do at least the same for me or even more. And worse yet is if she does more than that puts me in a position the next time to do more. It's a vicious cycle."

"I understand," he said. "But, Stacy, I don't buy things just to spend money or expect something in return. I buy things of need or, more importantly to me, things for sentimental reasons."

"I see, like my car and the high school trips," she said.

"That's exactly right. If I just wanted to blow money, I could have sent you two to Hawaii."

"Hawaii, that would be cool," Stacy joked. "Remember, Andy, I'm not the offended one." They both laughed. "So please come back to the house and see Heather," Stacy begged.

"No way. I'll figure out a way to get Heather, but I can't show my face to the O'Rourkes or to your parents for a while."

"Andy, you have nothing to be embarrassed about. Mr. O'Rourke has already said that and expressed his embarrassment over the situation, and my parents went home, and if I had to guess, I wouldn't want to be in my dad's shoes right now. My mom is probably ripping him a new one. Please do it for Heather. That girl is hurting real bad. She is blaming herself for everything, and she thinks that you dumped her."

"Are you sure they will let me in?" he asked.

"Are you kidding? They are so embarrassed they will probably give you the house! Where are you at?"

"The next block over. I didn't want to get too far away from Heather until I figured things out."

"Well, I'm out front. When you get here, I will walk you in."

"Okay, be there in a second."

Stacy was waiting for him when he pulled up. She grabbed his hand and walked him through the front door. Dan and Mary were sitting in the study, and when they saw them, Stacy put her finger over her lips for them to be quiet. Stacy was in charge now. She opened Heather's door. "Heather, I have something that'll cheer you up."

Heather was still sobbing and said with broken words. "Unless it's Andy, nothing—" Andy walked through the door. "Andy?" she said in a disbelieving whisper.

"Heather, I am sorry for having upset your family today. That was never my intention."

She just sat there, still shaking, and said, "I am so sorry that this happened today, and it was all my fault. I just didn't want you to think that I'm with you for money because nothing could be further from the truth. I thought I lost you forever."

"Heather, I would have never dated someone if I thought all they wanted was money. I have never thought of you that way. You need to realize that you may get embarrassed by receiving expensive gifts, but I get embarrassed by not buying them. Having money isn't always fun. It's a curse. So I just look for special things to do for people I care about."

"Am I allowed to hold you right now?" she asked.

"Well, it would be exceptionally awkward if you didn't," he replied.

She stood up and wrapped her arms around him and buried her head on his chest. "Andy, I'm so sorry that this ever happened. I love you, and I don't ever want to hurt you like that again. I don't think I could bear you leaving me."

"Heather, I love you too, but I wasn't going to leave you. I was parked the next block over trying to figure out how to get you without facing your parents or the Hannas."

"Andy, you had nothing to be embarrassed about. You didn't do anything wrong."

"Are you two decent?" Stacy texted Andy.

"Of course we are, why?"

"We are coming in."

Dan, Mary, and Stacy walked into Heather's room to find Andy sitting on her bed, holding Heather on his lap. Andy set her to the side, stood up, and said, "Mr. and Mrs. O'Rourke, I would like to apologize for my—"

Dan cut him off. "Andy, I can't allow you to do this. You do not owe anyone here an apology, nor should you ever feel embarrassed for doing something nice for people. I take full responsibility for what happened here today, and I am thoroughly embarrassed, and on behalf of my family and the Hannas, I am sorry. I am truly sorry I hurt you and for hurting my daughter." The two men shook hands.

"I don't know how I'm supposed to handle this in the future," Andy said. "I can't come to you folks and ask permission to buy something because you will just tell me no, and I don't want to offend anyone if I just go ahead and do it."

"Andy, you just be Andy, and we will learn to accept it. Is that fair?" Dan asked.

"Yes, sir," Andy replied.

Heather, still visibly shaken, asked, "Stacy, how did you get him to come back?"

"Well," she said, "I just texted him that he could buy me anything he wants."

"You said that to him?" Heather asked.

"Yes, I did, and he immediately texted back that it was funny, then we talked."

"Really?" Mary asked. "Well, you know, Andy, that PCH trip you gave me would be great with a stay at the Casa del Mar," Mary said as she laughed.

"Mom!" Heather blurted out.

"It's okay, Heather. It's just a joke." He looked back to Mary and said, "Well, if you go through your package, you will find a two-night stay at the Casa del Mar."

"Andy, I was just joking like Stacy to break the ice. I would never ask for something like that."

"Mrs. O'Rourke, I booked the exact trip for the two of you that I took Heather on. I remembered the first day I met you, you whispered to Heather that you wanted one. I didn't know if you were referring to the Mustang or the trip, so I chose the trip because, quite frankly, you can't have my Mustang."

"You heard that?" she asked.

"Yes, I did."

"Thank you, Andy."

Heather got off her bed and gave Stacy a hug. She whispered, "Thank you. You are always there for me."

"That's what best friends are for," she replied.

Captain Garcia's Fate

Ex-captain Jose Garcia was about to learn his fate in front of Judge Fallon. He had pleaded guilty to all counts and was throwing his mercy at the court. After an internal affairs investigation, he was terminated but was allowed to keep his retirement, most of which will be used to pay for his legal defense and divorce. Jose agree to plead guilty in exchange for a lighter sentence. Had he taken his case before a jury, he stood to get twenty-five years behind bars. He had been in custody for six months and hated it. The prosecution was asking the judge for a seven-year sentence, and the defense was asking for probation. "Mr. Baker, would your client like to make a statement before this court?" Fallon asked.

"Yes, Your Honor."

Jose stood up wearing the standard LA County orange jail jumpsuit with his hands cuffed in front of him. "Your Honor, I am here to ask this court for mercy. What I have done is terrible, and I deserve to be punished for it. I've disgraced myself and my family. I have disgraced and tarnished the reputation of the LASD, for which I have wanted to work since I was a little boy, and I know it will take the agency a long time to rebuild public confidence. But more importantly than all of that, I caused undue pain and misery to the O'Rourke family." He turned around to look at Dan, Mary, and Heather, who were sitting in the front row. Andy was in the courtroom but was seated in the back on the opposite side. "I can only imagine the pain that they suffered through with the murder of Deputy O'Rourke and the fact that Sergeant O'Rourke had to be the first responding unit on scene, that and the fact that my actions prolonged their agony. Sergeant O'Rourke, Mrs. O'Rourke, and Ms. O'Rourke, from the bottom of my heart, I am truly sorry, and I hope one day you can forgive me, although I realize if I were in your shoes I wouldn't."

"Your Honor," Jeff said as he stood up. "If I may, Your Honor. That was not the statement Mr. Garcia was supposed to read."

"I didn't think so," Fallon responded. "That doesn't help a mercy plea."

"Your Honor, I just wanted to take this opportunity to admit what I did but, more importantly, take the time to express my apologies to the O'Rourkes. Sir, I know your reputation, and you are a hard judge, so I already know that you are going to give me the max. But I just wanted to be sincere in my apology."

"Jose." Jeff turned to him. "You are not helping yourself, and as your attorney, I am advising you to stop."

Jeff turned back to Fallon. "Your Honor, I would like the court to keep in mind the fact that Mr. Garcia has fully cooperated in this case, and at no time did he ever deceive the investigators."

"Noted," Fallon said.

Fallon looked to the prosecutor and asked if she had anything to say. "No, Your Honor. We will let the facts speak for themselves."

"Mr. Garcia, please stand." Fallon continued. "Sir, you are right. I am very hard, especially on law enforcement officers who commit crimes and who violate their oath of office, especially in the egregious way that you did. Having said that, I hereby sentence you to seven years in the state pri—"

Heather let out a loud "Yes!"

Fallon looked over his glasses and, without saying names, said, "I will not tolerate outbursts in my courtroom."

Mary looked at Heather and said, "You can't do that in court. You could be put in jail." Heather's face turned red.

"As I was saying, prison, however, given your cooperation and the fact that you had an impeccable career going before you got involved in this case, I don't believe that locking you up for seven years is the best rehabilitation. I am going to suspend that sentence under the following conditions: You will spend sixteen months of house arrest with an ankle monitor based on the probation department's guidelines with credit given for time served. You will serve four hundred hours of community service. I have spoken with Sheriff Dixon, and he agreed to allow you to speak at the LASD academy to new recruits about this case and what not to do as a cop—an ethics class, if you will. That is how you will serve your community service. You will be responsible for all court costs and the cost of the ankle monitoring system."

"Thank you, Your Honor."

"Mr. Garcia, I do not want to see you in this or any other courtroom again. If you violate any provisions set up by the probation department, I will immediately remand you to prison for the remaining seven years. Do you understand?"

"Yes, sir, Your Honor, and thank you."

"You are dismissed."

When they walked him out of the courtroom, a deputy walked up to Heather. "Ms. O'Rourke, your presence is requested in the judge's chambers."

"Am I going to jail?" she asked.

"Ma'am, I don't know. Only the judge does."

"Fine," Heather blurted out. "I don't regret what I did. That man caused five years of unnecessary pain for my family, and I'll go to jail for it."

Mary looked at Dan, and before she could ask, he said, "No, Mary, she is not going to jail."

Heather followed the deputy to the judge's chambers. He knocked on the door, opened it, and let her in. The deputy left and closed the door behind him. Before Fallon could speak, Heather said as she stood with her left hand on her hip and her right finger pointed at the judge, "Uncle Tim, if you are going to put me in jail, fine, put me in jail, but I don't want to have to listen to a lecture as well. I'm not sorry for yelling in your courtroom. That man put my family through living hell for five years, and if I have to go to jail for it, fine. Heck, maybe you will give me a light sentence like you did for him.

Maybe something like house arrest at a fancy five-star resort while being forced to pet Labrador puppies!" Heather was worked up.

"That's the reason I had you come in here," he replied. "Why would you think I would put you in jail?"

"Because when I yelled out in court, my mom told me I could go to jail for doing that, then after it was all over, you had a cop bring me in here."

"Heather, I called you in here because I knew you would be the only one in your family pissed off over the sentence, and I wanted to explain myself. Apparently, I was right."

"Uncle Tim, why did you let him off so easy?"

"Heather, our justice system is based not only on punishment but rehabilitation. Garcia did a terrible thing, but prior to that, he was a standout cop, father, and husband. He volunteered his off time to at-risk teens and even assisted with softball practice for his two girls. His life is ruined, but I think there is a chance he will make it right. Keep in mind that he is a convicted felon, so finding meaningful work will be difficult. He has no money, his wife divorced him, and his daughters want nothing to do with him."

"Well, good, he deserves it."

"Heather, I know you are upset, but deep down you know this was the right thing to do."

"I just wanted to see him locked up," she said.

"Believe it or not, Heather, this sentence is far worse than being locked up. He has to spend the next seven years walking on eggshells and making sure everything he does is perfect, or he goes to prison. He is going to be humiliated every time he has to give an ethics class to cops realizing that he is no longer one and will never be one."

"I guess you're right, Uncle Tim. Hey, sorry about yelling at you earlier, but I wasn't going down without a fight." They both laughed.

The O'Rourkes, Judge Fallon, and Andy all met up at a seafood restaurant in Santa Monica for an early dinner. They wanted to celebrate the ending of another chapter in their ongoing nightmare. While they were waiting for their food to arrive, Tim told them the story of what happened in his chambers earlier. "Heather," Mary barked, "you can't go into a judge's chambers and disrespect him like that."

"Mom, when that deputy brought me in there, I thought I was going to jail. So instead of getting upset, I told myself that I would fight. I'm tired of getting upset every time something happens with this case. I feel like every time I do, they win. That jerk put us through hell for a long time for no reason, and originally, I was okay with the seven years even though I really wanted more. Then when Uncle Tim reduced it, I got worked up, so I was willing to go to jail but not without a fight." They all started laughing, except Heather, of course. "Besides, Andy would have bailed me out, right?" she asked, looking at him.

"I don't know, Heather. The judge sets pretty high bail amounts." He laughed while she poked him in the side.

Not getting the answer she wanted, she demanded, "So is that a yes or a no?"

"Of course I would have, but I would much rather prefer sweet Heather over convict Heather."

"I just thought of something," Tim said. "Having spent over thirty-five years on the bench, this is the first time that someone has ever yelled and pointed their finger at me in my own chambers!" All five started laughing.

"So you like Labradors, Heather?" Andy asked.

"They're my favorite. Do you like them?" she asked.

"I've always dreamed of having a black Lab named Blue, but with me living at two houses and traveling a lot, it wouldn't be fair to the dog to be alone or kenneled, so that's why I never got one."

RANCH CUCAMONGA— THE BREAKUP

Heather and Andy just returned to Andy's house after celebrating their one-year anniversary of dating at Vito's Italian restaurant. Both of them being Italian, they were very picky when it came to the cuisine, but they found that Vito's was the best around. Ironically, neither one of them ate much Italian because of the pastas and heavy sauces. However, when they did, they enjoyed good stuff.

The sun was starting to go down, and they decided to soak in the hot tub. After changing into their bathing suits—well, if you could call what Heather was wearing a suit—Andy lit a Padron, poured a glass of Four Roses for himself, and a glass of cabernet for Heather. Andy's backyard faced northwest, so they were able to watch the sun fade over the San Gabriel Mountains. His house was at the base of the foothills, which ironically had palm tree-lined streets. His view of the palm trees with the backdrop of the mountains created a beautiful scene. The winter was even better when the San Gabriel Mountains were snowcapped.

Heather didn't like the cigar, but she liked the man, so she didn't have an issue with it. For that reason, usually while they soaked in the hot tub, she always sat away from Andy while he smoked. Tonight was different. She huddled close to him and placed her left arm around the back of his neck. Andy wondered why.

After the sun set and the cigar was finished, they both went into their rooms to shower and change. It was about ten o'clock. After his shower, Andy poured himself another glass of the Four Roses. He wasn't sure if Heather wanted a drink, so he decided to wait to pour her one. Heather drank but generally not too much. She walked out of her room wearing a pair of sweats and a worn UCLA T-shirt. She looked comfortable. She sat next to Andy on the couch. They had been dating for one year, and Heather was heading into her finals week and would be graduating a week after that. She didn't have plans beyond school as far as work went and hadn't decided whether to continue her education. She placed her hand on Andy's thigh and spoke.

"Andy, I love you, but please hear me out before you say anything," she said. "It's taken me a lot of courage even to ask you this, but I feel I am getting mixed messages from you."

Andy looked at her and asked, "Is there something wrong?"

"Andy, we have been dating for a year now, and we have a lot of fun together. You have been the greatest person to me and my family. You tell me that I'm your princess, and you definitely treat me like one." He tried to speak, but she put her hand up as if to say, "Just a second." She continued. "I am not trying to pressure you, but where is this going, this between me and you?"

Andy looked into her eyes and smiled. "Heather, I love you too, and there isn't a day that goes by that I don't ask myself the same question, and I don't have an answer for it. There is a stumbling block for me that I have to deal with."

"Andy, I'm not asking to get married. I just want to make sure we are going somewhere," she said.

"Give me some time to figure it out, and I'll let you know."

"What is this issue? Maybe I can help," Heather said.

"I don't believe so, Heather. It's something I have to work out."

She started to feel frustrated with him. She had never seen him this indecisive before, and he had always been straight with her. She didn't understand what the issue was. She pried. "Andy, if it is something from your past, we can figure it out together."

Andy let out a small laugh, and that was the icing on the cake. Heather turned red and stood up and walked to her room. After a couple of minutes, she came out with her overnight bag and headed toward the front door. Andy ran to her and stopped her. "Where are you going?"

"I'm going home," she said.

"Why?" he asked.

"Andy, do you realize that I just poured my heart out to you, and all I got back in return was a laugh?"

"I'm sorry, Heather. The laugh wasn't directed at you. It was directed at me for what I had going on in my head at the moment."

"So you weren't even listening to me?" she asked in a hurt tone.

"Of course I was."

"Andy, do you realize that everywhere we go and every time I stay at one of your houses, we sleep in separate rooms? We have never even slept together."

He stopped her and said, "Heather, there is a reason for that, and I promise it is honorable."

"Do you mind telling me what that reason is?" she asked.

"Not at this time," he replied. With that, she opened the front door, walked to her car, and drove home in tears.

Andy didn't know what to do. He let her down but had no intention of it. They had never fought before. He wasn't even sure if this was a fight. He tried calling her but no answer. He even sent a rare text but no reply. In California, it was against the law to use a cell phone while driving. *Maybe,* he thought, *she would return my call when she got home.* At 2:00 AM, Andy realized she wasn't going to call.

ENGAGEMENT

Andy pulled up at the O'Rourkes' home at eight o'clock the next morning. He saw Mr. O'Rourke's truck in the driveway with Heather's car and her mom's parked on the street. He nervously walked to the front door and knocked. About thirty seconds later, the door was opened by Mr. O'Rourke. "Andy," he said, surprised he was there—not as in a welcomed surprise but one that said, "Why are you here?" Mr. O'Rourke said that Heather was asleep and that he wouldn't wake her because she had been asleep for only a couple of hours.

"Actually, Mr. O'Rourke, I came to talk to you. Do you have a few minutes?" Dan let him in, and they went into the study. Dan got a cup of coffee and offered Andy one. Andy took it out of politeness, but he never cared for coffee.

Andy started. "I don't know if you are aware, but Heather got upset with me last night and left."

Dan shook his head and said he was well aware of the situation as he was up when she got home. "We talked for several hours," he said.

"So you know everything?" Andy asked.

"I don't know everything," Dan replied. "I wasn't there."

Andy thought that was a sign that Dan had a level head on his shoulders. Any other father would have taken his daughter's side and not even worry if there was another side. Must be a cop thing, he guessed. "The problem is that I'm not quite sure what I did wrong." Dan let out a small laugh. "Well, I did do that," Andy said.

"Andy, you probably didn't do anything wrong. I told Heather that if you have a problem to work out, then she should give you space. You two seem very strong together, and I don't feel that you are stringing her along."

"Sir, I am absolutely not. I have nothing but the highest respect for your daughter."

"Then let time heal this," Dan said. "Heather will come around. If you don't mind me asking, is this a commitment issue that you have?" Dan asked.

"No, my issue is that I'm afraid for Heather's safety. If we were to have a future together and our relationship causes something bad to happen to her…"

At this point, neither Dan nor Andy saw Heather and her mom standing just outside the study.

"I don't understand what you mean by bad," Dan said.

"Mr. O'Rourke, you know what I do for a living, right?" he asked.

"Not exactly. My take is, you do opposition research on political candidates and government officials."

"Yes, sir. In a nutshell, that is correct," Andy said.

"So how does something like that equate to somehow being able to hurt my daughter?"

"Sir, my work angers a lot of people—losing campaigns and terminated government officials just to name a few. While it might appear that I have a lot of connections, which I do, but most of these people are only friendly to my face because they are either afraid of me or they owe me."

"So your line of thinking is that if you and Heather have a future together, they might somehow hurt her to get to you?"

"Exactly," he said. "I have had death threats. I even had a councilman in my town try to pick a fight with me in a restaurant. I don't want anything to ever happen to Heather because of me. Politics is a very dirty and dangerous game. That's why I was so perplexed when she left last night. I thought I was doing the right thing."

"You may have been, but you apparently had a crappy delivery," Dan said. "Have you told Heather any of this?" Dan asked.

"No, sir. I didn't want to worry her," he replied.

"Well, don't I get a say in this?" Heather asked.

Dan and Andy turned around to find Heather standing in the doorway with her hands on her hips, wearing the same sweats and

T-shirt she left his house in. Her mom was standing next to her with her arms folded across her chest.

"How long have you two been standing there?" Dan asked.

"Long enough," Mary replied.

Heather, standing now with her arms across her chest, started to speak. "Andy, I love you. You are the sweetest, most generous man I have ever met. Sorry, Daddy. I fell in love with you the very first time I laid eyes on you."

Dan jumped in. "And when was that?" Dan had always been suspicious of these two and their relationship. He felt they always had a secret to tell, but he could never break Heather of it.

"Dad, please." Heather continued. "You treat me better than any girl could ask. Last night, I just wanted to know if you felt the same way and where our relationship was headed. Why couldn't you just tell me you were afraid for me?"

"Heather, I meant no disrespect, and I definitely had no intentions of upsetting you. I have been battling this issue since the first time we had dinner together." Andy looked at Dan, whose expression said, "Bullshit. It had been longer than that."

"Well, shouldn't I be the one who gets to determine whether I should take a chance between happiness and a risk?" she asked.

"I just needed time to work it out and come to grips with it, that's all," he replied. "I need to go to my car for a second and get some fresh air. Will you excuse me for a minute?" Andy walked out the front door to his car. He brought the big gun, figuring he might need it.

While he was outside, Mary jumped in and gave her opinion. "Heather, I don't know what's going on in his head, but maybe you two should take a break, and let him figure it out. There is no reason to put any more time or effort into this relationship—if you want to call it that—if, in the end, he is just going to break your heart. Maybe he's just a rich playboy who got what he wanted from you, and now he wants to move on to the next girl."

"Mom," Heather shot back, "Andy is not a playboy, and he definitely hasn't used me. In fact, if you must know, we have never even slept together."

"Really? After all those hotel rooms, vacations, and stayovers at his homes, you mean to tell me you two have never slept together?"

"No, Mom," she said, a little embarrassed in front of her parents. "We have not. He had purchased my own room at the hotels, and I have my own room at both of his houses."

Mary thought about it for a minute and said, "Maybe his little thingy doesn't work."

"Mom!" Heather blurted out.

Andy knocked on the door, and Dan let him back in. This time, Dan had a lot more respect for him and now seemed to understand where Andy was coming from. If he had to guess, it was a modern version of an old-fashioned courtship. It made sense—treating Heather like a princess, upholding her honor, and now calculating how to keep her safe. Andy was smart and handsome, owned two homes and a very successful business, and wielded power and influence, all at the ripe old age of twenty-nine. He could have had any girl he wanted. He could have used Heather and tossed her away like trash, but he didn't. *Who the hell raised this kid?* Dan wondered.

Heather started to speak, but Andy asked her not to. Andy turned toward her and placed both of her hands in his and started to speak. "Heather, I have been enamored by you since the very first day we met."

"And that was when?" Dan tried jumping in.

"Mr. O'Rourke, may I please finish? You are a very kind, family-oriented girl. You are exceedingly attractive, smart, and you care so much about your family, which, as you know, means a great deal to me. You are not selfish and are always gracious. I couldn't imagine my life without you, but at the same time, I couldn't imagine my life if I were to cause harm to you. You and your family have been through great pain, pain I can relate to, so that is why I asked for more time."

With tears in her eyes, Heather said, "Take all the time you need, but you need to know—"

Andy cut her off. "I started this relationship with the best of intentions. I planned each step to be as romantic as possible. You were always the one, Heather. Do you remember our first kiss?"

"Am I allowed to talk?" she asked sarcastically.

"Of course," Andy said.

"Of course I remember it. We were on the lake on the Fourth of July during a beautiful evening, watching the fireworks show."

"That's right, Heather, and I picked that day because of the ambiance. Also, because I knew it was going to be a warm night, and the only thing I wanted you to remember was the kiss and the ambiance, not the weather or anything else, which apparently worked. Do you not think I wanted to kiss you before that? God knows I did, but it needed to be perfect. You only get one shot at a first kiss. That is the same reason we haven't slept together. And just to set the record straight"—Andy turned to address Mrs. O'Rourke—"my little thingy works just fine!" Andy had heard her through the front door.

"Oh, before I forget," Andy reached into his pocket and pulled out the shark ring. He handed it to Heather and said, "I found it on your bathroom counter this morning, so I wanted to get it back to you," he lied. He actually took it three months ago to have it sized. Heather thanked him. Andy continued. "So I have some real serious issues about our future and your safety, which is my responsibility." Heather again tried to intervene. "Heather, please," Andy said. "I know you think you will be fine, and I pray that you will be, but I just needed to come to grips with it."

At this point, Andy looked past Heather to her dad, who was now standing in the foyer behind her, and looked for permission. Dan knew exactly what he was asking for, and he gave him the okay. "Heather," Andy continued, "I love you, so if you're willing"—Andy dropped to one knee—"will you marry me?"

Mary's eyes went wide open, and she placed both her hands over her mouth. Andy had the words out so fast Heather couldn't comprehend what was happening. She started to state her case for them to stay together when it hit her. "Wait, what? You're asking me to marry you?"

"If you are willing," Andy replied.

Heather raised her voice and said, "Yes, yes, oh my god, yes!" Andy tried slipping the ring on her finger but was having a hard time because she wouldn't stop bouncing. "I want you to remember I have always been the willing one," she said.

"You're never going to let me forget that, are you?"

As she jumped into his arms, she said, "Nope."

"What does that mean?" Dan asked.

"Just an inside joke between the two of us, sir," Andy replied.

After the proposal, they were all sitting around and talking in the study when Heather asked, "Andy, how are you going to break the news to Jenny?"

"Who is Jenny?" her mother asked.

"Just the one true love of his life," Heather replied.

Mary sat there with a shocked look on her face. "There is another girl?" she asked.

Andy looked at Heather and knew she was jerking her mom's chain, so he played along because of the little thingy comment. "I can't just break it off with her. You know that, Heather. We have talked about this," he replied.

"I'm not asking you to break it off. I'm asking if I can be number one instead of always having to take a back seat. You are engaged to me now, not her," she replied.

Her mother's face went from concerned to building up with anger. "What are you two are talking about?"

Ignoring her mother, Heather said, "Andy, I don't care if you take her out. I would just like to think you would take my feelings into consideration."

Mary could no longer hold it back. She grabbed Heather's left hand and tried to pull off the engagement ring. "Heather, I am not going to allow you to be engaged to a man who won't break things off with his girlfriend, and, young lady, for you to sit here and allow this type of behavior is appalling. You were not raised that way!" After unsuccessfully trying to remove the ring, Mary turned to her husband and demanded, "Dan, do something. Say something. You cannot let this engagement go forward!"

Andy looked at Heather with eyes that asked, "How long you are going to let this go on?" Dan turned to his wife and said, "Calm down, Mary. I have a feeling these two are playing you, and it appears that you are falling for it."

"Andy," Dan asked, "who is Jenny?"

Andy looked at Heather for permission to end this, but he didn't get the look he needed. "Sir, Jenny is a love, a passion of mine for the past five years. She is classy and elegant, just like Heather." Andy turned and saw Heather's eyes go soft from the compliment. "Thank God," he said to himself. What better way to start in a new family than to piss off an Italian mother-in-law?

"So you are planning on having a *Three's Company* type of relationship?" Dan exclaimed, referring to the hit show from the seventies where one guy lived with two girls.

As Andy was about to let the cat out of the bag, Heather blurted out, "Jenny is a boat, Dad."

Her mother stood up, gave Heather a very disapproving look, and walked out of the room.

Dan looked at the two and said exactly what Andy was thinking. "Well, we should celebrate this. How about we meet up for lunch?" Dan asked.

"Tell me when and where, and I'll be there. I need to run to Rancho for a fast shower first and a change of clothes. Last night was not a very good one for me," Andy replied. "Heather, I will pick you up in two hours."

"The heck you will! I'm going with you. Wait here a second," she said.

She ran off to get her overnight bag. Dan walked up to Andy and shook his hand and said, "Well done."

"I didn't feel like I did a good job," he replied. "I normally plan these things for a positive romantic result, and this was way too spontaneous for my comfort level."

"You still got your positive result, didn't you?"

"That I did."

"Spontaneous can be just as romantic," Dan said. As Dan walked off toward the kitchen, he turned and looked back at Andy and said, "One of these days, we will talk about how you two really met and how long it really has been." He turned and walked into the kitchen. Andy was speechless.

THE BIG GUN

"Is that your car?" Heather asked as they walked out the front door.

"That's the big gun I didn't show you at the cabin." The big gun was a bright yellow Lamborghini Huracán Spyder convertible. Andy wanted a car that screamed Southern California as a toy—not that he didn't have other toys. A man's got to have toys.

"You said that you only use it when you need to break out the big guns, whatever that means," Heather stated.

"Well, after you walked out last night, I didn't know what was going to happen. I didn't have a plan. So I got up this morning, drove to the lake, and picked up the big gun, then I came here to get you back."

"I never left you, Andy. I was just upset with you," she said. "But how in the world did you think your car would have helped the situation?"

Laughing, he said, "I just thought if you rejected me, I guess I would just try to convince you with money. I don't know what I was thinking."

"Andy, you are a very generous man. You have given me a lot. You gave me thirty-five thousand dollars' worth of jewelry on our first date!" she said.

Andy interrupted her. "You had the jewelry appraised?" he asked, disappointed.

"No way. I would never," she replied. "Uncle Tim told me."

"Your uncle Tim really is a weak link." They both laughed.

"As I was saying, you bought me a car, you take me on fancy trips and out to expensive restaurants, and this"—she looked at her massive engagement ring—"was not cheap. You spoil me, and I am extremely grateful, but I am not with you because of your money. I am with you because I love you, and looking back, I knew it deep down that first day in your office. That's why I waited, Mr. Right Guy. So again, why did you feel you needed your big gun?"

"I was in territory that I had never been in before," he said. "And out of curiosity, what would have it taken had you rejected me?"

She laughed and said, "Certainly not your big gun. Maybe you could have tried your little thingy!"

"Great," Andy said. "First, I have to live with how you were always the willing one, but now do I have to live with the little thingy one as well?"

"Well," she replied, "there's one way I know of that you can get rid of one of those." He opened her car door, and she laughed.

As they were driving toward Rancho Cucamonga, Heather asked, "So how is Callie going to take the news of our engagement?"

"Callie who?" Andy asked, confused.

"Andy, you know darn well who I'm talking about. Your cute little Nebraska volleyball player Callie Schwarzenbach, that's who." Heather saw the surprised look on his face and said, "Oh, so you didn't think I knew about that."

Last September, the Nebraska Cornhuskers came to UCLA to play a nonconference match with the Bruins. The match wasn't close. Nebraska swept the Bruins in three straight sets, and the score was ugly for the Bruins. Judge Fallon and Andy attended the game together. Andy was impressed with Nebraska and had been secretly following them ever since. While Heather and Stacy were good, the Pac-12 as a conference really weren't contenders every year like the Big Ten Conference and, particularly, Nebraska. He knew that if Heather ever found out about it one day, he would be in for an ass-chewing. Apparently, today was that day.

"Why does she have anything to do with our engagement? I don't even know her," he replied.

"It is my understanding that you talk her up all the time."

"Okay, so what else did Tim tell you?" he asked. Andy knew Tim must have told her because he was the only person he had ever mentioned Nebraska to, and the both of them talked volleyball all the time.

"He told me that during that match last year, you were comparing me and Stacy to those girls, and then he said that you thought Callie was cute. And he also told me that you watch Nebraska play behind my back."

"First of all, Tim and I are going to have a man-to-man talk. I was comparing you and Stacy with them as a compliment, not as something bad. I thought you had a powerful swing like Madi and that your form and jumping ability is comparable to Lexi. I then told him that I thought Stacy had blocking skills like Callie, but she also could work the slide as well as Stiverns. So how can you be upset with me for that? And as far as Callie being cute, she is. I didn't think you were the jealous type. And I follow the team because they are very good, and it's very exciting to watch them play, especially when they are at home. Their fans are exciting."

"I'm not upset because you think she's cute. I just don't know why you couldn't have picked someone else like Lexi. She's pretty and a very good player."

"Let me get this straight. You have an issue with me because I called Callie cute, but it wouldn't be an issue if I called Lexi cute? What am I missing here?"

"Andy, in that match last year, Callie stuff blocked me four times. I couldn't get anything by her. I tried going high hands, going around her. I wasn't successful in anything I tried. Heck, I even tried aiming for her head, and even that didn't work."

"Isn't that what she's supposed to do?"

"Yes, but not to me." Andy laughed. "So who else do you think that is cute on that team?"

"Nice try, Heather. I'm not falling for that trap, but I will admit that most volleyball players are cute. It must be a prerequisite in that sport."

"Nice save, mister."

"So can I still watch them, or will that upset you?"

"Andy, I can't tell you what you can or cannot watch, and I wasn't upset with you. I just found it ironic that out of all the girls, you chose Callie, the one girl that I don't like. Actually, I'm pretty impressed that you have taken such an interest in volleyball, and it's ironic that you picked Nebraska to follow."

"Why do you say that?"

"Stacy and I had an opportunity to play there. They brought us up there, and we toured the facilities. They have a nice place, and you are right, their fan base is very loyal, and the atmosphere in the Devaney Center is electric. So when we sat down to talk to Coach Cook, he explained that he wanted me as a libero because I was too short to play outside hitter in the Big Ten, and he wanted to move Stacy to outside hitter because he likes his middles to be giraffe-sized like Callie Schwarzenbach." She said her name with a hiss in her voice. "So anyways, as you know, we ended up at UCLA, and I don't regret my decision. I just wanted to play outside."

Andy laughed. "She really got into your head."

"Andy, I was so frustrated with myself that night. Sure, I've had bad matches in the past, but I had never been shut down like that before. Callie had my number. Out of curiosity, why did you pick her?"

"I don't know. It's just something about her, I guess. She's a pretty girl, but it's something about her demeanor that I find interesting. I mean, watch her play. Obviously, she has great blocking skills," Andy said as he laughed.

Heather cut him off. "That's not funny, Andy."

He continued. "But when she is waiting for the next serve and the cameras are focused on her, look into her eyes. Something just gets to me. That girl's emotions are never too high or too low. Then when she's on the bench, pay attention to how she acts. You have girls like Stiverns and others dancing around and looking to see if they are on TV all the time, but watch Callie. She's either picking at her ears or her face or stares at her fingers, or she is sucking on her water bottle. One day, I would love to have a conversation with her just to find out what's going on in her head. You know that if Nicklin and Callie ever get their timing down pat, between them, Callie will be a force that will have to be reckoned with."

"So anyway, I enjoy watching the Cornhuskers. And as a matter of fact, this past January, I purchased a front row center court ticket to the national semifinals and finals in Omaha. I'm hoping Nebraska makes it at least to the semis so I can watch them play. I think they stand a good chance. The team will be more experienced, and it will be Stiverns, Sun, and Jazz's senior year, so I'm hedging my bets."

"You only bought one ticket?" she asked, confused.

"Yeah, I didn't think that you would be interested because it didn't have anything to do with UCLA."

"Andy, if Nebraska makes it to the semis, then you are not going to be in the same building as Callie unsupervised," she said with a smile and raised eyebrows.

"I bought two tickets. I just thought I'd have a little fun with you."

"Andy, you're a brat!"

ENGAGEMENT LUNCH

Andy and Heather arrived in Rancho Cucamonga where they both showered separately and dressed for the day. By the time they got done and were ready to meet the O'Rourkes, Mary had already invited ten more people to join them. Heather added Stacy. They were all to meet at the Langham Huntington in Pasadena. Dan had suggested the place because he knew that was where Andy and Heather had their first date, *or so they claimed,* he thought. And he knew that Andy liked the joint.

Dan had known Andy for a year now and had figured out a couple of things about him. For one, he was very loyal, and he had a certain attraction to certain people, places, and things. Places and people he would rather surround himself with than being fake and hang out with the elites. Dan made reservations for eleven thirty because that was the only time they could accommodate that many people on such short notice. In all, nineteen people showed up. Stacy had taken the liberty to invite three girls from the team and Coach Brown. Stacy figured Heather would love it because, after the embrace, Coach Brown always kept her positive that Andy would come back for her, and one month later, he did.

Andy and Heather arrived fifteen minutes late. Andy hated being late to anything, but he always drove the speed limit in the Lamborghini because it definitely looked like it was going faster than it was. They pulled up to valet, and George stepped up and with a gleam in his eye. "Nice car, Andy. Will you be parking it, or will I?"

"If it weren't for the fact that courtesy towards a lady outweighs courtesy towards a car, I wouldn't let you put one foot in this car." They both laughed. George had parked it before.

They walked into the lobby, and Amy was waiting for them. This time, she walked up to Heather first and gave her a big hug and kiss on the cheek and congratulated her on the engagement. She turned her attention to Andy, and when she extended the same gesture, she saw the car. Amy turned back to Heather, put her hands on her hips, and asked, "Did he do something to you? Did he upset you somehow?"

Heather looked a little perplexed and said, "No, why?"

"Because I have never seen anyone, let alone a woman, allowed to sit in that car. He only breaks it out when"—and they both said it at the same time—"he needs the big guns! So what did he do?"

Heather said, "Really, nothing. He just chose to drive it, I guess."

"I'm not buying it. Andy, you did something to her. I'll figure it out. You know I will. And when I do, there will be hell to pay."

"Love you too, Amy," Andy said as he grabbed Heather's hand and pulled her toward the Terrace.

"One day, I want to hear the story between you two," Heather said.

"One day, you will," Andy replied.

They noticed that everyone was on their first cocktail or whatever poison they chose. Heather noticed that Katlyn was drinking a beer. She was only nineteen years old. "Andy was right," she said to herself. "Rich people play by a different set of rules."

"I apologize for being late," Andy said. "Traffic was running a little slow this morning."

Heather laughed and told everyone that the only thing running slow on the road that morning was his 200 mph car. Everyone laughed. They all got up from the table and started congratulating the couple. Heather introduced Coach Brown to Andy. Andy reached out to shake her hand, but the coach quipped, "I don't get one of those embraces I witnessed on the court last spring?"

"Coach," Heather said, "you're embarrassing him."

"I'm sorry. I just thought that was the most romantic thing I had ever witnessed, including in the movies."

She shook Andy's hand and introduced herself as Linda. Andy looked up and saw Dan listening to the conversation and said "Crap" under his breath.

"What's wrong?" Heather asked.

"Your dad just heard that exchange with your coach." Andy had told her what her dad said to him earlier.

"Yeah, so?" she said.

"That embrace was before we supposedly met for the first time."

"Great," Heather replied.

"What is it with you and this place?" Judge Fallon asked Andy as he walked up from behind with a Jack and Coke in his hand.

"Actually, Mr. O'Rourke chose here, not me," he said. "And by the way, since when did you become a jeweler?"

"A jeweler? What do you mean?" he replied.

"Well, it's my understanding that you go around unsolicited and appraise other people's jewelry," Andy said.

Fallon knew exactly what Andy was talking about. He said, "It's not what you think."

"Really? Then what is it?" Andy asked.

"After you bought Heather that car for her twenty-first birthday, I was at the O'Rourkes having dinner. They were talking about the car and were telling Heather that you didn't need to spend so much on it. Heather actually agreed. So I opened my mouth and asked Heather if she had shown them the jewelry yet," Fallon explained. "Heather looked at me in a disappointed way. When she didn't answer the question, Mary insisted she get it and show it to them. She went to her room and brought the necklace and the earrings and showed her parents. Mary said that they were beautiful but looked very expensive. I said, 'Yeah, around thirty-five grand expensive.' I thought Heather was going to kill me. You pissed at me?" Fallon asked.

Andy replied, "Nah, you have known Heather since she was born. If she had a problem with it, she would have said something. But one day soon, the both of us will have a talk about ratting me out to Heather about Nebraska volleyball."

"Be easy on me, Andy," Tim replied.

As the luncheon was winding down, Andy asked Heather if she needed studying time this weekend for her finals. She stated that she had a few notes to go over for a couple of classes. "Why? Do you have something planned for us?"

"Not planned exactly," Andy said. "I figured you would be busy this weekend. I didn't realize I'd get engaged this morning, so I didn't make any plans."

"Wow, Andy DiPaola does not have plans? No organization!" she teased.

"I'll let you pick. I'll do anything you want," Andy said.

"Anything?" she asked with raised eyebrows. They both laughed.

"We can go to your parents' house, Arrowhead, Rancho, Disneyland, whatever you want," he said.

"Well, then let's go to Arrowhead and put the big gun away, take Jenny out for a spin, have some cocktails, and soak in the hot tub. Does that sound okay?"

"Sounds great to me," Andy said. He looked into Heather's eyes and said in front of everyone remaining, "I love you."

Heather jumped onto him and wrapped her legs around his waist, looked into his eyes, and said, "I love you." They kissed, and she whispered in his left ear very quietly. "After the hot tub, maybe we can try out that little thingy."

"Maybe we can," he replied. Heather felt the same warmth she felt when they embraced at practice.

Linda looked at the two and stated, "It would be wise to take a couple of cold showers first." Andy and Heather both blushed.

Heather was talking to Stacy and Katlyn when she saw her mom and dad talking to Andy. She walked up to see what was going on. Her mom explained that they were trying to set up an engagement party for them. "Party? I don't need an engagement party. We just had one," she said. "Today was fantastic, and it costs way too much."

Andy listened as the three of them bantered back and forth. Heather didn't want one, her mom was being insistent, and her dad was on the fence. But in the back of Dan's mind, he was counting the costs, but he would never dare say that to anyone. Today had cost him over two grand. Andy spoke. "May I make a suggestion?"

"Sure," Dan quickly jumped in.

"Heather, you always seem to put other people in front of yourself, and you are always gracious about it. You have concerns about the costs of today, and although I do not know the exact number your parents paid, it wasn't cheap. By the way, thank you, Dan and Mary. You are perfectly fine with today, but your mom has legitimate concerns. Your family has been in the same place since before you were born. They have lifetime friends that watched you grow up. Your mom has numerous church friends, and your dad has numerous cop buddies who all watched you grow up."

"I know that, Andy, but I never planned on a big wedding, and I certainly won't let my parents spend their retirement on one."

Andy continued. "Mrs. O'Rourke, approximately how many people you were thinking about inviting?"

"Well, we certainly can't invite all the people you just mentioned, but I think we can get away with fifty to sixty," Mary replied.

"No way, Mom," Heather barked. "Don't I get a say in this?" Dan was calculating the costs in his head. "Sixty people, a rented hotel venue—this could easily get to over ten thousand dollars. Now," he said to himself, "I'm on team Heather."

Andy stepped in and said, "I have a suggestion that might work. My place in Rancho Cucamonga is not that far from West Covina. It can easily accommodate sixty people. Keep in mind we also have a graduation to celebrate, so my thoughts are, we hold a graduation/engagement party at my house in Rancho. We can cater the food in. I have a large backyard and a large swimming pool. I can rent a bunch of tables and chairs. If we do it during the day, then we can cut down on people drinking too much and driving home late."

"Andy, I can't ask you to open your home to a bunch of strangers," Heather said.

Andy stopped her. "You mean open our home. You see, that ring on your finger with you, accepting it means we both made a commitment to each other. We will soon be one. If your parents feel that all these people are that close to you, then they are no strangers of mine. Then we can kill two birds with one stone."

Dan spoke first. "Heather, this is yours and Andy's day. I'll let you decide. Mary, what do you think?"

"I think it's perfect. The costs would be much lower, making Heather happy, but I will be able to bring a lot of people making me happy." Dan mumbled under his breath, "Thank God."

Plan B

Garcia-Hernandez was transferred to the California state prison in Chino two days before his new sentencing hearing. He was transported there from the San Quentin State Prison where most death penalty inmates were housed. He arrived at Chino at 1103 hours and had originally been placed in general population. Meal call was at 1800 hours. After his arrival, he was greeted as a hero by most of the inmates for being a cop killer. At approximately 1620 hours, Garcia-Hernandez went to use the restroom in the dormitory-style restrooms. Already in the room were two Mexican Mafia convicts serving life for narcotic manufacturing and murder. They were being held at Chino to wait for a murder trial where both were accused of another gangland murder. The first one shook Garcia-Hernandez's hand, and when he turned around to shake the second man's hand, the first one wrapped a rope around Garcia-Hernandez's neck. Both men pushed Garcia-Hernandez face-first into the toilet. One man still held the rope while the second one forced his foot on the back of Garcia-Hernandez's neck, smashing his throat against the rim of the toilet and at the same time continually flushing the toilet to drown him.

When Garcia-Hernandez did not report for meal call, the officials placed the unit on lockdown to search for him. He was found deceased at 1850 hours.

THE THIRD OPTION

"Or there is a third option," Andy said.

"What's the third option?" Dan asked. He wanted to let Andy speak because he understood people, and he was sure Andy was considering his finances.

"We can skip the engagement party, celebrate the graduation wherever you folks decide, have a short engagement, and get married late this summer."

"What? Wait, you want to marry me now?" Heather asked.

"Heather, I married you this morning when I put that ring on your finger and you accepted it."

Mary jumped in. "Guys, don't you want to give it more time to get to know each other? I mean, I was thinking about another year."

"Mary, I don't need any more time, but if Heather does, then I certainly will give her that space. I have dated her for a year now, and I know what I already know. Another year of dating isn't going to change anything for me, except one more year that I can't claim that I am married to her," he replied. "I was willing to do this earlier this year, but I didn't want to interfere with her schooling and volleyball."

"Heather." Andy turned to her. "You didn't lose that shark ring. I took it so I could have it sized. I just forgot to put it back. I have had that engagement ring for three months."

Heather looked to her mom and said, "Mom, I agree with Andy. I don't need any more time. Heck, I will go to the courthouse right now and marry him and skip all of this." She looked to Andy. "Is this why you peppered me with all of those questions this morning?"

"Yes, that was the extent of my engagement, just questions that we have never asked each other before."

The whole time, Dan was standing there and thinking about all those Benjamins he was saving the longer this conversation continued. He was woken from his daydream when Mary said, "No, no way! You are not going to get married at a damn courthouse." She looked at her husband and said, "Dan, say something!"

"Dammit, woman," he said to himself. "Mary, I have closely watched these two for a year now, and to be honest, they get each other. This is not a decision they are making out of urgency or need. These two are already really one and have been for some time. They seem to have some sort of special bond that I haven't figured out yet. I don't know how to say the words because I'm not a romantic—"

"That you're not!" Mary interrupted. She turned to Andy and said, "I got proposed to at a Winchell's doughnut shop at two o'clock in the morning while he was on duty."

"I never heard that story, Mom," Heather said.

"Why would I tell anyone that?" Mary replied.

"That was romantic," Dan said. "A cop at a doughnut shop, that's good stuff right there. Anyways, as I was saying," Dan continued, "if two people ever stood a chance of an everlasting marriage in today's society, it is these two."

"Ah, that was romantic, Dad," Heather said as she kissed him on his cheek.

"Having said that, have you two crossed all the t's and dotted the i's?" Dan asked.

"I believe we have, sir," Andy replied.

Dan continued. "What about kids?" They both responded yes. "Where will you live?"

Heather jumped in and said, "At both of the houses for now."

Andy admitted that that issue wasn't settled because he asked Heather if they could keep the Arrowhead house and sell the Rancho house and that they would build or buy a home wherever Heather wanted. Heather wasn't thrilled at the plan. She suggested they keep the Arrowhead house, sell the Rancho house, and not get another one. "But we felt that this was not really an issue at this point, and it definitely isn't a dealbreaker," Andy said.

Dan agreed. "Did you discuss the fact that there is an age difference?"

"Yep," Heather chimed in. "Not an issue for me."

"What about you, Andy? Is it an issue for you?"

"Well, I've never really thought about it." He leaned over into Heather's ear and whispered, "Should I go for someone with a little more experience?"

Heather looked up at him with raised eyebrows and said, "Really, Andy?" She started to laugh. "Would you like for me to give you an answer to that now, or would you like it in private later?" she said as she was poking him on the ribs.

Andy recalled the answers he received in Pasadena and Sedona, and he was not about to be on the receiving end of another one of those. "No answer will be necessary, sweetheart. I was just kidding. Dan, I certainly have no issue with that."

"Where will you work? What will you do with your life?" Dan asked Heather.

"I am going to utilize my literature degree, and I'm going to operate a travel blog. I am going to write about all the adventures that I have had with Andy and all the ones to come. I personally know someone who knows his way around a computer." They laughed.

"Now the ugly part: How will the prenuptial read?"

"Dad!" Heather yelled.

"Dan, really?" Mary asked.

Andy explained to Heather that her dad was 100 percent correct to ask that question. Finances were the biggest threat in a marriage and the largest cause of divorce. While an engagement party might not be the most appropriate time to bring it up, Andy said he brought this on himself by announcing the possibility of a short engagement. "Your father is right, and that was a very appropriate question to ask." Andy turned to Dan and stated, "There will be no prenuptial."

Heather and Mary both looked at Andy in disbelief and said, "What?"

"Sir, during our first dinner together, I had to explain to your daughter how beautiful inside and out she is because she is too gracious to see it for herself, and that was just one of the many words I used to describe her. I have bought her things that I know she was embarrassed to receive because of the cost, but she took them because of her grace. We are having this conversation because of her concern for spending money. One year ago, I opened a separate account and put money in it for her to use at her leisure with the intention of just replacing what she used each time so she would never run out. She could have used it for schoolbooks, manicures, clothes, shoes, lunches with the girlfriends, anything. I explained that to her and gave her a bank card. Do you want to know how much money she spent out of that account this past year?"

Dan squinted with a look like it's a number he didn't want to hear. "Not one penny," Andy said. "So I'm not worried about Heather and money. If she marries me and then divorces me for money, then I have made a serious mistake in her character, which I am 100 percent convinced I have not. Everything I have is hers, and everything we obtain from here on out is ours. I want us both to be invested in this marriage equally, and I don't want money to be a dividing issue. That's why I would like to sell the Rancho house and build or buy one together so we start our lives together and say it's ours."

"I think that's very romantic and sweet," Mary said. "Don't you think so, Dan?" she asked.

"I do," he replied. "Heather, it would make for a very strong bond between the two of you."

"I see what you're doing, Andy," Heather said.

Sheepishly, he said, "What?"

"You just used my parents for an advantage against me in the house conversation. Smooth, but it's not over yet." Andy just smiled.

"What do you think, Mary?" Dan asked.

"I'm not thrilled about no engagement party, but if the wedding is going to be within three months, then I understand it. Heather," Mary asked, "are you okay with this?"

"Of course," she replied.

"When should we start planning?" Mary asked.

Andy jumped in. "How about you guys spend next weekend up at the cabin? We can grill and discuss things then." They all agreed.

"If you don't mind, Andy, I'll do the grilling," Dan stated.

"Well, sir, you would be a guest in my home, but if you want to."

"You're damn right I want to because of your new rules. I don't want to have to do the damn dishes!"

They all laughed except Dan, who added, "Oh, and it might be a good time to talk about how you two really know each other."

CONNECTED SOULS

After saying their goodbyes to the remaining lunch attendees and to Amy, Andy and Heather walked to valet to retrieve the big gun. While they were waiting, Heather asked, "Andy, would you mind dropping me off at my parents' house? I have to pick up something I forgot for an overnighter, and I need to run an errand. I'll meet you at the cabin in a couple of hours, okay?"

"Of course I don't mind, but is it something we can do together?" he asked. George had pulled up in the big gun, and Andy held Heather's door open for her. "Congratulations on you two's engagement, Andy."

"Thank you, George," he replied as he handed him a twenty-dollar bill.

Andy pulled out of the Langham when Heather answered his question. "Andy, it's just something I do every year, and I don't want to waste your time. Besides, I don't want you to think I'm crazy."

"First of all, Heather, you can never waste my time. And secondly, if you are crazy, shouldn't that have been something you should have let me know before I proposed to you?" he said with a laugh.

"Andy, I'm embarrassed to tell you," she replied while putting her hands over her eyes.

"Heather, I love you, and I've spent over two years getting to know you. I don't think you're crazy, and whatever you are embarrassed to tell me is probably no big deal."

"Andy, today is my brother's birthday and—"

Andy cut her off. "Heather, I am so sorry. I didn't mean any disrespect. This is why I plan everything and don't do things spontaneously so I can avoid situations like this. Are you mad at me?" he asked.

"Why in the world would I be mad at you?"

"Because I disrespected Brian and your entire family by selfishly proposing to you on his birthday. Your parents must be pissed."

"Andy, settle down. No one's upset with you. That was a very romantic proposal. I definitely didn't see it coming. And besides, my brother would have been flattered, not mad. What I started to say is, every year, I visit him on his birthday and talk with him. I know it sounds crazy, but I wanted to stop by today to tell him you finally proposed to me. I go by and see him often. It comforts me, and hopefully, it comforts him."

"Why would you think that is crazy? I talk to my dad all the time."

"You do? Really?" she asked.

"Of course I do, and I couldn't care less if someone thinks it's crazy. Just because he isn't here physically doesn't mean he's still not with me. I'll tell you what, why don't we head to his resting place, then stop by your parents and then head to the cabin?"

"Thanks, Andy. I don't know how to get there from here, but I'll look it up."

"No need, sweetheart. I know exactly where it is."

"Why? Is your dad buried there also?" she asked.

"No, but that would have been one heck of a coincidence. Heather, you're not the only one who talks to your brother."

"What's that supposed to mean?" she asked. "Wait a minute, you've talked to my brother?"

"Several times," he responded.

"When? Why?"

"Heather, I have visited your brother's resting place several times. The first time was two days after you came to my office. I stopped by to tell him what you did and how brave you were and that I would make sure that he received justice. I told him that I would take care of you."

"Andy, you're so sweet. Can you tell me about the other times?"

"Sure. The next time was right after Garcia-Hernandez was arrested. I stopped just to let him know that I kept my promise. Then the day before I asked you out, I stopped by to ask his permission, and I assured him that I would treat you with respect."

"Andy, you're going to make me cry. Is that all of it?" she asked.

"No, I came by on the morning before I bought your engagement ring to let him know of my intentions. So, Heather, it's only right to talk to him today to let him know you accepted my proposal."

With small tears in her eyes, she turned toward Andy and said, "I love you, Andy, and to think this whole time I thought that I was the crazy one, jeez!" she said with a laugh. "You know, my dad was right when he said earlier that the two of us really are one," she said.

"I was just thinking the same thing," he replied.

Andy pulled up to the graveside and turned the car off. "Do you want me to wait here?" he asked.

"No, I want to tell him together," she said.

Andy opened the trunk and pulled out a beach towel. They walked hand in hand to the grave. He spread the towel out and sat down while Heather stood next to him. They stayed in silence for several minutes when Andy asked, "Aren't you going to talk to him?"

"I'm nervous, Andy," she replied.

"Okay, fine, I'll go first. Well, Brian, I just wanted to let you know that that issue we talked about has been handled. I know you would have preferred a different way, but I felt there was only one way to solve it. But on a lighter note, I did it. This morning, I—"

"No, Andy, don't!" Heather barked as she put her hand over his mouth to silence him. "Please let me," she said. Heather sat on Andy's lap and addressed Brian. "Well, big bro, he finally did it. Andy proposed to me this morning, and I said yes. Your little Tiggs is getting married, ah!" she yelled. She went on to explain how Andy proposed to her, and then she told him about the joke they played on their mom. "She wasn't too happy with us when we played her like that," she explained. She told him about the engagement lunch and that they were going to be making wedding plans next week to get married at the end of the summer. Andy just sat there listening to her talk. He could tell it really did comfort her to be talking with him. It seemed as though she didn't even know he was sitting right there with her.

"Whose car is parked by Brian's grave?" Dan asked Mary as they pulled up.

"I don't know, but it looks expensive," she said.

"That's because it is," Dan responded. "It's a Lamborghini."

As they pulled up behind Andy's car, Mary said, "Well, go figure. It must be Andy's because he is sitting with Heather by Brian's headstone."

When Dan and Mary got out of the truck, Heather heard the doors shut. She turned around to see her parents there. "Mom, Dad, what are you doing here?" she asked as she got up out of Andy's lap.

Andy stood also. "Andy, is that your car?" Dan asked.

"Yes, sir," he replied.

"Nice. So I guess that is the 200 mph car Heather mentioned at lunch earlier."

"That's the one, Dad," Heather replied.

"Well, it is Brian's birthday today, so we wanted to stop by to wish him one and to tell him about your engagement, but it looks like you beat us to it," Mary said.

"Mr. and Mrs. O'Rourke, are you upset with me?" Andy asked.

Before either one of them could answer, Heather explained to them how Andy felt he disrespected their family with his proposal this morning. "Andy, I never even gave it a second thought," Dan said.

"Andy, that proposal and the way it played out was something to witness. Brian's birthday or not, the circumstances and unplanned timing were perfect. Of course we are not upset," Mary explained.

"I was just telling Heather that's why I like to plan things out instead of being spontaneous to avoid conflicts like that."

"Don't worry about it," Dan said.

"Well, we were just leaving. I have to stop by the house to pick up something, then we are off to the cabin," Heather said. She gave her mom and dad a hug, and she and Andy drove off.

As they were driving away, Mary asked, "How much money do you think Andy has?"

"I don't know," he replied. "Bill said it was substantial, and at Christmas, when I was concerned that Andy would go broke spending all that money on us, remember Tim just laughed and assured us that that would never happen."

"Well, your daughter definitely did well for herself," Mary said.

"In my daughter's defense, she has a lot to offer also, so I think it's Andy who has done well for himself," Dan responded. "I think that they are both good for each other, and next weekend, I am going to push to find out their little secret."

"Dan, don't be too hard on them. Let's assume for a minute that they do have a secret between them. So what? I mean, if it created this great relationship and soon to be marriage, then let it be. Isn't is good enough to be confident in knowing that your daughter will be well taken care of and that she is very much loved?"

"Of course it is, Mary, but you know me. I have a lot of questions. Two in particular are what happened and why Heather can't tell us. We are a very close family. Hell, she even admitted to us this morning that her and Andy have never even had sex yet. Now if that's not close, then I don't know what is. So for her to hide something from us really piques my curiosity. Those two have been very tight from the beginning, and there is no way they did that after spending one sexless weekend together."

"I know, Dan. But keep in mind, she's not one of your deputies, so you can't order her to tell you, and you don't want to ruin your relationship with her over it."

"I won't let it get that far," Dan said.

THE DRIVE
FROM HELL

Andy and Heather left the cemetery and headed to her parents' house. "What issue did you solve that you told my brother about?" Heather asked. When Andy didn't answer right away, she continued, "Andy, I know there are things involving my brother's case that you cannot ever tell me, so if this is one of those, please let me know so I won't ask anymore."

"Heather, this is definitely one of those, and thanks for being so understanding."

"Andy, what you did for me and my family, I will never judge you for, nor will I ever tell anyone. You know that."

"I know, sweetheart. That's what makes you so special. So are you going to tell me about Tiggs?" Andy asked.

"Oh, you heard that," she stated.

"I was sitting right there. So what does it mean?"

"It's no big deal, really. When I was little, my dad nicknamed me Tigger because when I got excited or anxious about something, I would kind of bounce like that Disney character Tigger, so my brother shortened it and always called me his little Tiggs."

"That is a perfect name for you," Andy replied. They both laughed.

When they got to her parents' house, Heather ran inside; and in less than forty seconds, she was back out. Andy was holding the passenger's door open for her. Andy had the convertible top down. It was going to be a beautiful drive. They took Interstate 10 east and then merged onto the California 210 E Foothill Freeway. They exited

California State Route 18 N Waterman Ave in San Bernardino and headed up the mountain. St Rt 18 was a scenic mountain highway, but it could be dangerous—winding roads, falling rocks, forest fires, and during the rainy season, mudslides.

They were about two-thirds up the mountain when Andy noticed a California Highway Patrol car heading in the opposite direction. Andy watched him turn around and get in behind him. "I wasn't speeding, was I?" he asked.

"I don't think so. At the last passing lanes, an old VW bus passed you." They both laughed.

As Andy was approaching a turnout, a turnout that he was very familiar with, the highway patrol man turned on his red light. Andy pulled into the turnout confused. He turned the car off and put his hands on the steering wheel. The officer approached the driver's side, and Andy immediately recognized him. The patrolman spoke first.

"Sir, my name is Sgt. Jack Welch of the California Highway Patrol." Sergeant Jack was an ex-marine, six feet five inches tall and 250 pounds, and looked like an NFL linebacker with a crew cut. "Ma'am," he spoke to Heather, "I'm going to need to see your driver's license or California ID card if you are not old enough to drive."

"Me?" she responded.

"Yes, ma'am." Nervously she reached into her purse, pulled it out, and handed it to Andy, who in turn gave it to the sergeant. Andy had known Jack his whole life, but he had never seen him this formal with him. He also knew Jack to be a jokester, so Andy played along. Heather looked at Andy with eyes that said, "What did I do?" Andy told her to do just what the officer said and that everything would be all right. "Heather, may I call you Heather?" Jack asked.

"Yes, sir," she replied.

"I'm going to need you to step out of the car. Mr. DiPaola, I'm going to need for you to do the same. I want you two to walk to the right side please."

Andy looked at Heather, who was visibly nervous, and said, "It's okay. I know what's going on here."

They both did as the officer asked them to. When they got to the other side, Jack said, "I have never ever seen a woman in that car, Andy." Heather looked surprised that they were so personable. "Heather, I heard about the engagement, so when I saw Andy's slow ass driving up the mountain, I just had to screw with you." Jack gave both of them a hug and congratulated them. He handed Heather's driver's license back to her and said, "I don't know how you found this guy or got him to ask you for your hand in marriage, but my suggestion is, you need to hang on to this one."

"Yes, sir," she replied.

"The name is Jack."

Andy shook his hand, and then Sergeant Jack got into his patrol car and drove off. "Jeez, that was different," Heather said. "How long have you known him?"

"All of my life. He was fishing buddies with my dad." Heather knew Andy didn't like talking about his dad, so she didn't push the questions. Andy grabbed her hand and led her to a large boulder overlooking the cliff and sat down. "You know"—he turned to her— "this was where it happened. This was where my dad was killed." A small tear ran down his cheek.

"No, Andy, don't. It's okay."

"Heather, it's okay. I'm now at peace with it. Our engagement this morning lifted a serious load off my shoulders. I cannot keep this bottled up anymore around you, and I don't want you to feel like you have to walk on eggshells every time the conversation comes up." Heather didn't respond and let him talk. "He was rear-ended by a drunken sheriff's deputy and forced down this cliff."

"I know, Andy. You don't have to do this. I know how painful this is for you, and I don't want to see you upset," she said as tears were running down her face.

"It's time," he replied. "The San Bernardino County sheriffs were the first units on scene. A captain with the department had his dispatch call the highway patrol and cancel their responding units. They told the highway patrol that they would handle it. Jack was on duty that day and was dispatched to the accident. When dispatch called him off and said the sheriffs were handling it, Jack immediately figured something wasn't right. He doesn't like the sheriff's department, but for them to accept a possible fatality on a state highway, something didn't add up. Jack always felt that they were all lazy bastards and always tried to get out of assisting other agencies. When he got here, the fire trucks had just arrived.

"There were four sheriff's cars, including the captain's unit. Jack approached the captain and asked what was going on. The damaged sheriff's unit was already starting to be loaded on the back of a flatbed tow truck. Seeing the front-end damage, he asked the captain where the driver was. The captain refused to answer and told Jack that the sheriff's department was handling it, and he told Jack to basically leave. Jack had already run the plate on the Crown Victoria, and it had come back as a sheriff's unit. Jack contacted his dispatch and requested additional units. I guess there was a heated debate between Jack and the captain, so Jack told him that it was his jurisdiction and that if the captain didn't get out of his way, he would arrest him for obstruction.

"That captain still didn't back down, so he threatened Jack that he would call his station chief. Jack called his bluff and told him to do it. That's when Jack saw the driver sit up in the passenger's seat of the sheriff unit. When Jack asked the captain if that was the driver, he told him it was none of his business. At that point, a highway patrol sergeant unit pulled up along with another unit and two motor officers. The patrol sergeant walked up to Jack and asked him what was going on. Jack explained everything up to that point. The sergeant went to the sheriff's captain and told him to remove the driver in his car. Jack had already tried, but the unit was locked. The captain refused to open the door to his unit, so Jack arrested him for obstruction and evidence tampering. He grabbed the captain by the back of his neck and shoved him against the unit. He had his arm twisted so far up his back the captain thought it might break. He placed him in handcuffs, removed his guns, and everything on his person. Jack escorted him to his patrol car.

"As he was buckling him in, Jack removed his captain bars off of his lapel and removed his sheriff's badge, telling the captain, 'You won't be needing these anymore.' The other three deputies didn't make a move. Jack used the keys he got off the captain, unlocked the door, and removed Deputy Ortega. He reeked of alcohol and even had thrown up a little. Field sobriety tests weren't even an option.

Another patrolman called in a telephonic warrant to the on-call judge for them to draw blood when they got back to the station. His blood came back four times the legal limit, and he was on duty.

"Jack was there for everything—the deputy's vehicular homicide trial, the captain's obstruction and evidence tampering case, and all of the civil cases that went on after that."

"Does that mean you had to relive that day numerous times?" Heather asked.

"More than I care to count. I understand that suspects have rights in this country, but why do victims have to be traumatized by them numerous times?"

"I don't want to pry, Andy, but you never talk about your stepmother."

"Didn't know her that well. I was working a lot between Fontana and Yuma. My dad met her at Woody's Boat House one weekend. They dated for only six months prior to getting married at the courthouse about three weeks before the crash. I was there for the wedding. My dad seemed to like her a lot. I just think it was a matter of convenience because I was gone a lot, and he wanted female companionship."

"And your real mother?" she asked.

"My mom left us when I was six years old, and I haven't heard from her since." Andy explained that his dad had taken his mom to a concert at the LA Coliseum one night. She got up to use the restroom and never came back. He filed a missing person's report, and two weeks later, LAPD told him that they found her in Florida and that she was fine but did not want to be contacted. "It took my dad three years for the courts to allow him to divorce her."

"What about grandparents?" she asked.

"Well, my mom's parents live in Berkeley. I never knew them. My dad said they were at the hospital when I was born, and they showed up to my first and second birthday parties, but we never saw them again. My dad always referred to them as lost hippies. Then my dad's mom died of breast cancer when I was eight. Shortly after her death, my grandfather took his own life. They were high school sweethearts, and he couldn't bear living his life without her."

"No aunts, uncles, or cousins?" she asked.

"My mom is an only child, and my dad's only brother died three years ago from lung cancer. He never married or had kids."

"I'm so sorry, Andy. You have gone through hell."

"We both have, Heather."

She thought for a second and realized that Andy had no family, so she stated, "Andy, you have a family now. I will never leave you. I promise." Tears were running down her face.

"I know that, Heather. That's why I chose you," he replied.

"Come here," Andy told her. "I want you to see something." He looked over the cliff. Heather acted a little nervous. She was hoping there wasn't a car down there. "I want you to bend over the railing and look what's right below and under the pavement."

"Andy, am I going to fall?"

"No way. I will wrap my arms around your waist and hold you."

She trusted him, so he grabbed her waist from behind, and she bent over to see what he wanted her to see. As she was looking, she felt him again, so she wiggled her butt a little, pretending to act like she needed a new angle. "I see it," she said. Andy pulled her upright. "What is that?" she asked.

Andy had bought a small angel water fountain and modified it to look like it was peeing. He then built a base for it. It was battery-operated, and Andy came by frequently to fill it with water and to change the batteries as needed. "Did you see what it was peeing on?"

"It looked like some sort of a badge," she said.

"Compliments of Jack Welch. He obtained the deputy's badge that killed my father, so I thought, as a tribute to my dad, it was appropriate." They both laughed.

Heather can still see the bulge in Andy's shorts and asked him, "Do you need to sit for a moment?"

Blushing, Andy said, "Maybe for a few." He sat on the boulder and opened his legs. She sat in front of him. When he reached around her to hold her waist, he missed and grabbed her breasts. He quickly removed his hands and found her waist. "I'm so sorry, Heather. That was an accident."

Heather picked up his right hand and placed it on her right breast. "This isn't," she replied.

They kissed, and Andy removed his hand. "While that is great if I continue with it, I'll never be able to get off this rock." They both laughed.

They got back into the convertible and headed to the cabin. When they got there, Andy told her he needed to take a cold shower, and she replied she needed the same. "Why do you need one?" he asked. She replied as she was headed toward the master bedroom, "The physical and emotional effects of what happened at that turn-out are not exclusive to men."

DOING IT

They took Jenny out for a spin. Heather was seated next to Andy with her arms wrapped around his waist. "I see why you and your dad spent so much time up here. It's beautiful."

"We love it, but the only drawback are the rich idiots. Are you hungry?" Andy asked.

"Not really, but I could pick at something."

"Name it," he said.

"I don't know. Maybe a shrimp cocktail or a fruit salad."

"I know just the place." He turned Jenny around and headed to the resort. They walked into the bar area, which overlooked the lake, and grabbed the only available table. Andy usually preferred sitting in bar areas of restaurants because, normally, it was open seating, and you generally didn't have to wait to eat. He ordered a glass of red for Heather, a beer for himself, two shrimp cocktails, and a bowl of fruit. "Well, that was a heck of a day," he said.

"How so?" she asked. "I mean, I know we got engaged."

"Well, let's see. It all started with my girlfriend leaving me."

"I never left you, Andy, and I never will. You have to know that." Heather felt that she might have come on a little strong, especially since Andy had just confided in her the story of his mom and the loss of his dad, stepmom, and his grandparents, but Andy didn't seem to mind.

"Okay, when my girlfriend left my house upset with me, I chased her down, got engaged, had an engagement luncheon, got pulled over, explained my life's history, got sexually harassed on the side of the road, had to take a cold shower—"

Heather interrupted. "I didn't sexually harass you, and you grabbed my breasts!"

"Really? The butt grind," he said. Heather blushed. "All in all, it was an interesting day."

She reached over and kissed him on the lips and said, "Your day isn't over yet. Well, let's see," she started. "Mine began when my boyfriend kicked me out of his house."

"I didn't kick you out."

Heather laughed. "Two can play at this game. Okay, when my boyfriend hurt my feelings for the second time in our relationship."

"Wait, when was the first time?" he asked.

"At a certain Fourth of July breakfast," she replied.

"Oh yeah, I don't want to play anymore," he said.

Heather continued anyway. "Then shows up at my parent's house and has a conversation with my dad about me without me being present, then tries to make up for it by asking my hand in marriage, apparently making me wait three months longer than I should have had to." Kidding, she looked at Andy. "Then I get engaged to this great guy, have an engagement party—yes, I said party—get pulled out of a car by a cop, try to seduce my new fiancé only to be rejected again, and had to take yet another cold shower, and here we are. Pretty much sums it up."

"Your day isn't over yet," he said.

They got back to Jenny and started heading to the cabin. "Hey, Andy, I just thought about something," she said.

"What?"

"You showed up this morning with your big gun because you hurt my feelings, right?"

"Well, I'd prefer not to have to relive that, but yes."

"Amy somehow knew you did something like that. How does she know you so well?"

Andy laughed and said, "Thank God. I thought you were going to yell at me for hurting your feelings."

"No way. That's over, and now I understand why you did what you did. It was just a communication failure, but I do still owe you an answer to your question about my lack of sexual experience."

"Please, that won't be necessary, dear," Andy pleaded. "So Amy, she used to work at the resort," Andy started. "She started in the kitchen and worked her way up to general manager. She was the best. One weekend, the owners of the Langham came up for a retreat, and they noticed the way she treated all the guests, whether she knew them or not, so they offered her the general manager's job and working for them. Her and her husband moved down the hill, but they still maintain their cabin up here."

"So that's how she knows you so personally?" Heather asked in confusion.

"Oh sorry. After my mom left, my dad had no one to really turn to with me other than Jack and his wife, Jill, but they worked a lot, so Amy stepped up and took over. She drove me to school, attended all my sports practices and games. She was there for everything. Our families became very close. Then when my dad died, her and Jack handled everything for me to make sure I didn't get screwed over by attorneys or the court system."

"Boy, Andy, she is a good woman."

"She's the best," he replied.

"What is she going to do to you when she finds out you upset me?"

"She won't find out because we aren't going to tell her, are we, Heather?"

"I don't know, Andy. I might have to hang on to this one for a competitive advantage in the future, like maybe over a certain real estate conversation." They both laughed.

As the sun started to set, Andy and Heather sat in the hot tub enjoying the early evening. "So what do you want to do for the rest of the night?" Andy asked her. "Did you bring your notes to study for exams?"

Heather turned to him and splashed water in his face. "I thought we had this day planned out," she said.

"If we did, then I don't remember it."

"Andy! You are not getting out of this. Earlier in Pasadena, we said we were going to do something, and I expect it to be done. You have made me wait for over two years for this, and you are not backing out. I'll tell Amy!"

"So you are going to blackmail me into having sex with you?"

"I wish you had told me the story about Amy on our first date," Heather said.

"Why?" he asked.

"Because," she explained, "then that day when you hurt my feelings over your boat, I could have used that leverage to not only get a first kiss but to also have sex or a first kiss during sex."

Andy let out a laugh. "But I thought we should wait until we were married."

"I understand you wanted to wait until we were married, and I agree with you," she said.

"So we are both in agreement that we wait for our wedding night," he stated.

"No, we are not. I married you this morning when you put this ring on my finger and I accepted it. That was what you said to me earlier in front of my parents, was it not? I win. Now go shower up."

They both showered separately. Andy finished first, so he lit a fire in the fireplace. It was a relatively warm evening, so he opened one of the patio doors so the room wouldn't get too hot. He just wanted to create an ambiance. He was wearing a pair of gym shorts and nothing else.

When Heather finally came out of her room, Andy couldn't believe what he saw. She was wearing a short flannel shirt that barely covered her white panties. She looked sexy. "Your room or mine?" she asked playfully.

"I was thinking right in front of the fireplace." She walked up to him, and they both looked into each other's eyes and said I love you. Andy pulled them both down to their knees. He unbuttoned her shirt and slid it off her shoulders. He could sense that she was nervous, so he joked while looking at her breasts, "Where have I seen these before?"

"I'm surprised you can remember them since you covered them up so fast last time," she replied. They both laughed. "Andy, I'm nervous," she said.

"Heather, if you don't want to do this, we can wait."

"Nice try," she said. "I just don't know what I'm supposed to—"

He silenced her with his lips. He laid her down and spent thirty minutes kissing, caressing, tasting, and pleasuring her entire body, and when he was certain that she had been satisfied, he took her. After he finished, he asked, "Are you okay?"

"I'm fine," she replied, "just a little sore, but I expected that, but I'm definitely not going to be calling you little thingy anymore, jeez." She smiled. "Andy, thank you for being gentle and taking your time with me."

"Heather, I will never hurt you," he replied.

"I think I made a big mess. I need another shower, then how about after the shower we get a drink and sit in the hot tub again?" she stated.

"Sure," he said, "but let's use the one on the lake this time."

Heather thought about that for a second and remembered that she had never been in that one and wondered why. "Okay," she said. "You go take a shower, and I'll meet you here in ten."

"I have a better idea." Andy picked up her naked body, carried her into the master bedroom, and said, "This is our room now." They took a shower together and attempted to bathe each other. Not being able to keep their hands off each other, they made love again. After the shower, they grabbed a bottle of wine, a bottle of Four Roses, a couple of glasses, and headed for the lakeside spa.

"It's gorgeous down here," Heather said. The hot tub had a full view of the village and the open lake. The moon was shining its reflection on the water.

As they were sitting there enjoying the views and drinking their respective drinks, Heather reached down and grabbed Andy's groin. He looked at her and said, "Again? I thought you were sore."

With a sexy grin, she said, "You have a lot of making up to do." She removed her bikini bottoms and then his shorts. She climbed on top as he removed her top, and they made love for the third time in as many hours. They stayed in the hot tub drinking, kissing, and touching until about eleven o'clock. They walked back to the cabin naked with no cares in the world. They were both a little tipsy. They took a fast shower to rinse the hot tub chemicals off. Heather dressed in that same flannel shirt. They were sitting on the couch in front of the fireplace when she asked, "So did you like the shirt and panty combo? That is what you like, isn't it?"

Andy thought, *That is exactly what I like, but how did she know?* "That look is the sexiest thing I know, and with you wearing it makes it even better," he said. "How did you know I liked that look?"

"Remember our first date?"

"Of course I do."

"Well, when we were just walking through the shops, I noticed you looking at a mannequin wearing this. Something in your eye screamed sexy. So when we walked down the street and back, I saw you glance in the same store. Remember when I asked you if I could go back inside for something?"

"Yes, I do."

"Well, I bought it."

"You thought about having sex with me on our first date?"

"Please, Andy. I thought about it the first time we met. I know when I offered myself in your office, that was because I didn't know what to do to get your help, but during my car ride home, I seriously thought about it. I've thought about it every time we went somewhere and every time I came to one of your houses. It wasn't until this morning that I understood why you were waiting. I have been carrying around that shirt for a year hoping I would be able to use it, and that's why I had you stop at my parents' house earlier, because I left it there."

"You are a very sweet person, Heather."

THE TALK

Dan, Mary, Heather, and Andy walked into the great room in Andy's cabin after he gave them a tour of the cabin, garages, and surrounding grounds. They were there for two reasons, and Heather and Andy didn't like one of them. They had talked about it for a week now, weighing the pros and cons, and they finally decided to give a redacted version.

"So," Dan started, "how did you two first meet?"

Andy spoke first. If anyone was to get picked apart, he wasn't going to allow it to be Heather, although he thought she did start this! "Heather came to my office approximately two and a half years ago asking for assistance with my connections to see if there was something that I could do to help your family out. She didn't understand why Garcia-Hernandez hadn't been arrested, and she was concerned for your job and for your health and the emotional wellbeing of your family. She was very emotional yet very brave."

"What? I can't believe what I'm hearing," Dan said. "Is this some sort of joke?"

"No, sir, it is not," Andy replied.

"So are you telling me that the two of you were responsible for the arrest of Brian's killer?" Dan was moving his finger back and forth between Heather and Andy. Mary's eyes opened wide as she placed her left hand over her mouth in disbelief. Heather and Andy turned toward each other, looked into each other's eyes, and turned back to Dan, but neither one of them answered. "Am I supposed to take your silence as a yes or no?" Dan asked. Again, no answer. Realizing that they weren't going to answer him, Dan continued. "Heather, how did you know to go see Andy?" he asked.

"Dad, I can't tell you that. I gave my word to never reveal the person's identity, and I never will."

"Heather, that was a very dangerous and potentially criminal thing you did, and I would like to know who sent you."

"Dad, Andy and I thought about what we were going to tell you today. We thought about just making up a fake story so we wouldn't have to get into this because we knew that it would lead to a bunch more questions that, frankly, we aren't willing to answer. But I have never lied to you before, and I don't plan on starting now, so please don't make me. You have to respect that I gave someone my word, and if you push me, you will force me to lie to you, so please don't."

Andy looked at Heather and thought, *This really is one trustworthy woman. She really wouldn't tell Amy on me, would she?* Dan backed off the request. "So you drove out to Rancho Cucamonga by yourself for an appointment with Andy?"

"Well, it was in San Bernardino, and I didn't have an appointment or anything, and I had no idea what I was doing or what to expect. I was frightened and desperate, but my connection told me that if there was anyone who could help us, it would be Andy, so I had no choice. I had to try."

"Why didn't you come to me? I would have gone with you, or I would have gone by myself," Dan said.

"Because, Dad, if things didn't work out and they found out that you were involved, they would have fired you, and you could have lost your pension. They were treating you like crap as it was. I didn't want to make things worse for you." Heather continued, "So I showed up unannounced. Andy had no idea I was coming. In fact, I almost wasn't able to see him. His secretary wouldn't allow it. I was finally able to convince her into letting me see Andy."

"So that's when Andy agreed to help?" Dan asked.

"No, not at first. I went in there and just bluntly asked for his help. He told me that there was nothing he could do for me. I got upset and started crying and shaking uncontrollably. I was so expecting a positive result and was crushed when he told me no. He was our only hope. No one else would help us."

As she was telling this part, she started shaking and crying as if she was reliving it. Andy got up and sat next to her on the couch. He lifted her up and placed her in his lap and gave her a comforting hug. He whispered in her ear, "Do you want to tell him what you offered?" She pulled her head out of his neck and gave him a look that said no as she giggled. Andy could always calm her down.

"What was that?" Dan asked.

"Nothing, sir, just a little inside joke between us."

"You two seem to have a lot of those."

Andy took over. "So Heather left my office with an assurance that I will at least look to see what I can do for her."

"So you agreed based on a damsel in distress kind of thing."

"Yes and no. Heather was so hurt that I actually felt her pain, so I thought about it and recalled a time in my life when I could have been in the same shoes. When my dad was killed, there was a huge chance that he would have been denied justice just like you folks were, but one man had the wisdom to see through it all and put an end to it, so my dad and I got our justice. Your family was still living it, so I asked myself, if one man was able to help me, why couldn't I help her? I certainly had the means and the ability."

"I'm sorry, Andy, but you have me at a disadvantage. I know about the death of your father, but I don't know any of the details."

Heather spoke up. "Dad, you know that his dad was rear-ended and forced off of a cliff by a drunk deputy, right?"

"Yes, you told me that part."

"Well, the sheriff's department was going to cover it up and make it look like Andy's dad had an accident and just drove off the cliff by himself. If it weren't for the fact that a highway patrolman, a very big and intimidating highway patrolman. Trust me, I have first-hand experience with him"—Heather and Andy laughed—"sensed that something wasn't right. So he responded to the scene and blew up the cover. If it weren't for Jack, Andy would have never known his dad and stepmother were murdered."

"You are pretty good with this stuff," Andy said.

"I learned from the best."

"So," Andy continued, "I made the decision right there that I was going to do everything in my power to help. I also made a commitment to myself that when I was able to see Heather again that I would make sure she would never have to feel any more pain like the pain and hurt that she expressed in my office that day."

"So you thought about seeing me in the future on that first day?"

"Not only thought about it. I kept tabs on you until I was able to see you again."

"You never told me that." Then she whispered in his ear, "Other than the part when you cheated on me." She giggled.

"Another inside joke, I assume," Dan asked.

"Yes, sir," Andy replied.

"How did you do that?" Heather asked.

"Your friend Stacy is a chatterbox on social media."

"So that's how you knew her."

"Yes, it is, and it is also how I sort of kept a connection with you."

"So when you told me that you loved me from day one, you weren't kidding."

"No, I wasn't, Heather. It wasn't a pickup line. So," Andy continued, "Heather was given instructions to never call me or show up at my office again, which she honored. That was to protect her and give her plausible deniability. Three weeks later, Garcia-Hernandez voluntarily reentered the United States east of Calexico."

"Really?" Dan sarcastically interrupted. "So he voluntarily drugged himself, pinned a note on his chest, and zip-tied himself to a railcar? How did he really get here?"

"Dan, I am not at liberty to discuss this," Andy stated.

"Bullshit," Dan quipped.

Mary, who had been sitting there quietly the whole time while emotionally listening to what her daughter went through for her family, jumped in and said, "Dan, I do not give a damn how that piece of shit got here. I don't care if Andy dragged him behind a damn horse with a rope tied around his neck. Hell, I wouldn't have cared if he snuck into Mexico and put a bullet in the back of that son of a bitch's head. He murdered my son. Then to make matters worse, I had to sit through a jury trial and a sentencing hearing and victim impact statements and had to relive it all over again. You had to also, and I know it was hard on you. And then we almost had to do it all over again. It was a nightmare that wouldn't end."

Heather had never seen her mother explode or curse like that and later apologized to Andy for it. "She wasn't venting at me," he explained. "She was just venting. She sure saved us from a lot of questions."

Mary started tearing up, and Heather sat next to her for comfort. Begrudgingly, Dan conceded, and Andy continued. "Garcia-Hernandez made statements in Mexico about how his sister had been protecting him from prosecution and that he actually stayed at her guesthouse in San Dimas after the shooting before she helped him get to Mexico," he explained. "So I started doing some research and made some inquiries."

"So you were the one who tied the sheriff, his wife, and brother-in-law to the suspect?" Dan asked.

"Yes, sir, that's exactly right."

"I'm at a loss for words right now," Dan said. Mary was just looking at Andy in disbelief. She thought of how Andy had done more for justice for her son than the largest county agency in the world. "So you had no contact with Heather that entire time until you showed up at the courthouse and asked her out?"

"No, not quite. About a month prior to the trial, I couldn't take not seeing her any longer, and I thought enough time had passed. So I showed up unannounced to one of her volleyball practices, and we talked."

"Was that the embrace everyone was talking about at lunch last week?" Dan wanted to let Andy know he picked up on it.

"Yes," Andy said, slightly blushing. "I made up an excuse that I needed for her to get me a name at LASD I could trust."

Dan interrupted. "I remember that. Did the name help?"

"Yes and no. Truth be told, the investigation was already wrapping up, and the feds and the LA District Attorney's Office were preparing warrants for their arrests. But I just had to see Heather, and I'm glad I did."

Heather and Mary were still sitting next to each other, each of them with tears in their eyes. Heather got up and sat on Andy's lap and gave him a kiss.

"Heather, tell me about this embrace everyone keeps talking about," Mary said.

"Mom, it was great. We had just finished a practice, and I was in the locker room getting ready to take a shower when our equipment manager came up to me and told me Andy was waiting for me when I was done. My heart immediately began racing, and I screamed 'Andy is here' in disbelief. I was so excited that I ran out of the locker room, not realizing that I had on only my sports bra and panties, and jumped into his arms, wrapping my legs around his waist and my arms around his neck like an octopus. I held him forever. I didn't want to let go. And then I leaned back, and I looked him into his eyes and thanked him. He stood there holding me as we got lost in each other's eyes for a very long time. My heart melted. Mom, I can't tell you how I ended up in his arms. When that girl told me he was there, everything went blank. I don't remember my feet even hitting the ground as I ran to him."

"That is the most romantic thing I have ever heard," Mary said.

"Well, it would have been more romantic if Andy had kissed me, told me that he loved me, and asked for my hand in marriage during our embrace," Heather said as she was poking at his chest.

Andy whispered into her ear, "I didn't say anything about a proposal. I just said that I loved you."

She whispered back, "I know, but I just added it because had you asked, I wouldn't have waited so long for sex." They both laughed.

"You would have said yes had he asked you?" Mary asked.

"Without a doubt," she replied.

Mary thought about something, then asked, "Heather, did you ever figure out the meaning of those eighteen rose arrangements that Andy bought you?"

"I never did, and Andy won't tell me either," she replied as she hit him on the shoulder. "Why do you ask?"

"Because I think I just figured it out," she replied.

"Tell me, Mom, please, because this brat won't."

"Heather, after listening to you guys' story, if I had to guess, they represent the seventeen and a half months that you two couldn't be together."

"Seriously? Is that true, Andy?" she asked.

"That's exactly what they represent," he replied.

She reached up and grabbed him around his neck and gave him a long kiss. "I love you, Andy."

"I love you too."

Andy looked at Dan and continued, "The next time I saw her was at the courthouse, and you know the rest."

Andy was satisfied with the somewhat short explanation, but Dan wasn't. "This isn't over," he said. "How did the DA and feds get involved?"

Mary stopped him and stated, "Dan, you had only asked for the truth on how these two met and under what circumstances because you had suspicions. Your suspicions proved to be correct. I believe they have truthfully answered your questions, and the rest of your inquiry is not necessary. They could have lied to you, but they chose not to. I feel that they went well beyond what was asked of them, and if you continue, it will only lead to more questions that you are not going to get answers to."

"Fine," Dan mumbled. "Can I ask one more?"

"Sure," Andy said.

"Did you play any part in Garcia-Hernandez's sudden jailhouse death?"

"Dan!" Mary yelled. "That's enough of this. I will not allow you to continue. The bottom line is, he is dead, and that's all we need to know. I am grateful Andy came into our lives, and I am so proud of you, Heather, for bringing him into our lives. You made a very brave decision to seek Andy out." Mary looked at Dan and said, "That's the end of it. We have a wedding to plan."

Andy was grateful for that intervention, but deep in the back of his mind, the ten grand that was anonymously placed into those two convicts' legal defense funds was well worth it. He wasn't about to let Heather and her parents sit through another trial and have to relive that fateful day all over again. Real justice had been served.

WEDDING PLANS

For the past week, Heather and Mary had been going back and forth over wedding details. Mary wanted a large church wedding at the family's Catholic church, a reception there, and a second reception at a hotel venue. Heather, while wanting a much smaller wedding, had already conceded to the larger one because her mother didn't get the engagement party. However, she wanted an outdoor wedding at a low-key place, like a local park, and a small reception for close family and friends.

"You are not getting married in a public park," Mary explained to her.

So when Andy had invited them to the cabin to discuss all this, he already knew of their concerns. Andy figured he could get Mary her large wedding and reception, still utilizing a church resource, and get Heather the outdoor park wedding. They did accomplish one thing together during the week: They already bought the wedding dress. As Andy was pouring the girls a glass of wine and getting a beer for Dan and himself, he asked, "How are the wedding plans coming?" Heather and Mary started pitching their own versions. "May I make a suggestion?" he asked.

"Please do," Dan replied. Dan didn't want this to go on forever, and if anyone could shorten the conversation, it would be Andy.

"Why don't we get married here?"

"Here?" Mary asked.

"Yes. It would make you both happy. We can decorate the backyard and have a wedding that overlooks the lake, so Heather will be happy. We can accommodate at least two hundred people, so you will be happy," he said as he looked at Mary.

"No offense, Andy. Your home is beautiful, and your backyard can certainly handle the people, but inside here might be a little too small for that amount of people for a reception."

"No offense taken, Mary, and you are right. That's why I figured we can have the reception at the resort's ballroom."

"And when did you come up with all of this?" Heather asked.

"A while ago," he responded.

"Why didn't you tell me about your plan?" she asked.

"Heather, this wedding is very important to your family, so I wanted you two to come up with the wedding plans. But when you got to an impasse, I tried taking both sides' concerns into account and tried to come up with a solution."

"Andy, this is your wedding also," she said.

"True, so then here is my suggestion. Nobody has to make a decision now, but if either one of you is interested even a little bit, I have an appointment to check out the ballroom in two hours." He reiterated, "Just to check it out. Heather, are you mad at me?"

"No, I'm not mad. This is just getting overwhelming. I just wish we can have something simple, like maybe just get married at the resort and host a reception there for close friends and family. That would be cheaper and easier."

"Let's go look at that ballroom and then make up your mind," he said.

"Okay, let's go," she said. "But before we do, do I have time to shower and freshen up? I'm still a mess from having to relive that San Bernardino meeting."

"Sure," Andy said. "But we have to leave in about forty-five minutes."

Heather stood up and reached for Andy's hand. "Would you like to join me?" she asked. Andy's face turned red because she asked right in front of her parents. He was speechless, so Heather grabbed his hand and pulled him toward the bedroom.

Mary spoke out. "I thought you two stayed in separate rooms."

Without looking back, Heather replied, "Not anymore, Mom."

"Well, Dan, looks like your little girl is all grown up," Mary said.

"From the sounds of it, Mary, she grew up a couple of years ago in an office in San Bernardino." While they were waiting for the two to get ready, Dan turned to Mary and asked, "Do you think I did enough to get justice for Brian?"

"What are you talking about, Dan?"

"I tried for five long and agonizing years to get justice for this family, and our daughter managed to accomplish it in three weeks. And the worst part of it is, the answers were right under my nose, and I didn't even see it." Dan thought of something. "Mary, do you remember the press conference one year after Brian was killed?"

"Of course I do," she replied.

"Remember when Heather refused to shake the sheriff's hand because she didn't trust him?"

"Yes, I do."

"She knew something was wrong then. She sensed it."

Mary could tell he was starting to get a little emotional. "Dan, you tried everything you could. You had a bureaucracy to fight and rules to play by whereas Heather made the decision that she wasn't going to play by those rules and found a man who agreed with her."

"Maybe I could have done the same thing," he said.

"What, go rogue and lose your job? Dan, you did right. Listen, I don't know how Andy pulled off what he did, and he and Heather made it perfectly clear we will never know, but what I do know is, I appreciate everything he did. And your daughter is a very brave woman. Remember on Christmas when we called Tim and Heather said that even if Andy broke up with her that he would always be a part of her life and family? I just chalked it up at the time to a schoolgirl being in love, but that wasn't the case, and now I know why she said what she said. I know you are upset with her for going to Andy in the first place, but, Dan, you really shouldn't be."

"I'm not upset with her. I am very proud of her. I'm just upset that she accomplished something that I should have."

"Maybe you should tell her that. You don't want her thinking you're mad at her. Oh, and, Dan, you can put to bed that special bond question you have between these two. You just had that answered."

"No shit," he replied. "Their story is better than anything Hollywood could come up with, but unfortunately, this one can never be told, but I have a feeling that there is a whole lot more to it than we are being told," he said.

"Let it go, Dan," Mary said. "Of course there is, but we will never know it, and believe it or not, I kinda like it this way."

After the shower, Heather and Andy walked back to the great room only to find Dan and Mary sitting on the back patio. Dan spoke first. "You two have a moment?" Heather and Andy looked at each other and thought, *Oh no, round two.*

"Of course, Dad."

"Heather, are you under the impression that I am upset with you?"

"Just a little, Dad. I know you don't like the fact that I wouldn't reveal names, but I was hoping you would understand. And I think you're upset with me because I didn't come to you when I found out about Andy, but I explained my reasoning behind that decision."

"Heather, I am not upset with you. In fact, I am very proud of you. As far as the names go, I do understand why you can't tell me. I think it was the cop in me who just wanted all the answers. And as far as you going to Andy, I just got upset at myself because I have always felt that I could have done more to get justice for Brian, and maybe I should have been the one to go see Andy."

Andy spoke up because he didn't want this conversation to gain any momentum. "That would never have worked, sir.

"Why not?" Dan asked.

"Because then I would have never met Heather, and quite frankly, you are way too big to be wrapping your legs around my waist in a romantic embrace." The four of them broke out in laughter.

"Dad, don't worry about it. Everything worked out perfectly. I love you."

THE RESORT

"You really do have a beautiful place up here, Andy," Dan said.

"Thanks, Dan. My grandpa bought it a long time ago when things up here were still affordable."

"Andy, don't we have to get going?" Heather asked.

"Let's take Jenny. It'll be faster," he replied. Mary gave Heather a sideway look. She still hadn't forgotten the little stunt Heather and Andy played on her last week.

They walked down to the dock, and Andy pulled the cover off. "Wow, she really is beautiful, Andy."

"Thank you, Dan. My dad had bought her years ago, but he wasn't able to restore her, so after his death, I had it restored back to as original as I could."

"He would have loved it," Dan stated.

Since they still had an hour, Andy drove them along the lake's shoreline. They pulled up to the docks at the yacht club. "Andy, are we allowed to park here?" Heather asked. "It says Private, for Yacht Club Members Only."

"It'll be okay," he replied as he was tying the boat down.

He was assisting the ladies out of the boat when Heather said, "Let me guess. You are a member here."

"Yes, I am."

"You never told me that."

"My dad bought a lifetime membership, and I just keep up the yearly dues because it's real convenient to park here to go grocery shopping. I don't like hanging around these stuffy people. The way they act and treat people makes me feel dirty. I only show up when they have their annual classic wooden boat get-together."

The four of them introduced themselves to Maria Lopez, the wedding specialist at the Lake Arrowhead Resort and Spa. She showed them the ballroom and asked for a head count. Heather spoke up and said, "Fifty to sixty."

Immediately, Mary spoke up and said, "Approximately two hundred."

Maria sensed the tension between the two. She saw it a lot.

"Well, however many you decide, we can accommodate. Heather, we do have a minimum of twenty people, and, Mom, we have a maximum of three hundred." Dan, Maria, Heather, and Andy laughed. Mary wasn't impressed.

"Maria, is this place available for the end of August?" Heather asked.

"Yes, that's a fifteen-month reservation window to work with. I'll have to check our calendar, but I'm sure we can accommodate that."

"I was talking about this August."

"Oh, Heather, I will go check the computer, but I doubt there will be an opening."

Andy gave her a wink that no one else noticed and asked her to go check and give them a few minutes to discuss it. They went into the bar area and ordered drinks. "Well, what do you think?" Andy asked.

"It is a beautiful setting, and I will concede the church if Heather will allow me the large group that I want," Mary stated.

"I love this place, but my two concerns are money, and now it doesn't look like it will even be available," Heather replied. "And how would all this work logistically, and how much money will it cost?"

Andy looked at all three of them and asked, "If all that were to be worked out, is that something you three could agree on?" All three of them said yes. "Well, then," Andy said, "let me explain the plan."

THE PLAN

Andy started explaining. "At the cabin, we will set up the stage by the water and all of the chairs in front of it facing the lake. Mary, you and Heather can decide on how to decorate it. I mean flowers, anything you want. We can replant the flower beds with whatever flowers and colors you choose. We can invite Father Cleveland for the ceremony." Mary smiled. "My plan is to have two charter busses stationed down the hill, and hopefully, we can bus in most of the people. They will be dropped off at the cabin, and after the ceremony, they will be brought to the resort. For all the others, in order to condense traffic and parking, they can park at the resort or in the village, and we can ferry them on the Arrowhead Queen. Then we give people about an hour to get settled in and hold the reception. Again, Mary and Heather can pick out the decorations and menu."

"I'm still concerned about the costs," Heather said. "This is not going to be cheap."

Dan stepped in. "Honey, if this is what you want, then this is what you'll get. The both of you deserve it after what you did for this family. That is, if we can keep Bonnie and Clyde here out of jail."

"Dan, that's enough!" Mary yelled. Heather and Andy just laughed and pointed finger pistols at each other.

"I was kidding, Mary, come on. After what I was told today, aren't I allowed to at least joke about it?"

"Fine," she replied.

Andy continued. "Besides, between the four of us, we can work the finances out."

"The three of you maybe," Heather said. "I don't have any money. Heck, I don't even have a job." They all laughed.

"While the job part might be true, you do have money," Andy said.

"How's that?" she asked.

"May I see your wallet please?" She handed it to him. He opened it and took out the debit card he gave her. "Remember this?"

"Of course I do."

"Well, you still haven't spent a dime of it."

"I didn't plan on it."

"Well, Heather, how much do you think is in this account?"

"I don't know," she replied. "A couple hundred bucks, I guess."

"By my accounting, you have ten thousand dollars in your account."

"Why would you put ten grand into an account for me?" she asked.

"Well, I never went to college, but I hear it's pretty expensive. So if you are willing, we all can pitch in for this." Dan mumbled to himself, "Thank God." "One more concern I have is, Dan and I will have to work out the bar situation."

"Are you thinking of a cash bar or open bar, Andy?"

"That's what we have to work out, sir. I don't want anyone getting drunk and driving these roads."

Heather and Mary teared up.

"I love it, Andy," Heather said. "But what if we can't get the ballroom?"

"If we can get the ballroom, is everybody here in agreement?" He got a firm yes from all three.

Andy went to get Maria and brought her back to the group. Heather asked her if there were any open dates at the end of the summer. "I'm afraid there isn't, Heather."

Heather's excitement faded. "I understand," she said.

Andy looked at Maria and asked, "What about the possibility of a cancellation?"

"Well," Maria responded, "a couple reserved the venue nine months ago, and we still haven't heard from them. They left a deposit, so we have to wait until the cancellation period has expired."

"Are you allowed to tell us who they are?" Andy asked.

"I'm not supposed to, but there was supposed to be a DiPaola-O'Rourke reception."

Shocked, Heather couldn't comprehend what she just heard. "Wait a minute," she said. "You booked this place nine months ago?"

"Last August," Andy replied.

"But we had just been dating for less than three months," she said.

"Heather, like I told your folks last week at our engagement luncheon"—he didn't want to call it a party because they would have to listen to Mary gripe about how she was denied one—"I knew everything about you then, and my mind was made up."

"So it's still on?" Maria asked.

Andy looked at Heather, and she said, "Yes, it is!" Maria gave Andy a hug and congratulated him. "Wait a minute, Maria. You knew about this the whole time, didn't you?" Heather asked.

Maria went over to Heather, gave her a hug, and replied, "Only for the past nine months. You have a keeper on your hands."

Heather smiled and said, "Yes, I do."

THE WEDDING

Temperature for the one thirty wedding was around eighty-two degrees. There was a slight breeze off the lake, so it felt around seventy-eight degrees. The busses had arrived at around noon. The guests were directed up the front steps to the cabin where there sat two tall bronze pots with pine tree branches flowing out of them with a bouquet of pine cones wrapped with subtle white lights in the middle of them on either sides of the steps. As a cute touch, Heather purchased a wood-carved bear holding a welcome sign and had placed a top hat on its head. Heather wanted an elegant mountain wedding but didn't want it flashy or cluttered.

As they walked into the cabin, the first thing the guests saw was the baby grand piano decorated with a honeysuckle vine garland running across the middle of it and hanging off both sides. In the middle of the piano was a dark wood-carved duck with a brass beak. The curved stair railing had honeysuckle vine garland intertwined with white lights going all the way up and pine cones hanging between each stair rung. The vibrant green forestry and the clear lake set the tone of their elegant mountain wedding. All the guest chairs were facing the lake. On each end chair facing an aisle, there was a tan-and-brown-plaid bow tied with a two-dimensional white wooden duck hanging down from it.

People were mingling around. Andy was introducing himself to the people he didn't know. His five groomsmen were all grumpy and were dying for a beer. Andy explained that none would be consumed prior to the wedding. Heather, her six bridesmaids, and Mary were in the master bedroom getting ready. At 1:00 PM, Father Cleveland asked the crowd to start taking their seats. At one twenty, the bridesmaids and groomsmen walked down the aisle. The bridesmaids were wearing beautiful pale-yellow summer dresses that were sassy but classy. The length was just a little longer than midthigh, the bottom of the dress ruffled a little, and the top was a V-neck. Their bouquets were made of pine cones and baby's breath. All the bridesmaids' hair was worn down and slightly wavy. Andy had purchased matching diamond necklaces and earrings for the girls.

The groomsmen were wearing black tuxedos with yellow ties. Andy was wearing the same with the addition of a white honeysuckle boutonniere. They were one groomsman short, so Andy took the liberty of walking Coach Linda himself. They all stood on the temporary stage. The organist started playing the wedding music, and out came Heather. She was stunning. Her dress was simple and elegant, and she was wearing the earrings and necklace that Andy had given her on their first date. Her bouquet was made of white honeysuckles, baby's breath, and some green leaves to add a little color to it.

Dan walked her down the aisle with a smile on his face the whole time. When they reached the stage, he kissed his daughter and handed her to Andy. He shook Andy's hand and stated, "I know this is where I'm supposed to tell you to take good care of her, but I have zero concerns about that."

Jack and Rick spoke at the same time. "You shouldn't!" The crowd laughed.

Dan started to turn to walk back to his seat next to Mary but suddenly turned around to Andy and spoke. "I know this is unprecedented, Andy, but I see that you are one groomsman short. It would be an honor if you would allow me to stand in for you." Heather's eyes filled with tears. She looked at her mother with a look that asked, "What is happening here?" Her mother shook her head side to side as if to say, "I have no clue." She turned to Stacy, and Stacy did not say a word, just shrugged. Heather knew Andy was one short, so she offered to cut one of her bridesmaids. Andy insisted that he would work it out.

Heather turned back to Stacy and asked, "By the way, who walked Coach Brown down?"

"Andy did it himself," she replied. In the back of Heather's mind, she said, *I hope she didn't touch anything.*

Andy responded, "Mr. O'Rourke, have you ever golfed at the Lake Arrowhead Country Club?" Everyone had a questioning expression on their face. Father Cleveland didn't understand what was going on, but nobody interrupted.

"Years ago," Dan answered, "why?"

"Do you remember who you played with?"

Dan turned to look at Judge Fallon standing on the stage and said, "It was with the judge."

"Was it a twosome or a foursome?"

"A foursome. I remember a guy named Brad, who all he did was talk about money and screwing people over for it."

"And the fourth man, do you remember his name?"

"He was a little quieter, but I do remember he couldn't wait to get away from that Brad fellow."

"Was his name Paul?" Andy asked.

"Yes, as a matter of fact, his name was Paul," he answered.

"That was my father you played golf with that day. It would be my honor if you stood in for me."

They shook hands, and Andy turned his attention back to Heather, who was standing there with tears running down her face. She whispered, "God, I love you, Andy."

He grabbed both her hands and said, "I love you, Heather." They both turned to Father Cleveland for the ceremony.

When it was time for their vows, Heather spoke first. "Andy, I took a long time writing my vows because I wanted to be able to express my true feelings towards you." Stacy tried handing her the vows, but Heather put her hand up. "Thanks, Stacy, but I won't be needing them." Heather continued. "But the problem was that the list kept getting longer, and it started resembling more like a book than wedding vows." The crowd laughed.

"Andy, you are the most kind, gentle, and loyal man I know. You treat me like a princess, and you put everyone else in front of you. I can go on all day with these types of examples, but I realized something more from just standing up here today. I realized that even though I don't know all the men standing up here for you, I am confident in knowing that each and everyone one of them have a connection with your father. I know that entire brick wall behind you"—she was referring to the size of the men standing there—"hold a special place in your heart. You don't have any drinking buddies, politicians, or any of those type of people standing there for you. You have loyal people. Andy, I don't think I will ever be able to determine the depth of your heart." She started tearing up.

"But what I and everyone else here witnessed was the courtesy and generosity that you extended to my dad knowing that since he lost his only son, my only sibling, and would never be able to stand in for him, I"—she started shaking—"don't have the words for it. You are a great man, and in front of all of these people and God himself, I promise that I will never leave you, nor will I ever hurt you. I love you, Andy." Andy turned to the crowd, and there wasn't a dry eye in the place.

Andy started. "Heather, anyone here who knows me, which is very few because your mom took most of the seats for your side"—everyone laughed—"expects for me to have a detailed written vow, but I don't. Spontaneity can be romantic too." He looked at Dan, who was smiling, and gave him a nod. "But I do have a question for you. Why are you always crying and shaking?" Andy then got real close to her ear and whispered, "But you're not half naked this time, so we'll have to let my little thingy work on that."

Heather hit him in the chest and started laughing. "Andy!" She looked around to see if anyone heard him. She calmed down. Stacy and Coach Brown got it. Father Cleveland was close enough to hear it and wasn't impressed. Andy always had a way of calming her.

"Heather, you are the most important thing to me, and I promise that I will never hurt you or ever cause you pain. I couldn't even if I wanted to because you see that brick wall behind me? Anyone of those men would take me behind the woodshed and physically explain to me how to treat a lady."

"Include me in that list also, Andy," Amy yelled out.

"I love you too, Amy." Everyone laughed. In a couple of sentences, Andy was able to calm everyone down by using himself as a punch line. "Heather, you are right. Each and every man standing up here does hold a special place in my heart, and each one of them have been affected by our tragedies. Heather, I don't know if you realize it, but it was those tragedies that brought us together and, I believe, which also bonds us together. And I know that your brother and my dad are looking down on us right now, blessing this marriage. My love for you will never fade. Each day, I get closer to you. Frankly, I don't deserve someone like you, but I promise you that I will work each and every day and throughout every chapter of our lives together to earn it. I love you, Heather, but I do have one regret."

"Oh no," Rick said to himself. "Kid, you had it going. Don't fuck this up."

"Is that I didn't do this sooner," Andy finished. Heather lifted her veil, and the two of them embraced in a long and passionate kiss. The audience stood on their feet, and a thunderous clap followed. There were numerous boats floating off the shoreline watching the wedding. They were blowing their horns.

The kiss, horn blowing, and clapping lasted for several minutes. When it started to die down, an annoyed Father Cleveland spoke into the mic. "May I remind everyone that this ceremony is not over, and the couple is still not married. Now please, can everyone return to their seats and positions so I may continue. And can we please have some normalcy here."

"Not with these two," Dan shouted out to the amusement of everyone, everyone except Father Cleveland. Dan wasn't fazed by the father's annoyance. After all the years he had been going to his church and the tithing he had paid, Father Cleveland still demanded a two-thousand-dollar church fee and a case of Jack Daniels to conduct the wedding.

After the vows, Father Cleveland continued with the ceremony. Heather and Andy were both holding hands. She was so excited she couldn't stand still. She kept bouncing like a little girl waiting to ride her first pony. Finally, Father Cleveland asked, "Heather, do you take Andy to—"

"Yes, yes, yes, I do."

An annoyed Cleveland didn't even try to finish. It was no use. Heather turned to Stacy and got the ring. She placed it on Andy's finger. Father Cleveland continued. "Andy, do you"—Father Cleveland waited for Andy to interrupt him, but he didn't—"take Heather to be your lawfully wedded wife"—Heather kept making motions with her hands for Andy to hurry up—"in sickness and in health till death do you part?"

"I do!" He retrieved the ring from Jack and placed it on Heather's finger.

"By the powers vested in me by the archdiocese of Los Angeles and the state of California, I now pronounce you"—Heather jumped into Andy's arms, and they embraced in a long kiss—"man and wife."

When they finally stopped kissing, Andy picked up Heather as if he was carrying her across a threshold, carried her offstage, up the aisle, and to the back porch while everybody stood and clapped. The bridal party followed. The back porch was decorated and set up for drinks and appetizers. About an hour into it, Dan and Mary started rounding up people for the bus or boat ride to the resort. What they didn't plan on was, most people wanted to take the boat, so it took a little longer than expected. The bridesmaids and groomsmen took the bus since Jack convinced them that it was the fastest way to more beer. Andy and Heather stayed behind and relaxed.

About an hour before the reception was to begin, they were ready to leave. As they walked to the front door of the cabin, Andy asked Heather to cover her eyes. She didn't even hesitate. He held her hand and walked her out the front door. He told her to open her eyes. "Are you serious? That's beautiful!"

Andy had rented a Cinderella carriage with two horses and a driver for the trip to the resort. "I told you that you are my princess, and I meant it."

She gave Andy a kiss, and he helped her into the carriage. During the ride, she grabbed his hand and said, "Thank you for what you did for my dad."

"You're welcome," he replied.

"How were you able to play that off? Was my dad involved in it?"

"Absolutely not. I came up with the idea when we were looking at the resort a couple of months ago. Do you remember when you were concerned about how much money was going to be spent and your father told you not to worry about it? He said"—and Andy quoted him—"'Honey, if this is what you want, this is what you'll get.' Then I thought about something—that this wedding is the only chance your father would have to see one of his kids get married. The other chance was taken from him. So I said to myself, my dad's chance was taken from him also, but why couldn't your dad have a shot?"

"Why didn't you tell me?" Heather asked.

"Because I didn't want to stir up the emotions if that was something your dad didn't want to be involved with. So I went to Judge Fallon. Coincidentally, Tim told me that your dad confided in him about the same thing but didn't want to ask me out of respect for my dad. So I contacted my sixth man and told him of my idea, and he was more than willing to step aside to make room for your dad."

"You mean you had a sixth man the whole time, and he gave up his spot for my dad?" Heather asked.

"Yes. He's a great guy. You will meet him soon. I felt uncomfortable asking your dad, so Tim talked to him but didn't tell him I knew. It almost fell apart after your dad shook my hand earlier and turned towards his chair. But when he turned back around, I knew that Tim had convinced him to ask. Tim had told me the story about the golfing outing, and it all fit together."

"Andy, I couldn't love you any more than I do right now." She put her arm around his and lay her head on his shoulder. She looked up at him and asked, "Do you want to do it?"

"Right here, right now?" he asked.

"Yes, right now."

"Heather, that would be very romantic, but the gentleman in the car behind us escorting us in uniform and flashing red lights, I think he might have a problem with it."

"Just remember, Andy. I have always been the willing one." They both broke out in laughter.

Old Wounds

The ride took only forty minutes, so when they got there, the wedding party was inside the resort. Andy called Jack and had him round them up. Andy and Heather wanted quick pictures with the carriage and wedding party. Andy helped Heather out of the carriage, and he went off to the ballroom to help round up the wedding party. While Heather was waiting for them, she heard two girls scream and then shout, "Heather O'Rourke!"

"Girls," their mother barked, "that is very rude. Miss, I'm sorry for that interruption on your special day."

"Don't worry about it. We still have to round up the wedding party for pictures," Heather replied. "How do you two know me?" she asked the two excited twins in front of her.

"Everybody knows who the best outside hitter at UCLA for the past four years is!" Hannah replied.

"And who holds the record for having the most kills in the school's history," her sister added. Heather felt embarrassed. "Dad, look, it's Heather!"

"I see," he replied.

"I'm sorry, Heather. My girls are volleyball nuts and have followed your entire college career. This one is Hannah, my outspoken one, and this one, ironically, is Heather, my quieter one. I'm Abby, and this is my husband Jim."

"Well, it is nice to meet you folks."

"So is it safe to assume your last name isn't O'Rourke anymore?" Abby asked.

"Not as of about two hours ago. I am now officially Heather DiPaola."

"DiPaola?" Abby asked with a concerned look on her face.

"That's correct. And here comes my new husband as we speak."

As Andy approached the group, he immediately recognized Abby. "Well, isn't this a surprise. Hello, Abby," Andy said as he offered her his hand.

"Hello, Mr. DiPaola," she said as she shook his hand. "Congratulations on your wedding."

"Thank you," he replied, "but I prefer to be called Andy. How are things in your life?" he asked.

"Well, thanks to your generosity, I've been able to rebuild my life and keep a stable home for my girls. I also found a great man," she said as she pointed to Jim.

Andy looked at him and stuck his hand out and said, "Andy DiPaola."

"Jim James," he replied.

"And these are Heather and Hannah," Abby said.

The twin girls were both six-feet-one-inch tall with dark brown hair and slender frames. They were getting ready to start their senior year at Redlands High School. Both were starters on the volleyball team, Heather a middle blocker and Hannah an outside hitter. Jim whispered something into Abby's ear, to which she just nodded as an answer.

"How do you guys know each other?" Heather asked.

"It's a long story, and now is not the time or place, so I'll catch you up later," Andy explained. "So what brings you to the mountain?" Andy asked.

"Well, as you are aware, we have to leave our house next year, so we started looking around and thought we would check Arrowhead out. We just drove up here unplanned, really hoping to get a room and spend a couple of days looking at houses, but this was our last stop."

"There isn't a room to be found anywhere around here," Jim said.

"Will you folks excuse us for a moment? Wait right here. Heather and Hannah, I'm counting on you not to let your parents wander off. If you keep them here, I have more surprises for you."

"Yes, sir, we won't move."

Andy walked away with Heather and explained his plan to her. "I have no problem with that, Andy. I would rather stay at the cabin than here anyways, but why are you doing this? How do you know them?"

"Heather, let's get through the reception, then later in private, I will explain everything to you. I promise."

"Okay, Andy. You truly are the most generous man I have ever known."

Andy walked up to the carriage driver and spoke with him for a couple of minutes. He reached into his pocket and pulled out three one hundred dollar bills and handed it to him. He then grabbed Heather by the hand, and they walked back to the family. "Abby, we booked an extra room here that we won't be using, so we would like to offer it to you guys."

"Andy, that is not necessary, but I appreciate the offer," she replied.

"Well, I insist. Girls, help me out here." Andy turned to the twins.

"Mom, Dad, please. One more day here would be fantastic," Hannah said.

"What do you think, Jim?" Abby asked.

"If it's extra, then we could sure use one," he replied.

"Settled," Andy said. "I want you to ask for a girl named Maria. In about two hours, she will have everything set. The downfall is, it only has an oversized king bed, so, Jim, you might have to sleep on the couch or a rollaway bed."

"That's fine. It's worth it," he replied.

While Andy was talking to them, Heather texted Stacy and had her gather up all the girls and bring them outside. "Girls," Heather started, "we have two surprises for you."

As she said that, she saw Hannah's eyes leave hers and look past her. Hannah elbowed her sister and pointed to the front door of the resort, and the excited screams started all over again. "Girls, calm down," Abby barked.

"Mom, Dad, look!" The whole gang came walking out of the resort—Stacy, the Jazz, Katlyn, and the rest of the previous year

UCLA team, including Coach Brown. The girls ran up to them and introduced themselves and started rambling their knowledge of each of the college women's personal statistics.

"Boy, your girls know their stuff," Heather said to Abby.

"They have lived and breathed volleyball their entire lives. They have dreams of playing for UCLA, but I don't know if that'll work out."

Twin Heather asked Heather, "How did you get all the girls to come to your wedding?"

Coach Brown interrupted and answered the question. "Heather, a volleyball family just doesn't end on the court. You play as a family, and you live as a family. That's how you win matches. Remember that."

"Yes, ma'am," Heather replied.

Unfortunately, the twenty-minute shortage was long enough for most of the wedding guests to leave the ballroom and check out the commotion. After the wedding party took photos with the carriage, Heather invited the twins to take a picture with all the volleyball girls. They gladly accepted. While they were taking the pictures with the twins, Jack, Rick, and Dan used their rough voices and intimidating bodies to get everybody back into the ballroom. "Okay, girls. One more surprise as we promised," Andy said. He whispered into each of their ears.

"Seriously," Hannah said, "this is the best day of my life."

Andy explained to Abby and Jim that they had an hour's worth of time left on the carriage, so they could take the girls for a short ride around the village. "Andy, I certainly didn't expect any of this. I thought that you would never talk to me."

"Why wouldn't I talk to you?"

"Because of our history," she said.

"Abby, you and your girls didn't do anything wrong. We all went through a terrible time, and what happened hurt a lot of people and destroyed families. I am just happy to see that you have done well for yourself."

"Thanks, Andy, but I owe a lot of that to you."

"You don't owe me anything," he said. "Well, we have to get this reception going. Enjoy the carriage, and we would appreciate it if your family joined us for brunch tomorrow morning here at the resort. We have reservations for ten thirty."

"How can we say no?" Jim asked. "We will see you in the morning."

"Heather," Abby spoke out, "sorry to have interfered in your wedding day."

"You didn't interfere. Your girls made this day even more memorable. Thank you," Heather responded. As they walked to the ballroom, Heather asked, "Andy, what history do the two of you have? Please tell me those twins aren't yours."

Andy busted out a laugh. "No, Heather, they are not mine, and our history is the complete opposite of that. Please, let's have our reception, and I will tell you everything, but, Heather, erase all those types of thoughts out of your head. I know what you are thinking, and it's nothing like that."

"Okay, Andy." She reached and kissed his cheek. "I love you."

"I love you too."

RECEPTION

The ballroom was elegant, and the floral decorations immaculate. Mary, Heather, and the bridesmaids did an excellent job. Heather insisted that they do the labor to save costs. Mary gave in just to make Heather happy. On one wall, they had the long table for the wedding party. Circular tables were set up around the dance floor. They hired a local band who performed a lot of weddings. For the menu, Heather wanted the cheapest package, which was priced at $95 per head, but she was overruled by Dan, Mary, and Andy. They selected the most expensive Diamond Package, which was priced at $195 per head. They explained to her that since they decided to have a cash bar to hopefully minimize people getting drunk, they figured they would treat their guests to an excellent meal. To keep Jack appeased, they had a list of the wedding party and Dan and Mary at the bar for free drinks. After the dinner was over, the festivities began. Stacy stood up to give the maid of honor speech.

"I have known Heather my entire life. We grew up two blocks away from each other," she started. "We started playing volleyball at the age of eight and always played on the same teams, including playing for UCLA. She is the most elegant girl you could ever ask for, she is generous, and although she is very pretty, she doesn't act it. I don't know the story of how these two met. I'm not quite sure anybody does. And if someone does know, they sure are keeping it a secret. I've asked Heather numerous times, and all I've gotten was a dinner in Pasadena. But that story doesn't add up because I was a witness to an amazing embrace these two had at volleyball practice, and that was a month before this dinner date. So I was a little annoyed that she wouldn't tell me.

"All I saw was this storybook relationship between two people that I love, and I just wanted to know how it started so maybe a girl like me could get one. However, after listening to Andy's vows today, something struck me and made me feel very selfish. Andy mentioned that tragedy had brought them both together. When he said that, I felt embarrassed for ever having pried. I am so sorry, Heather."

Heather stood up gave her a hug and said, "I had no idea you were upset with me. I am sorry you had to go through that. I would never hurt you."

Stacy turned back to the crowd. "This is what I'm talking about. I acted selfishly towards her, and she apologized to me for causing something she didn't even do. Andy, I know you have heard this numerous times, but you've got yourself a great girl, more girl than a guy could ask for. I'll pray for nothing but happiness for the both of you."

Jack stood up and said, "I'm not one for all this mushy stuff, so I'll keep this short. Andy, I've known you your entire life. I've seen you go through things that no young man or woman"—looking at Heather—"should have had to go through, but each and every time, you came out a stronger person." Looking back at Heather, he added, "And you, young lady, did the exact same thing. You see, Stacy, I do know the story behind these two, and I understand why they keep it a secret. But let me assure everyone in this room those tragedies that Andy spoke of did in fact bring these two together, and that is why they are both so humble. Heather, do you remember what I told you the first day we met?" he asked.

"Yes, sir," she replied.

"Call me Jack. What did I tell you?"

"You told me to give you my driver's license or ID card if I wasn't old enough to drive, and then you told me to get out of the car!"

The entire room broke out into laughter, including Jack. When the room calmed down, Jack said, "Funny, very funny. Okay, smarty." Looking at Andy, he said, "She gets that crap from you. You know that." Andy and Heather looked at each other, smiled, and winked. "I told you to hang on to this one."

"That's exactly what you said," Heather replied.

"Well, I meant it then, and I mean it now. Hang on to him. You will never find another like Andy."

"I plan on it, sir." Jack looked at her sideway for calling him sir. "Well, you are a very intimidating man." Everyone laughed. Andy stood up and shook Jack's hand. Jack pulled him in and gave him a big bear hug.

Maria introduced the new couple and initiated the first dance. Andy had asked Heather if he could pick out the first song. She agreed. They walked to the dance floor, and the band started playing Frank Sinatra's "The Way You Look Tonight." As they danced, camera flashes continued. Maria then announced that it was time for the father-daughter dance. Heather and Dan started dancing. As they were dancing, Dan whispered into his daughter's ear, "Remember what you said earlier today that you may never know the depth of Andy's heart?"

"Yes, I remember."

"Well, sweetheart, I don't believe you ever will."

She looked at her dad, and he motioned for her to look over her left shoulder. She turned to see Andy asking her mother to dance for a mother-son dance. She heard him ask, "May I have the honor of a mother-son dance?"

"Of course you may," Mary responded. Heather thought that she had seen less tears at a funeral than she had seen at this wedding. Then she watched Andy waltz away with her mother.

When the father-daughter and mother-son dance ended, Maria made an announcement. "At the request of the bride and groom, we have one more dance prior to the wedding party dance." Stacy brought a dozen red roses and handed them to Heather. Andy and Heather walked over to Amy, and Heather handed her the roses. "What's going on?" Amy asked. "Did you do something to Heather?"

Andy spoke. "Amy, you have been the only mother I've ever known. You have always been there for me without hesitation, and you still are to this day. If anyone in this room wants to know who raised me well, my dad taught me what was expected of me and what rules he demanded, but Amy here enforced it!" The room broke out in laughter.

Dan whispered to Mary, "Well, that explains a lot."

"May I have the honor of a mother-son dance?" Amy broke out in tears. She handed Andy her hand, and they both walked onto the dance floor.

Maria instructed the bridesmaids and groomsmen to join in. Dan had to cut Heather short to dance with Coach Brown. Andy and Mary had finished, so Andy and Heather sat this one out. They were both watching all the groomsmen stumble with their dance partners. They were all big men, and the bridesmaids were fairly petite. But the funniest one to watch was Jack and Stacy. Jack looked so uncomfortable. While they were watching the pair, a very handsome man walked up to them, tapped Jack on the shoulder, and asked, "By your leave, sir."

Jack looked at him and said, "Be my guest." Stacy looked at her new dance partner and thought, *He's cute.*

"Who is that?" Heather asked.

"That is Jack's son," Andy replied.

"Look at the way they are looking at each other," Heather said.

"He's a great guy," Andy replied.

After Maria invited everybody to the dance floor, the wedding party took a break. Stacy came bouncing up to Heather all giggling. "Did you see that?"

"I did," she responded.

"Who is he?"

Heather looked to Andy to answer. "He is a great friend of mine. We grew up together. His name is John, and he is Jack's son."

"Is he dating anyone?" Stacy asked.

Andy said, "There is one girl in his life." Stacy's excitement diminished. "Stacy, John is a great guy, but he does have some baggage. Don't tell him I called it baggage. I was just trying to use a familiar term."

"What is it?"

"He has a six-year-old daughter."

"Was he married?"

"No."

"Did he just get a girl pregnant?"

"No."

"I don't understand," she said.

"He has a cousin that got heavily involved into manufacturing methamphetamines. She gave birth to Charlie and was arrested when

Charlie was a year old. The system took Charlie away from her, and the county placed her in foster care. When John found out about it, he petitioned the courts for custody. They didn't want to give her to him because he was not married, nor was he in a steady relationship. The judge gave him three months to work it out. Well, John didn't want to get married, and he certainly didn't want to get a girlfriend just to use her. I found out about all of this about two weeks prior to that next scheduled hearing while they were at my cabin for a BBQ. I asked who the presiding judge was, and John told me Linda Sanchez. I smiled because Judge Sanchez owed me a favor. I'll explain that later. To make a long story short, John was granted custody of Charlie. Stacy, I would not have set you up with him if—"

"Wait a minute. You set that whole thing up?" Heather asked.

"I did," Andy admitted. "Stacy is your best friend, and she hasn't had good luck with men because guys her age aren't real men. They act like spoiled little boys. Heck, a lot of them don't even know what gender they are." Stacy and Heather nodded. "If I thought you would get hurt…" He finished, "Go for a coffee. Talk to him. I can assure you will not be disappointed."

"I don't know if I'm ready for an instant family, and I certainly wouldn't want to hurt Charlie any more than it appears she's been hurt."

At that moment, a little blue-eyed blond girl came running up to Andy. "Uncle Andy, will you dance with me?" He scooped her up and gave her a big hug.

"Heather, Stacy, this is Charlie."

"Heather, are you going to be my new aunt?"

"I believe so," she replied.

"You two girls are very pretty," Charlie said.

As Andy carried her to the dance floor, he turned back to Heather and said, "Oh, by the way, sweetheart, John was number six."

Andy had Charlie stand on top of his shoes, and they started dancing. "What did that mean?" Stacy asked.

"Stacy," Heather said, "we need to talk."

FIGURING HIM OUT

Heather explained to Stacy what the sixth man comment meant. "Really?" Stacy asked. "John gave up his place in your wedding as Andy's best friend to allow your dad to stand in on your wedding stage?"

"Yes, Stacy," Heather said. "These men are very loyal to each other. Andy felt that it was important to me to have my dad in our wedding, so John stepped aside without hesitation."

"That is the sweetest thing I've…I feel like crying," Stacy said.

"So what do you think?" Heather asked.

"He's cute, but what about Charlie? I don't want to start dating him and then, if it doesn't work out, hurt Charlie."

"Well, I would tell him that up front. Maybe you can start dating him without Charlie's knowledge until the relationship grows." Then it hit her. "Wait a minute," Heather said, "I know what's going on here. Stacy, I don't think Charlie is going to be an issue if you date John. I'll bet Andy has been working on this for a long time, and him and John has this whole thing planned out, and John probably already knows all he needs to know about you."

"What makes you think that?" Stacy asked.

"Remember last fall when Andy picked me up at the dorm the weekend before Thanksgiving?"

"I remember that," she replied.

"Well, when he asked me where I wanted to go, remember when I said Arrowhead because of the mountain air and hot tub?"

"Yes, but where are you going with this?" Stacy asked.

"What did Andy tell you when you said, 'I want one'?"

"I don't remember," she said.

"Well, I do. He assured that you would get one but to be patient."

"I do remember him saying that," Stacy replied. "But that was what nine months ago. It took him nine months to introduce John to me."

"Listen, Stacy. Andy, and if I'm right John, plan these things for memorable outcomes. You've seen what Andy has done for me these past fifteen months."

"Yeah, he treats you like a princess. That's why I want one."

"Well, I think John is your prince. Stacy, Andy booked this place a year ago, only three months after we started dating, so it takes a while for their plans to come together. Although these guys are technically millennials, they were raised old-school and are expected to act that way. You heard what was said during Andy's vows with the woodshed comment. John was raised in the same circle. So I think I've finally figured out how Andy operates."

"Do you think you're right?" Stacy asked.

"I think I am, but I'm not positive. But if I had to bet on it, I would. So are you going to give it a try?" Heather asked.

"Heck yeah," she said as she started acting excited. "I don't want to give up a chance there might be another Andy out there."

"Okay, listen, Stacy. Let's keep an eye on Andy. Try not to stare, but watch him. I have a feeling he has been watching us for your reaction."

Andy had been watching them out of the corner of his eye while dancing with Charlie. When he saw Stacy excited, he knew she was game. Andy looked over at John, and when they made eye contact, Andy just nodded.

"I knew I was right. Did you see that?" Heather asked.

"I can't believe what I just witnessed. You were right, Heather. God, I hope this works out," Stacy said.

"I think you'll be fine," Heather replied.

"What happens next?" Stacy asked.

"If I had to guess, he will probably come over here and ask you for a dance and then ask you out."

The girls watched John walk over to Stacy's parents. "Why is he talking to my parents?"

"Man rules," Heather replied. "I forgot about them."

"What man rules?" Stacy asked.

"Stacy, there are a lot of things you're going to have to get used to when dating someone like these guys. They live by a set of rules that require a man to do certain things."

"What kind of things?"

"Well, I still don't know all of them. But when you guys go out, just expect him to pay for everything, and don't even bring it up because it will insult him. Don't open any doors, including your car door. That will be done for you. You will be seated first, and they will get up every time you need to. Heck, Stacy, they won't even take a bite of their food until you have been served. They treat girls with respect."

"You mean what I call like a princess?" Stacy asked.

"Exactly right, and there are consequences if they break those rules," Heather explained.

"So why is he talking to my parents?" Stacy asked.

"That's the number one rule. You can't ask someone's daughter out until you introduce yourself to her parents," Heather explained.

"Did Andy do that?" Stacy asked.

"No, he didn't, and he caught hell from both of my parents and Bill and Marsha because of it. I found out that my parents could have made him stop dating me because of it. They take those rules very serious."

"Really? I don't think my dad cares. He'd be happy if I found someone to take me so he wouldn't have to feed me anymore." They both laughed.

"Stacy, may I have this dance?" John asked.

"Of course," she replied.

"So how long have the two of you been planning this?" Heather asked Andy as they watched John and Stacy dance.

"Planned?" Andy asked. "What do you think, there is some sort of conspiracy between me and John?"

"Andy DiPaola, don't play dumb with me. I figured you out. But the only thing I can't determine is how long this has been in the works. I know it's been at least since Thanksgiving."

"Okay, I'll make a deal with you. You prove to me that you figured it out, and I will answer all of your questions," he said.

"Ha! You lose, Andy. I figured you out when right after you saw Stacy's excitement, you turned to John and gave him a head nod, then John went straight to Stacy's parents."

"Very good, Heather. What do you want to know?" he asked.

"How long has this been in the works, why today, and how are they going to handle Charlie?"

"I told John about Stacy one year ago when he came with me to reserve this place."

"Wait a minute. John was involved in the planning of our wedding?"

"Of course he was. He's my best friend," Andy replied. "Answer number two is, two people's best friends get married, and on their wedding day, their best friends start dating. And Charlie will not be involved at first to make sure the relationship is going to last, which it will unless Stacy determines that she doesn't like John, and then she will slowly be involved. We don't want her to get her hopes up of having a mommy if it doesn't work out."

"So let me guess. John has spent the last year figuring Stacy out, and he knows what he already needs to know about her," she stated.

"You catch on fast," Andy replied.

HEATHER'S SECOND DECISION

During the reception, Andy had asked Bill and John if they would go to the cabin and bring Jenny to the yacht club so he and Heather could have a ride back after the reception. They were able to change before the boat ride so they would be more comfortable. As they drove away from the dock, Heather didn't waste a second. "Okay, Andy. Who is she?"

Andy chuckled. "I'm surprised it took you this long," he replied. "And I hope it didn't ruin your reception, but if I told you in advance, then I know it would have."

"No way. That was the best time of my life. And with those two twins fawning all over me, John asking Stacy out, and you having a mother-son dance with my mom made it even better, but obviously, I'm very curious."

"Heather, as we both know, each of us went through hell. And frankly, mine only started getting better the day you showed up in my office. That one encounter changed me forever. Sure, I had money and a successful business, for which I am grateful, but I wasn't happy. You showing up in my office and the events that happened today made me the happiest and luckiest person alive."

"Andy, you are the sweetest." She gave him a kiss. "So how does that fit in with Abby?" she asked.

Andy put the boat in neutral and turned to Heather and looked her straight in her eyes. "Heather, it was Abby's ex-husband that killed my dad."

"Oh god," Heather said as she put her hand over her mouth. She put her arms around Andy's neck and hugged him. "Now I wish that you had told me those twins were yours."

"I knew that you would be thinking that the whole time," he said. "Heather, I would have been, what, ten to eleven years old?" He laughed.

"Andy," she said, "then why were you so pleasant with her? You even gave her our honeymoon suite and invited her family to brunch tomorrow."

"Heather, neither Abby nor her girls did anything to me. I can't hold them responsible for what their father and her ex-husband did, but I made them pay for it, and I feel a little guilty about it."

"What do you mean made them pay?" she asked.

"When my dad was killed, I became a hermit for a couple of months. I had just lost the only family I had, and my dad was the greatest. When I got done feeling sorry for myself, I went into an angry phase where I was going to make everyone even remotely connected pay for my father's death. Tim hooked me up with some very high-powered lawyers. I sued everybody—the county of San Bernardino, that captain, and the three deputies that were on scene. I sued the guardrail company, the company that installed the rails, the state of California, and then finally, I sued the deputy and Abby. I was on a terror. So the case against the deputy and Abby had been decided by a judge, and he awarded me five million dollars. They didn't have that kind of money, but they did have boats, Jet Skis, nice cars, and a beautiful home in Redlands, so I took them. The deputy was sent to prison, so Abby and the girls were the ones who really lost everything.

"After the judge made his ruling, I saw Abby turn to her dad and say, 'I'm sorry, Daddy. I should have listened to you,' and she broke down in tears. As I was leaving the courtroom, her dad, Buck, asked if he could speak with me. My attorneys advised me against it, but I didn't listen to them. Buck explained the history of the house in how that when Abby was a little girl, they would go to Redlands to pick oranges at the groves. He said Abby loves the smell of orange blossoms, so he purchased a piece of land in Redlands with the intent of building her a house in the future. He started building the house when she was in high school and gave it to her when she graduated. He built it with his own two hands. He had dreams of his daughter being married there, which she was, then he hoped his granddaughters would also be married there. He had told Abby to get a prenuptial to protect the house, but she wouldn't."

"Is it a nice house?" Heather asked.

"The house is beautiful. It has five bedrooms, a guesthouse, a pool, and a tennis court, which they converted into a volleyball court."

"How much is the house worth?"

"Well, when I took it from them, it was worth nine hundred and fifty thousand. It's worth almost one point five million today."

"Holy smokes, that's a lot of money," Heather said. "So why are they still living there if you took it from them?" she asked.

"Well, when Buck talked to me, he told me that he wasn't mad at me for suing them, but he asked if we could make some sort of deal for his daughter and the girls to stay there at least until they graduated high school. He said he couldn't afford rent on nine hundred thousand dollars and asked if I could make it reasonable, so I agreed to let them stay there for one dollar a month until the twins graduate."

"That's it, one dollar? Why would you do that for them?"

"Heather, I was becoming a monster going after everyone, so I thought about it and said although I didn't regret suing them, I had to look at how that incident hurt them too. They were victims as well, and their lives were ruined, so I thought the least I could do is let them stay in the house that her dad built with his own bare hands. In the end, it was still appreciating in value."

"You truly are a very generous man, Andy," she said.

"I'm glad you said that, Heather, because I would like to give them the house back," he said.

"What? Why would you do that?"

"Heather I...I'm sorry. We don't need the money, and maybe Buck will get to see his granddaughters get married there, but I can't give it to them without your approval."

"No way, Andy. That is your house that you got because of the death of your father. I have no say in it at all."

"Heather, like I said at our engagement lunch, everything I have is ours. So from here on out, we make the decisions together as one."

"Andy, I don't know. Other than making the decision of building a new house in Rancho, the only other decisions I had to make in life was whether to buy generic over brand-named at the grocery store." Andy laughed. She continued, "I understand where your heart is, but 1.5 million dollars is a lot of money. I know you don't like talking about your finances with other people, but just this once, would you mind if I get advice from my parents?"

"Not at all," he said. "We are just about there, so we can talk to them now."

Andy pulled up to his dock and helped Heather out of the boat. As they walked up to the cabin, Heather said, "Andy, do you realize that we are homeless? Where are we going to sleep?"

"Crap, I didn't think that one through," he said. "Don't worry. I have an idea." Andy had given the master bedroom to her parents, and all the bedrooms were taken by others.

When they walked into the cabin, Mary, Dan, Stacy, Coach Brown, Charlie, and John were sitting in the great room, talking. "Well, there you two are," Mary said. "Why did you give up your hotel room?"

"Mom, it was for a good reason. Besides, I would rather be here than in a hotel," Heather replied.

That's when Andy heard it. "What was that?" he asked. "What was what?" or "Nothing" was all everyone said back. "It sounded like a dog whimper," Andy said. No one answered.

"Heather, Andy, Mary, and I got you a little something for your wedding."

"Dad, we asked for no gifts, and besides, you guys paid for a lot of the wedding."

"I know, honey, but it's just a little something." Heather and Andy told all the wedding invitees that no gifts or money were to be given. Dan got up and walked to the garage. When he returned, he was holding a black Labrador puppy. "Here's Blue." Andy's eyes lit up, and Heather started bouncing. Andy was speechless, so Dan said, "That's right, Andy. You aren't the only one who can give thoughtful gifts. I know you held back on getting one because of your travels, but we thought that when you two are gone, Mary and I can watch him since we are now empty nesters."

"Dan, Mary, thank you. I have wanted one for a long time."

"Thanks, Mom and Dad."

Andy, Stacy, and Charlie were playing with the pup as Heather took her parents into the master bedroom to talk. John was sitting there admiring Stacy and the way she interacted with Charlie. Heather explained everything to them about Abby, the girls, Buck, and the house.

"Well, Heather," Mary started, "first of all, what are the odds of them showing up and running into you on the day of your wedding? God must have had a hand in that. But that being said, we all know that Andy is a very giving man, but 1.5 million dollars is a lot of money, and maybe you guys should be thinking about your future with kids and the costs associated with that."

"I know, Mom, but Andy says we don't need the money."

"Has he explained your finances to you?" she asked.

"Not yet. We have an appointment in three weeks with his CPA to go over everything."

"Well, in my opinion, that's a lot of money, and I would keep the house. You might need the money in the future."

"What do you think, Dad?"

"I don't think money is an issue. Andy would never jeopardize your guys' future to give something away, so I say go with your heart."

"These decisions suck," Heather said. "First I had to make the decision to build a new house, which is costing a fortune, and now I have to make a decision to basically give away 1.5 million dollars. Hell, yesterday I didn't have a dime to my name." Dan and Mary laughed. "It's not funny. Andy is right. Having money is a curse."

"How are you leaning, sweetheart?" Mary asked.

"I have to ask Andy one question before I make up my mind. I'll be right back." She walked out of the room. "Andy, do you have a minute?" she asked.

"Of course I do." He picked up Blue and started walking toward the back patio with Heather.

"Hey," Stacy yelled, "Blue stays with me and Charlie!" Andy returned the puppy and walked out back.

"Andy, I know we have an appointment with your CPA, but for me to make an informed decision on the Redlands house, I kind of need to know where we are at. I know you said we don't need the money, and of course I trust you, but 1.5 million dollars is a lot of money to give away. And I won't say anything to my parents." Andy leaned over and whispered a number into her ear and kissed her on the cheek. Heather stood there in shock. "I don't suppose you're kidding," she asked as she started to shake.

"Well, that was the last time I checked, so it's going to be a bit higher by now. And, Heather, that number doesn't include real estate and the value of our business, and it's your money too. You can tell your parents. They are family now. Now can I please go back and play with Blue before Stacy and Charlie get too attached?"

When Heather didn't return to the room, Dan and Mary went to go look for her. Dan wanted to finish the conversation so he could play with Blue. "Where's Heather?" Mary asked.

"She's on the patio," Andy replied. "I think she's trying to absorb what she was just told."

Dan and Mary walked out back to find Heather sitting on a chair, staring into space. "What's the matter?" Mary asked.

"Mom, I'm giving Abby and her girls the house back."

"But what about the future and your guys' needs?"

"Mom, Andy just told me what his net worth is, and Abby needs that house way more than we need the money. Our kids will never have to worry about anything."

"I'm so proud of you for the way you handled this whole thing, Heather," Dan said. "I have a feeling you are in for a whole lot more of these types of decisions in your future."

"That's what I was just thinking about, Dad, but I finally figured out why Andy does what he does. Guys, he can afford anything, and I mean anything, yet he doesn't blow it. He lives well below his means. He would rather do nice things for people than himself. Giving the Redlands house back is the right thing to do."

"Heather, I know it's none of our business, and you don't have to tell us if you don't want to, but how much money are we talking about?" Mary asked.

"Mom, not counting real estate and what his business is worth, Andy said we have over 156 million dollars."

"Oh dear God," Mary said as she covered her mouth with both hands.

"This day has been so overwhelming. First, I had a fairytale wedding on a beautiful mountain lake and married the most generous, sweetest man. My dad got to stand on my wedding stage, then a Cinderella carriage ride to a resort where I had an amazing reception. I met the ex-wife of the person who killed Andy's father and got fawned on by her twin daughters. Andy danced a mother-son dance with my mom, my best friend got asked out by Andy's best friend, we got a Lab puppy, and then I'm told that I am wealthy beyond my wildest dreams. And I give away 1.5 million dollars like autumn leaves blowing in the wind. Mom, Dad, I don't deserve any of this," she said.

"Well, sweetheart, I know of a man sitting in that living room"—Dan turned to point at Andy—"who is wrestling with a little girl over a puppy." Mary and Heather looked and saw Andy and Charlie tackling each other so neither one of them can reach Stacy who was holding Blue in her lap. They started laughing. "Who would disagree with you? And quite frankly, sweetheart, I am on his side on this one."

"Thanks, Dad."

They walked back into the great room, and Heather jumped on Andy's back and started tickling his sides. "Let go of that little girl," she demanded. When Andy couldn't take the tickling anymore, he released Charlie's leg. Charlie grabbed Blue out of Stacy's lap, then turned around and sat in her lap. Dan sat on the floor waiting for his turn with the dog. Andy rolled over, and while Heather was sitting on his stomach, she said, "Okay, Andy, you can give Abby the house."

"Not me," he replied. "Tomorrow at brunch, you can give it to her. You need the practice."

"Me? But… You know what? I can do this," she said. Andy excused himself to make a call. He was hoping it wasn't too late. While Andy was away, everyone looked at Stacy and couldn't believe what they saw. She was sitting on the floor Indian style with Charlie in her lap holding Blue. Stacy was curling Charlie's hair in her fingers and smiling. Heather looked to John and saw him smiling at the sight.

HONEYMOON SUITE

"What is this?" Heather asked as they pulled up to their dock.

"That is your honeymoon accommodations," Andy replied. Prior to taking Heather on an evening lake cruise, Andy pulled John and Dan aside and asked them for a favor. He had them set up a tent next to the lakeside hot tub. Earlier, Andy had the rental crew on standby. So after the wedding was over, the backyard was immediately cleaned up. The rental company had removed the stage, all the chairs, and the sound system. Inside the tent was a queen-size bed with sheets and blankets, a portable fan, a lamp, two grocery sacks each filled with clothes for each of them, pillows, a bottle of Four Roses, and two bottles of wine. They lit a path of candles from the dock to the tent and had red rose petals all along it. Dan had asked Stacy and Mary to pick out clothes and a bathing suit and anything else they felt that Heather might need for the night. John grabbed Andy's essentials.

"Are you serious?" she asked.

"Are you disappointed?" he asked.

"Disappointed? No way. Just when I thought this day couldn't get any more memorable. Andy, I will never forget this. It's way better than staying in a hotel room. How romantic. Well, Mr. Romance, how is tonight going to go?" she asked.

"Well, the way I see it, we change into our bathing suits, soak in the hot tub, drink whatever we want, and make love as many times as we can."

"Well, mister, you're in for a long night. And unlike your swimming abilities, you better be able to keep up," she said with a sexy grin.

Andy had yet to beat her in a race. "You're a bully," he responded.

As they sat in the hot tub, Heather turned to him and said, "Andy, I have a question for you. You don't have to answer it if you don't want to, but it's been bothering me for a long time, and now that we are married, I would like to get it off my chest."

"Is something wrong?" he asked.

"Nothing is wrong. I just kinda want an answer, but now that I brought it up, I'm afraid to ask you."

"Heather, you don't have to be afraid to ask me anything. If I don't feel like I can give you an answer, then I'll explain why I can't. Fair enough?"

"Okay, here it goes. But I think I already know the answer, but I just want to confirm it. Why didn't you have sex with me that day in your office?" Andy let out a long laugh. "What's so funny?"

"Heather, when you said that you needed to ask me a question, all kinds of scenarios went through my mind, but you asking why I didn't have sex with you when we first met was not one of them."

"Andy, aside from the day my brother was killed, that day in your office was the worst day of my life. And when I offered myself to you and you turned me down, it made it even worse, so I'm just curious as to why."

"So why do you think that I didn't?"

"Well, knowing you like I know you now, I don't believe that you would ever take advantage of a girl. Am I right?"

"Heather, you were so desperate that day there was no way in the world that I could have lived with myself had I taken you up on your offer, but there was way more to it than that."

"Like what?" she asked.

"Heather, I wanted you. I wanted your heart, and I wanted the whole package, not just quick sex." Heather turned beet red. "I had spent a long time looking for someone like you. In just that short albeit chaotic meeting we had, I made the determination that I was going to do everything to get you. And if we had sex that day, then I figured that we could never be together again. You would have never respected me because you got what you wanted out of it, and I got to have sex with you. In that case, I lose. I wanted to earn your respect and heart, and I wanted you to love me for me and not because I did a favor for you. And likewise, I wanted to love you for you and not because we had sex together."

Heather threw her arms around his neck and gave him a big kiss. "Boy, just when I thought I couldn't love you any more than I do, you surprise me. Thanks, Andy. So what are we going to do, jump in the tent for round one?" she asked.

"Not so fast, missy. It doesn't work like that. You asked a question that's been on your mind. Now it's my turn."

"Really? There is a question about me that you don't have an answer to?" she asked while giggling. "Andy, you're slipping." They both laughed. "Okay, so what's your question?"

"Well, our first dinner night together, when we were in the Tap Room with Tim, he asked you how you made something happen, and you responded power prayers. What did that mean?"

She thought about it for a second, then told him about the conversation she had with Tim the day after Garcia-Hernandez was arrested. "So," she said, "I told him that I would say an extra prayer every night for you to come back into my life. Uncle Tim told me that in order for me to get what I wanted, it would take some serious power prayers. Then one day, out of the blue, you showed up at practice. That's why I hugged you so long. I didn't want to let you go. Then when you left again for a month, I prayed even harder, figuring it worked the first time, then it had to work again. And sure enough, it did."

"You are the sweetest, Heather. I love you."

"I love you too." They both hugged and kissed.

"One more question," he stated.

"Be careful, Andy. You only asked for one, which was asked and answered. Are you sure to want to continue?" She laughed.

Remembering the debacle during their first dinner date, he thought about it and said, "Come on, Heather. Just one more."

"Andy, you can ask me anything. I won't beat you up again over it," she replied while still laughing.

"During that same conversation with Tim, he whispered something in your ear, and you responded that you didn't understand what he meant."

She rolled her eyes back into her head, thought, then said, "I remember that. He was referring to that conversation I just told you about because I got upset that you did what you did for me and my family and that you got nothing out of it, so he whispered something like, 'And you were afraid that he got nothing by helping you.' I still don't understand what he meant by that."

"Heather, you are a very smart girl. Think about it. I got more than anyone else in that deal."

"What?" she asked, confused. Andy raised his eyebrows at her and nodded toward her. "Me?" she asked as she was pointing at her chest. "You got me?"

"That's exactly right, sweetheart."

"Oh jeez, Andy, you're making me cry."

After saying that, she took her bathing suit off and climbed on top of him. Andy fumbled with his suit and finally managed to get it off with her sitting on top of him. "I thought you wanted to have round one in the tent," he said.

"I can't wait that long," she replied as she put him inside of her. They made love for the first and only time that night. After the tub, they climbed into the tent naked and fell asleep in each other's arms. It had been a long and exhausting day.

EPILOGUE

By the time Heather and Andy walked into the hospital room, Mary, Bill, and Marsha were already there. Heather immediately walked up to Dan and gave him a hug. "Are you okay, Dad?"

"I'm fine, sweetheart," he replied.

Bill saw Heather's face turn serious and knew what was coming. "Come on, Marsha. Let's wait in the hall."

"Heather, would you like for me to wait in the hall as well?" Andy asked.

"No, Andy. We are a family, and we will deal it as one."

Standing with her infamous hip-finger action, Heather started. "Dad, how many times were you shot?"

"Twice, dear."

"Don't lie to me. How many times?"

"Well, I was hit in the chest, but my plate stopped it."

"Dad, you have to get out of that job and retire. You have been there over thirty-seven years, and enough is enough. This family has sacrificed enough for that agency. You lost a son, and we almost lost you," Heather stated as tears started in her eyes. "Dad, I need you. Mom needs you. Andy, Stacy, John, and Charlie need you. I'm trying to have children, and what do you want them to do, grow up without a grandfather?" Dan tried interrupting, but Heather was having none of it. "Dad, if you stay with that agency and something happens to you, then you are just being selfish. Let me ask you a question. Where did you spot the suspects?" Bill had already told her of the circumstances surrounding the shooting to give her ammunition to use against Dan.

"I was on Fifth just south of Lincoln."

"Dad, where was Brian killed?"

Dan thought about it and started tearing up. "Fifth and Lincoln."

"And what time was it when you spotted them?"

"Around one thirty."

"And what time was Brian killed?"

"One thirty."

"Dad, God is telling you to get out. If those aren't signs, then I don't know what is." Jack, Stacy, and Charlie were standing with Marsha and Bill outside the door and heard every word.

"Heather, calm down for a minute," Andy said.

"Andy, I am right, and everybody in this room knows it."

"Heather, you are right, but can I get a few words in?"

"I'm sorry, Andy. Go ahead."

"Dan, Heather is right. I know you've been there a long time, and it's my understanding that you are excellent at what you do, but can I ask a question?"

"Sure, go ahead."

"What keeps you there? Why won't you even consider retirement?"

"I'll be honest with you guys. I know of several cops that retired, then passed away shortly after that. I wouldn't know what to do with my life. The only thing I know is police work. I have spent my entire life doing it, and I don't want to retire just to sit on my couch and drink myself to death."

"But, Dad—" Heather started. Andy cut her off and whispered something into her ear. "Are you serious, Andy? Do you promise?"

"Yes, dear."

"Thanks, Andy." She reached up and gave him a kiss on the lips. Heather calmed down.

"That's it, sweetheart? I figured there would be more," Dan stated.

"Not for now, Dad, so long as you make the right decisions. Besides, Andy has a plan."

About the Author

Scott Burnell can usually be found at the gym, burning off the beer he consumed the previous day. Writing a novel was always on his bucket list. Due to his own hardships, interests, creative mind, and support from his wife and three kids, Scott was able to create *Unintended Consequences*. He was so inspired by checking this item off his bucket list that he continued writing two more novels, making *Unintended Consequences* the first in a series of three. When not absorbed in the writing of novels two and three, Scott enjoys kayaking and the great outdoors. He lives in North Texas with his family.